FREY FELT HERSELF HELD IN THRALL . . .

unable to resist the call of her senses. He wove a magical spell that robbed her of all strength of will and made her wish only that he would continue to work his enchantments until she drowned in delight.

Then, when she was totally bewitched and almost beyond thought, he spoke softly, mockingly in her ear, saying, "So shall the Norman dog tame the Saxon wildcat."

For a moment her mind refused to comprehend him, so enraptured was she. Then as the meaning of his words penetrated her euphoria, a black fury of shame and self-disgust swept through her.

"You will never tame me, sir," she managed in a voice thick with loathing.

His eyes seemed to burn with a dark fire that hovered between anger and amusement. He shook her a little, as if in exasperation. "So the challenge is laid. So be it. Deny me if you will, though you will regret it, mistress, before you grow old. You forget who I am."

"I do not forget!" Frey spat at him. "You're a foreigner, an upstart, a treacherous Norman—a lackey of Hugh the Wolf!"

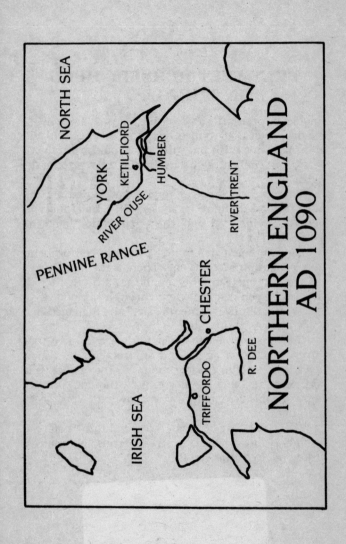

NORTHERN ENGLAND
AD 1090

NORTH SEA

YORK

KETILFIORD

HUMBER

RIVER OUSE

PENNINE RANGE

RIVER TRENT

CHESTER

R. DEE

TRIFFORDO

IRISH SEA

MARY CHRISTOPHER

Dark Conqueror

LEISURE BOOKS ❧ NEW YORK CITY

A LEISURE BOOK

Published by

Dorchester Publishing Co., Inc.
6 East 39th Street
New York, NY 10016

Printed in the United States of America

I

On a September day in the year of Our Lord 1090, the sun shone again on the Saxon settlement of Ketilfiord after several days of rain. The manor lay among the gentle shire hills east of the city of York, quite near the coast and the great estuary of the Humber. It was a quiet place, far from the great strivings of nobility and the king's court, but while most of the people were glad to be away from the arrogant gaze of their new Norman overlords, to one youthful member of the household Ketilfiord increasingly seemed a stagnant backwater where nothing happened. The maiden Aelfreya longed for adventure.

Delighted by the return of fine weather, Frey lifted her green linen skirts clear of the muddy track as she walked swiftly down the hill and through the village, making a stern effort to curb her spirits. She must not arouse suspicion by appearing too eager and hasty. Her coppery hair, worn in two thick braids, fell down either side of her face from under a light veil held round her brow by a band of green wool. About her slender waist a length of plaited leather, its ends threaded with glass beads, formed a girdle, and over her arm she carried a soft reed basket. She was seventeen years old, busy with her familiar chores—the

Saxon maiden Aelfreya, Wulfnoth's daughter, off
with her basket to pick herbs for the pot and the
medicine chest.

Or so everyone would believe.

In actuality, the veil that fluttered against her
cheek hid the glint of mischief in tawny eyes and
her teeth were clamped on her lip to stop laughter
from bubbling out. Once again she had managed to
delude the entire household. She had escaped without arousing the least suspicion as to her real purpose.

The village with its cluster of wood and wattle
houses stood quiet but for the crying of a baby, the
humming song of an old woman at her loom and
the clucking of chickens as they scratched in the
dirt. One or two dogs snoozed in the sun, but most
of the manor people were busy at the harvest. Frey
could see them on the slope of the hillside, men
bending with sickles to reap the corn which
women caught up and bound into sheaves, while
children came behind setting the sheaves on end
and propping them up into tented "stooks" to dry.
Older women and smaller children gleaned among
the stubble for fallen ears, gathering as much as
possible for the winnowing and the milling that
would turn the grain into flour to keep the village
in bread through the winter.

On a gentle rise of land commanding the valley
stood the manor house that was Frey's home.
Sturdily built of wood and plastered wattle, with a
high sloped roof whose thatch was ornately woven
into knots and braids, the house and its courtyard
were guarded by a thick hawthorn hedge. Outside
this prickly defense, more hedges guarded the enclosures where the horses were kept; Frey's people
had long been masters at breeding and training
swift, sound horses for the saddle. Even the
Normans were beginning to appreciate the worth

of a mount bred on the manor of Ketilfiord.

At the edge of the village, Frey came to a growth of bushes where washing had been spread out to dry. She glanced around to see if anyone might be watching but saw no one close enough to take note of her. Swiftly she snatched a homespun tunic from the bushes, tucking it away in her roomy basket. A few seconds later a brown mantle joined it, and then a pair of loose, grayish breeches. The clothes were still slightly damp, but would answer her purpose. Taking another quick look to make sure she was unobserved, Frey laughed to herself and with her basket now bulging with illicitly "borrowed" clothing she ran lightly to the stepping stones that spanned the stream.

On the further side of the stream, a path wound across meadows and up into the woods, skirting the edge of the fallow field. The village sheep were grazing there, with a few cattle belonging to Frey's older brother, Reynold, who was lord of the manor or, in the native Saxon tongue, "thane" of Ketilfiord. A hurdle fence enclosed the valuable livestock, guarded by a herdsman who seemed half asleep as he lounged in the grass, with a bronze watch-horn thrust into his rough rope belt. He squinted up at Frey as she approached and, recognizing her, got clumsily to his feet. Guilt at his own laziness showed all over his broad red face as he grinned sheepishly, showing broken teeth, and touched a tow-colored forelock.

"Mistress."

"Good day to you, John," Frey greeted, blessing her fortune. A more intelligent herdsman might have been curious, but simple John atte Water would scarcely remember having seen the lady Aelfreya, much less pause to wonder at her haste and her bulging basket. It seemed to Frey that the angels must be with her. Perhaps they winked at mischief born of youthful high spirits and a desire for a little adventure in a humdrum life.

Cheered by the thought of heavenly support for her exploit, she climbed the hill briskly, passing a thorny growth of gorse bushes before finally reaching the dappled shade of the woods. One last glance behind assured her that she was not being followed or spied upon and her eyes sparkled as she hurried deeper among the shade of the trees. When she was far from the danger of prying eyes, she stopped by a thicket and hurriedly began to undress.

Her kittle with its tight sleeves caused her to sweat as her fingers fumbled in sudden anxious haste. Having come this far she was impatient, and anxious in case Nicol might not wait for her. These snatched meetings made him nervous as a faun. A few moments could mean the difference between seeing him and missing him—assuming that he came at all. Oh, he would come. He *must* come!

Stripped to her linen shift, she scrambled into the baggy breeches and knotted the drawstring tightly at her slender waist. The rough tunic went on next, much too large for her, but that didn't matter. With the mantle over it, held at the throat with her own bronze and enamel brooch, she would pass for a peasant at a distance.

Bundling her own clothes into the basket, she hid it under a bush and paused to tie her long red braids behind her head; then she pulled up the mantle's hood to complete the disguise, ducked out from the thicket and began to run through the woods, leaping tussocks and laughing to herself, full of the joy of being seventeen, abrim with life and off to a forbidden meeting with her sweetheart.

As she neared a clearing she knew well from previous trysts, her heart flipped in pleasure as she

saw two horses waiting there. Beside them was a
young man wearing a long, washed-blue cloak. She
saw him glance at the sky as if to gauge the time by
the angle of the sun, and then he must have heard
her coming for he swung around, half alarmed
until he recognized her beneath her disguise. As
she burst, breathless, into the clearing, he stared at
her in shock, scandalized to see her wearing the
garments of a male peasant.

"Frey!" The name jerked out of him as his face
paled with his eyes dilated in disbelief and vexation.
"Are you mad?"

"It's better this way," she replied, irritated that
he chose to censure instead of applauding her
ingenuity. Sometimes she wished Nicol were a little
more daring, less worried by what people might
think. For herself, she didn't care a fig for the
opinion of others, not if it interfered with her own
plans and wishes. "If we're seen, no one will know
who I am."

"But if someone *would* recognize you—" He was
almost incoherent with outrage. "It will make a
terrible scandal, Frey! We shall both be disgraced!"

Nicol of Linscote had long brown hair brushed
back from a high brow like a dome above eyes of a
pale iced-blue. Frowning, he looked like a sulky
little boy and Frey was suddenly bored with his
timidity. Pique made her want to remind him that
he ought to be grateful, not angry with her; she was
taking a chance just by being here. "After last time,
you should be pleased that I risked coming at all.
Reynold was furious with me. He forbade me to see
you again."

Nicol's sulky mouth turned even further down
at one corner. "I know. He sent a message to my
father. I've been sternly warned to stay away from
you."

So he, too, had dared to take a risk in order to

spend time with her. The thought drove away Frey's ill temper and she laughed up at the young man. "But still you came to meet me."

"Only to say goodbye."

The blunt words, spoken so flatly and with such finality, doused all her enjoyment of the escapade. For a moment she gaped at him, then as the import of his news pierced her disappointment she thrust out her full lower lip in a pout. "You're going back to Wales?" she asked dully. "Oh, Nicol! So soon?"

"You knew I could not stay here in Yorkshire for long," he said, his own lips curled in bitterness. "My duty beckons. Hugh the Wolf, my liege lord and master, is anxious for my return."

The name of Hugh the Wolf, Earl of Chester, made Frey's hazel-gold eyes narrow with distaste and she clenched her fists, exclaiming loudly and passionately, "How I hate the Normans!"

"Aye, so do we all," Nicol agreed, though his own voice was low and he glanced about the empty woods as if afraid of who might be listening. "But speak such thoughts softly, Frey."

Her freckled face set and her thoughts turned bleak as she recalled the depredations inflicted on her people since the coming of William of Normandy twenty years ago. He had slain the Saxon king Harold, set the English earls to flight and decimated the fyrd, the great army of Englishmen who had rallied to Harold's banner; then after his great victory at Hastings the Norman conqueror, William the Bastard, had marched to lay the north of England to waste by fire and the sword, to teach his new subjects a lesson and to impose his authority on them.

The thane Wilfrith, Frey's grandfather, and his son Wulfnoth, who had later become her father, had ridden with the fyrd against the invaders. Wilfrith had been slain, leaving his family impover-

ished and at the mercy of the Earl of Chester, a
Norman lord named Hugh d'Avranches—called
Hugh the Wolf—whose territories, generously
granted to him by the Conqueror, included parts of
Yorkshire. The Norman earl of Chester was, there-
fore, now overlord of Ketilfiord.

Nicol and his family at neighboring Linscote
were in a similar situation, bound in the service of
Hugh of Chester, and Nicol as a younger son without hope of inheritance had been obliged to seek
service among the earl's knights. Saxons had few
rights left, it seemed. Normans ruled everything—even Frey's own personal destiny.

"When will you come home again?" she asked.

"I don't know." Nicol stepped closer, watching
her with eyes that were suddenly ardent as his
voice deepened to a vow. "But be sure I will come.
I'll not forget my promise. As soon as my service is
rewarded by a grant of land, then I'll return to you
and we'll be married. Sweet Aelfreya!" He swept
his arms round her and pulled her to him with a
clumsiness borne of haste and inexperience. Frey
allowed him the liberty of holding her, but when
he bent his head and sought to kiss her mouth she
evaded him and wriggled until she was free of his
embrace.

Feeling uncomfortable, for reasons she could
not define, she turned to the horses and grabbed the
gelding's trailing bridle. "Let's ride, Nicol."

"That's all you ever want to do," he muttered,
but he linked his hands for her foot and she leapt
lithely to the saddle—throwing her leg over to sit
astride, which made Nicol look shocked again.
"Frey!"

"But I'm wearing breeches!" she cried. "Oh,
don't frown so, Nicol. You remind me of Reynold.
He disapproves of everything I do, too. I was taught
to ride astride when I was three years old. What

difference does it make?"

"It's not ladylike!"

"Who is there to care? Oh, if you don't stop being such a bore I shall wish I'd never risked a beating to meet you today. I'm in disguise! I'm supposed to be your body servant. Have you ever seen a body servant riding sidesaddle?"

Before he could think of an answer she kicked her heels and urged the horse to a gallop, glad to get away from Nicol for a while. Now he would have to ride hard to catch her; her skill at horsemanship easily matched his.

How she loved to ride like this, with the wind in her face and the sun sparkling behind the swirling leaves in the woods. It reminded her of the days of her youth, when she had ridden wild beside Wulfnoth. Sadness tugged at her with the thought. How she missed him, Wulfnoth her beloved father, who had adored and ingulged his headstrong older daughter, revelling in her high spirits, encouraging her to be independent in an age when convention demanded that a woman be meek and subservient. Would there ever be a man who would understand her and make her feel as loved, as secure, and yet as free as she had felt while Wulfnoth was alive?

She rode fast until she came to the edge of the woods where the land sloped away to a lush expanse of river marshes thick with wild ducks and geese. The river Ouse shone in the autumn light as it met the broad waters of the Humber estuary. Wheeling gulls swooped around a few fishing skiffs, and in the marshes the figures of peasants moved on punts, gathering the long, strong reeds to use for thatching.

Frey drew rein and brought her horse to a halt under the eaves of the wood, reality returning with a rush. She was no longer a child, no longer the spoiled darling of thane Wulfnoth. Wulfnoth was dead and his older daughter had become a grown woman of seventeen—a woman whose future must soon be decided. The alternatives were plain—marriage or a nunnery.

She glanced round as Nicol rode up beside her, his face reddened from the exertion of trying to catch her. The sight of him made her heart soften with affection. Nicol was the only man who had ever discussed marriage with her; as the sister of a poor Saxon thane, her dowry was not sufficient to attract a flock of suitors. And since she must either wed or take the veil—an alternative her sister Emma was considering—she had to conclude that Nicol would make as good a husband as she could hope for, once he had been granted some lands of his own and therefore the means to support a wife. When—if—his lord the Earl of Chester rewarded his services and enfeoffed him with a manor then, she had no doubt, her brother would be only too pleased to give his consent to the match.

However, Frey was in no hurry to enter the wedded state. Her life at Ketilfiord was, for the present, pleasant enough. The thought of becoming a wife held certain terrors which she was reluctant to examine too closely.

But it was not marriage, or even courtship, that Nicol had on his mind at that moment; he was worried about the welfare of the gelding he had brought for her to ride. He looked askance at the pony, saying, "I hope you haven't winded him. I'll be in trouble if you have."

"I've never winded a horse in my life!" Frey exclaimed. She leaned to stroke the gelding's pulsing silken neck, enjoying the flow of strong muscle beneath the short thick coat. It occurred to her that once Nicol had gone back to the Welsh marshes it would be many months before she could enjoy another afternoon of stolen pleasure with him as a willing accomplice. Thinking that she ought to appreciate him more, and be kinder to him, she said, "I shall miss you, Nicol."

"Will you?" Giving her a hooded look, he swung down from his horse and tethered it to a branch before holding out his arms to her. "Then prove it to me. Come down and let me make a proper farewell to you."

Reading his meaning in his eyes, she knew a moment of near panic. During previous encounters he had occasionally grabbed her and kissed her, clumsily and wetly, in a way that disquieted her and made her feel unclean so that when they parted she had often scrubbed at her mouth to rid her skin of the feel of him. Now he wanted more than that—perhaps he wanted of her what Reynold demanded of his wife Edith behind the thin walls of their bedchamber at the manor. The very thought made sweat break out on the palms of Frey's hands as she tightened her grip on the reins.

To cover her alarm, she summoned a laugh and kicked at the horse, making it spring into a trot. "You must catch me first," she called over her shoulder as she spurred away along the hillside above the marshes and turned back into the woods.

Bent low over the tossing mane, she urged the horse ever faster, praying that she might outride Nicol long enough for his ardor to abate. With the wind in her ears, the rough mantle flying and hooves thudding on damp turf, she flew through greenwoods touched with autumn's gold, startling birds and small creatures. She gave herself to the pleasures of speed and motion, forgetting her apprehension.

Aware that Nicol was still some distance behind her, she burst suddenly on a break in the woods where a cart track ran between settlements. Frey glimpsed a horseman riding there, less than a furlong away. The sight of him made her check her speed in the instant before she remembered how she was clad—she must not be seen close enough for anyone to recognize her, or to guess that she was female. Instinct made her pull the wide hood closer round her head. Discovery would lead to trouble, to shame and perhaps even a beating from her brother Reynold.

Urgently she dug in her heels, making the gelding leap forward with fresh impetus, taking her into the shelter of the farther woods. Was Nicol close behind?

After a while she glanced back, hoping for a sight of Nicol, and in that moment a low bough caught her shoulder. The blow jolted her from the saddle, though her clutching hands kept hold of the reins. She was tossed momentarily against the gelding's flank as the horse bolted in fright. Frey tried valiantly to regain her seat but felt herself slipping. A yelp escaped her as the ground came up and hit her. Threatened by flying hooves thudding close to her face, she was dragged through the greenwood, tossing helplessly until her aching hands loosed the reins and momentum threw her aside with a breath-robbing thump amid the broken branches of a hazel bush.

For a moment or two she thought she would never breathe again. Her lungs seemed to have stopped working. Then just as her mind began to spin she was able to draw a long, ragged breath. The trees above her seemed to be revolving and as she closed her eyes against the dizzying sight she heard the sound of hoofbeats approaching. The soft thudding came closer, slowing to a halt not far from where she lay. Nicol had come, she thought in relief.

But as her eyelids fluttered and lifted she glimpsed the legs of a huge black horse, and a swirl of black cloak as the rider dismounted. It was not Nicol! Horrified, she remained as she was, half under the hazel bush, huddled in her peasant's clothing with a wary hand drawing the roomy hood well round her face and hair in order to maintain her disguise. *Now* what was she to do?

The hard toe of a riding boot dug none too gently into her ribs as if to test whether she was alive or not, making her wince. "Winded, are you?" a deep voice asked in derisive tones. "Come out from there and let me take a look at you, lad."

Frey groaned a little, feigning recovery from unconsciousness, and prompted by another dig from that boot she crawled painfully out from the bush, wincing a little as a sharp pain reminded her of the tumble she had taken. She would bear the bruises of this escapade for weeks. Slowly easing to her feet she stood huddled in her rough clothing, rubbing her aching shoulder and snatching a glance at the stranger from behind the edge of the concealing hood.

That first glimpse was enough to send a chill of unease through her. Though he had addressed her in Saxon English, the man was a Norman—that was evident from the way his hair was cut, cropped very close at the back but falling in thick dark locks across his brow. He seemed to be all darkness— black clothes, sable hair and eyes, bronzed skin—with the gleam of gold in brooches holding the heavy cloak. His face was strong and good-looking apart from its frowning, forbidding aspect and he was older than Nicol by several years, taller and more muscular, with broad shoulders and long legs. He stood with his feet set apart, as if braced for action, with one hand on the hilt of his sword, gazing narrowly at Frey with his sun-browned face set in stern lines.

Nor was his horse any less impressive. Brought

up to recognize and appreciate fine horseflesh, Frey saw at once that it was a mettlesome stallion, bred for speed and stamina—a horse on which to cover the miles. Its long black ears pricked intelligently, light gleaming on its mane as it shook its elegant black head and snorted as if aware of her scrutiny.

From behind the sheltering shade of her hood, Frey regarded the stranger with apprehension, wondering who he could be. She had never seen him before, of that she was certain; such a man would not have gone unremarked by every maid and goodwife for miles. There was something about him—a tautness, a stillness, a self-composure that said he was used to wielding authority. In his belt she glimpsed a dagger whose hilt was crusted with red gems, and the scabbard that bore his sword was studded with gold. These things marked him as at least a knight of the realm, and not a poor one like Nicol.

Why was a Norman knight travelling alone through the woods so near to Ketilfiord? Could she continue to conceal her identity—and her gender—from him?

"So what have we here?" the knight asked wryly, staring down at her with those dark-brown eyes glinting like wetted stone. "A horse-thief?"

"No!" The denial was shocked out of her as she straightened indignantly.

"Then why were you being pursued?"

So he had seen Nicol.

And where was Nicol now? Why didn't he come to her aid? A fine protector he, to leave her to the mercies of this Norman! But when she thought about it she hoped that Nicol would remain hidden. If he came he would surely betray her; he was not the most quick-witted of men. "I was not being pursued," she denied.

"Sir," the Norman reminded her of the respect

due to his rank.

"Sir," Frey muttered, irritated.

He peered at her more closely, then glanced thoughtfully behind him at the now-silent woods. "He does appear to have vanished. Yet I saw him clearly enough. Strange . . . If he was not chasing you for some misdemeanour—"

"He's my master," Frey said, the lie coming swiftly and convincingly to her lips. "Perhaps he took a fall. I must go back and look for him." As she spoke, she glanced about for the gelding she had been riding and was dismayed to find it out of sight. It must have gone on running, frightened out of its wits, after she fell. It might be leagues away by now. A despairing "Oh, no!" came from her. Nicol had brought the horse from Linscote! If it were lost, or found wandering riderless, there would be awkward questions to answer!

Belatedly, Frey wondered why she never considered consequences before embarking on these escapades. Her wildness had led her into trouble before and though Wulfnoth her father had laughed about it and admired her spirit, her brother Reynold was of a different mettle—he only found her wilfulness an irritant. If he learned about this he would be very angry with her. Again.

She was unaware that the Norman knight had been watching her closely, his sharp, intelligent brown eyes probing the shadows beneath her hood. He said softly, "So what am I to do with you, *lad*?" The slight mocking emphasis he laid on the last word told her he had guessed she was no boy!

Alarmed, Frey spun around and tried to dart away, but the knight threw out a hand and grasped her arm, his other hand reaching for her hood to jerk it back, revealing her pale freckled face and startled eyes. Her long red braids fell down across one shoulder, betraying her femininity.

She was discovered. There was no point in continuing the pretense. Summoning all her fiery temper and youthful dignity, Frey straightened her spine and glared right into the knight's eyes, daring him to find fault with her. But to her disgust his hard expression wavered and a disconcerting gleam started in his eyes; amusement tugged at his mouth as he looked her up and down, taking in every detail of the way she looked—the baggy breeches, the ill-fitting tunic, the coarse mantle . . . Finally, after considering her furious, blushing face and tawny-gold eyes that spat hatred at him, he threw back his head and laughed aloud with uncontrollable mirth.

If there was one thing Frey hated it was being made the object of someone else's scorn. Her dignity was wounded, her pride trampled, her vanity vanquished. Now she was disgraced, Wulfnoth's daughter caught out in a foolish, childish deception. And laughed at—by a Norman!

She reacted instinctively, as she did so often, without thought for consequences. Her hand lashed up with all the force of her arm behind it. The knight's mocking laughter choked off as her palm cracked across his face.

For a moment everything was still. Even the birds in the woods seemed to stop their singing and hold their breath. The knight glared at her, his eyes burning with a glow of building fury at the mortal insult she had offered him. And she hung there, horrified now by what her temper had made her do, hardly daring to breathe for fear of what *he* would do in retaliation. Her palm tingled with hot pain and on his cheek the mark of her insolence showed stark white, rapidly filling with red as blood rushed back to the surface of his skin.

He snarled something in French, biting the words off through his teeth; to judge by his

expression the curse boded no good for her.
Suddenly realizing what a rash thing she had done,
Frey tore free of his detaining hand with a strength
born of fright. She turned on her heel and ran,
ducking away from him. She cried out as he caught
a corner of her mantle, impeding her momentarily
before the worn material tore free from the brooch
that held it and she ran on, driven by fear and
despair.

Panic lent her feet a swiftness she had not
known she possessed. She fled wildly, through
clawing branches and thorns, leaping bushes and
tangles of brambles, until her lungs were bursting
and her legs unsteady. Then her foot caught in a
tree root. She stumbled and fell, pitched head first
into a grassy hollow where she lay feeling sick and
weak, her head spinning.

Slowly the earth stopped whirling, the trees
stood straight, the breeze cooled her face. She
looked up to see long legs straddled on the edge of
the hollow, black-stockinged and thonged with
leather, braced apart in an arrogant, angry, determined stance and topped by a black tunic that
heaved as the broad chest beneath it drew breath.
Hands braced on his hips made the cloak a billowing black frame for his lean, sturdy body, and from
a face darkened by hot blood his dark eyes glinted.

"Wait!" The voice came from Frey's right and
as she glanced round Nicol came running beneath
the trees, his dagger already drawn in her defense.
Part of her admired his bravery even while she
knew it was foolhardy. She despaired of herself.
Now her waywardness had brought danger to
Nicol, too; Normans were known to be cruel and
unforgiving and this one seemed a particularly cold
specimen. The consequences of this day's doings
would be dire, for both her and her sweetheart.

The knight considered Nicol coldly, with a

slight curl of scorn on his lips. "Would you pitch that puny knife against my sword?" he demanded in a harsh voice that expressed both anger and disgust. "Faith, man, the maid must mean a great deal to you."

"She's my betrothed," Nicol stated, though he sheathed his dagger as if realizing that continued aggression would be asking for trouble. "I'm sorry, sir, I didn't realize who you were."

"No," the knight agreed dryly. "Betrothed or not, a wanton like this is hardly worth the risk of a charge of murder." As if suddenly tiring of the whole affair, he stepped back, away from the hollow where Frey crouched. "Take her, then. Take her and give her the thrashing she deserves. I don't envy you the life you'll have with such a strumpet."

With that, he swirled his dark cloak around him, turned on his heel and strode away with long, ground-eating strides, heading back to where he had left his black stallion.

Frey could hardly believe her good fortune. Was the Norman actually going to leave without demanding some recompense for the insults he had suffered? Were she and Nicol safe from punishment, after all? Relief made her feel lightheaded and she rested on her arm for a moment, feeling weak. But behind the relief came a resurgence of spirit, a return of hot blood to the head . . . The Norman knight was not the only one who had been insulted.

On a wave of indignation, she found the strength to stumble to her feet. She glared at the Norman's receding form with a fury that made her grind her teeth. "How dare he! Strumpet, indeed! You should have killed him!"

Nicol gave her a hooded sidelong look. "For what reason?"

"He insulted me!"

"From wounds inflicted by words you'll soon recover. There was no one else to hear. And he was right—I dare not take the risk of harming him. If a Norman is found slain it's declared to be murder. The culprit has to give himself up, or admit his guilt by running away to outlawry, else his whole parish is punished. You know that. It's the law, Frey."

"*Their* law!" she spat. "If a Saxon dies they don't care who killed him. He's as unconsidered as a dog. But let one of their precious breed come to harm and—" She shook herself, trembling with a mixture of emotions that dissolved into impotent anger. That anger had no outlet but to spill itself over Nicol. "And where were you all this time? Hiding from him?"

"I—" He couldn't meet her eyes. "I had to go after the gelding. I daren't risk losing it."

"You mean you were ashamed to be seen with me!"

Nicol looked her up and down from the corner of his eye, his expression sullenly accusing. "You must admit that—"

"I dressed like this for your sake!" she cried. "For your sake I defied my brother to meet you."

"No, not for my sake!" he returned, his pale eyes flashing. "You dressed like that—and defied your brother—because it amuses you to play the hoyden." His pride had been punctured and his own temper was rising with frustration as he rushed on, "If you had any real regard for me, you would not spurn me and run away when I wish to—" He stopped himself, though his meaning was clear enough.

"When you wish to what, Nicol?" Frey challenged him with a toss of her copper braids, standing straight and defiant before him. "To make me in truth a strumpet, rutting in the woods with a man who can offer me no marriage contract unless some Norman upstart graciously deigns to grant him an acre of our Saxon England?"

He had no answer for that; he only glowered at her, disgruntled and ill-tempered, his lust thwarted yet again.

"So where are the horses?" Frey said, turning away. "You had best take me back before anyone else sees us."

Before they left, however, she retraced her steps to the hazel bush where she had first fallen from the horse. There was no sign of the Norman knight, but the rough mantle he had torn from her lay in the grass. She picked it up, looking askance at the ragged tear on the shoulder. Only now did she consider the garment's owner and wonder what he, and his wife, would think when they found the garment in need of patching. Belatedly, she was sorry for her thoughtlessness. The afternoon's adventure had turned into a lesson her conscience would not easily forget.

As they rode back to the clearing where they had met, Frey maintained a chill silence while Nicol seemed sunk in gloom. Only as she slid from the saddle did her downcast swain find words to say.

"This is not how I imagined our parting, Frey. Will you wait for me still?"

Sighing, she said, "I might. Unless some wealthy lord comes asking for my hand in the meantime."

Nicol managed a wry, unhumorous smile. "Such a thing is not likely, I fear."

"Then you have your answer." She shrugged, and turned away. "I have no choice but to wait for you—or go with Emma to the nunnery at York and incarcerate myself there, hiding my tears behind the gray veil of piety." The thought of it made her pause, her hands clenched tight in the material of her rough cloak as her stomach tightened. "I should hate it!" she said through her teeth, and swung back to face him. "Come back safely to me, Nicol. You are my only hope!"

"Oh, Frey!" He threw himself from his horse and ran to comfort her. "You know I love you. If I were a wealthy lord, I . . . I wouldn't care that you have no dowry. I'd marry you for yourself. Frey, it may be months before we meet again. Don't send me away without some token of affection. Please, Frey . . . Please—"

Frey squirmed uneasily in his grasp, wishing he would not always insist on being so amorous. His expression as he gazed at her mouth reminded her of a hungry dogfox and brought prickles of panic to her skin. "Give me a kiss," he pleaded. "One kiss in farewell?"

Partly out of pity, partly out of guilt, she allowed him to draw her closer and as he bent over her she closed her eyes, blotting out the sight of his rapacious expression. She felt his mouth hot and wet over her closed lips, his teeth scraping, but when his arms came round her and he tried to drag her in more tightly against his body she stiffened and pushed him off, crying, "One kiss, you said! That's enough, Nicol!" Disturbed, and wanting to rub away the feel of his lips, she backed away.

Nicol was breathing heavily, flushed and bright-eyed. He turned to remount his horse and sat looking down on her possessively. "Farewell, my love. Pray God it will not be long before I come home again."

"Amen to that," Frey answered fervently, and stood waving as he rode away into the distance leading the gelding behind him.

When he was gone from sight, she scrubbed at her mouth with the back of her wrist, grimacing at the memory of Nicol's hot, wet kisses. She assumed herself to be in love with him; he was the only man she had ever been close to in that way—the only one who seemed likely to offer her marriage—yet his physical nearness was distasteful to her. She hated it when he wanted to hold her and kiss her. But that was always the way, for any woman who was not a whore or a strumpet, or so her experience had led her to believe.

She thought of her sister-in-law, Edith, and the times that lady could be heard pleading fatigue, or pains in her side at night when she and Reynold were in bed, or uttering choked cries of pain and disgust when Reynold would not be held off. Was that how marriage was? Was that what love came to, in the end?

For one shocking moment, she caught herself remembering the dark Norman knight and wondering if a man such as he might overcome her maidenly fears and make marriage something joyous. There had been something about him—a quiet, deep strength that made Frey imagine how it might be to lean on such a man, to feel his strong arms enfold her and his mouth on hers . . .

Realizing what she was doing, she tore her mind away from such thoughts, clapping her hands to suddenly burning cheeks. Such fantasies were immodest, especially when they concerned a man whose birth and breeding made him an enemy, one of the vile conquerors of her people, slayers of her kin, despoilers of Saxon lands—a Norman! To imagine loving him and lying with him was a betrayal of everything she held dear.

Besides, Frey was fairly sure that true love, such as minstrels sang of, was only a fiction. Hadn't old Ula, her nurse, told her it was so? "Love is for dreams, for stories and songs, my maid. Marriage is for security. A woman must bear her lord's demands, care for his home and comforts, warm his bed and bear his children, in return for the shelter

of his home. Yet at times love grows amid the daily
round of duties. Your father came to love your
mother very well. Which is why he cherished you.
You're like her in looks with your red hair and
your queer cat's eyes. You're no beauty, it's true—all
freckled like a thrush—but I dare say you'll find a
husband some day, and if you're a good wife he
may come to love you as his nature allows it."

Frey hoped that was so. She might dream of a
lover more exciting than Nicol of Linscote, but she
knew that reality made the fulfillment of her
dreams unlikely. Nicol offered her only prospect of
marriage. The alternative—being sent to lifelong
seclusion in a nunnery—made her feel cold and sick
just to think of it. It was Nicol or nothing.

By the time Frey emerged from the woods
wearing her own green gown, the sun was low in
the west. Banks of white cloud layered the blue sky,
limned with light that was shading to pink near the
horizon and all the valley lay serene. John atte
Water was still at his post, but sound asleep and
snoring, and in the fields men and women eased
their aching backs and began to think of supper.

Keeping a sharp watch for observers, Frey
returned her homespun disguise to the bushes,
hoping that the rent in the mantle would be blamed
on too vigorous a pounding on the stones. It was a
thin, old garment. Perhaps—the thought occurred
belatedly as ever—its owner was too poor to afford
another. The more she thought about it the more
guilty she felt. She promised herself that this was
the last time she would behave so thoughtlessly.

The afternoon had brought her no joy after all.
She told herself she would confess her sins to the
priest and do penance for her wilfulness. The saints
had been too kind, watching over her and allowing
her to escape unscathed but for a few bruises and

scratches. Those slight wounds would heal; they were not nearly so bad as discovery and consequent disgrace. But fortunately no one would ever know she had met Nicol in secret that day, or that she had been seen wearing the clothes of a male peasant by a Norman knight.

At least . . . no one would know so long as her luck held until she reached the safety of the bower. Should either Edith, her sister-in-law, or Ula, her nurse, enquire too closely into the contents of her basket, Frey's escapade might still be uncovered; the basket contained only a few of the more common herbs, hastily snatched at the last minute along with handfuls of grass.

Ah, me! she sighed to herself, shaking her head over her own capriciousness. She was thankful that the fates had allowed her to evade the worst consequences of her folly.

But the worst Edith or Ula could accuse her of was daydreaming and laziness. Neither of them would come near to guessing the rest. The thought made Frey bite her lip to prevent a smile from forming. It had been quite an adventure, meeting with Nicol, riding wild in the woods—and slapping the face of a Norman knight! As she remembered it all in detail, laughter bubbled out of her, but she curbed it and demurely inclined her head as a cart laden with logs creaked by and the driver acknowledged her presence by knuckling his brow.

Her natural high spirits reasserted themselves as she strolled lightly after the cart, following it up the incline to where on a ridge of higher ground the thatched manor house stood. It was surrounded by a stout hawthorn hedge and a deep ditch crossed by a plank bridge over which the cart rumbled.

The courtyard was bustling with activity as serfs and peasants went about the final chores of their long day. Chickens scratched in the dirt by the

big thatched barn and a couple of dogs came
wagging their tails to greet Frey. From the kitchen
hut drifted appetizing scents of cooking; smoke
poured through the hole in its roof and beyond the
open door Frey glimpsed the gleam of fires and
sweating scullions hurrying about their tasks.

The manor house itself was raised above stone
cellars which contained storerooms and a prison
cell. The upper section of the house, where the
thane's family and retainers lived, was built of
wood with an ornate thatched roof.

As Frey approached the flight of stone steps that
would take her up to the hall, she saw one of the
housecarls—what the Normans called a man-at-
arms—leading a horse toward the stables. The
sight made her pause, dismayed as she recognized
the threat that loomed again just when she had
thought herself safe; the horse was a sturdy stallion,
a magnificent beast, its muscles rolling beneath a
coat that shone like black silk.

Frey had seen that same stallion not two hours
ago. The mount belonged to the Norman knight
who had called her a strumpet!

If he were here at the manor then she had no
hope of keeping her afternoon's adventures a
secret. The Norman would tell her brother all about
it. Well of course he would; it would be a sweet way
of wreaking vengeance for the insults she had
offered him. And Reynold would be so angry that
Frey didn't dare think what the consequences
might be.

II

Catching Frey's eye, the burly housecarl who was leading the black stallion to its stable nodded at the manor house. "We've a visitor, mistress. A Norman." With a glance to see who might be watching, he spat feelingly onto the uneven cobbles of the courtyard, expressing the distrust and resentment most Saxons felt toward their overlords.

Sharing his unease more closely than he guessed, Frey asked in an undertone, "What does he want?"

"Come to do a deal over some horses, from what I can gather," the man replied. "It's lucky that Thane Reynold got home early from the wapentake court. Normans don't like to be kept waiting."

Frey caught her breath. "My brother's home? So soon? We did not expect him until tomorrow!" Not waiting for a reply, she hurried on and climbed the steps to the manor door, which was made of solid oak and studded with great iron nails forged by the manor smith. The door stood open to the September warmth and beyond it a sturdy wooden screen, carved and painted with flora and fauna, guarded the main part of the hall from prying eyes and cold drafts.

Cautiously, Frey peeped round the screen, took

one look and pulled back, afraid to be seen. The
bower—the chamber she shared with her sister
Emma and old Ula the nurse—lay at the far end of
the hall. In between, with much clatter on straw-
scattered floorboards, servants were erecting the
trestle tables ready for supper, setting them length-
wise down the hall. And on the dais, behind the
high table and framed against painted linen
hangings on the wall, Reynold sat conversing with
the dark Norman knight.

Flattening herself against the screen, Frey
frantically sought for a way out of her dilemma.
The Norman was sure to recognize her, even
though she was now dressed properly for her
station and her gender. What he would say, and
what Reynold would make of it, she dared not
think. Still, there was no help for it; to reach the
bower she must cross the hall.

Knowing she had no choice, she straightened
her shoulders, lifting her veiled head proudly. She
would show herself and have done with it, for good
or ill. She had never been one to hide in corners and
play the coward. Let the Norman do his worst.
She, Aelfreya of Ketilfiord, Wulfnoth's daughter,
was not afraid of him.

Leaving her basket by the door, for one of the
servants to take away, she stepped from behind the
screen and began to stroll across the rushes that
covered the floor. She prepared to give Reynold a
warm greeting, as though nothing untoward had
occurred. But before she could go anywhere near
her brother his wife Edith appeared, her veil
fluttering from a bronze circlet worn around the
brow of a thin face pinched with suspicion.

"And where have you been?" the mistress of
the manor demanded shrilly. "I have asked everywhere. No one has seen you all afternoon."

Wide-eyed with feigned innocence, Frey met

her sister-in-law's snapping blue gaze calmly.
"Why, Edith, you know where I have been. I was in
the woods and meadows, collecting herbs as I often
do."

"Too often!" Edith snapped. "It doesn't take half
a day when *I* do it."

"But then, Edith," Frey said sweetly, "you have
not been as well-educated in herbal lore as I have,
under the tutelage of Ula from my earliest days. The
medicine chest has to be restocked before autumn
withers the best leaves and roots. And I know
where to find them. Some of them are a great
distance away."

"Indeed, you do know more of herbs—and of
spells and other enchantments—than I do," Edith
sneered. "I have no desire to learn more of such
heathen arts. I prefer to keep myself pure in the
name of Our Lady, who would have scorned to
practise such witchery."

"Witchery?" Frey laughed, aware that jealousy
was at the root of Edith's vitriol. "If so, it's white
magic—good magic."

"The priest might not agree with you!"

"Edith!" Reynold's curt voice cut into her
complaints. His boots thudded on the floorboards
and straw went flying as he came striding down the
hall, a tall, thin man in his mid-twenties, with
frown lines already driven into his brow beneath a
fringe of lank fair hair. Glaring at his wife, he said
in an undertone, "Enough of this. We have a guest.
Remember your manners and hold your tongue. Or
would you have him think all Saxon women are
shrews and scolds?"

Edith shot him a look of hatred and said, "What
do I care what he thinks?" and spun away to stalk
across the hall to her bedchamber. In her wake,
Reynold glanced at Frey, taking swift note of the
way she was dressed and groomed.

"At least you're not too untidy. Come, let me
present you to our guest before you prepare yourself for supper—and don your best gown, sister. I'll
not have Sir Blaize going back to the earl with tales
of ill-breeding at Ketilfiord."

"The earl?" Frey breathed with a jolt of dismay.
"The Earl of Chester?"

"Aye," her brother confirmed tersely. "Our
visitor is in the service of Earl Hugh."

It was worse than Frey had thought. By
slapping the face of an arrogant stranger she had in
fact insulted an emissary of the powerful Earl of
Chester, who held Ketilfiord and all its people,
including its thane and his family, in the palm of his
hand.

Hugh d'Avranches, Hugh the Wolf, held total
power in his own lands, dispensing justice as if he
were a king. Indeed, in all England he was second
only to the king, and not even William Rufus
himself had the right to interfere in the affairs of
Chester. The earl was said to be a ruthless man,
demanding total obedience from all who served
him; he made a harsh and frightening overlord.

As with the master, Frey thought with a
sidelong glance to where their influential visitor
waited on the dais, so with the man. If she knew
Normans, this dark knight mightly easily decide to
seize the opportunity to discredit Reynold and
perhaps take the manor for himself, merely as
restitution for the insults Frey had offered. Such
things often happened now that Normans held
power, so it was said. How she wished she had
curbed her temper more firmly.

But it was done. No use wishing time to fly
backwards. The mistake had been made. Now came
the retribution.

With a fatalistic feeling, she numbly followed
her brother across the hall to where the "guest"

rose politely from a chair that had been carved by village craftsmen from good English oak—the only armchair the manor possessed; other seats were stools and benches. How tall the dark knight was, impressive as he straightened to his full height: tall, well-made, a fine specimen of Norman manhood, secure in his own arrogance. He might already be the master here, she thought bitterly.

Briefly, her gaze met his opaque dark eyes. He knew her, without doubt, though nothing in his manner betrayed it outwardly. Detecting a glint of mockery in those obsidian depths, she felt hot color rise to warm her cheeks. Oh yes, he knew her, and he knew she knew it.

Reynold introduced her almost apologetically. "My sister, mistress Aelfreya."

She made a deep, graceful curtsey, unable to prevent herself from overplaying the deference, though she kept her eyes modestly downcast as she murmured, "My lord."

"Sir Blaize is come to buy horses," her brother added with a note of pride, seeking her approbation. "It seems the fame of Ketilfiord colts has reached the ears of our lord of Chester."

"Then I trust we shall not disappoint him," Frey cooed, regarding her adversary through a veil of lashes as she wondered how he intended to play this scene.

Considering he was a Norman, he was extraordinarily good to look upon, as finely made as any man she had ever seen. But now that she saw him again she was not sorry she had slapped his handsome face. He had deserved it, and more. Look how he carried himself with such an air, as if he owned the world, when in reality he was nothing more than an errand boy, even if his lord was one of the most powerful men in the land.

Perhaps her scornful thoughts showed in her

face, for she saw his lips twitch in sardonic humor and there was a gleam in his eyes as he made her an elaborate bow and taunted her with the grave, formal Latin greeting of, "*Domina*," adding in a soft, deep voice, "Ketilfiord seems blessed with more than its share of grace and beauty. You're a fortunate man, Sir Reynold."

Reynold made demurring noises, but he was obviously pleased by the flattery, much to Frey's irritation. The Norman was amusing himself at the expense of ignorant, unsophisticated Saxons, couldn't Reynold see that?

Keeping up the pretense that nothing was amiss, she made excuses about needing to change for supper and Sir Blaize politely moved aside to let her by. He gracefully swept his cloak out of her way, but as she glanced to thank him his free hand rubbed his cheek, sharply reminding her of the blow she had struck. Sparks of mutual challenge flowed between them but Frey guessed that the knight had decided to keep their earlier meeting secret—at least for the time being. A feeling of elation filled her as she tilted her chin and swept past him, her back tingling as she felt his dark velvet gaze following her.

After walking the few yards that seemed more like a furlong, she shut the bower door behind her and leaned on it, taking a deep breath to still her thudding pulses. The Norman still had her at his mercy. One word from him would evoke Reynold's fury at her scandalous behavior of that afternoon. She did not understand why he had kept silent so far, though she was relieved that he had.

But if he continued to hold his peace she would be forever beholden to him, which was galling. She could not decide which prospect pleased her least— his talking or his silence. While she had no wish to be punished for her misdeeds, neither did she relish the thought of being obliged to feel grateful to a Norman!

In the bower, her younger sister, Emma, was being laced into a yellow gown by stout Ula, who had cared for both of the sisters since their mother's death when Emma was still a baby. The old nurse frowned at Frey, demanding, "And where have you been, mistress?"

"I was out collecting herbs. You know that." Frey brushed by and poured water from a bronze jug into an earthenware bowl, sluicing her face and hands in the cold liquid drawn from the courtyard well. She felt unsettled. A gauntlet had been tossed down between herself and the Norman knight and she had no idea how it might all end, except that almost inevitably there must be disgrace in it for her, one way or another.

"Have you met our visitor?" Emma asked, her hazel eyes clear and guileless in a pale face framed by mouse-colored hair. She was a slight girl of fifteen, with long, fluttery hands, a plain face and a way of looking through people as if she saw distant vistas of beauty and delight that were hidden from ordinary mortals. The effect was in fact caused by extreme shortsightedness, but it gave her an unworldly air which rode well with her proclaimed intention to become a nun. "Sir Blaize of Bayonne is his name," she added. "He comes from the earl's court."

"So I understand," Frey said, reaching for a towel and scrubbing her face dry on its rough, sun-bleached weave with unnecessary vigor. Her thoughts were bleak.

"Such grace and beauty," Sir Blaize had murmured, the liar. Poor Emma was too colorless to be called beautiful; Edith, despite her desirable yellow hair and blue eyes, had a hard face and a shrewish

twist to her mouth; Frey herself was cursed with
ugly red hair—the witches' color—and her face was
speckled like a thrush, with odd golden-brown
eyes. No doubt, she thought bitterly, Sir Blaize
would return to the earl's castle at Chester and
beguile the ladies there with amusing tales about
awkward, ill-favored Saxon women.

Feeling irritable, she began to change her
clothes, remembering Reynold's injunction that she
wear her best so as not to disgrace him.

Eventually, having tossed aside most of the
articles from the wooden chest that held her
clothes, Frey chose a kirtle in a pale violet. An
expensive fine wool, dyed with a costly dye, the
fabric had been one of the last gifts her father Wulfnoth had given her before he died. Unfortunately
she had grown curves since then, so the gown had
been altered, with coarser wool let into the side
seams, dyed with blackberry juice, which was
nothing like the original color. But it was the best
she possessed.

She bade Ula comb out her long hair until it fell
like a coppery mantle round her shoulders, then
she added a light veil held by a circlet of polished
bronze. Bronze brooches, polished until they shone
like gold and enamelled in red and green, pinned a
dark blue cloak at her shoulders. She wished she
had a mirror to see her reflection, but polished steel
was too expensive for Ketilfiord's coffers.

Considering her charge's nervous preening
with a jaundiced eye, old Ula said, "Handsome, is
he, this Norman knight?"

"Reynold told me to look my best!" Frey
snapped, her face flaming. "Haven't you anything
else to do, Ula? Won't baby Lucy be needing your
attention?"

Ula headed for the door, glancing over her
shoulder to say darkly, "The babe's asleep. She's not

well, though I doubt you'd care about that, my maid." At that point, she exited.

"She treats me as though I were still a child!" Frey fumed.

"Well, you do behave like one at times," Emma said mildly. "Why are you so upset? Usually you come in singing after being out in the woods."

"There's nothing wrong with me," Frey denied. "It's Ula. She must have eaten something that didn't agree with her. I always get the blame for her liverishness."

"Be charitable, Frey," gentle Emma begged. "Ula's concerned for little Lucy."

"Why? I thought she only had a colic."

"It seems to be something else," Emma sighed. "And . . . my puppy died this afternoon, poor thing."

"You knew it would die," Frey said impatiently. "It was the weakling of the litter. I don't know why you bothered to nurse it."

Emma regarded her with gentle eyes, smiling in a way that was at once sympathetic and chiding, as if she were by far the older of the two. "Dear Frey. Sometimes you're very selfish, you know. Is there anything you really care about—apart from horses, and riding, and picking herbs, and enjoying yourself? By the way . . . I hear that Nicol of Linscote will soon be returning to his duties."

"Of what interest could that be to me?" Frey asked stiffly.

Her sister regarded her blandly, knowingly. "Why, none, of course, since Reynold forbade you to see Nicol again and you would never disobey our dear brother, would you?"

"Then why mention it?"

Emma shrugged and smiled to herself, one of her faraway looks on her face. "No reason, Frey. It was only a piece of gossip that I happened to hear."

At supper at the high table, Frey found herself placed beside her brother, with Edith on his other side, next to their Norman guest, and then Emma. The two men discussed horses at great length, though Blaize found ample opportunity to charm and flatter the two ladies who flanked him. He spoke scarcely a word to Frey and hardly even glanced in her direction, for which she told herself she was thankful; she had no wish to be the object of condescension. Even so, she was irritated by the way Emma and Edith kept blushing and flirting with the handsome young knight.

With so much noise from the housecarls and retainers who were eating at other tables on either side of the fire, Frey caught only snatches of the conversation along the high table, though in a quieter moment she heard Emma's future being discussed.

"To me it seems a waste for a young woman to shut herself away from life," Blaize commented.

"But the choice is my own," Emma replied with her usual earnest sincerity. "To serve God, sir, is surely one of the finest things a Christian can hope for?"

"Of course," Blaize agreed. "If it's a vocation it's to be envied. Not all of us are so blessed with a clear vision of our future road." He turned to glance along the table, leaning forward a little to look at Frey as he asked, "And what of the lady Aelfreya? Surely she must be betrothed?"

His deep voice sent a shiver like a breeze across Frey's flesh. Suddenly she was remembering how Nicol, out there in the woods that afternoon, had claimed her as his betrothed. Now Blaize was probing the truth of that assertion. With what purpose in mind?

Reynold, unaware of her thoughts, was saying,

"Not yet, I fear. Her dowry, like Emma's, is very small. But no doubt I shall find her a husband one of these days."

In face of this revelation, the look in Blaize's eyes sharpened to speculation and it was clear to Frey that he was wondering just what her relationship with Nicol was. Knowing that her face was scarlet, Frey carefully put a piece of bread in her mouth; she almost choked on it when Blaize said smoothly, "You're wise, Sir Reynold. A nunnery would hardly do."

Noting the fury in Frey's spitting eyes, he allowed his own eyes to gleam sardonically at her before he added, "I mean, it would be a shame for both of your sisters to be forced to take the veil."

He didn't mean that at all, Frey thought hotly, he meant that a life of penitence would hardly suit such a hoyden. He was reminding her of her unladylike escapade that afternoon. This was how he planned to have his revenge, with sly digs sharp as his sword, keeping her on edge and at his mercy. It was intolerable! She would not be toyed with in this way.

Only once after that did she allow her eyes to stray openly toward Blaize of Bayonne and then he returned her glance with cool, dark, glimmering eyes that seemed to hint at a secret they held in common. He lifted his brows in quizzical amusement and she met the look with a disdain that was spoiled by the hectic color in her cheeks.

In all her seventeen years she had never felt so unsettled, so deeply restless and unsure of herself. Blaize of Bayonne was the cause. He was a Norman, a man to be feared and despised, but he managed to disturb her more deeply than any man had before.

After examining the horses at the stud, Sir Blaize left Ketilfiord the next morning with

promises that the Earl of Chester would definitely
wish to purchase several colts. With Frey he exchanged no more than the politeness demanded by
the situation. She assumed the dark knight would
return to complete the transaction when a price
was agreed by the earl his master.

But when, that October, soon after the feast of
St. Ethelreda, a party of men arrived and took the
horses away, Blaize of Bayonne was not among
them.

Suddenly, for no accountable reason, Frey was
aware of little to look forward to, only the winter
days ahead, her chores and her embroidering by
the fire with stiff fingers, while smoke eddied in
chill drafts. She had always disliked the cold dark
days of winter but that year the months before
spring loomed ahead like an endless dank tunnel.
Life seemed very drear.

Before Christmas, Reynold's baby daughter
Lucy died—a tragedy which distressed Edith so
much that even Frey felt sympathy for the sister-in-
law with whom she shared a mutual dislike. But
many young children did not live beyond babyhood
and as it happened Edith soon discovered she was
with child again—Reynold had twice persuaded her
to allow him his husbandly rights, as Frey and
Emma had been forced to hear through the thin
partition wall which separated the bower from
their brother's private chamber.

Reynold had thought he was fortunate in
securing Edith for a wife. She had brought with her
ten hectares of land, and she was considered a
beauty with her blue eyes and yellow hair. But she
had proved to be shrill and vinegarish in
disposition. Neither she nor Reynold seemed to
derive much joy from their union.

"I think I shall never wish to marry," Frey said

to Emma one day in summer.

"Oh, of course you will," her sister replied with a laugh. "Nicol's bound to be granted a fief sooner or later. Only be patient, Frey."

"Patient?! I shall probably be old and rheumatic before Hugh the Wolf even deigns to notice Nicol. He has hundreds of men in his service. He can't grant lands to all of them."

"Then perhaps," Emma said slyly, "you'd prefer to come to York with me—to take your vows at St. Winifred's convent?"

"Ugh!" said Frey, a grimace expressing her feelings. She had not the makings of a nun and she knew it. But neither was there any immediate prospect of marriage. She was eighteen years old. Her life was rapidly drifting by.

Edith's second child was born in September, a fine healthy boy who was named for his grandfather Wulfnoth. Reynold was very proud of his son; every man wanted an heir to follow him. He began to speak more seriously of finding a husband for Frey, so that she too might give some man the joy of an heir, but he seemed unsure where he might find a man willing to take a maid of little dowry. One time when the subject arose, Frey was incautious enough to mention the name of Nicol of Linscote, which made her brother angry.

"You're to stop thinking of Nicol of Linscote!" he told her. "While he remains a household knight, without lands of his own, how can he possibly support a wife? Forget him. I'll find someone else. You may be sure of that."

However, another winter arrived, with no sign of any prospective suitor. Nor was there any word of comfort from Nicol.

During that winter, Reynold began to make

frequent mention of a man named Geronimus, a merchant he had met on his visits to York. The two of them seemed to be on very friendly terms and the merchant proved to be a generous man, often sending gifts of small luxuries like real wax candles and costly dyestuffs to the household at Ketilfiord. Edith in particular was impressed that her husband had acquired such a wealthy, openhanded friend.

In the spring, this Geronimus spent a night at Ketilfiord and held his hosts spellbound with his tales of journeying across the sea to strange lands to buy exotic merchandise and to expand his contacts among foreign dealers. But though Frey was as fascinated by his stories as the rest of her family, she felt strangely uneasy in the fat merchant's presence, for reasons which were only vaguely definable even in her own mind.

What mainly disturbed her, she decided, was the way he looked at her, his deep-set eyes straying over her body as if to probe through her clothes to the tender curves beneath. That bold stare made her want to go and wrap herself in an all-concealing cloak. She was glad when Geronimus departed.

"A fine man," said Reynold. "But for all his wealth he has no sons, though he has wed three wives. Sadly, all have died."

Privately, Frey wondered if the unfortunate wives had been crushed to death beneath the merchant's great weight. She could not understand her brother's leaning toward the man, nor Geronimus's keen and beneficent interest in a poor Saxon thane who held only one small manor and could be of little use to him in the way of trade. It was a riddle which bothered her greatly whenever she thought on it.

As midsummer approached, and with it the time of her nineteenth birthday, Frey sensed changes in the air. Emma was preparing to join the nunnery of St. Winifred in York before harvest and Edith was again great with child, about to produce a sibling for little Wulfnoth.

Reynold's small son slept in his carven cradle in the bower with his two aunts, with old Ula to attend him. Fortunately he was a sunny baby who slept well and gave little trouble. Frey found herself drawn to the child's one-toothed grin and often when she held him she wondered what it might be like to have a child of her own. Such thoughts inevitably led her to remember Nicol and to wonder where he might be. Had he made his mark yet with the earl? Would Hugh the Wolf ever grant lands to his faithful soldier Nicol of Linscote? As the months passed, the possibility seemed ever more remote.

Frequently, too, her thoughts turned to Blaize of Bayonne as she relived their encounter in the woods and recalled the supper when she had been alive to his every word and gesture, aware of him as she had never been aware of any man before.

Her older self now derided those memories. What a thoughtless child she had been! Blaize must have found the incident diverting—a childish escapade hardly worth his notice, except to amuse himself by goading her a little to enliven an otherwise dull visit to the wilds of Yorkshire far from the glittering court of the Earl of Chester. Even so, on many nights Blaize of Bayonne invaded her dreams with those compelling dark eyes, though as the months passed she found that, waking, she could no longer remember his face in clear detail. The loss of even his memory was a cause for secret sorrow.

She could not understand why she should wish to be able to picture Blaize of Bayonne. Whatever the emotion he had stirred in her, it meant nothing. It had been a dream, that was all—an unattainable dream.

As an added irritant that only served to increase her restlessness, she was informed by her brother that the merchant Geronimus was to pay another visit to Ketilfiord. With Edith so near her time, the tasks of hostess would fall on Frey; Reynold ordered her to take great trouble to make Geronimus feel welcome. The best food must be prepared, the hall cleaned and freshly lime-washed, and the ladies must have their best gowns ready to wear, their brightest smiles at call.

"Anyone would think this fat, fawning merchant was a member of the nobility!" Frey chafed to Emma. "The arrival of the Earl of Chester himself couldn't cause more fussing."

"No, indeed," Emma replied.

The soft, knowing tone of her voice sharpened Frey's attention. Suspiciously, she said, "You never say much about it, I note. Don't you agree that Reynold is demeaning himself? He may be poor, but his blood's as noble as many a prancing Norman's. Our forefathers have been thanes here for generations. Why does Reynold pay court to this lowborn merchant?"

Emma's calm hazel eyes fixed on Frey's face with a gentle, pitying expression. "Do you really not guess why Geronimus is coming to Ketilfiord, sister?"

"I've not the least notion!" Frey stated.

"You mean you choose not to recognize the truth."

For a moment Frey stared at her sister's pale, plain face with its vague and sorrowful eyes; then she spun away, nervously pulling at an end of her veil as her flesh shuddered in response to overpowering waves of heat and cold that rippled over her skin, raising all the tiny hairs. How blind she had been—perhaps deliberately blind, as Emma charged. She had not wanted to recognize the truth. But all at once she was seeing clearly and the solution to the conundrum was evident: Reynold needed a husband for the older of his sisters, but no man of rank would offer for a maid without dowry: The merchant Geronimus of York had need of a wife to bring him prestige, and the money to buy the favor of an impoverished thane. Put the two together and both problems were solved at once.

No! Frey thought as cold sickness churned in the pit of her stomach. It could not be true! That fat, obsequious, oily, *elderly* man . . . Surely Reynold could not expect her to agree to such a fate?

In the full heat of midsummer the sweating merchant arrived with a pack-train of mules, a whole string of servants and an escort of men-at-arms—an entourage that would not have disgraced a great lord.

Geronimus himself wore robes of the finest linen trimmed with silk. A gold necklet hung heavy at his breast, along with brooches and an ornate girdle twined with gold thread; his plump hands were thick with rings of gold, some studded with precious stones, trumpeting his wealth. He wore his hair in the old Saxon fashion, long and brushed back from his face; there was much gray in it, and in the long moustache and forked beard which he had a habit of stroking.

But above all it was his eyes that disturbed Frey—eyes whose color she could not determine, so deeply were they embedded in the fleshy face; little, sharp, gleaming eyes that seemed to be watching her rapaciously whenever she appeared. Those eyes told her that the repulsive man burned with desire for her; he could hardly wait to get his hands on her. The thought made her sweat with panic and revulsion.

At the noontide meal, Frey found himself placed beside the merchant, obliged to endure his fawning and his ogling. Once his hot, damp palm covertly spread across her thigh beneath the edge of the table cloth, kneading and exploring her flesh while he made unctuous conversation with Reynold, who appeared delighted with himself.

Nauseated, Frey waved away the dish of blackbird pie that was being presented to her. Pretending to settle herself more comfortably on her stool, she managed to jab a sharp elbow into the merchant's flesh-padded ribs, which made him wince and remove the errant hand from her thigh. He sent her a questioning sidelong look to which she replied with a cool, haughty stare that made his eyes narrow as if with approval. He did not expect a high-born lady to welcome his attentions, it seemed; but he intended to enjoy the battle he foresaw. It was a battle he would win, once she became his wife.

Feeling ever more sickened by the prospect, Frey was relieved when the meal ended and she had good reason to move far away from the merchant. Hurriedly she sought the shelter of the bower, sharply closing its door behind her.

"Why, mistress!" Stout Ula looked up in surprise from feeding young Wulfnoth his bread and milk.

The sturdy child waved his arms and grinned at Frey, but for once she was unable to respond to his merry appeal. She turned away in distress and went to the window, leaning her forehead on the smooth cool wood of the open shutter. A summer breeze flirted with her veil and a bee stumbled in briefly, lost on his way to the hives in the gardens. She wished she, too, had wings to fly away, over the wooded hills, away from fat, lustful merchants and unfeeling brothers.

"What's amiss, my maid?" Ula asked.

"You know, don't you?" Frey said dully. "Everyone knows. How can Reynold do this to me?"

The click of the latch made her glance around as Edith came in, her blue eyes flashing, her face puffed with the bloating of the late stages of pregnancy. Closing the door carefully, she moved into the room, a hand laid protectively on her distended stomach as she scolded Frey, "You're a fool if you refuse him! Think of the jewels you could have, the fine house, the clothes . . . With no dowry to commend you, you should think yourself fortunate. Your face could never be your fortune. You're nineteen years old. If you don't take Geronimus you'll have to go with Emma to St. Winifred's. No other suitor is likely to present himself."

Frey swung away from the window, her tawny eyes ablaze. "You don't have to remind me. I know what my choices are!"

"Then what is it you want?" Edith demanded. "Some handsome gallant to sweep you off into a world of courtly love? Tosh! You're a dreamer, Frey, that's your trouble. Though I daresay that if you wed Geronimus there could be flirtations enough in York for a young wife whose husband is forever off about his travels. You'd have more freedom there than you'll ever have here in Ketilfiord."

Shocked to hear her brother's wife express such outspoken views, Frey protested, "Edith!"

Edith's face twisted into pinched, resentful lines. "Do you deny that you enjoy flirtations? I seem to recall a man named Nicol of Linscote—"

The thrust went deep and Frey turned away to hide her pain. Edith knew how to wound with words. Almost two years had passed without word from Nicol, despite his vows of love and constancy.

"We all have hopeless dreams in our years of innocence," Edith said in a hard voice. "But reality must be faced sooner or later. You, at least, could have a life of ease—a life of wealth and luxury, with servants to do all your bidding and lovers sighing round you. Think on it. You have a little time to ponder your answer. The men are planning to go off hawking until suppertime. But tonight Geronimus will ask to speak alone with you."

"And I shall have my answer ready!" Frey said, her face blotched with angry color.

"Don't be a fool!" Edith exclaimed. "You will accept him. You *must* accept him—unless you really have a yearning to take the veil of abstinence and piety—for the rest of your life!"

The door closed with a bang behind her, startling the baby and making his lip tremble until Ula distracted his attention. Frey exchanged a glance with her one-time nurse, whose broad face was gloomy beneath its blue kerchief.

"She's right, my maid," the old dame said. "You have no other choice—unless your brother will take you in my place when I grow too old to care for his children. Do you want to end up like me—a nursemaid growing old on charity?"

"Edith would never agree to that," Frey sighed. "And even if she did I couldn't bear to be beholden to her. No, I can't stay here. One way or another, I must leave Ketilfiord. But—" Tears gathered behind her eyes and she threw out her hands in distress, exclaiming, "But I *do* have prospects! I'm promised to Nicol, Ula!"

"Not legally, you're not," the nurse argued. "And, besides, you know your heart won't break over that young man."

"But it will!" Frey insisted. "I love Nicol. I shall always love him."

Ula shook her head and turned back to the baby

as he grabbed her sleeve and shouted in his wordless way. He was a darling, Frey thought, but soon he would be joined by a brother or sister and the bower would become a nursery. With Emma gone, the manor would have no room for Frey. Her choice was simple: Geronimus or the nunnery.

Waiting until Reynold and his guest had ridden away on their hawking expedition, Frey fetched her soft reed basket, intending to go out for herbs. The pastime always soothed her when she was upset. Perhaps in the peace of the woods she might find the wisdom to decide what her future should be.

She took the track that led along the valley, past hay meadows where men with scythes were slicing down the tall grasses. A pig had escaped into the meadow and three men were chasing it. One of them dived to catch it only to have the pig slip away with an alarmed squeal, while the men cursed the young hayward for his lack of vigilance. Normally the sight would have made Frey laugh, but today she was too tense to appreciate the humor of it.

"Frey!" The clear voice drew her attention to where Emma was standing by the hurdle fence of a temporary enclosure containing a mare and her newborn, sickly foal. Frey sighed to herself; Emma always had to be mothering something—a puppy, a foal, a bird with a broken wing. With her quiet, caring nature she would fit well into the life of the nunnery.

"Look at this poor little thing," Emma breathed, bending to stroke the head of the listless foal. "He's almost too weak to stand. Oslac says he'll die."

If Oslac, the horsemaster, had given up hope, then the foal was doomed, Frey thought. But she said aloud, "Do you disagree?"

"I don't doubt Oslac's skill, but he has so many

other things to tend to. If I nurse the foal with care, and pray hard for it, it may yet recover."

"Then I, too, will pray—for your success."

Emma looked up, a hand shading her eyes against the sun. "Once you would have scoffed at me, Frey."

"With age, one learns tolerance," Frey said dryly. "Besides, now that I'm soon to lose you, suddenly I appreciate you more. I sometimes wish I were more like you. More . . . tractable. Instead I'm cursed with a headstrong nature to match my witch's hair."

Answering her sister's hidden tension rather than her words, Emma said, "What will you do about the merchant?"

"I don't know. I can't decide. I wish—" She sighed and, torn by conflicting emotions, threw out her hand, adding with a rush, "Oh, I wish some prince would ride out of the west, throw me over his saddle and carry me away to the gilded turret of his castle!"

"I remember that song, too," Emma smiled. "Last Yuletide. It was a favorite of that young minstrel who came. He was a bold fellow. He had a roving eye."

"So he did," Frey said with another heavy sigh. "And a roving nature, so it seemed. A pity he didn't stay longer. *He* might have carried me away. A life on the road would be preferable to living with Geronimus."

"You must pray for guidance," her sister advised, suddenly serious. "God's purpose is not always clear to us. Perhaps He has good reasons for wanting you to marry this merchant. And think—if you are living in York, you might visit me sometimes."

Frey bit back an impatient reply. It was all very well for Emma to talk piously of accepting the will

of the Almighty; Emma was happy with the life
ordained for her. Frey was more inclined to use all her
strength and ingenuity to fight against her own
fate, even if in the end it overwhelmed her.

From somewhere on the hill came the sharp,
high notes of a watch-horn as one of the shepherds
caught sight of something that alarmed him. Across
the manor, everyone stopped what they were
doing, alerted by the call; in the kitchen, scullions
paused and held their breath; the haymakers
paused to stare; the pig-chasers lay still, their
quarry squirming in their grasp. Shading her eyes,
Frey peered along the valley, looking for a sign of
whatever trouble threatened.

Where the track merged with the trees, a lone
horseman suddenly burst from the shelter of the
woods, coming at such a pace that his long dark
cloak flew out behind him. The hounds of the devil
might have been on his tail, though as yet there was
no sign of any pursuit as far as those watching could
see.

"Is it a hue and cry?" Emma asked.

"I can't tell, though . . . he doesn't look like any
runaway I ever saw." Frey squinted against the
bright June sun as the man came closer. "Look at
that horse, how swiftly it covers the ground. It's a
high-bred—" She forgot to end the sentence as a
shock of recognition swept through her.

Refusing to believe what her senses told her, she
instantly derided herself. Of course it wasn't Blaize
of Bayonne. So many times over the past two years
she had thought that some dark stranger riding a
black horse was familiar to her; always she had
been wrong. But now . . . now the illusion refused
to fade. The nearer he came, the more he resembled
her recurring fantasy.

And Emma, it seemed, was seeing the same
apparition. "Why, it looks like Sir Blaize of

Bayonne!" she exclaimed. "Do you remember him, Frey? He came here near two years past, bargaining for horses for the earl."

"Yes," Frey managed through stiff lips, a strange churning excitement keeping her rooted to the spot. "Yes, I remember him."

"Why do you suppose he's come again?" Emma said. "And why is he in such a hurry?"

Chills and fever ran through Frey, color ebbing and flowing in her face. The charging black stallion drew nearer, and nearer, bringing his rider too close for his identity to be in question. After all, now that she saw him again she realized she had not forgotten what he looked like. He was familiar to her from many unsought dreams.

III

The oncoming horseman had noticed Frey and Emma standing by the side of the track. He checked his mount to slow it from full gallop to canter, finally bringing it to a halt not far away.

Sweating and quivering, the black stallion tossed its head and stamped restively until Blaize of Bayonne leaned forward to stroke its neck with a soothing hand, speaking softly until the animal quietened. Flecks of sweat beaded its glossy coat beneath which muscles still twitched from exertion; evidently the stallion had been ridden hard.

Over its wild black mane, a pair of deep brown eyes met Frey's with a directness that startled her and set her heart to pounding erratically. He had come, at last. He had come in haste, on the very day when she was to be plighted to fat Geronimus. She hardly knew what to think of it. His sudden arrival could not possibly have anything to do with her imminent betrothal; in her reasoning mind she knew that. But try as she would she could not quench the tiny hope that Blaize's coming might somehow save her from the fate that waited.

"Sir Blaize!" Emma was the first to recover her composure enough to offer greeting. She bobbed a curtsey, smiling up at their visitor. "You are well come."

He inclined his head courteously, replying, "Good day to you, Mistress Emma," though his grave eyes never left Frey's face. His gaze searched her every feature, as if he were trying to read the thoughts that swirled crazily in her mind. He said, "Mistress Aelfreya. Is all well here?"

"Why . . . yes," Frey croaked, wondering why he, alone of humankind, had the power to wipe all coherent thought from her head. She cleared her throat and moistened her dry lips before adding, "Had you heard otherwise, sir?"

"On the road I met a pedlar who spoke of seeing sea-rovers off the coast," he told her. "Ketilfiord is vulnerable, so close to the estuary."

So that was what had brought him, the need to bring warning and possibly save valuable property which, after all, belonged finally to his master the Earl of Chester. But was that his only reason? Despite herself, Frey detected another purpose. Behind his explanations his eyes seemed to be alight, speaking messages other than his words imparted—messages that were at once intimate and concerned. Or was she being foolish and imagining more than was there?

Realizing that she ought to make some reply, she again ran the tip of her tongue across her lips, saying, "It's many years since Vikings troubled us here. Perhaps they were heading further south."

"Perhaps so," he agreed. "But one can never be sure with these pirates. They have a knack of appearing where least expected. Thane Reynold would do well to ready his defenses."

"You may tell him that, sir," Emma put in, pointing down the road where Frey now saw her brother riding in haste, his favorite hawk poised on his wrist. Fat Geronimus rode behind him, heels and elbows working as he urged his struggling mount on. Reynold must have been close enough to hear the alarum of the watch-horn; he had left his sport to investigate the cause of the disturbance.

The anxiety on his thin face lifted a little as he drew near enough to recognize his latest visitor. He reined not far away, exclaiming, "Sir Blaize! We're honored."

Geronimus labored to a halt beside him, hauling vigorously on the reins so that Frey felt sorry for the poor beast that carried the immense and ungainly rider. Its back would ache that night, no doubt. The merchant waved his hand in pantomime of a flourishing bow, his little eyes gleaming almost as brightly as the jewelled rings on his fingers. "Sir Blaize! My eyes rejoice to see you again."

Did they know each other? Frey wondered in surprise. She slanted a veiled look at Blaize and saw that he seemed not to share the fat merchant's delight in the meeting. His face looked stern and cold, his eyes shuttered as he returned the greeting: "Master Geronimus. You're far from home."

"Visiting good friends," the merchant laughed. "A man must have some respite from business, however successful. How fares it with you, my lord? And the good Earl Hugh? I trust he was pleased with the bales of silk I sent him."

"I know nothing of that," Blaize said shortly, and turned his shoulder to exclude Geronimus as he added confidentially to Reynold, "I heard tell of a squadron of Viking ships off the estuary. I came to make sure you were prepared, in case they choose Ketilfiord as their next quarry."

"That was good of you, Sir Blaize," Reynold replied. "But of late the sea-rovers seek richer pickings elsewhere. We have little treasure left for them to plunder. However, I am grateful for your concern, sir. We should be honored if you would sup with us and take shelter in our hall for the night. Tell me . . . What brings you this far into Yorkshire?"

Blaize seemed confounded by the question, though his hesitation was so slight that Frey fancied only she had noted it—she who was alive to every fleeting expression on that pleasingly fashioned face, every nuance of his deep, caressing voice. Perhaps she was the only one who guessed that he was concealing some secret, personal motive for being here.

But on the surface Blaize was smiling, saying smoothly, "I had business to attend to in the area—a mission for my lord the earl. But I confess I had hopes of finding hospitality under your roof tonight, Sir Reynold. I've ridden far today. This saddle begins to feel like stone."

"Come up to the hall," Reynold suggested, evidently flattered that the earl's emissary had sought out his humble home for shelter. "My lady will be pleased to welcome you. Frey! Emma! Make haste, your help will be needed."

"We shall come at once," Frey said, feeling almost sick with excitement mingled with dread. There was something strange about Blaize's arrival at such a moment. She tried not to think that it must have some connection with her future, but the hope refused to die.

A movement of Geronimus's hand caught her eye and drew her attention to where the merchant sat astride his snorting, shaking horse. He was stroking his beard, his eyes running covetously over her, as though anticipating his full possession of her. Tonight he will ask for my hand, she remembered with a shock, drawing her light mantle closer as if it were armor to protect her.

Glancing at Blaize, she saw that he had witnessed, and perhaps accurately interpreted, the silent exchange. His dark gaze pierced her, sharp and questioning, before he spurred his mount and rode off beside Reynold, with Geronimus behind saying fulsomely how pleasant it would be to enjoy the company of such an eminent friend.

"Geronimus had best take care not to let his tongue drip too much honey," Emma commented. "Sir Blaize is not the man to be flattered by a toadying merchant. Did you see his face?"

"I saw it," Frey replied.

"Aye—in truth you did," Emma observed softly. "In fact, sister, you saw little else but him from the moment he came in sight."

Alarmed that her feelings had been so apparent, Frey of course denied it at once. "Nonsense!"

"Scoff at me if you will," Emma responded, "but I was watching you. I know you too well. But Frey—" Her hazel eyes clouded with concern. "Do not forget who he is, and who you are. He's a highborn knight, used to the ways of the court. He probably has ladies dangling by the dozen—and probably also a good wife waiting back in Normandy. You could be nothing more than an hour's dalliance to a man of his station."

Knowing her face was scarlet only heated Frey's temper even further. She did not understand the thoughts and emotions seething inside her, but she knew they were unwelcome and she wished them gone as she turned on Emma in anger. "Why should I want to be anything to him? I hate Normans!"

Returning to the manor, Frey went about her housewifely tasks in place of the pregnant Edith, organizing the household for a supper at which two important guests would be present. As she moved about the hall instructing the servants on what cloths to use and what goblets to get out, she caught snatches of conversation around her. Near the

ornately painted screens by the main door, Reynold
was talking with his sergeant-at-arms, a grizzled
man named Grimwald, advising him to station his
men in hiding in the woods because Sir Blaize had
heard rumors of pirates.

"They've not attacked us here in twenty years,"
Grimwald objected. "Not since William the Bastard
harried the north and took everything of value we
Saxons possessed."

"I know." As if afraid that such talk might be
overheard and reported, Reynold cast a hooded
glance down the hall, to where under one of the
high window openings Blaize of Bayonne sat on a
bench talking with the gravid Edith, who had
young Wulfnoth on her lap. "But to placate Sir
Blaize," Reynold went on, "we'd best take proper
precautions. We don't want to give the earl cause to
chide us for not guarding his lands as well as we
may."

Expressing his disgust, Grimwald spat upon the
rushes that strewed the floor, though when he
spoke his voice was low despite its angry gruffness.
"*His* land! When Saxons wrested it from the forests
before the Normans ever dared dream of invasion.
Very well, my lord, I'll set the men on watch. At
least it's a fine evening to be out, even if they will
have to be content with a supper of bread and
cheese."

As Frey made for the bower to change her
gown, she saw that Edith had set the baby on the
floor. He was crawling rapidly and gleefully amid
the rushes, his head flung back to grin his one-
toothed grin at Blaize, who had left his seat to
follow. All at once, to Frey's astonishment, Blaize
bent and picked the child up, tossing him into the
air. Wulfnoth chortled and shrieked as he was
caught again in strong, safe hands, and Blaize, too,
laughed in undisguised enjoyment of the moment.

"Have you any children of your own, my lord?" Edith asked.

Blaize held the child closer, his laughter dying as he looked down into Wulfnoth's bright face. "Aye," he replied quietly. "A daughter."

Suddenly he seemed not to know what to do with the chubby baby, who had become an embarrassment. Perhaps he regretted the impulse to play with the child, which had revealed more of his deeper feelings than he had intended.

Frey stepped forward, so stunned by the news that he had a daughter—and therefore, perforce, by all the laws of logic and common sense, a wife—that she hardly knew what she was doing. Emma had warned her that Blaize probably had a wife, but she hadn't really listened. She hadn't wanted to listen.

"I'll take him," she offered, holding out her arms and fixing her gaze on Wulfnoth in order to avoid Blaize's eyes.

He relinquished the child willingly enough, but somehow during the transfer a ring he was wearing caught in a thread of her sleeve and as he sought to uncouple it there was an unsettling moment when he came very close, his hand touching her flesh, his bent head brushing the veil that covered her hair. Her chest felt constricted, so that she could hardly breathe, and her face was afire with awareness of him. From the place where he touched her a jolt like lightning seemed to sear up her arm to invade all her body, disturbing her intensely. Never had she been so tinglingly affected by a man's nearness, nor so acutely aware that such feelings were wrong. Wrong!

As he at last freed himself and drew away, their eyes met briefly and she saw from the naked, startled glance he gave her that he was equally aware and affected by that kindling contact; scorched by the sudden intimate knowledge that

flared between them, Frey cuddled the squirming
baby close and hurried with him to the bower,
where Ula took charge of him.

Frey stripped to her shift and washed her hands
and face at the earthenware ewer on its stand,
pausing with her hands in the cold water as a
shudder sent pimples racing across her skin. It was
wrong of her to let Blaize disturb her so. He was not
free. He had a wife. But of course he had a wife! She
had known that all along, though she had chosen to
ignore the obvious truth. He was a mature man, not
a green, untried boy. His rank had probably bought
him a rich heiress.

Why should it matter to her, anyway? He was
highborn, and Norman, and she just a poor Saxon
maid without dowry. For her even to think of him
in such intimate terms was folly.

But she couldn't help it! She *did* think of him,
dream of him. For two long years now he had
always been there in her mind, entwined with her
sweetest maidenly fantasies. Such thoughts, in his
absence, had been innocent enough; she had never
expected to see him again.

But now he was here, in the pulsing, vital flesh
that set her senses on fire and her thoughts
whirling. Why had he come back to Ketilfiord?
That moment in the hall just now had told her that
his interest in her was not all in her imagination.
And yet it frightened her, because nothing good
could come from it. She would be wise to avoid him.

An hour's dalliance, Emma had warned. Was
that all that Blaize wanted? Then he had sadly
misjudged his quarry. Aelfreya of Ketilfiord, proud
Wulnoth's daughter, would never be any man's
momentary toy.

Dinner on that fine summer evening was as rich
as Ketilfiord could provide, several courses of meats

and dainties, stews and roasts, followed by pies and confections laced with honey. Despite her efforts to avoid it, Frey once again found herself beside Geronimus, though this time he was too busy trying to impress Blaize to take insolent liberties under the cloth.

Blaize, while being polite, appeared unmoved by the merchant's fawning; and Reynold was almost floating with the pleasure of two such eminent guests.

Eventually the servants cleared away the food, leaving wine jugs and goblets on the table. Blaize drank sparingly, but Geronimus enjoyed his wine; it made him even more expansive.

"With your permission, my lord," he said unctuously to Reynold, "I've organized a diversion for your—and your ladies'—pleasure." Forcing his great bulk to rise from its stool he shook out the folds of voluminous robes and beat on the table with the gilded hilt of his knife, causing a ripple of silence to spread across the hall as all attention slowly focused on the high table and the portly merchant standing there. Having achieved the desired effect, he ordered his servants to, "Bring in those packs!"

As the burdens were carried in, Geronimus left his place on the dais to supervise the untying of lacings that bound weatherproof packaging. By now, the occupants of the hall were agog with curiosity. Behind carved wooden posts that supported the roof, the household servants lurked and gaped and a few children peered round the screens; even the housecarls had remained in groups to observe the spectacle and the dogs padded round sniffing, while Frey felt the interest and speculation among her family.

What Blaize might be thinking was difficult to assess. From the corner of her eye she could see him beyond Reynold, lounging on the manor's only armchair, toying with a goblet, his dark eyes narrowed as he watched the merchant's theatrical performance. His face was still, his expression unreadable.

In the center of the hall, Geronimus made a resplendent figure in his fine linen robes edged with pure silk. The garments flowed round his great belly as he moved and spoke, constantly gesturing with hands on which every finger bore a jewelled ring. And at every pause he would stop and stroke his beard, his little eyes sparkling as he enjoyed the effect his show was having.

With a flourish he drew aside an oiled cloth to reveal a wondrous saddle of polished, tooled leather, generously trimmed with silver. The sight of it brought gasps of wonder from many in the hall. "For you, my lord," the merchant declared with a flourishing bow toward Reynold. "A saddle from Araby. They say the Sultan himself has one just like it. A Norman baron at the king's court offered me twenty marks for it, but even though he was a friend I told him it was bespoken, whereupon he offered me thirty marks—and forty." His belly heaved as he laughed and pulled at one wing of his beard. "A rare saddle indeed, my lord."

"A gift fit for a king," Reynold agreed, clearly stunned by the lavishness of such an offering.

For Edith there was a generous length of blue silk—"to match her shining eyes." Frey saw her sister-in-law almost drooling over it. And for Emma the merchant produced a jewelled silver crucifix, offering it with a reverence that sat ill on him. "For your devotions, my lady."

Emma softly spoke her thanks, but as the merchant turned away she shot an unhappy look at Frey. The sisters shared misgivings about the meaning of this extraordinary largesse.

"And now—" Geronimus was declaiming, picking out a heavy leather bag which he opened and upturned over the table. "For my lady Aelfreya—" A glitter of gold and green fell with a jangling thud onto the tablecloth—arm-rings, brooches, pins, and a triple row of green glass beads. "I heard that you once expressed a wish for such a necklace," the merchant murmured, letting the beads run through his hands like water. "Would that they were emeralds. Perhaps one day—"

Frey tore her eyes from the scatter of expensive trinkets and looked up into his bearded face. The small eyes embedded in his flesh seemed to be those of a merciless, ravening animal, hot and predatory.

Nothing could explain this extraordinary ceremony of gifts but that Frey was being bought—bartered for like a mare at market!

Suddenly the room felt stifling. If her father had been alive, she thought, this revolting man would never have been allowed to make such a show. Wulfnoth's noble blood would have recoiled at the very idea of a lowborn merchant displaying his wealth so freely—and for such a purpose—in the great hall of Ketilfiord. Unfortunately Reynold was of a different mettle from his father. He had only one concern—his own advancement and prestige.

Muttering, "Excuse me, I feel unwell!" she fled to the bower and slammed the door behind her, ignoring Reynold's exclamation of outrage at her lack of manners.

Ula sat on the floor by young Wulfnoth's wicker cot, rocking him to sleep, her eyes full of sympathy as she watched Frey. But not even the old nurse could advise her now, Frey knew. No one could help her. The decision was hers alone to make.

She sat on her bed, her fists clenched fiercely in
her lap as she fought back tears. She would not
marry Geronimus. She would not! But the alternative was a life of contemplation and prayer, a life
spent behind the high walls of a nunnery—not
necessarily as one of the nuns, not unless she
wished it, but certainly as their guest, immured
with them amid their cloisters and their quietness.

And she would take with her the guilt of
knowing she had refused a match that might have
helped to restore her brother's fortune; Geronimus
had made it clear that he would be generous to
Reynold if she accepted him. On Frey's answer
rested the future of all the heirs of Wulfnoth her
beloved father. Could she doom them to continued
poverty? Would they ever forgive her if she did?

As the noise from the hall abated, the tables
having been cleared and stacked away and the
household settling down to amuse itself during the
final hours of the long midsummer daylight, Emma
appeared in the bower. Grave-faced, she brought
the summons Frey had been dreading.

"Geronimus craves that you grant him the
honor of your attention for a speech he's most
anxious to make to you," Emma announced in
formal tones and screwed up her little nose in a
grimace of distaste, adding in a more normal voice,
"At least, that's what he said. He has our brother's
full permission to speak with you, Frey. I don't
think you can refuse to see him, even if you want to.
He'll be waiting in the garden for you. Frey . . .
what will you say?"

"I don't know." Hopelessly, she glanced at Ula,
but the nurse now seemed intent on the child; not
knowing what advice to offer, the old woman was
feigning deafness.

"God will guide you," Emma said with confidence.

Frey suppressed a quiver of irritation. She wished she could feel equally sure of divine guidance but her faith had never been as strong and sure as that of her sister. On reluctant feet she set out to meet the man who wished to have her as a wife—the man whose very appearance made her flesh crawl with revulsion.

She had still no idea what answer she would give him.

With her head down and her gaze on the floor, she hurried across the hall. She dare not look up for fear of meeting a dark brown gaze that would only add to her confusion. She didn't even know whether Blaize was still in the house; he might have gone out to take the air or check the guard. Someone was blowing a plaintive melody on a reed pipe and the young men and women of the household were making trysts to meet later when chores were done. Frey heard laughter and quiet gossip, the comfortable sounds of a warm summer's evening with twilight still an hour or two away and time to relax in the busy round.

At the top of the steps she paused to look out over her home, seeing a final cartload of that day's hay come rumbling home over the plank bridge with children dancing round it and dogs barking. As the horses clopped onto the cobbles, a chicken went screeching and fluttering out of the way, launching itself in ungainly flight to reach the safety of the thatch roofing the kitchen hut.

Beyond the thorn hedge lay the village, rows of wattle and daub cottages set each in its small vegetable patch. A clutch of women gossiped around the well, old folk sat in the evening sun, and against the church wall a group of men took their ease, passing round a jug of mead. Surrounding it all lay the fields and the meadows that provided food and work for the people of the manor, the cultivated acres stretching in all directions to where the woods circled protectively, enclosing the valley.

Contemplating that familiar view, Frey found her thoughts dark and unhappy, clouding her eyes and making her freckles stand out on pale skin. This had been home for her for all of her nineteen years. She knew no other home. But now she must leave Ketilfiord, one way or another.

It was a choice she did not want to make. Not yet. Not yet!

She would ask for time, she decided. Yes, that was the answer. Surely Geronimus would grant her a little time to consider all the implications of his offer?

The garden lay behind the hall, a place of apple trees and bee hives, reached by a path that skirted the kitchen huts and barns and passed through beds of lavender and other cultivated herbs. Very slowly and reluctantly, Frey set out to meet her fate.

But as she reached the corner of the manor house, Blaize of Bayonne appeared from the direction of the stables and, seeing her, lengthened his stride to join her. His ill-timed appearance had to be a coincidence, she thought; her impression that he had been watching for her, waiting for her to appear, must be erroneous. Whatever her foolish heart might choose to imagine, Blaize could not be interested in the fortunes of a simple Saxon maid.

Nevertheless, her heart was beating fast and suffocatingly in her breast as she paused and watched him approach.

He greeted her with a formal bow and a smile he must have practiced on all the ladies at the earl's court. "Mistress Aelfreya! If you're out to enjoy this fine fresh air, I'll join you. It's too pleasant an evening to be within doors." He caught himself, the smile turning deprecating as he realized his boldness and tried to amend it, affording her a little mocking bow. "With your permission, of course, mistress."

Frey felt as if she were a piece of living statuary, immobile but with every sense suddenly alert, every nerve quivering. Tiny beads of nervous sweat dampened her upper lip and her throat felt paralyzed. Part of her welcomed the intervention, though she knew that her interview with the merchant could not be prevented—only delayed. But there was more to it; whatever lay between herself and Blaize—and she knew there was something—it could not be. It *should* not be. It promised only shame and betrayal for herself. Even marriage to Geronimus was preferable to disgrace.

Quietly, firmly, wondering if he heard the slight hoarseness of her voice, she said, "I must refuse that permission, sir."

Blaize stared at her, his brown eyes slowly widening as though he didn't believe his ears; then suddenly he laughed aloud, evidently not taking her seriously. "Spoken like a countess!"

His laughter reminded Frey of the first time they had met, in the woods above the estuary, when he had uncovered her peasant disguise and laughed at her so heartily that she had slapped his face. She was older now, wiser, but still his mockery hurt her pride. Lifting her head proudly she faced him with blazing eyes in a face gone white but for two angry spots of color on her cheekbones.

"Even a peasant may choose the man she walks with!" she said in a cold voice that tempered his amusement and made him regard her with fresh interest. "Be careful, sir. My brother is within call and though you are his guest he does not take kindly to insults to his family."

His eyes had narrowed, though there remained a gleam deep in their depths, as if he didn't entirely

take her seriously even now. "But is your brother
so careful of your honor that he would object to a
man's merely walking beside you? With only the
most sincere of intentions? And—" His gesture
swept the courtyard, where servants were busy
about their tasks. "And in full view of your household?"

Her mouth set, she looked up at him through
her lashes, saying in an undertone charged with
anger, "I believe you know well enough why I
refuse you, sir. I know no way of making it clearer.
Besides . . . I am to meet someone in the garden."

"I know," he replied, all trace of mockery gone
from his face. And for a second time she was aware
of a silent communion between them, mind to mind
and heart to heart. It made her stomach perform a
strange, unsettling twist that seemed to clog her
lungs and make it difficult to breathe.

As she turned away to conceal her agitation, his
hand fell lightly on her arm, preventing her from
moving on, and when she looked up at him again
she found his dark eyes intent on her face. "Tell me,
mistress Aelfreya," he murmured, "is this match to
your liking?"

"I would rather die!" she admitted, low-voiced,
before she could stop herself.

"Then you'll refuse him?" His fingers tightened
about her arm, the touch shocking her by its
intimacy even while it made strange tremors interfere with her heartbeat and her breathing.

To cover her nervousness she summoned all her
dignity, lifted her head to look him in the eye and
said coldly, "This conversation is unseemly, sir. By
what right do you question me?"

"By the authority I hold from the Earl of
Chester—your liege lord!" His lips compressed as
his temper rose, but the hand on her arm relaxed
and fell away, taking with it the last stiff pretense

of formality between them. "Do not play the haughty maiden with me, mistress Aelfreya. I remember well that you disregard 'seemliness' when it pleases you."

Her head felt hot as she recalled the day when she had played the hoyden, dressing in peasant's clothing, meeting a man in secret, and daring to slap the face of a Norman knight.

"I was a child!" she said. "A headstrong child! If you had any notions of chivalry—"

"I was chivalrous enough to hold my tongue for your sake!" he reminded her in a charged undertone. "But I have not forgotten—not one instant of it."

Her thoughts in disarray, Frey turned from him, only to have him lay hold of her arm again and swing her back to face him.

"Is that your answer—to run away?" he demanded. "You ran away that day, too, as I recall, and your lover came valiantly to your rescue. To whom would you fly now—a lardy merchant?"

Betraying tears scalded her eyes. "Where else can I go—except to a nunnery? Please, sir!" Unable to bear his touch a moment longer she tore her arm away and fled from him—not toward the garden but back toward the house and the security of the bower. Geronimus would have to wait for his answer; she was too distraught to think clearly.

Somehow she composed herself sufficiently to cross the hall without attracting attention to her distress, but in the bower she had to face Emma's perceptive eyes. The younger girl was too astute not to notice her sister's pallor and the sheen of tears on wild, haunted eyes.

"You refused him?" Emma asked. "Was he angry?"

"I didn't see him!"

"Then what happened?"

Brushing past her sister, Frey sat down on her bed, trying to control a trembling that had seized her. She sat folded into herself, her head bent and her hands tightly clenched at her brow. "Don't ask me, Emma. Please don't ask!"

She could never speak of what had been said out there in the courtyard, especially not to Emma; the unworldly girl would never understand how it had been. The tension, the panic, the fright and—yes—the excitement of that lightning connection that kept flaring between her and Blaize. But what was it he expected of her? Even if he had been free, he would still never contemplate marriage with anyone but an heiress—a rich Norman heiress, not a penny-poor Saxon. The facts of reality and convention precluded any relationship between them except one that would bring shame to Frey.

Besides, she told herself frantically, repeating the belief as though it were a spell that could protect her against Blaize's sorcery, it was Nicol she loved, Nicol she wanted. She had been promised to him since childhood when they had first been sweethearts and friends. She would remain faithful to him until he came back for her, as he had promised he would. She had no intention of letting any man eclipse Nicol in her affections, especially not an arrogant, overbearing Norman!

"Geronimus is still in the garden," Emma said, looking down from the window. "Sir Blaize is with him now."

Frey looked up, astounded. "He is?!" Her curiosity piqued, she leapt to her feet and went to the narrow window opening, staying back where the men below could not see her. Beneath the leafy branches of an oak tree, the fat merchant was pacing restlessly, gesturing with stubby, beringed hands, while Blaize lounged against the bole of the tree watching him, apparently relaxed. They were deep in conversation, but though the murmur of voices drifted up to the bower Frey could not make out what they were saying.

"Geronimus looks agitated," Emma said. "I wonder what's wrong. Can they be talking about you?"

At that moment a scratching at the door announced the arrival of a maid with a message that Reynold wished to see Frey at once, in his chamber. Perhaps he had learned that she had not kept her appointment with the merchant. He would be angry, she knew, but she had best face him and give him some kind of explanation, if she could.

In the private bed-chamber next to the bower, Edith lay pale-faced on the bed with sweat glazing her upper lip and a hand to her distended stomach as if the child's kicking pained her. Reynold stood by his dressing chest, sweeping a hand again and again through his lank fair hair.

Frey had expected to face the force of his temper, but her brother didn't look angry; to her puzzlement he looked grievously worried.

"Is Edith unwell?" she asked in concern.

"She's tired," Reynold said shortly. "She's near her time. That's not important now. Aelfreya—" He looked at her sidelong from under his lashes, almost shiftily. "Has Geronimus spoken with you?"

"No," she admitted. "No, I—"

A sigh of relief escaped him, cutting off her excuses as he made a wide sweep with his arm and turned fully to face her. "Perhaps that's for the best. I seem to have been hasty, sister."

"Hasty?" She hardly believed her ears. Was there to be a reprieve? "You mean, over the subject of my marriage?"

"What else could I mean?" he demanded testily.

"God's wounds! My plans are frustrated at every turn. Now Sir Blaize tells me that the new law requires me to ask permission of our overlord before the matter of your marriage goes any further. Earl Hugh must be told the terms of the marriage contract, so that he may fix the bride-price—the tax I must pay before the marriage can take place."

"Which means," Edith muttered peevishly, raising herself on one elbow, "that the Earl will squeeze as much money out of us as he can, since Geronimus is prepared to be generous with his settlement." She looked at Reynold, adding, "But I still don't see why the earl should care what becomes of Frey."

Frey didn't understand that, either, though she could make a cynical guess: "No doubt it's the bride-price that interests him, not the fate of one insignificant Saxon maid."

This theory caused Edith to thrust out a sulky underlip. "As if his coffers weren't already over-flowing!"

"According to Sir Blaize," Reynold said, "the earl takes a close interest in all his fief-holders, high or lowly." His mouth twitched bitterly. "We, of course, are among the most lowly. But I believe Sir Blaize was taking the opportunity to remind me of my position as a vassal of the earl. If I disobey the rules—Norman rules—I may find myself, and my children, disinherited of even these remnants of the lands we once held."

Frey caught her breath in disbelief. "Reynold, no! It could never be as bad as that. The earl couldn't do such a thing!"

"But he could, Frey," her brother informed her flatly. "Many Saxons have found themselves reduced to the status of serfs on lands they have owned for years, on the most feeble of excuses. If we remain here it is by good fortune, and by the fact that Ketilford is a small and unimportant vill. So for the sake of prudence, before I allow Geronimus to speak with you, I must take Sir Blaize's advice and seek the earl's blessing on this match."

Glad as she was of any excuse for a delay, Frey could not help but feel bitter at the way her future could be altered on the slightest whim of the men in whose hands her fate lay. First her brother and now the powerful Earl of Chester. With a sharp, unhumorous laugh, she said, "A pity you did not think to seek *my* permission, brother, before you ever gave the merchant cause to cherish hopes. There were times, so I've heard, when a woman could not be given in wedlock against her will."

"Those times," Reynold replied, thin-lipped and hard-eyed, "are gone forever, like so many things of the past. I'll hear no more argument on this subject, Frey. If I'm to rise in this world—and my son after me—I need money to increase my holdings. Geronimus will help me. By marrying him, *you* will help me. Wulfnoth our father would have wished it of you."

"Do not call on Father's name!" she exclaimed in disgust. "He would have died sooner than give me to that revolting man, however wealthy. Wulfnoth our father had pride—pride that you seem to have abandoned, brother!"

He did not deny the charge, though his expression became even more pinched and cold. "I shift as I must in a changed world. You have won a delay—but a brief delay only. Sir Blaize will take details of our agreement to the earl, and when I've paid the tax he demands then the marriage will take place. At once."

"And suppose the earl refuses his permission?" It was a faint hope, she knew, but she had to voice it if only to comfort herself.

He snorted derisively and his mouth twisted into a smile. "He will not. As you yourself said, his only interest is the profit he might make from the transaction. He doesn't care about your fate, either way. Never forget how insignificant we are now. My people still call me thane, as they called my father and my grandfather before me, but in truth I'm nothing but a minor vassal of a great Norman magnate who holds my life and my welfare in his hands. And you—a girl without even a dowry to interest him—are less than nothing. Now go. Go to bed. There'll be no more discussion of this matter."

As twilight ended the long midsummer day, Frey and her sister retired to their narrow beds in the bower. In the darkness old Ula snored as she slept on her pallet beside the cot where young Wulfnoth was peaceful.

Emma's breathing came slow and regular and eventually Frey, too, slept. She slipped into unsettling dreams woven around eyes and hands—Geronimus's mean little eyes, set deep in his pudgy flesh, glittering rapaciously, and his hands, plump, sweaty, loaded with rings . . . and then Blaize, intent dark eyes hiding most of his thoughts, and *his* hands, lean, strong, brown, caressing . . . In her dream he was very close to her, mesmerizing her with his eyes while his hands moved on her. She realized she was naked but she felt no shame, not with Blaize . . .

She woke suddenly, shocked to hot wakefulness by the intimacy of her imaginings. Confused by the emotions those dreams had brought she sat up, trying to clear her head.

The other occupants of the bower remained oblivious in sleep, their breathing scarcely audible. Frey could see nothing in the total darkness imparted by the closed shutters, but she strained her ears to listen, needing to be assured of normality so that she might forget her disturbing dreams.

Everything seemed still—perhaps too still. Some sixth sense warned her that something was amiss. Then onto the silence faint sounds impinged themselves—a disturbance along the valley, centered on the distant whinnying of nervous horses. And then a shout.

Frey sat up, listening intently as her heartbeat quickened with apprehension.

Suddenly the night was split by the fast, penetrating notes of an alarm horn. Another joined it, closer at hand, and from the hall came scuffling and then a rising commotion as the household awoke to danger. There were cries of, "My lord! My lord Reynold!"

Throwing back her sheet, Frey groped in the darkness for the robe she had left hanging on a pole beside her bed. She covered her nakedness with it and went to the window, throwing back the shutters. Beyond the narrow window opening a half moon rode low and large in the sky, shedding faint light across the valley. The bright flare of torches was springing out here and there and she could discern the flow of movement among the horses against the hillside. Something was disturbing them. As her eyes adjusted, she made out dark figures among the herd, some already leaping astride the horses. Moonlight glinted dully on polished helms, and slanted ice along the blade of a broadsword that slashed down at some obstacle. A thin cry reached Frey's ears.

Vikings! Blaize had been right to bring warnings. The Vikings had come!

The knowledge screamed through Frey's head and made her scalp tingle. But, frightened though she was of the sea-raiders, her fear mingled with a strange elation, as if part of her welcomed the excitement.

A rush of flames beyond the barn caught her attention as the night lit with an orange glare and a scatter of golden sparks. The thorn hedge was alight! After the dryness of past weeks it burned fiercely, crackling and smoking, the flames rapidly spreading on the breath of a breeze. Even as Frey watched, a flaming torch sailed through the air toward the high thatched roof of the main barn. Fortunately it bounced off and landed in the courtyard where it could do no harm, but other brands would follow and the thatch was dry.

Was Ketilfiord doomed to die in a blaze of Viking fire?

"Frey?" Emma's voice came softly on the darkness as she joined her sister at the window and stared out with wide eyes, her pale face illumined by the growing flames. "Dear God! Is it the Vikings?"

"They're after the horses," Frey said. "That's why they're setting fires—to distract our men while they get away with the horses." A fierce knot of anger was building inside her at the injustice of it. After the depredations inflicted by William the Bastard and his armies twenty years ago, Ketilfiord was left with little of value—apart from the horses. Must they lose the herd, too? Life was so unfair!

"But why do they want the horses?" Emma asked. "They can't carry them off on their ships."

"No, of course they can't," Frey said impatiently. "But since they come from the sea they must travel on foot—unless they can steal horses that will take them swiftly inland. Then they'll go back to their ships and leave our horses scattered and broken-winded. God curse them! The sea-rovers care for nothing and no one but themselves and their plunder."

The baby had woken. His cries sounded plaintive in the night, mingling with Ula's sleepy shushing as she rocked him.

"Holy mother!" Emma moaned. "The foal is out there! The sick foal!"

Even as the meaning of the words reached Frey, Emma moved swiftly away from her side. Frey cried, "Emma!" but her sister's slender form slipped out of the door into a hall lit by yellow torchlight. Ula was there behind her, blocking Frey's way, crying after Emma, "No, my maid! No, don't go!" to no avail.

"Let me pass!" Frey gasped, but as she tried to get by Ula in the narrow space between the beds, the nurse whirled and caught hold of her with big, strong hands that fastened painfully about Frey's arms.

"No, no! Don't go. She's run mad! You mustn't go after her. There's danger, my maid. Danger!"

"Let me pass," Frey repeated, her voice low but filled with authority. "I know you mean well, Ula, but I can stop Emma. I know where she's gone. You take care of the baby. He's Reynold's heir. He's what matters most. Now, please! Move out of my way!"

With a strength born of fear she tore free from the old nurse's grasp, thrust her aside and ran on slippered feet into the hall.

IV

Most of the men had already grabbed weapons and gone to help fight off the attack, but the women of the household were still in the hall, huddled in wide-eyed groups. In a corner, Geronimus comforted a sobbing Edith.

Evidently there was to be no bravery from the fat merchant, Frey thought in disgust, though since there was no sign of Blaize of Bayonne she concluded that he had not scorned to go to the defense of humble Ketilfiord. She had expected no less of him. Ignoring cries of alarm from the women who saw her, she ran out into a night lit by a fitful half-moon and by soaring, crackling, smoke-belching flames.

Men hastened hither and yon, shouting instructions, intent on saving their settlement in whatever way they could. Arms were being handed out from the storeroom cellars beneath the hall and most of the men now wielded a sword, a lance, or a cudgel. Some of them had formed a chain of water buckets to and from the well, in an effort to stem the fire that had now got a hold in the barn roof. Smoke belched skywards from the blazing thatch. But most of the activity was centered beyond the thorn hedge, outside the gates, where weapons clashed and men shouted as the well-drilled housecarls repulsed the raiders.

Gathering the long skirts of her nightrobe clear of the ground, Frey ran straight for the half-open gate and the plank bridge. A man called to stop her, but before he could do anything he was diverted by another torch which came spinning over the hedge and landed against the wall of one of the huts. Frey saw no more. She was through the gate, searching the smoky, flame-shot darkness for a sign of Emma.

In the back of her mind, sending terror coursing through her, was the thought that it was not only horses the Vikings prized. They made a habit of capturing women, too. Frey had heard stories of the treatment such captives received—slavery was the very best to hope for. If the raiders caught Emma and dragged her off . . . Frey couldn't bear to think what rape and violation might do to gentle Emma.

For herself she didn't care. She was older, stronger, tougher. Without thought for her own safety she made for the horse enclosures, intent only on saving her young sister.

As Frey had guessed, the Vikings' main purpose was in stealing the Ketilfiord horses to use as mounts for a foray further inland from the coast, where unsuspecting manors slumbered peacefully that midsummer night. If the guard had not been alert in the woods, thanks to Blaize's timely warning, the sudden raid would have caught the manor with few defenses and by now the pirates would have stolen what mounts they needed and been heading away in search of richer pickings. As it was, they had a struggle on their hands. Their first assault on the herd was being strongly repulsed.

All of this Frey gathered as she searched for her sister, slipping from shadow to shadow, keeping on

the edge of the fight, her whole mind fixed only on
the need to find and protect Emma.

In darkness shot with the glare of firelight,
swathed with drifting hands of thick smoke, it was
difficult to make out exactly what was happening.
Here and there, seen as dark shapes amid the swirl
of smoke, backlit by flame, housecarls struggled
with Viking invaders who came running with
flaming brands to add to the confusion around the
manor house. Further off, the shrill neighing of
panicked horses and the clash of steel on steel joined
the soft thunder of hooves as the herd turned this
way and that across the hillside.

Some of the Vikings had already captured a
mount, using crude rope bridles and riding bare-
back on highbred animals unused to such treatment. But those of the raiders thus mounted had an
advantage over the defenders; they turned back for
the manor to aid their fellows in the struggle.

Frey saw a mounted Viking come galloping out
of the smoke and darkness. Firelight glared along
the edge of the axe he swung in his hand as a housecarl charged with a lance. The axe flew, missing its
target. The lance sank home. The raider was jerked
from his mount and the horse came on, forcing
Frey to dodge aside from its flying hooves.

But in ducking she saw Emma's robed form
among the shadows, making her way along the
fence that guarded the hay meadow toward the
enclosure where the sick foal was being kept with
its dam.

"Emma!" Frey yelled, but the cry choked off as
a billowing cloud of smoke hid her sister's slight
form. The smoke bit at Frey's eyes and caught in
her throat, making her cough and throw up her
arms as if to ward off the acrid cloud. For a moment
she was blinded, choking until she was almost sick
as she stumbled on and found herself up against the

hurdle fence of the meadow. She leaned there, blinking and gasping for breath, lungs sore and eyes streaming.

Emma appeared to have vanished into the livid night.

A bellow of triumph alerted Frey to renewed danger for herself. Through aching, bleary eyes she saw a giant horseman come swooping out of smoking darkness into the glare of firelight, a figure from a nightmare, thick-bearded and fierce-eyed, wearing a horned helmet that gave him the appearance of a demon. Directing his horse straight to where Frey cowered helplessly against the fence, he bent low and scooped her up in one massive, iron-muscled arm.

A scream tore out of her as she was lifted from the ground and carried away. She struggled in his grip but he held her fast, his arm like a band of steel clamped about her slender waist as he urged his horse on and away. She was jolted against hard muscles, borne through a melee of frightened horses and fighting men, all lit by the fires and smoke of hellish night. Then the battle faded behind them as the Viking thundered with his prey out into the darkness of the valley.

Impotently Frey screamed and struggled, straining to break the iron grip about her waist, but her efforts proved futile. She was tossed like a rag doll against the Viking's massive thigh, jolted and jarred until every bone and muscle ached. The man stank like a goat. The stench of him assailed her with waves of nausea. His arm threatened to crush her ribs. Her senses protested and faintness threatened to bring oblivion as a surcease. She felt herself slipping into a black tide of unconsciousness.

Then dimly, as if it happened far off from her, she felt her captor straighten with a jerk. His hot

grasp slipped. He seemed to fall backwards. Frey
was released. Helpless, she jounced off the flank of
the flying horse and the ground came up and hit
her, rolling her over and over until she fetched up
against a rut of ground.

Winded, she lay for a moment recovering her
breath. Her faintness had fled, leaving her weak but
fully aware, so that slowly her senses accepted that
all motion had ceased and the immediate danger
was over. Then, her mind still dazed and incoherent, she instinctively leapt up and, driven by
pure terror, began to run up the hill for what
seemed the best hiding place—the woods, thick
with impenetrable shadows under the moon.

All at once, to her horror, she heard a shout
behind her—someone was after her. She heard his
heavy breathing, heard him curse in an alien
tongue as he blundered into a gorse bush. The
Viking! Aided by faint gray moonlight and her
own knowledge of the terrain, Frey followed an
uneven course up the hillside, past bushes and
bracken, her heart pounding in her throat. She
must escape. She must not stop! The pursuer
followed.

Panic spurred her on to greater effort as her
mind worked in wild spurts. The Viking who had
caught her had been riding without a saddle or
proper bridle. He must have been unhorsed, probably unbalanced by her struggling. But he wasn't
going to let go of his prize so easily. The sea-raiders
were known to be merciless in their dealings with
captive women; they took their pleasure and
carried their victims off into slavery.

That was the fate that waited for her—her
tender body violated by the lust of a stinking pirate.
She must run. Run! In the night-dark woods she
might escape him.

Reaching the first of the trees she swung under

a low branch with all her weight, letting the branch spring back behind her as she leapt free. It caught her pursuer full across the chest and stopped him in his tracks. She heard his, "Oof!" of surprise and pain as she darted into a tangle of undergrowth.

But she had not gone much farther when, in the darkness, her foot in its thin slipper stamped hard on a twig. The twig snapped and a sharp pain pierced the ball of her foot.

Biting back a cry, she checked the rhythm of her stride and inevitably stumbled. In the same moment a hard hand snatched at her from behind, closing like the jaws of a trap about her upper arm. Off-balance, she fell. Her feet tangled with the man's legs. He toppled with her, landed on top of her. His weight winded her. His hands clawed at her. His body pinned her down.

Numbly, she waited for what must inevitably come. When the red rage of lust was on a Viking, he forgot everything else.

For what seemed like endless moments the man lay gasping for breath, his chest heaving, then his voice came deep and soft through the blackness under the trees. "You still run like a deer," he observed dryly.

Surprise and relief tore a gasping sigh from her; she knew that voice well. "Blaize!"

There was a moment's silence during which she realized she had afforded him no title but had addressed him intimately by name and somehow she knew that the significance of it was not lost on him, either; then he said, "Even in the darkness you know me. As I knew you, through all the confusion of battle and night."

"You . . . attacked the Viking who had me?" she asked, remembering how the man had jerked and fallen backwards from his horse as he dropped her—as if, she realized now, he had been injured by a blow from a weapon.

"And lost my sword in the process," Blaize confirmed dryly. "Aye, mistress."

"Then I'm grateful, sir. I . . . I owe you my life."

He let out a breathy laugh that was almost a snort of derision. "I doubt it was killing he had in mind. It's not your life you owe me, mistress Aelfreya."

"Then what?" She was still too dazed to think clearly.

There was a moment's hesitation, then he said softly, meaningfully, "Your chastity, perhaps?"

Self-consciousness ran hot and alarming through her veins, bringing fire to her cheeks. A note in his voice made her vividly aware of the intimacy of their situation; he was lying virtually on top of her there in deep shadow under a canopy of trees. He had made no attempt to move away and free her from his weight, and since he was lightly clad in little but a shirt and breeches she could feel every contour of his strong body—as he must be aware of her firm and tender young curves through her thin robe. She was glad that darkness hid her blushes.

He bent his face closer to hers, his breath fanning warm against her face as he said in a throaty voice, "And how will you repay this debt of honor?"

Feeling hot, Frey twisted her head away, protesting. "Sir! It is unworthy of you to take advantage when—"

"But a man deserves some reward," he murmured huskily, and brushed his lips against her arched throat. "Come, mistress."

Sparks of delight seemed to leap through all her veins, centered on the place where his lips had touched her. Her body was trembling in response to the nearness of a lean, muscular male frame, but her mind recoiled from acknowledging the pleasure in the experience. Her willingness to respond shocked her with its pagan heat. She would not give in to his shameful demands. She would not!

Controlling her voice with an effort, she muttered, "You're no better than that Viking!"

"Hush!" the answer came sharp.

"I will not hush! Do you think I—"

The words choked off as without further ado his hand clapped firmly across her mouth, silencing her for sure. Infuriated by such errant handling, Frey squirmed beneath him, moaning protests in her throat. Then suddenly her struggles ceased and she became still, for she had heard the sound that had made him hush her—a pounding of hooves, running like thunder through the earth, growing in volume as riders headed straight toward the place where she and Blaize lay concealed in the woods.

The Viking raiders were leaving the fight. They had the horses they wanted. They were moving on.

The horrified Frey lay motionless and half-stifled beneath the knight, with his hand still painfully clamping her mouth, as the Vikings swept up the hill on their stolen horses. Raucous laughter and shouts of triumph joined with the first faint twitterings of birds. The riders crashed into the woods, calling to each other in rowdy enjoyment as they swept by not many yards from where Frey and Blaize lay hidden.

A cold chill of fear cleared Frey's mind. What had happened at the manor? Was everything burned—house, stores, granary; the horses stolen, the people slain? And her family—? Reason told her that the raiders had been too few to inflict much damage, that they had stayed only long enough to steal the horses they needed. Ketilfiord boasted sturdy defenders, loyal to Reynold, who would have fought hard to save what they could. But Frey felt sick as she remembered how Emma how run into the darkness after the sick foal. What had become of her? Had she died with a sword in her breast, or under the galloping hooves of stolen stallions? Or, worse still, been swept away by some rough raiders from the sea, to a fate that would destroy her by slow inches?

If anything had happened to the gentle Emma, Frey thought, then her own stupid life was not worth living.

As the earth ceased shaking under the beat of hooves, Blaize shifted slightly. The pressure of his hand on her mouth eased enough for Frey to part her teeth and sink them into the side of his palm.

He tore his hand free with an oath. "She-cat!"

"So take me!" she hissed. "Take me and have done with it. Isn't that what you want?"

He bent closer, saying in a hard voice, "Aye, mistress, indeed it's what I want—what I have thought of often these past long months, waking from dreams to lie sweating and sleepless. Why else do you think I returned?"

Appalled to discover she had been right about his intentions, she began to struggle, pummelling his back and ribs with her fists. "Norman dog! French fiend! Ravisher of—" Again the words choked off as he silenced her—not with his hand this time but with his mouth, hot and hungry over hers.

For a moment she was frozen with shock and outrage, and then she began to fight him. He was as bad as Nicol! No, he was worse. At least she had gone freely to spend time with Nicol. This Norman was stealing favors she had no wish to grant.

She pounded him with her fists, pulled his hair. Her nails sought to gouge out his eyes. But he captured her hands one at a time and held them on either side of her head while he pillaged her mouth with hard lips and a serpentine tongue whose attempts at invasion horrified her. She kept her mouth clamped shut, determined to deny him as she had always denied Nicol.

But when, finally, he lifted his head to look down at her, the deep desire in his eyes affected her deeply. The sky was lightening fast with the early June dawn, the birds rousing the woods with their merry chorus. For a long, silent moment Frey lay still, staring in bewilderment at a dark face that for almost two years had haunted her dreams.

She had never been more confused as to the true nature of her feelings for Blaize. All she knew was that with Nicol she had never actually wanted to give in to him; her reluctance had never been feigned. But with Blaize . . . with Blaize the argument was all from her head. Her heart, and her physical self, were only too eager to explore the new emotions that he created.

"Aelfreya!" He spoke her name very softly, in a vibrant, trembling croak that spoke straight to her heart. He held her entranced with opaque, pleading eyes as he bent closer again, until her sight blurred and she closed her eyes, unable to resist the spell he wove on her.

This time his mouth moved gently, coaxing her lips to part. The tip of a warm tongue slid across her underlip, tasting the honey of her mouth. Strange sensations began to course through her, like nothing she had ever known. Her body had come alive to the shape of Blaize against her, her hands of their own accord were caressing him, and she felt her lips soften eagerly to answer the sweet pressure of his mouth.

"Aelfreya!" he murmured hoarsely, and something stirred deep inside her, a languorous flow warming her veins as he laid soft kisses across her face to the hollow below her ear. Every touch woke fluttering responses across her skin, sensual pleasure dampening every desire to resist him.

Frey felt herself held in thrall, unable to resist the call of her senses. He wove a magical spell that robbed her of all strength of will and made her wish only that he would continue to work his enchantments until she drowned in delight.

Then, when she was totally bewitched and almost beyond thought, he spoke softly, mockingly in her ear, saying, "So shall the Norman dog tame the Saxon wildcat."

For a moment her mind refused to comprehend him, so enraptured was she. Then as the meaning of his words penetrated her euphoria a black fury of shame and self-disgust swept through her. What a fool she was. How nearly he had made her believe that his tenderness meant he truly cared for her, when all the time he had been working his wiles for his own ends. But he was mistaken if he thought he could make her subservient to his will, as if she were any common serving wench. She must never let him know how deeply he had moved her with his kisses.

"You will never tame me, sir," she managed in a voice thick with loathing.

Blaize laughed sharply and rolled away from her, lithely coming to his knees. He bent over her, grasping her shoulders to pull her into a sitting position as he argued, "And I say it shall be so."

"Never!"

His eyes seemed to burn with a dark fire that hovered between anger and amusement. He shook her a little, as if in exasperation. "So the challenge is laid. So be it. Deny me if you will, though you will regret it, mistress, before you grow old. You forget who I am."

"I do not forget!" Frey spat at him. "You're a foreigner, an upstart, a treacherous Norman—a lackey of Hugh the Wolf!"

His brow furrowed in a swift black frown. He looked so angry that she feared he might strike her. But she had been gathering her feet under her and she sprang up, taking him off guard. A little push and Blaize went sprawling in the undergrowth while Frey made her escape.

Or tried to. She had forgotten the thorn in her foot. Each step brought agony to sear up her leg, but she moved on in a curious lopsided, half-hopping gait, limping heavily on her right foot and constantly biting back exclamations of pain. She was aware that Blaize was following her and could easily have caught up with her, but he remained a pace or two behind, saying nothing, apparently content to let her stubbornness have its way.

Frey pressed on, her pride forcing her not to acknowledge the knight's presence.

The morning light was bringing color back to the world, lighting the sky to hazy blue and restoring the rich greens of summer to the woods. Birds clamored joyfully among leaves wet with early dew. Soon Frey's thin nightrobe was damp, threads pulled and torn by prickly branches. She had begun to feel chilled and weary as the strains of the previous night took their toll.

Coming to the low bough of a mature oak tree, she leaned on it, closing her eyes against shaming tears as she lifted her sore foot to clasp the ankle, seeking a moment's respite from the throbbing pain.

"How much longer do you think you can go on?" Blaize asked from directly behind her. "Be sensible, Aelfreya. You're hurt."

"Save your concern!" she snapped, but a sob escaped her, weariness and despair combined. It was no good resting here. She must go on.

But when she put her foot again to the ground a sickening shaft of pain shot up her leg. White mists of oblivion gathered like clouds across her mind. As she fought the faintness her knees weakened and she sagged with fatigue, finding herself supported in Blaize's arms, her cheek against his linen shirt. Half swooning, she thought how much easier it would be to stop fighting him, to lean on him and let him order her life as he wished.

Resenting her own weakness, she told herself sternly that she must be mad—mad with pain and with the distress of wondering what had happened back at Ketilfiord. But she had no more strength to help herself. A choked laugh sobbed out of her as Blaize knelt with her, gently laying her down among soft, dewy grasses. When he was sure that she was comfortable, he gave his attention to her wound, carefully removing her slipper to examine the sole of her foot.

"It's bleeding!" he informed her accusingly, dark eyes flashing a stern glance at her face. "You have a thorn in it. Gone deep."

"I can feel it," Frey said.

"Then lie still and let me remove it."

He sounded angry, but beneath the anger lay a genuine concern and perhaps a touch of guilt because he had not realized sooner just how much discomfort she was enduring. His sudden kindness, coupled with her own feelings of sheer helplessness and vulnerability brought more tears to her eyes. She flung an arm to cover them. She would not allow Blaize of Bayonne to see her weeping.

Though he was as gentle as he could be, still his ministrations made her sweat as he sought to gain purchase on the thorn embedded in her sole. Her

teeth clamped tight on her lower lip to prevent a
cry from escaping, the pain she inflicted helping to
take her mind from the agony in her foot. Then at
last she heard Blaize exclaim in satisfaction and the
torment lessened. She lifted her arm from her eyes
and blinked at him from under it.

"Is the thorn gone?" she asked.

"Aye. All gone." He rested her foot on his knee,
absently massaging her throbbing ankle as his dark
glance flicked over her, moving from her pale
freckled face down the slender length of her body.
That look reminded Frey of how lightly she was
clad—in a thin, damp nightrobe knotted with a girdle
at her waist. The robe had parted over her leg and at
her bosom, revealing too much of her tender flesh.

All at once the warm intimacy of his touch became unbearable.

Grasping the edges of the robe, she drew it
tightly about her throat and sat up, freeing her foot
from his grasp and gathering the robe to cover her
limbs. Hot color flooded her cheeks as she tossed
back her tangled hair and met his eyes defiantly.
His gaze was veiled, hiding all his thoughts.

It was full light now, with the sunrise beyond
the trees sending a golden glow across the sky. Frey
saw dirt smudged across the brown face of her tor-
mentor, and a smear of blood trailing from a slight
cut on his brow. His dark hair was dishevelled, his
shirtstrings hanging loose. Evidently he had
dressed in haste when the alarum notes rang out
their warning of danger, though he had found time
to don his sword belt. He had, she remembered, lost
his sword in saving her from the ravening Viking.
His scabbard now hung empty, though a smaller
leather sheath contained his jewelled dagger.

Challenges of a sexual and personal nature
flared between them, transmitted by the lightning
glance they shared, but the words Blaize spoke

were of other matters. "You have courage, mistress Aelfreya. Many a lady would have screamed aloud from the pain that thorn must have caused you."

"Not I." Proudly she tossed a lock of copper-red hair back over her shoulder, fixing him with a fierce glare that belied the sheen of tears in her tawny eyes. "I am Wulfnoth's daughter, with the blood of Danish kings in my veins."

"And on your lip," he observed. "You've bitten it through." He glanced down at his hand, flexing it in remembrance. "Your teeth are sharp as knives."

Frey's eyelids flickered and dropped as she looked away from him, reddening. She had bitten him, to add to other insults. She knew he would not forget, or forgive, easily.

Nervously, she licked her dry lips and found the sore spot where she had bitten herself. She soothed it with her tongue, causing his gaze to be drawn to her mouth. Realizing it, she clamped her mouth shut as a wave of hot awareness surged through her.

She had never felt so alive before and it troubled her that Blaize should be the cause. Chasms divided them, but at that moment they were simply two human beings, a man and a woman, alone together in woods full of dawnsong, stripped of the usual barriers of comfortable formality. Her skin seemed to ripple in that knowledge, her womanhood responding to his masculinity in a way that shocked her. If he guessed how he affected her, he would probably believe he had been right to call her strumpet. She must use every device at her command to correct any wrong impression her earlier behavior might have given him.

"What do you mean to do with me?" she asked, hating the catch that was quite audible in her voice.

Blaize widened his eyes, parodying innocence. "Why, take you home, mistress. What else do you expect?"

He picked up her slipper, reaching for her bare foot, but Frey recoiled from him as from a viper, afraid of restirring the feelings his touch could evoke. In response, he glared at her darkly. A wordless snarl broke between clenched teeth as he tossed the slipper at her.

"You were glad enough of my touch when it freed you from the thorn," he reminded her roughly. "Aye—and back there in the thicket when you quivered so charmingly beneath my hands."

"If I trembled, it was with revulsion!" she flung at him, denying her own memory of those moments. She must have been mad to let him enchant her, however briefly. "I would never willingly submit to any Norman."

Deep brown eyes veiled by dark lashes surveyed her from a face like stone. Quietly, deliberately, his voice deep with threat, he said, "You will submit, my lady. Sooner or later, willing or no. This I vow by all the saints—you will submit!"

Before she fully comprehended this threat, he straightened to his full height, glowering down at her with one hand resting tightly round the jewelled hilt of his dagger. Eyes widening, she stared at his whitened knuckles, suddenly afraid for her life.

Her thoughts must have shown in a face from which all color had drained. His mouth twisted in response. "No," he said, his voice deep and silky. "Not with a blade. I have subtler weapons, as you will learn."

Subtler weapons? she thought, remembering the spell he had cast on her with his kisses. Did he intend coldly to set out to seduce her? The thought of it sent ripples of heat and chill across her skin as the blood came and went.

Watching her blush and grow pale by turns, Blaize smiled to himself as if satisfied by her reaction. "Now, put on your slipper and let us be gone. Your betrothed will be anxious about you."

Dragging the slipper on, Frey looked up, her heart sinking in despair as memory returned. "My betrothed?"

"Aye. The merchant Geronimus."

"Oh," she said dully, remembrance dousing her in cold reality.

He bent and slid a hand beneath her arm, lifting her to her feet, and before she could move away his arm snaked round her, pulling her in close to his side as he added meaningfully, "A fine husband the merchant will make for you. Such a fine, fat, *wealthy* man." A long finger under her chin forced her face up until she was staring deep into his glinting eyes.

His body felt taut and hard against her, sending an uncontrollable shiver of response through her. Sensing it, Blaize softened his expression and let his gaze caress her face as he said softly, "Unless, perhaps, I might persuade Earl Hugh to forbid the match."

Frey stared at him with wide, questioning eyes, her mind working. Just what was she expected to deduce from that enigmatic remark? Did he mean that he would attempt to influence the earl—perhaps in return for certain favors from her? He had made no secret of his desire for her. She ran her tongue across dry lips, appalled that he could think of using his position for such unscrupulous purposes. "Why should he do that?" she breathed.

"He can do anything, if it suits his whim," Blaize replied, and added, tightening his arm about her as if to emphasize his meaning, "Anything." He surveyed the tender mouth so close beneath his own and she saw the flicker of hunger gleam again in his eyes. "And you, mistress Aelfreya, have already told me that you would rather die than accept this merchant as your husband. Is there someone else you might prefer to wed?"

His nearness was confusing her, his chest, hip and thigh pressed close to her own so that her brain refused to work properly. She felt she could hardly breathe as she stared at the firm curve of his mouth and tried not to remember what his kisses felt like. "Any woman," she managed, "would prefer a husband of her own choice."

"And have you someone in mind?" he asked in a husky undertone. "Some lusty lover that you dream of in the lonely darkness of your bower?"

What was he implying? Was he referring to himself—offering himself as a spouse? Oh, it couldn't be! That was too unlikely. No, he obviously had some more devious notion in mind; it could not be marriage he was offering, not to Aelfreya of Ketilfiord.

"What of the lad who so boldly claimed you as his betrothed that day in the woods?" Blaize demanded. "Or is he only one of many?"

"No!" Her eyes widened in outrage and she began to struggle to be free, but he only tightened his hold about her waist, drawing her in even closer to him while his free hand spread at the side of her face, holding her so that if she kept her eyes open she could see nothing but his dark, taunting face.

"He alone, then?" he asked. "Is he a true lover, to whom you are forever faithful?"

Her emotions were in turmoil. The longer he held her the more she wanted to wilt against him, to have him kiss her again. Panicked by that thought, she answered passionately, "Yes! Yes! The only husband I ever want is Nicol of Linscote!"

His grip loosened so suddenly that she almost fell, but as she sagged against him he bent and swept her off her feet, carrying her bodily in his arms. "Then we had best go back," he said through bared teeth. "I to my duty and you to your Geronimus. Come."

In the aftermath of the Viking raid, Ketilfiord
counted its losses. Men-at-arms carried their
wounded fellows to shelter while similar sorry
parties cared for the dead. The barn had burned
down and the thorn hedge had blazed fiercely for
several paces before the flames had been extinguished by people wielding a chain of water-
buckets. What was left was a tangle of spiky,
blackened branches bereft of leaves. The horse
pastures stood empty but for the body of a Viking
impaled with a lance; those of the stock that had not
been stolen had been driven off, scattered into the
woods. Oslac the horsemaster was organizing a
search for them. Most of this Frey discerned as
Blaize carried her down the hill and along the track
toward the manor.

As he strode steadily past the enclosure where
the mare and her foal had been kept, Frey saw the
fence was broken down. The body of the foal lay on
its side, sprawled lifeless in the grass.

"Emma," she breathed.

Blaize looked down at her for the first time
since he had started the homeward walk with her
in his arms. "Mistress?"

"My sister," she muttered, resting her aching
head on his shoulder in her distress. "She came out
to save the foal. What can have become of her?"

Blaize said nothing—he knew the possibilities as
well as she did—but briefly his hold tightened as if
to comfort her. Oddly enough, she did feel comforted, but then nothing was as it should be on that
bright June morning.

Though the defensive hedge had been partly
burned the plank bridge remained secure, as did
the gates, standing open now to allow the flow of
people about their work of clearing and repairing.
Though the barn was a blackened mass of ruined
timber and thatch none of the other buildings had

taken much harm apart from a few scorch marks across their plaster. As Frey had guessed, the Vikings had wanted only the horses; since Ketilfiord possessed no treasure to arouse their greed, once their object had been achieved they had withdrawn. She supposed she should be thankful for that. It could have been so much worse.

But as it was it was bad enough. If any ill had befallen sweet young Emma then Frey would never believe in God's mercy again.

Several people exclaimed in relief at seeing Frey return alive to her home. Despite the confusion of the battle the previous night, her capture by the Viking had been witnessed and reported, the story spreading to every corner of the manor. Everyone had believed her lost forever.

Now, as Blaize carried her into the hall, Reynold came hurrying up, saying, "Thank God! Thank God you are safe, Frey! But, are you hurt?"

"A thorn in her foot," Blaize replied.

Frey saw relief sag through her brother as spots of color returned to his pale face. "God be praised if that's the worst she's suffered. Thank you, sir. Thank you for bringing her home. Indeed, thank you for all your aid in our troubles."

"Reynold—" Frey reached out to clutch at his sleeve, finding herself unable to put her fear into words. "Reynold, is Emma—"

"She's safe," her brother assured her, causing her to be as relieved as he had been a moment before. "She's over there, look—tending the wounded with Ula. God protects his own, it seems. And, Sir Blaize, your sword is here. It was found still in the body of one of the raiders. We owe you a great debt, sir."

Seeming embarrassed by the praise, Blaize muttered something about merely doing his duty as a knight of the realm.

At that moment, the merchant Geronimus swept up in his long robes and winged beard, expressing great concern over Frey's well-being. "Mistress Aelfreya! Oh, sweet mistress, how afeared we have all been for your safety."

"She needs to rest," Blaize said curtly, brushing the merchant aside as he strode with Frey to the bower. Over his shoulder, Frey saw the merchant's fat face go blank. He began to waddle in pursuit, only to be excluded when Blaize reached the bower and kicked the door shut in the man's face.

The bower was empty but for the tumbled beds. Frey directed Blaize to her own pallet by the window, where he gently laid her down and straightened beside her, watching her face.

Much comforted to know that her young sister was safe, Frey lay back among sheets that were still thrown back untidily, just as she had left them the previous night. Disturbed by the intensity of Blaize's gaze, she closed her eyes and gave way to the hot throbbing that pounded in her foot. It seemed to be swollen to twice its normal size. Sighing, she murmured, "I'm grateful, sir."

"Grateful?" he repeated dryly, his tone making her open her eyes to find him leaning over her, an elbow on his knee, a booted foot up on the side of her bed. His mouth curved in a rueful smile, lighting his eyes in a way that did strangely warm, unwelcome things to her emotions. "Grateful to a Norman dog? A French fiend? Grateful to a ravisher of women?"

Frey could find no reply to that. She watched him dumbly, wishing he would leave and yet wanting him to stay. Her feelings were confused, her thoughts cloudy with pain and exhaustion. She no longer knew what was right or wrong.

To her dismay, Blaize sat down on the bed beside her, stroking the tousled hair from her face.

His thumb brushed her lips and he bent closer,
making Frey catch her breath with a heady
mixture of sweet anticipation and frantic alarm.

"Sir!" she muttered. "We are in my bedchamber! My brother—"

"Will rush in and slaughter me if you so much
as raise your voice," Blaize finished for her, a smile
in his dark eyes. "I know it well. So scream,
mistress."

The silence lengthened. She could feel her heart
thudding in time with the pain that throbbed in her
foot, but mostly she was alive to the warm hand
cupping her chin, and the darkly handsome face so
close to hers, so very close . . .

As her eyelids drooped she felt his lips touch
hers with the softest, sweetest pressure, his mouth
moving on hers until he had the response he
sought. Frey felt as though she were drowning,
bathed in the sweetness of that kiss. She wished it
could last forever.

When Blaize eventually drew away she opened
her eyes and saw him searching her face intently, a
questioning frown puckering at his brow. He got to
his feet, backed away a pace still watching her, then
swung on a booted heel and strode out, closing the
door softly behind him.

Frey lay for a moment wondering why, this
time, she had not even tried to repulse him—had
scarcely thought of it. She must be mad. This wild
fascination that Blaize exerted was so wholly
against everything she knew and believed that it
could not be real. It must not be real! She must
exclude it from her heart, from her soul, cleanse
herself of all unseemly desires. The web he wove
about her could only entrap her in disgrace and dis-
illusion. She would not be an hour's pleasure, not
for him or any man.

V

With the help of Ula, who left off tending the wounded to serve her mistress, Frey bathed her foot carefully and laid fresh woodruff leaves against the wound before watching the nurse bind it with linen strips. Then she drew on her stockings, her shift, undertunic and plain green kirtle, and much against Ula's advice limped out into the hall to see what help she could offer.

Two of the housecarls were dead and seven others hurt. Among the wounded was tough old Grimwald, the sergeant who had fought beside Wulfnoth against the Normans in the early years after the Conquest. The village carpenter had been killed, too, but against these losses could be weighed five Vikings slain. It was generally agreed that the attack might have been much worse. In violent times, the Saxons believed in counting their blessings.

For Reynold, the loss of his horses cut deepest. Some of the scattered ones might be injured, or lost forever to wild animals in the woods; those that the Vikings had taken could be anywhere.

"They'll turn them loose on the shore when they go back to their ship," Grimwald advised, a clean bandage binding the wound in his scalp. "We'll search for them, my lord. With luck we may find at least some of them."

This assurance seemed to comfort Reynold, but not much; he went about with a frown on his face that only increased when it was discovered that his wife Edith was starting in labor a month before her time. The excitement of the previous night must have caused the child to stir too soon.

Having borne two children with great toil and pain, and being fully aware of the risks to her own life, Edith was terrified and consequently even more vivious than usual. When Frey went to her bed-chamber to help her, Edith screamed at her to get out.

"I'll not have you in here putting your witch-curse on me!" she shouted. "I want Emma to stay. And Ula. You get out, Frey. Get out, get out, get out! Witch! Witch!" The tirade ended on a high-pitched wail as Ula urged Frey from the room.

"You know what to do, my maid," the nurse muttered. "Take no mind of her ravings, now. Go and prepare the draught. We'll tell her I had it ready by me just in case. And get Mildgith to look after young Wulfnoth. We may be in for a long night."

As Frey limped across the hall she encountered Blaize, who gave her a bright, teasing look and murmured, "Witch? Ah, perhaps that explains it."

"I've no time for foolery," she returned, brushing past him. The epithet of "witch" hurt her, as Edith knew full well. There was little reason for it, except that red was held to be the witches' color and Frey's hair was vividly, undeniably red; add to this a certain skill with herbs—and a certain envy—and Edith had her grounds for name-calling.

As she hurried down the steps, she saw that Geronimus and his party were preparing to leave. She would have avoided the merchant but he espied her and came padding to set his huge bulk in her path, his hands spread out as if to detain her. But the look in her eyes made him pause, turning the gesture into a flourishing bow.

"Lady Aelfreya—" he greeted her fulsomely. "As soon as we have word from Earl Hugh I shall return to Ketilfiord for your answer. I trust I may rely on it's being favorable."

"For that," she said, "we must both wait on the earl's blessing, master Geronimus. Fare well. I trust you will not meet with any stray Vikings on your journey back to York."

Geronimus paled visibly, but before he could say any more she dodged past him and made for the kitchen store.

Preparing henbane was never a pleasant business. The plant stank so much that it turned Frey's stomach and the servants kept holding their noses as they passed. But experience had shown that only a decoction of henbane flowers would calm Edith during labor. It would lull her into a drugged half-sleep, making the work of her attendants much easier. The herb was poisonous if wrongly used; if Edith had known Frey was preparing it, she would no doubt have doubled her accusations of witchcraft and refused to take the medicine, imagining that Frey planned to kill her.

After a while, Ula appeared to complete the preparation of the draught. She remarked to Frey that Edith's behavior was worse than usual this time; Edith kept vowing that if she survived this birthing she would never let Reynold anywhere near her again.

"At least when this potion works it will spare your brother's blushes," the nurse added. "Shouting like she's doing now, Lady Edith can be heard right across the valley."

But those within earshot of the lady of the manor's hysterical outbursts had other things to

concern them by the time Frey returned to the hall:
the steward from the neighboring manor of Linscote—Nicol's home—had arrived in great distress,
with marks of tears still visible on his pale face. He
was seated in the armchair, with Reynold and
Blaize bending either side of him.

Frey saw her brother looked stunned while the
Norman's darkly handsome face was grave. The
sight made her heart turn over with unease. What
tragedy had befallen Nicol's home and family?

"Rest, fellow," Blaize was saying to the steward,
a hand on his shoulder as the man in his agitation
would have left his seat. "Take food and drink, then
I'll ride back with you and see what can be done. I'll
go and ready my horse—with your leave, Sir
Reynold."

Reynold seemed caught in some distraction; he
took a moment to understand then he nodded,
passing a weary hand across his brow. "Of course.
Yes. If there's anything we can do—"

"You appear to have enough on your hands,"
Blaize said. As he turned to leave he saw Frey and
swept her a bow, straightening to regard her with
deep dark eyes that asked questions but gave no
answers. "Fare well, mistress Aelfreya," he
murmured, and strode out.

There was a terrible finality in his voice. For no
reason at all, Frey was stricken by the sudden
conviction that she would never see him again.

The Ketilfiord steward, Bron, took charge of
comforting and refreshing his peer from Linscote
while Reynold drew Frey aside.

"Linscote was attacked by the Vikings," he told
her. "Half the village is burned, the manor house
destroyed. The thane and his family . . . They're all
dead, Frey."

Frey caught her breath, unable to believe such

terrible news, though the truth was written clearly in her brother's somber eyes. "Dead? All of them?" She pictured them in her mind—the kindly thane Heric, his gentle wife, their pretty young daughter Guendolyn, and their older son Philip—fair-haired, merry Philip, who in years past had pretended to rival his brother Nicol for her affections. It was impossible to believe that they were all gone.

"Poor Nicol!" she sighed, her eyes flooding with tears.

Reynold's face stiffened with disapproval. "Your thoughts fly straight to him, I notice. Well, no doubt now that Philip's gone his brother will inherit the manor."

"What?" she breathed. "You mean Nicol . . . Oh!" That eventuality had not occurred to Frey, who had been too distressed by the news to think coherently. But now the possibility became clear: with his father dead and Philip, the older son and heir, also gone, Nicol would have his inheritance, his lands—he would be free to marry. At last!

But why didn't the notion bring her more joy? It was what she had always wanted, what she and Nicol had dreamed of for many years, wasn't it? But she had never wished for her own dreams to come true at such a tragic price. That must be why she felt dismay instead of delight. How could she rejoice when all the Linscote people were dead?

Watching her, Reynold's pale blue eyes flashed and hectic color showed in his cheeks. "Much good it will do you, sister, because by the time it happens you'll be wed to Geronimus! Be sure that I shall see to that. You will wed Geronimus as soon as we have permission from the earl. I'll brook no argument. I've given him my word!"

"I have not given mine!" Frey said fiercely. "Not to your friend the fat merchant! But you wrong me, brother. I was not thinking of myself.

Our neighbors are dead. Our friends! Guendolyn, so sweet and pretty. And Philip . . . Philip was so strong, so alive last time I saw him. You speak as though I wished them dead. It's not so. Not so!"

Nevertheless she could not help but wonder what difference this would make to her own life. But before she could imagine the possible consequences she was assailed by a wave of nausea and faintness that made her reach out to lean giddily on her brother. The last thing she remembered was hearing Reynold shout for Ula's help.

For Frey, the next three weeks were made hazy by the poison that had got into her foot through the agency of the thorn. Her foot swelled to a puffy, pain-wracked horror and her mind wandered in the virulent fever that resulted. Vaguely she was aware of Emma and Ula tending her with herbal potions and prayers; she heard the mewling of the newborn babe from the next room where Edith lay in childbed; and once she woke to find the bower full of acrid smoke and the village wisewoman there chanting spells. Frey wondered if this was what dying felt like. Then the fever reclaimed her.

She dreamed vivid visions of Wulfnoth her father, and of the Viking attack—and she dreamed of Blaize of Bayonne, always Blaize somewhere there amid the mists, though in lucid moments she remembered being told that he had gone. He had done what he could to help the folk of Linscote and then he had returned to take a full report of events to his master the Earl of Chester, far away on the other side of England.

So he was gone, and as she began to recover her wits she remembered how his leave-taking had seemed so final. In the depression that came with the aftermath of her illness, she was certain she would never see Blaize again.

And that, she told herself, was fit punishment
for the sin of daring to think of him as anything
more than a bright unattainable star shining briefly
in her life.

On a day in July when she was sufficiently recovered, Frey was carried out to the garden to sit
under an oak tree with Emma beside her. Emma
read aloud to entertain her sister, squinting at the
book, slowly and painfully enunciating the Latin
words with a finger following the script on the
thick yellow paper of the leather-bound volume—
the only book the manor of Ketilfiord possessed. It
was a beautiful, precious book, lavishly illuminated
by some scholarly monk in colored inks and occasional gold leaf, its leather binding darkened by
grease from many hands and pitted with scars. The
writing in the book concerned the lives of the
saints.

Though the subject matter only served to make
Frey aware of her own shortcomings—she was no
saint and never could be—she envied Emma's
ability to read. In earlier years, Emma had sat
entranced when the priest came to give Reynold his
lessons, but Frey had always found excuses to
neglect her education and be out-of-doors. To her,
the lore of herbs, and seeking them in the woods
and fields, was of far more use and interest than dry
Latin tomes. But she appreciated her sister's efforts
to amuse her in her convalescence and smiled at
Emma's serious demeanor as she frowned over the
words and made a halting translation into English.

After a while, Frey's restless thoughts
wandered to the world around her. Bees droned
among the lavender and the roses and a blackbird
shrilled his song from the sturdy oak branches that
gave her dappled shelter from the sun. She remembered that Blaize had sat here talking with

Geronimus on that last evening before the Vikings had erupted into her peaceful world.

Incautiously she allowed herself to linger over memories of Blaize. She thought of his lips on hers, his strong body blending with her softness, his hands caressing her, waking heady new feelings that had both excited and dismayed her. The vision was so strong that she felt her stomach jerk as it had then, both in guilty shock and discovered pleasure. She was sure her guilt must show in the staining of her cheeks and she prayed that Emma would not look up from the book.

Angrily she reminded herself that her feelings for Blaize, and the intimacies she had allowed him, had been wrong—sinful—and would bring disgrace to her entire family were her behavior to be discovered. She knew that. But she also knew that it was beyond her power to have resisted the call of her heart and her senses. For that reason, because she feared her own weakness, she was glad that Blaize had gone away. She hoped he would never return.

Yet the thought of never seeing his dark face again made her desolate. How gravely he had spoken that last farewell.

Drifting over the valley came the sound of a horn warning of the presence of strangers within the bounds of the manor. As always, Frey's heart jumped, her senses became alert and she wondered if the visitor might be Blaize. But it was not—it was merely a messenger looking for Reynold. Sighing, Frey settled back against the tree and closed her eyes, letting her mind drift again.

Emma read on, her voice soothing against an aural backdrop of the sounds of summer: from the kitchen huts came the clatter of pots, the chomping of a pestle and mortar, scolding voices and the scraping of a knife against a whetstone; the hum of bees was a counterpoint to the singing of birds and the barking of a dog; and from the manor came the thin, high wail of the new baby demanding attention—it was another boy, much to Reynold's delight. The child had been named Eadric and it seemed he would survive his early arrival in the world.

The book slapped shut, making Frey open her eyes to see Emma grimacing as she tucked a stray strand of brown hair under her veil. "That's one thing that won't be a distraction at the Abbey—a baby crying," she sighed. "Oh, I wish Reynold would make up his mind when he's going to take me to York. The sooner I'm gone, the happier I shall be."

"Are you so anxious to leave us?" Frey asked.

Emma gave her a troubled glance. "It's not that. With each day that passes Ketilfiord seems dearer to me. I often wonder if I'm going to be able to leave it. Yet leave it I must, and I do want to go. I just wish the day would come and the journey be over. Then I may put my mind entirely to my vocation."

"Certainly the bower will be less crowded without you," Frey teased, covering her own sorrow. She knew she would sorely miss her sister's companionship.

"Will it?" Emma returned. "With young Wulfnoth growing, and Eadric to join him soon? But surely it can't be long before you, too, must leave. We shall soon have word from the earl."

She might as well have slapped Frey, who was grateful for the few moments when she could forget the future that loomed ever nearer. She had no wish to be reminded that a message from the earl would seal her doom.

But Emma's mind, it seemed, was more on her own future. "Maybe that's what Reynold's waiting for," she mused. "Perhaps he'll take me to York

when he has good news for Geronimus—it will save
him having to make the journey twice." But her
face clouded as she realized what that must mean
for Frey. "It won't be good news for you, sister, I
know. But at least you'll be in York, too. We'll be
able to see each other sometimes."

Frey found herself still unwilling to accept the
inevitability of her fate. Until all was settled, a
stubborn part of her refused to accept that marriage
with the merchant was her only choice. "Perhaps
not, sister," she argued. "I may decide to become
mistress of Linscote instead. Nicol will soon come to
claim his inheritance." She spoke hopefully, telling
herself that it would be good to see Nicol again.
More and more she had forced her forlorn hopes to
be centered on her childhood sweetheart. Familiar
and predictable, Nicol was a man she understood
and could manage.

"Nicol?" Emma queried.

"He always promised he would come back and
seek my hand in wedlock as soon as he had lands of
his own."

Emma was watching her closely, looking
troubled. "That may be so. Frey . . . I've never
mentioned this before, but . . . it was not Nicol you
cried out for in your fever."

The news struck Frey like a physical blow and
she knew her color had heightened. "Then who did
I cry for?" she demanded, though she knew full
well whose name must have come most readily to
her lips—the same man who filled her dreams,
waking and sleeping. Hard as she tried to exclude
him from her thoughts, Blaize of Bayonne was
entrenched there, seemingly forever.

But whatever Emma might have replied was
prevented when Reynold's voice interrupted them
and they both glanced round to see their older
brother approaching. His swift, jerky stride and

pallid face told of his high temper, and he held in his hand a parchment, which he waved impatiently in Frey's face.

"I don't believe it!" he exclaimed. "I simply do not believe that this can happen. This is your fault, Frey. If you had agreed at once, the wedding could have taken place before ever the earl knew anything of it."

"The wedding?" she faltered.

"Yes, the wedding! God's teeth! Was ever a man more ill-served by the fates! What a fool I shall look. And Geronimus will demand some recompense. He has been generous with us only because he fully expected to gain a wife in return."

Astonishment and an incredulous creeping hope made Frey enquire, "You mean, the earl . . . Reynold, has the earl refused to give his permission for the marriage with Geronimus?"

"He has!" her brother confirmed, his pale eyes snapping with annoyance.

Frey bit her lip, though the joy sparkling in her eyes betrayed her. Wondrous news! She was not to be forced to wed the fat merchant after all.

"Don't look so pleased with yourself," Reynold rasped. "There's more—and this you certainly will not like to hear."

"Oh?" Faint disquiet curbed her delight. "And what is this bad news, brother?"

"Not only does the earl withhold his consent for your marriage, he directs that you be sent to the nunnery with Emma, until he can find a more suitable husband for you."

Frey caught her breath, stunned by this news. "What?"

"That is what he decrees," her brother replied. "And since I doubt that a more suitable husband exists—*I* certainly couldn't find one—it probably means that you'll be there forever." His frustration

made him want to strike out and his mouth thinned
as he added harshly, "Well, why should any man
want you, without dowry or beauty?"

When Frey winced, the bolt gone surely home,
Reynold slapped the parchment testily and began to
pace the grass, muttering almost to himself, "This is
another example of Norman oppression. Hugh the
Wolf will not allow me any means of advancing my-
self—as I might have done with Geronimus's help.
And meanwhile *you* will molder away at St.
Winifred's for want of good dowries. Both of you."
He spat viciously onto the ground. "A curse on all
Normans!"

"Hush, brother," Emma cautioned. "Be careful
what you say."

He silenced her with a brusque gesture. "None
of my people would spy on me for a Norman
shilling." Again he turned on Frey, adding, "And
do not think that this means you're free to wait for
Nicol of Linscote. The earl has his talons there, too.
I've just heard that Linscote is to have a new
lord—another Norman!"

If she had not felt so weak she might have leapt
up to dispute this statement face to face with him.
On top of all the rest she could hardly take it in.
"That can't be true! Nicol is the rightful heir after
Philip."

"You mean he *was* the rightful heir!"

Frey blinked at him, not understanding. "Was?
Reynold, what can you mean? What has happened?
Has some evil befallen Nicol?"

"You might call it evil," Reynold snorted, not
without a certain relish. "Nicol of Linscote has been
stripped of his rights. He has been disinherited."

This news made Frey blanch. Her mind went
blank and as if from a distance she heard Emma
exclaim in horror. It was impossible, terrible news.

"But why?" Frey cried. "What excuse did they

use?"

"The earl believes that Philip was involved in a plot—a planned uprising against the Normans," her brother told her.

"Philip was?" she repeated. "Merry, laughing Philip? Oh, I don't believe it!"

"Whether or not you believe it, sister, that is the reason the earl has given to the folk at Linscote. Philip plotted treachery, so his lands are forfeit to the king. God's blood!" But his anger was not on Nicol's behalf; it was for himself and the chance he was about to lose, as his next words proved. "Now we shall have to return the gifts that Geronimus gave us. In all faith we cannot keep them if the marriage is not to be. By the time my sons are grown there'll be nothing left for us Saxons but serfdom!"

Red in the face with rage, he took the parchment and tore it across and across, hurling the pieces to scatter on the breeze. "*That* is for Hugh the Wolf!" he exclaimed, and swung on his sisters with a gesture of futility. "So—prepare yourselves, both of you. As soon as Aelfreya is strong enough, we journey to York, to the Abbey of St. Winifred. At least you'll be companions for each other behind those gray stone walls."

In the darkness of a chill March dawn, the Prime bell woke Frey and as she stirred the straw pallet beneath her rustled and she felt the rough caress of woollen blankets against her skin. She had learned, after seven months at the Abbey, to ignore the Matins chime at midnight and the Lauds bell an hour later, but Prime at the seventh hour never failed to disturb her from slumber, however black and cold the morning.

In common with a few other women—all of them guests of the Abbey—she slept on a straw pallet on the bare floorboards of a loft over the nuns' dormitory. Now she heard the nuns stirring below, hastening to don their habits and answer the bell—the call to further prayers in the great Abbey church of St. Winifred, just beyond the cloisters.

Frey imagined her sister Emma among the nuns, her young face solemn and yet serene, with an inner glow of conviction, framed by the severe gray wimple; Emma was very sure of her calling. During the time they had been at the Abbey, the sisters had grown further and further apart, not from choice but from inevitable change as Emma merged more deeply into her life as a novice.

In some ways Frey envied her sister's certainty. Emma had known exactly what she was doing; she had come gladly to embrace a life that had long appealed to her gentle nature. There were times when Frey, out of sheer frustration, had thought that she too might as well take the veil, but she shuddered at the thought of giving up so many worldly pleasures.

To begin with she could not bear the thought of having her hair cropped—the sin of pride was strong in her, even if her hair was red and not the more desirable yellow which a woman must possess to be considered a true beauty. And she still thought of Nicol of Linscote with a wistful, nostalgic fondness, and of Blaize of Bayonne with . . . with a curious sick, guilty, shaming need that made her flush all over every time she experienced it. She tried to rid herself of such wanton yearnings, but memories of Blaize continued to torment her and in her dreams at night she knew again the awful bliss of being held against a firm male body and kissed by a warm mouth that fired her blood.

No, she was not made to be a nun.

The ladder rattled and a coiffed head appeared in the opening in the floor of the loft as one of the nuns placed a rushlight on bare boards. The small flame danced and flickered in a draft, sending uncertain light around the figures rousing themselves from their thin straw pallets and scratchy blankets.

"Prime has rung, my ladies," the nun carolled cheerily. "Mass in half an hour. Be ready."

As the head disappeared, Frey pushed back her blanket and sat up, rubbing her eyes. The girl beside her yawned and stretched, groaning, "Do we have to go to mass this morning?"

Frey smiled in sympathy. "Sister Annora won't speak to me all day if I'm absent. You lie a moment longer, Constance. I'll wash first."

As she doused her face in icy water from a bowl, shivering, Constance said from behind her, "I still don't see why we have to say mass every morning. Praying never did me much good. Maybe the old Gods are better—the Gods of our pagan ancestors. Did you know you're named after one—Freya? Colin told me of her."

Having dried herself on a harsh towel of coarse hempen weave, Frey reached for her shift and shuddered into it, making no reply. Every conversation, so it seemed, led Constance back to thoughts of her lost lover, Colin; it was an old wound that she seemed determined to keep unhealed.

Constance had been in much the same position as Frey, the daughter of an impoverished Saxon family, with two brothers and no dowry; her father had arranged to marry her to an older man who already had grown sons and wished for a young wife to delight his jaded senses. But Constance had fought against her father's decision; Constance had been in love—with one of her father's housecarls, Colin by name. The pair had for months indulged in secret trysts that had only fuelled their hopeless passion for each other.

Denied hope by their difference in station, a few days before Constance was to be forced to wed her dotard the lovers had run away. Her father, brothers and all the men of their household had raised a hue and cry in pursuit. In the fight which ensued when the runaways were caught, Colin had been mortally wounded and Constance dragged away from her dying lover by main force, her reputation stained forever. The disgrace had scandalized her elderly betrothed, who had withdrawn his marriage offer. Constance's punishment was incarceration in the nunnery.

Trailing blearily to the washstand, Constance said, "What does today hold, I wonder? More sewing for me, more hours in the infirmary for you. And salt fish to eat. Ugh! I shall be glad when Lent is past. We shall all grow gills if this diet continues."

"It's not much to my taste, either," Frey agreed. "I never thought there might come a day when the very thought of Ketilfiord mutton would set my mouth to watering."

"At least you may hope to taste such fare again some day," Constance said, absently rubbing her wet hands together as she stared off into the distance. "I'm here forever—in disgrace." Her eyes welled with tears that got into her voice and made it sound choked. "Oh, why is it so wrong to love? Colin was fine, Frey, even if he was a peasant by birth. And because of me he died."

"Hush." Concerned, Frey put her arms around the weeping girl. Every time she spoke of her lost lover it ended in tears, but she seemed unable to forget him. Trying to comfort her friend, Frey said, "I do know how it feels. Once . . . once there was someone—"

Constance lifted drowned, astonished eyes. "There was? Who?"

Nicol, Frey thought, hardening her will against intrusive thoughts of Blaize of Bayonne, though it was to him her mind had first flown. "Just someone I couldn't have. I don't know where he is, or even if he's alive or dead. I shall probably never see him again."

She meant Nicol. Of course she meant Nicol!

"Did you—" Constance ventured, and dropped her voice to a whisper. "Did you and he ever—"

"No!" Wide-eyed, Frey felt her face flame at the very thought.

Her friend regarded her sadly. "Then you don't understand, not really. If you had truly loved him you would have wished to lie with him."

"Unwed?" Frey asked in horror.

"Wed or unwed, what difference does it make?"

Frey could find no answer. Such thoughts were alien to all she had been taught to believe.

"Is it because of him that you're here?" Constance asked, eager for further confidences. "I thought you were waiting for them to find a husband for you."

"So I am—so they said." She sighed, turning away from a subject that continued to vex her; there were times when she suspected that she might be just like Constance—that with the right man she would not be able to resist the lure of sensual pleasure. With Constance it had been a good-looking peasant; for Frey it could so easily have been a handsome Norman knight. Both of the choices were equally shaming. In sober fact, she and Constance were sisters in sin. It was a chastening thought.

"Don't you believe they'll find you a husband?" Constance asked.

"I doubt that Earl Hugh so much as recalls my existence," Frey sighed. "No, I'm tied here, just as you are—neither fish, nor flesh, nor fowl. We're not of the sisterhood, we're not servants, exactly, and we're certainly not honored guests. We have no place in the world, Constance. We've both broken the rules. Now please—get dressed or we'll be late."

"Get dressed, and go to mass and pray for humility to accept my fate, is that what you mean?"

"That's what the nuns would say," Frey replied wryly. "It's my misfortune, but meek acceptance was never in my nature."

When her knowledge of herbal remedies had been discovered by the nuns, Frey had been assigned to the infirmary. She worked under the offices of stern sister Annora, whose skill with medicines was surprisingly slight, though the best the Abbey could furnish. Annora was willing to learn from Frey but refused to utter the charms and spells that went with some of the cures. For Annora, prayer was the only permitted way of encouraging the herbs to work, even though Frey knew that certain spells, spoken in the right way and with the correct passes and gestures, could be very efficacious. But perhaps they only worked for peasants who believed in them.

That morning, Frey was busy with pestle and mortar pounding dried succory root to make an infusion for the easement of sister Gunhild's rheumatism when one of the serving maids came anxiously running with news that a visitor was asking to see her.

"Really, this is most inconvenient!" sister Annora chafed. "Who is this visitor, girl?"

The young maid hopped from foot to foot under Annora's beady eye. "His name is Sir Reynold, Sister. Sir Reynold of Ketilfiord—mistress Aelfreya's brother. He says his errand is of great importance. So the holy mother sent me to fetch mistress Aelfreya straight away."

Reynold! Frey thought, delighted at the prospect of seeing her brother and hearing news of home. She only hoped that no ill fate had befallen anyone at Ketilfiord.

"Best go," the nun instructed, glancing at Frey with a gesture of her wimple-covered head to the door. "But don't be long. You're needed here."

Hurrying through the cloisters, Frey gained the passageway to the courtyard and thence to the outer parlor next to the gatehouse, one of the few places in the nunnery which male visitors were permitted to enter. It was a plain, whitewashed room whose only adornment was a silver crucifix on the wall above a wooden bench—the Abbey did not encourage casual visitors to linger.

Reynold was pacing the pounded clay floor, looking ill at ease. He wore thick stockings, a padded jerkin and a cloak lined with lambskin against the March chill. As Frey appeared he stopped his pacing and looked her over with a frown.

"You've grown thin," was his first comment.

"Well, it's Lent, and a diet of salt fish does not encourage one to eat heartily," Frey said with a smile, not wishing to worry him over her unhappiness. After all it was not Reynold's fault that she was without dowry and therefore unmarriageable; besides, he looked as if he had troubles enough. A warm wave of pity and affection shot through her. "Oh . . . it's good to see you, Reynold!" Impulsively she ran to him with outstretched arms and they shared a brief, half-embarrassed embrace; Reynold had never been one to encourage displays of sisterly affection.

"How is everyone?" Frey asked as she drew

away. "Edith, and Ula, and the little ones? Have you asked for Emma to be sent for? She'll be happy to see you, too."

"No." He looked troubled. "No, I shan't see Emma this time. It's you I came to see. Yes—everyone's well. Ula asked me to give you her best love. Edith, too."

Frey stared at him. "Even Edith?"

"Don't mock, Frey," Reynold sighed, and turned away to stare out of the narrow, barred window which looked out onto the muddy road that wound beside the Abbey walls. A fine drizzle was falling like mist, drenching everything. "You've been missed. Both of you. I know Emma is content with her lot, but you—" He glanced at her over his shoulder, seeing again how thin she was and that much of the animation had gone from her face. "You were never meant to be in a place like this."

"Then why did you agree to leave me here?" Frey asked, her bitterness asserting itself.

Her brother seemed not to hear her; he was caught up in dark thoughts of his own as he watched a pedlar, soaked through with rain, drive a pack-mule up the road toward the city walls. "Geronimus is wed, had you heard?" he said. "He married the widow of another merchant."

"No, I hadn't heard. Is this why you came? To tell me this?"

He swung around, his face set in lines that expressed anger, though it was an anger that covered feelings of guilt for the fate to which he had consigned her. "I had thought this place might alter you, but you're still the same—still wilful as an unbroken colt. But this time, sister, you must not be headstrong and selfish or it will be the worse for us all. Think of young Wulfnoth. Think of little Eadric."

His earnestness sobered Frey, making her still and watchful. Whatever he was trying to say, it boded no good for her. "I think often of my nephews, brother. I miss seeing their bright faces. Now tell me your news plainly."

As though he couldn't bear to watch her reaction he turned away again and leaned on the stone ledge of the arched window. A cutting wind sliced past the opening, driving the misting rain across fields where corn showed green tips and peasants bent at their weeding in the shadow of the great walls of York.

"The earl of Chester has found you a husband," Reynold said.

Frey was stunned into silence. She had been so sure she had been forgotten that she could hardly believe she was hearing correctly. Questions swirled in her head, but which one to ask first?

The most important one: "Who?"

Flinging her a look from the corner of his eye, Reynold said, "His name will mean nothing to you. He's castellan of one of the earl's outposts at . . . Triffordd, or some such name. Or so said father John, who translated the message for me. My Latin is poor. I scarcely believed my own reading of it, so I had the priest confirm it."

"One of the earl's castellans?" Frey said in a voice that sounded as dead and cold as her blood felt at that moment. "You mean, I'm to be forced to wed a Norman?"

"A lord—a baron."

A Norman! Her spirit rebelled at the thought. Whatever his rank, it was his foreign blood she detested. "If he's a baron why is he content to have me for a wife?" she demanded. "Will no one else have him? Is he old? Is he deformed?"

Impatiently, Reynold flung out a hand as he turned to face her fully. "I don't know! The earl sent no explanations. Why should he? He commands, we obey—if we value our lives and our livelihood."

The earl can do anything, Blaize had said. *Anything.*

Blaize . . . was he behind this? Was this his way of punishing her for scorning him, to get her married off to some old man in some far corner of the land where she would be lost to all she knew and loved? Oh, surely he wouldn't be so vindictive!

But the wild imaginings ceased as she reminded herself of reality: Blaize could not possess so much influence with the earl. Blaize was merely a knight, one of many in the earl's service. This could have nothing to do with him; it was Earl Hugh's whim, and who could fathom the purposes of the most powerful Norman lord, second only in the land to King William Rufus himself?

"And think, sister," Reynold was saying, trying to encourage her to think positively. "If you wed an old man, you may soon be widowed. As a widow you'd be entitled to one third of his lands. You'd be free to take a husband of your own choice, should fitzHugh die first. That's the law."

"FitzHugh?" she queried, disquiet quirking at her heart. Among the Normans, sons born outside marriage were often known by their father's name with the prefix "fitz." "Is that his name? He's not . . . he's not the earl's son, is he?"

Reynold gestured irritably. "Don't be stupid, Frey. Would the Earl of Chester marry his own son—even a bastard son—to a girl without dowry?"

No, he wouldn't, she thought dully. It had been a foolish question. The name Hugh was not uncommon; many a man had given the sobriquet fitzHugh to some by-blow got on a mistress. The name told her nothing.

"Where is Triffordd?" she asked.

"It's on the borders of Wales, in the Welsh marches." Seeing her start, he added, "Yes, I've heard of the troubles there, too. The Welsh folk are still struggling to stem the spread of Norman rule. But you'll be safe enough in the fortress. And since fitzHugh is a marcher lord he'll be away fighting a good deal of the time, so you'll be mistress of your own domain—chatelaine of the castle of Triffordd. And if your husband should perish under Welsh arrows—" He did not complete the thought in words but his meaning was clear enough: widowhood meant attaining the nearest thing to freedom that a woman could hope for. "Frey . . . it will be better than spending your life behind these walls. Will you accept this marriage?"

She looked down at her hands, stained green and fragrant from the herbs she had been pounding. "Have I any choice?"

"Very little, I fear."

After a moment, Frey drew a deep breath and lifted her head, looking him straight in the eye as she said quietly, "Then I'll take fitzHugh—for you, and for young Wulfnoth."

A swift frown drew his brows together, as if he could hardly believe her easy compliance; Frey had always been a recalcitrant sister over whose willfulness Reynold had fumed and fretted. But she had made up her mind. Abbey life was not for her—seven months of it had assured her of that—so she might as well accept her fate. As a woman she had no real choice.

Besides, when Reynold mentioned the Welsh marches it had not been thought of the wars that had made her start, it had been the realization that Nicol was somewhere on the borders of Wales. By marrying Lord fitzHugh, Frey might be paving the way for a reunion with her childhood sweetheart.

"Do you mean it?" Reynold asked, not

attempting to hide his relief. "Ah, Frey, you've learned some wisdom at last. Then you must ready yourself. Lord fitzHugh is escorting the countess of Chester from the king's court back to her husband's demesne. They'll rest here in York over Eastertide. Since it's convenient, the marriage will take place on Easter Sunday, in the Abbey church, and then you'll go on with your husband to Chester."

Frey's face had grown pale. It was all arranged, she thought in dismay. And Easter Sunday was only ten days away! "So soon?" she breathed.

"That's what the earl decrees. And isn't it better to have it done with?"

"Before I change my mind?" she asked with a touch of acerbity.

"You wouldn't—"

A humorless laugh escaped her, cutting him off. "Oh, have no fear, brother. For once I'll bow to my fate and go quietly. Will . . . will you be here to see it?"

"Of course. It will be my place to exchange contracts with Lord fitzHugh's witness. I'll bring Edith, too, and Emma will be here with us. You won't be alone. And thank you, Frey. Thank you!"

You won't be alone, she thought. No, not until after the wedding, when she would be obliged to journey across England into unknown territory, in care of a total stranger. Would he be kind or cruel? Young or old?

Having no notion what her husband would be like was so frightening that she shut it out of her mind and set her thoughts to a further future, when in the Welsh marches she might find Nicol again. Who knew what might result from that meeting?

VI

Desperately needing to share her fears and mis-givings, Frey discussed the news of her impending marriage at length with Constance, and also with Emma in the brief hours when the novice nuns were free from their routine of work and prayer. Much speculation surrounded the person of Lord fitzHugh, but speculation it had to remain without any further clue to the nature or identity of the man. The conclusions to be drawn from the few facts available were not comforting: a marcher lord would hardly demean himself to take for wife someone like Frey unless there was something wrong with him—so wrong that no other woman would have him. He had to be a monster of some kind, if not physically then in his character, perhaps cold and cruel, perhaps even perverted in some way which young women of their limited experience could only guess at.

"We may be entirely wrong," Emma said, trying to comfort her sister. "He may well have wealth enough of his own not to desire an heiress to bring more lands to his estate. Perhaps he is a man who needs only a good wife to tend him when his duties are burdensome."

"Perhaps he is a saint in disguise," Frey added dryly. "The blessed fitzHugh, friend of dowerless

Saxons!"

This made Constance giggle, though Emma reproved her sister for making mock of sacred things. But laughing about it was the only way Frey could cope. If she thought on the matter in sober reality it filled her with terror.

The days were passing all too swiftly. Hardly had Frey had time to accustom herself to the idea of this marriage with a stranger than the Abbey was buzzing, preparing for the imminent arrival of the countess of Chester with her escort and her entourage.

Countess Arlette, exhausted after the strain of a winter spent at the king's court in Winchester, had apparently chosen to pass Easter quietly and contemplatively within the confines of the Abbey, in preference to facing the rigors of the garrison castle in the city. When the holy days were over, she and her companions would travel on to rejoin her husband, the earl, at Chester.

"I wonder where fitzHugh will stay?" Constance mused. "At the castle, probably. But neither that, nor a guest room here, seems a fitting place for a wedding night."

Wedding night, Frey thought with a jolt. The physical consummation of this marriage was another thing she was trying not to think about. She had tried to persuade herself that her new husband might be content to wait until they were alone at his castle at Triffordd, but she knew she was deluding herself.

She could only pray that fitzHugh, however monstrous, would be chivalrous enough to remember and make allowance for her innocence.

Foul weather during the week before Easter delayed the countess on the road, so that she and her company did not arrive in York until late on a

wet and dismal Easter Saturday. From the window
of the infirmary, the apprehensive Frey saw the
escort approach through a veil of driving rain. Her
heart began to beat heavily, causing a nervous pulse
to flutter in her throat as she watched the countess's
train approach.

First came a company of mounted knights and
men-at-arms, helmeted and mailed as if for battle,
with crimson pennants fluttering. Behind them
walked packmen wearing weatherproof, hooded
cloaks, leading a train of packhorses laden with the
essentials of a countess's life—furniture for her
comfort wherever she might stop, even her great
bed, hangings, clothes, pots and pans, and of course
equipment and food for the massive army that
travelled with her. Behind the packtrain a force of
infantry bearing spears and axes marched rank
after rank, and in the midst of them four horses
supported a swaying, curtained litter around which
rode several figures heavily bundled in cloaks and
hoods against the weather, some of them evidently
ladies since they rode sidesaddle on palfreys.

Among so many, and through the mist of rain
that obscured details of form and face, Frey could
not pick out which, if any, of those shrouded
figures might be Lord fitzHugh.

Only the countess and her ladies were staying at
the Abbey; the rest of her train went on, winding
down the road toward the city gates and a night's
sojourn at the castle.

Frey waited with a sick feeling in the pit of her
stomach, but when an hour passed without any
attempt by her prospective bridegroom to present
himself she was forced to conclude that he had gone
with his men to enjoy the hospitality of the castle. It
was a clear signal of his indifference toward his
intended bride, who was evidently of as little
account as any other of his goods and chattels.

But she was soon to discover that she had not been forgotten: that evening just before she, and everyone else in the Abbey, retired to bed with the waning daylight, she received a message bidding her to present herself at the countess's apartments after mass the next morning, to be readied for the wedding.

Countess Arlette, along with her closest attendants, occupied the largest guest suite off the main courtyard of the Abbey. When Frey tapped timidly on the door it was opened by one of the countess's ladies, who gestured Frey to enter a solar that was now richly furnished with padded stools and embroidered hangings—the countess carried such items with her to add suitable comfort to whatever place she graced with her presence.

Three other ladies waited inside the room, dressed like the first in velvets and silks with much jewelry, their noses high and thier eyes full of curiosity as they stared at Frey. Ladies-in-waiting to a countess were inevitably highborn Normans themselves. They chattered like magpies together in Norman French, whispering and laughing, obviously discussing Frey's poor clothing and conjecturing about her, much to her discomfort.

The countess swept in from her bedchamber, a tall, slender woman in glowing scarlet. Dark hair in thick braids hung from beneath her veil, twined with ribbons and jewels, and her gown was crusted with gold embroidery. She was quite young, not so very much older than Frey, but she bore herself haughtily, conscious of her rank, and she spoke in short bursts, giving orders and waving her hands peremptorily, accustomed to being obeyed at once.

A Saxon maidservant took Frey into the bedchamber where a tub of water had obviously provided a warm bath for the countess. By now it

was only of blood heat, but having been undressed
by the maid Frey slid into the tub and washed herself.

"Your hair, too," the maid said, clearly under
instructions to cleanse every inch of this insignificant person in preparation for her marriage to a
powerful Norman baron. Even the maid looked
down her nose, as if wondering how on earth Lord
fitzHugh could lower himself to take such a wife.

Her face burning with humiliation, Frey did as
she was told, then sat wrapped in towels as the
maid dried her hair and combed it out. At this
point, two of the ladies-in-waiting came in, obviously amused by the vivid color of Frey's hair.
Both of them, naturally, were fair-haired and blue-
eyed, as true beauty demanded, though one of them
had a pronounced squint. Their gestures and ex-
pressions—and their giggles—were eloquent, even
if Frey did not understand a word they said.

Few Normans bothered to learn English; the
Saxon tongue was considered to be fit only for the
lower classes.

But—Frey realized with a spurt of alarm—Lord
fitzHugh was Norman, too! Dear heaven, was she to
be married to a man with whom she could not even
communicate? Her spirit clamored in revolt but it
was too late now for second thoughts; she was
trapped in a fate woven by her loyalty to her
family. She would accept that fate, but still she felt
like a lamb being readied for the slaughter.

The two ladies eased Frey into a sheer muslin
shift and a yellow undertunic with tight sleeves and
long flowing skirts. Embroidered stockings were
gartered above her knees with silk ribbons, and
then one of the ladies produced a gown of dark
green velvet embroidered with flowers around the
neckline and the flowing cuffs—the most beautiful
gown she had ever seen.

She fingered the fabric in wonderment. "But where did it come from? To whom do these clothes belong?"

The ladies shrugged, not comprehending, then the maid, who had been hovering in the background watching the excitement said, "They're yours, lady. They're a gift from Lord fitzHugh. Well, you could hardly marry a baron looking like a goosegirl, now could you?"

The girl was only mirroring the contempt of the two ladies, but nevertheless the insult stung Frey. None of these women considered her a fit bride for a Norman noble, however old or ill-favored he might be. Realizing how close the hour of her marriage was drawing, with no backing out now, Frey was seized by a panic that tightened her scalp and made her hands sweat. But the preparations went inexorably on.

The rich, heavy gown slid over her head, fitting tightly down to the hips before flaring out, shorter than the undertunic and caught up in front in order to show the yellow skirts beneath. The attendants tightened the side lacings, so that the velvet clung snugly to Frey's slim curves.

But she gasped as one of her helpers pinched her viciously.

The lady murmured what might have been an apology, but as their eyes met Frey saw spite burning in cool blue depths. Those eyes told her the pinch had been deliberate. This woman, whose name seemed to be Melissande, was not only disdainful, she was as actively hostile.

Shaken by the discovery of an enemy among the countess's ladies, Frey allowed herself to be led back into the solar, where she sat by the fire while the maid combed her hair to finish its drying. Around her, Arlette of Chester and her pretty companions took their ease, conversing together in their unintelligible language.

Frey closed her eyes, letting her mind sweep her far away from this nightmare in which she seemed to be trapped. When a tear escaped her control she surreptitiously wiped it away, angry with herself. In this world, self-pity served for nothing; a woman was a slave to the laws of men, a piece of property to be disposed of as men decreed. But she still had her own thoughts, her own dreams. However dreadful the future might be, she would cling to her dreams.

Through spangled tears she watched the fire. Inevitably, the flames produced a picture of a man with thick dark hair, deep brown eyes, a strong, handsome face . . .

Her attendants left her hair flowing unbound, a shining curtain the color of squirrels against the forest green of her gown and its bright flower embroidery. The four ladies completed her toilette with a gossamer veil for her hair, held by a silver circlet, then they stepped back and looked her up and down, three of them with smiles of satisfaction, clearly pleased with the result they had managed to achieve from such unpromising material.

The exception was the lady Melissande, whose eyes remained cold and unfriendly. Frey wondered what she could possibly have done to make Melissande hate her on sight.

Issuing an order, the countess flicked her hand toward the door and Frey was dismissed. The maid escorted her across the courtyard to the outer parlor where, to her relief and joy, her family waited for her—Reynold and Edith, and Emma in her grey novice's gown. Constance was there, too, quiet and subdued; she was losing her best friend and she empathized with Frey's fears. But they all exclaimed in amazement over Frey's gown. Reynold even said she looked beautiful, and Edith could not conceal her envy.

A table had been prepared for them to dine, but Frey could eat nothing. She was swimming in unreality, imagining that at any moment she must wake up and find this all some terrible dream. She drank some wine, however, as her family wished her good fortune; then she sat staring unseeingly into the goblet, wishing it had borage flowers floating in it, such as a woman should offer to a husband who was riding away to war. Borage—for courage and forgetfulness.

After what seemed an interminable wait, Frey and her companions were summoned to the porch of the church, where they stood to await the coming of the bridegroom. The courtyard was crowded with curious onlookers who had come to see the spectacle, but Frey's eyes were fixed on the door of the countess's apartment, where a small knot of guards waited, clad in the crimson tunics that marked them as the Earl of Chester's men.

At last the door opened, the escort formed into twos, and the countess and her ladies issued forth in a flutter of veils, smiling and chatting, accompanied by several men. But with the onlookers jostling for a good view and the guards walking in front of the wedding party, the person of the bridegroom remained hidden.

Suddenly, through a momentary gap in the crowd, Frey caught sight of a dark face she knew well—a face she had thought never to see again. Her heart seemed to fumble, stop, and then race at breathless speed . . . Blaize of Bayonne was among the group. He must have agreed to be one of fitzHugh's escort.

"God's blood!" Reynold muttered to himself, and Emma grasped Frey's arm in hard fingers, whispering, "Sir Blaize is with them. It's Sir Blaize!

Oh, Frey!"

Now, as the bridegroom's party approached the porch, the crowd fell back leaving an area of the cobbled courtyard clear. Across that gap, Blaize of Bayonne returned Frey's stunned, wide-eyed look with a steady gaze that both mocked and chided her.

The sight of him distracted her and her thoughts scattered confusedly, searching for answers. What was he doing here? Why had he agreed to accompany fitzHugh to his wedding? Was he a personal friend of the bridegroom? And had he known she was to be the bride this day?

Oh, yes, he had known—the thought fell like a stone, numbing her. Whatever emotions that enigmatic expression might be hiding, surprise was not a part of the recipe.

"But which is fitzHugh?" Edith asked.

The bridegroom, Frey thought, must be the solid, soldierly man walking beside Blaize—a man in his sixties, with close-cropped gray hair. Despite all her fears he was not, thank God, obviously deformed or disfigured in any way. He reminded her of Grimwald, the sergeant at Ketilfiord, except that Grimwald had never worn clothes so fine, nor such magnificent jewels and gold trappings. Evidently fitzHugh was a man of some wealth.

His escort comprised the countess and her ladies, together with five knights of the realm—five knights including Blaize, his tall, broad-shouldered frame garbed in brown velvet embroidered in gold, with gold studs in his belt and gold brooches holding his flowing cloak. His dark hair lifted in the breeze, framing a tense, unreadable expression with eyes that never left Frey's face.

How could she marry fitzHugh with Blaize standing by? she thought in despair. Or had he arranged it after all? Suddenly she was mortally afraid that she was going to faint.

As the guard fell back, keeping the gaping crowds from coming too close to the porch, the countess and her ladies paused in a little group with four of the knights ranged in an arc to guard them. Blaize and the older man came forward to the porch, where both of them made formal bows to the bridal party.

Not only was Blaize one of the bridegroom's escort, he was actually going to stand witness for fitzHugh, Frey thought with a sick emptiness churning in the pit of her stomach. Veils of mist seemed to drift across her mind. Had he come to see her humiliated? Was this his means of revenging himself on her? She could not read his thoughts behind the bright opacity of his eyes.

"Greetings, my lords," the voice of her brother Reynold intoned in her mind as if from great distances. "Welcome to this meeting. I am Reynold, son of Wulfnoth, thane of Ketilfiord in the shire of York. I speak as witness for the bride, my sister Aelfreya, who is here."

To Frey's bewilderment it was not Blaize who answered but the other man, announcing his identity formally in French. She gathered that he was declaring himself to be Gilbert of York, King William's castellan in the city, now acting as spokesman for the bridegroom of that day, whom he named as, "Blaize fitzHugh, seigneur de Bayonne, castellan de Triffordd."

The sonorous titles echoed in the porch and across the hushed courtyard as Frey and her family caught their breath. Her sense of unreality deepened. Blaize was to be her bridegroom. It couldn't be so. It couldn't be so! And yet it seemd that it *was* so. Was she dreaming? She felt numb. A trembling seized her limbs and all blood drained from her head, so that even her lips went white. Watching her, Blaize narrowed his eyes, as if puzzled by her pallor, and signalled his spokesman to continue.

his sleeve and spoke again, loudly and formally, still in baffling French.

"My contract," Blaize translated for the benefit of the stunned Ketilfiordians. "My protection for the lady Aelfreya while she and I live, and one third of all my estates and possessions should I die before she does."

Seeming dazed, Reynold accepted the scroll and produced another from his own sleeve, speaking the required speech by rote: "And this contract from the lady my sister—her person, her obedience, and her dowry." He hesitated before adding in a quiet, half-shamed voice, "Two bronze bowls, three silver spoons and a silver knife."

Blaize glanced at Frey, who was standing as if frozen, her head down, her eyes on the cobbles, unable to comprehend any of this. "Her dowry is of no importance," he said. "I accept the contract."

Gilbert took the scroll from Reynold and secreted it in his sleeve. To all legal intents and purposes, they were now married.

Now the door of the church swung open and Frey saw the nuns of St. Winifred all gathered inside, an array of black robes and wimples with a few novices in gray, standing below the vaulted, painted ceiling of the Abbey church, with beyond them the ornate high altar where candle flames swayed and danced and where the tonsured priest waited to solemnize the spiritual contract between Blaize fitzHugh and the lady Aelfreya of Ketilfiord.

The countess moved forward, glancing neither right nor left as she passed between Blaize and the bride's party to take Gilbert of York's arm and enter the church. Her ladies and the escorting knights followed.

Again Frey glimpsed cold hatred in the eyes of Melissande as she went by, but then all else faded as

Blaize bowed formally and solemnly to her, offering her his arm. As if sleepwalking, she laid her hand lightly on his velvet sleeve and together they proceeded into the church. Behind them crowded most of the eager onlookers who had gathered to watch the fun.

The church felt cold. Feet shuffled on its marble floor. Blossom-covered branches filled every space and the altar glowed with gold and color. Sweet voices raised in plainsong chant, praising and exulting, sending a shiver down Frey's spine as the high roof took and magnified the sound.

The wedding mass had begun.

News of the wedding had brought all the peasants of the area flocking to the Abbey to enjoy a stare at nobility on a fine, brisk Sunday. In the clamorous courtyard, Frey was kissed by her family and by a bitterly weeping Constance before Blaize helped her up onto a delightful gray palfrey and himself mounted his black stallion. The onlookers tossed handfuls of blossom and wildflowers, calling and cheering lustily as the bridal pair moved off with mounted escorts riding in front and behind.

If Frey needed proof of her husband's real status it was here in full measure, in the shape of the mounted knights and men-at-arms who now accompanied him and owned him as lord. Blaize fitzHugh, lord of Bayonne, castellan of Triffordd, the titles repeated in her mind, unreal and terrible. He was far more powerful than she had ever guessed. And she was his now, to do with as he pleased.

Some of the crowd called out bawdy comments, wishing the bridegroom strength for his coming labors and the bride the fortitude to bear with them. Still feeling frozen, numbed by all the strange things that had happened so swiftly she had

not had time to comprehend them, Frey saw Blaize
watching her and the darkly speculative gleam in
his eyes sent a shaft of fright through her as she
remembered an earlier encounter with him.

You will submit, he had threatened. *Sooner or
later, willing or no. This I vow by all the saints—you
will submit.*

They passed beneath the arched gateway,
leaving the confines of the Abbey. The road ran
between fields and trees that were budding green
with spring; the way was lined with laughing,
excited people. It seemed as though most of York
had come to gape and follow the bridal procession.
Some threw flowers, some tossed grains of corn as a
hope of fertility. To Frey, it all seemed to be
happening beyond a thick veil that separated her
from reality. She felt cold to the bone. Even her lips
were chilled.

Amid the soft rain of good wishes Blaize edged
his stallion nearer to Frey until his knee brushed
hers. The contact sent a shock of heady awareness
through her, heat like wine spreading along her
numbed veins.

"So silent, my lady?" he said softly. "Have you
no word for your wedded lord?"

Keeping her eyes on the tossing cloaks of the
escort ahead, Frey forced her stiff lips to reply, "I
may find words when I awake."

"Does it seem like a dream?" he enquired.

"A nightmare!" she whispered.

Blaize said nothing in reply to that. Though she
knew he was still watching her intently she could
not bring herself to look at him. A part of her was
seeking wildly for a path of escape but there was
none. After a moment, her new husband edged his
horse away and they rode on, approaching the gates
of the city, which stood open to admit them.

In her stupefied state, with her mind refusing to

work adequately, Frey assumed that they were
heading for the castle, which towered beyond the
church steeples and thatched roofs of the city.
Along twisting streets, wooden houses leaned together, washed with a white lime coating, their
gables overhanging boarded walks where people
had gathered in groups to observe the spectacle.
Urchins played in shadowy alleyways, pigs rooted
in the rubbish, dogs sniffed about . . .

Always before, on the few occasions she had
visited York, Frey had found the city exciting. Now
she fancied the crowds might suffocate her. The
smell from the garbage in its open sewer down
the road made her feel nauseous.

The street they were following led eventually to
a grassy open space that Frey recognized as the
marketplace. It too was crowded with people.
Youngsters kicked an inflated pig's bladder about
while adults idled their Sunday away in gossip and
gaming. The wedding party drew all eyes as the
escort stopped outside one of the few stone-built
houses the city possessed. Servants emerged from a
passage doorway to bow and curtsey, welcoming
Lord fitzHugh as he dismounted and came to hold
out his arms for his bride.

Feeling like a helpless puppet dancing on
strings, as though she no longer had any say over
her own actions, Frey laid her hand on her new
husband's shoulder as she unhooked her knee from
the pommel of the palfey's saddle. She expected
Blaize to lift her to the ground and set her on her
feet. Instead, he swept an arm under her knees so
that she fell right into his embrace, held clear of the
mud by her bridegroom's strong arms, much to the
delight of the watching crowd, who enjoyed the old
traditions. Thus protected from any evil spirits that
might be gathered round the doorstep, she was
borne into the dark passageway and thence to a

room where a fire burned in a stone hearth.

Blaize kicked the door shut behind him, shutting out the grinning faces of the servants; then he carried his bride to a high-backed settle by the wall, where he gently set her down among embroidered cushions and straightened to remove his cloak.

Aware of his tall figure towering over her, watching her, Frey kept her head down as she stole a glance around the room. A table had been laid with a jug of wine and sweetmeats, a loaf of bread, and some pieces of chicken. The fire had been freshly made up with logs, so the room was comfortably warm. Tapestry hangings covered most of the walls except for the chimney breast, where a crimson shield with a gold boss was displayed—the blazon color favored by the Earl of Chester.

Evidently Blaize was held in high honor by the earl his master.

"What place is this?" Frey asked tentatively.

"The house belongs to my father," Blaize replied, tossing his cloak across the back of the settle.

Very slowly, doubting her own senses, she lifted her head to look up into his frowning face as she said hollowly, "Your father?"

"Earl Hugh of Chester."

A roaring in her ears deafened her. Dear God, he *was* the earl's son! Illegitimate, yes, but evidently acknowledged and held in esteem or they would not be here in the earl's house, nor would the earl's wife have graced their wedding day with her presence.

Suddenly Frey's eyes were scalding with tears and a sob wrenched from deep inside her. She flung her hands to her face, rocking back and forth in an agony of pain, weeping helplessly and soundlessly. She felt totally alone, at the mercy of the man who

was now her husband. He had arranged all this—
arranged it so that she would not know what was
happening until it was too late. Such power was
terrifying.

All at once it seemed that she had never known
him at all.

How sweet her innocent, ignorant dreams had
been of love and romance with a handsome, dark-
eyed knight riding alone amid the Ketilfiord woods.
But now, here in the flesh, Lord fitzHugh of
Triffordd, honored offspring of the Earl of Chester,
was too grand, too powerful, too unreachable for
her to believe he might care for her. To have his
will of her, oh yes, that he would want, but to care
for her—no, never that. And suddenly she knew
that she very much wanted to be cared for. As if a
river were overflowing inside her, she wept
bitterly over lost, hopeless dreams.

Blaize's silence said he was baffled by the flood
of tears that ran over her hands and face and
dripped onto the glossy velvet of her wedding
gown. Setting one booted foot on the edge of the
settle, he leaned on his knee and watched her
impotently.

"Aelfreya—" he ventured at length. "What
have I done to cause such distress?"

"Nothing!" she wept, certain that he would
never understand. "Nothing at all, my lord. Only
misled me, cruelly tricked me, taken from me
everything I hold dear."

"That is not true!" he protested.

"It *is* true!" she wept. "But what is that to you,
my lord? You have what you desire. I'm at your
command. Why should it trouble you if I am disgraced?"

"Disgraced?" he repeated, as if he had never
heard the word before.

Frey lifted streaming eyes, staring up at his

dark figure—all darkness through a shimmer of
tears, all powerful, all demonic. She was terrified of
him. She had to use any means to make him keep
his distance. "You already have a wife!"

"What?!" He stepped back, his booted foot
slamming to the floor. "God's teeth! Ignorant girl,
do you think me so base?"

The outrage in his voice sounded real enough.
Blinking, she choked, "You said you had a
daughter."

"Aye, so I do! Her name is Guenevere. She is
being brought up in the household of the duke of
Normandy, King William's brother."

Understanding nothing but that she was hurt
and frightened, Frey cried, "Then who was her
mother? Some kitchen wench?"

He bent over her with an expression so
ferocious that she flinched away from the blow she
felt sure was coming. But the only force he used on
her was verbal. As she cowered against the back of
the settle, she heard him growl, "I'll not have
viperishness from you, my lady. Aye, *lady*. Lady
fitzHugh, because I made you so—as I can *un*make
you if I choose! And don't weep! I thought such
maidenish tricks were against your nature."

Frey had always thought so too; she had always
been driven to temper, not tears, but on this day
when all the world had run mad her eyes seemed to
have untapped a spring that might fill an ocean. As
Blaize moved away, she collapsed across the
cushions on the settle, sobbing bitterly and un-
controllably.

"Faith!" her husband of an hour muttered to
himself, grabbing up his cloak and swirling it
round him. "A fine wedding day! My lady, I'll leave
you to compose yourself."

As she heard the door slam behind him, a sob of
bitter laughter broke from her. Her unexpected

tears had unmanned him: Lord Blaize fitzHugh could not cope with a distraught woman. But at least he had demonstrated how very little she meant to him. *Ignorant girl*, he had called her. *I made you a lady, I can unmake you if I choose.* And of course he could. If it suited him, he could abandon her, as many men before him had abandoned recalcitrant wives, leaving them to loneliness and misery in a purgatory that was neither the true state of marriage, nor widowhood, nor yet spinsterhood.

Was that the fate that waited for her now—a limbo of lifelong nothingness?

And he still hadn't satisfied her curiosity over his daughter. If he had no wife, then the child must have been conceived and born outside wedlock, as he himself had been fathered by the earl. But what woman had borne Blaize's child in her womb? Where was that woman now? What barrier prevented him from making her his wife? Did he still keep her as mistress of one of his castles in Normandy? Did he visit her when his duties took him to France?

Such frantic speculation, one question piling unanswerable on top of another, only made Frey feel more desolate. After the storm of weeping abated a little, Frey must have slept for she came awake suddenly and wondered where she was. She found herself still on the settle in the main room of the earl's house in York, where all had been made ready for an intimate interlude between newly-weds. And on the third finger of her left hand a gold ring shone bright and new. It had all been true, then. She had not dreamed her marriage to Blaize of Bayonne.

As she sat up, easing stiffened muscles, she heard the servants whispering in the passageway. Judging by the angle of the sun beyond the high, narrow window, Blaize must have been gone for some time; the afternoon had drifted toward evening.

Eventually a timid knock came on the door and when Frey answered a maid appeared, a woman around thirty, buxom and red-cheeked with bright, inquisitive eyes. She took immediate note of the untouched food and wine, and the marks of tears on Frey's face.

"Is all well, my lady?" she asked with a look of concern. "Is there anything you need?"

"No, thank you," Frey sighed.

"Lord fitzHugh will be back shortly, I'm sure," the maid said. "He had some arrangements to make at the castle, so he told us."

"Yes, I know," Frey lied, not wanting to encourage more gossip than was necessary. "You might pour me a glass of wine. And tell me where my belongings have been put. I assume they've been sent from the Abbey?"

The servant moved to the table to pour wine into an ornate silver goblet. "Yes, my lady. Your clothes chest is upstairs in the bedchamber. I unpacked a robe in case you should need it."

"Bedchamber?" Frey repeated, hearing the word echo hollowly in the sudden emptiness inside her. Before long, Blaize would expect to claim his husbandly rights. All she had won was a brief reprieve.

"Yes, my lady. Would you like to see it?"

"Why not?" Frey said, pulling herself to her feet.

The stone passageway was cold and dark. At the far end of it Frey glimpsed trees in a garden, pink with blossom and washed with slanting evening sunlight. A kitchen lay off to one side, where more servants chattered together and aromas told of supper being prepared, but between the kitchen and the solar a dark flight of stairs led to an upper chamber.

The maid led the way, taking Frey into a room with a low, beamed ceiling that gave glimpses of the thatch above it. Its shuttered window looked out across the marketplace and its floorboards were scattered with fresh, sweet-smelling rushes and herbs. Frey's own clothes chest, which had been brought to York from Ketilfiord, first to the Abbey and now to this house, stood in one corner. Two larger chests, ornate with carving and gilding, stood by the wall. But what mostly caught her nervous attention was the bed.

Such a bed—low and wide, with a plump down mattress, linen sheets, fine wool blankets and a coverlet of fur. Fit for an earl. Or an earl's son, she thought. Her own nightrobe, thrown across the fur, looked poor by comparison with the rich brocade hangings fastened back at four bedposts, intended to be hooked across at night to screen its occupants against drafts.

Frey swallowed thickly, recoiling from a picture of being enclosed by those curtains with Blaize beside her. All at once she was swamped by memories of a dawn when the woods had been full of birdsong and a strong male body had been urgent against hers. *Yes, it's want I want,* he had declared in fierce passion. *What I have thought on often these past long months.* Recalling how her senses had been fired by his kisses until she was all willingness, she swayed a little, feeling weak in every muscle. Now he had the right to claim what he had wanted for so long. By tricking her into marriage, he had made sure she could not refuse him.

"You'll be cozy here, my lady," the maid said with a sidelong glance and a knowing gleam in her eye.

"It will do very well," Frey replied, and hurried back down the steep stairway to the solar, where she emptied the goblet and poured more wine, needing its warmth and its wondrous ability to numb her thoughts and her fears.

After a while, unable to sit still, she refilled the goblet yet again and was surprised to find that she was emptying the last of the wine from the big jug. Carrying the silver goblet in her hand, she went out into the garden to watch sunset gild the sky.

Blossoms drifted from the trees—apple trees, she now saw, like those that grew in the gardens at Ketilfiord. There were rose bushes in the garden, abud with March, and beds of yellow crocuses, and herbs that Frey recognized with pleasure, as if they were old friends—marjoram, rosemary, thyme, invaluable comfrey, and the aptly named son-before-father, whose golden flowers came before its leaves. Beside it she saw feathery fennel, and bitter rue. With the coming night in mind, she was tempted to gather some of these last two plants, which were held to be efficacious as a protection against enchantments and evil spirits. Not that Blaize of Bayonne was an evil spirit. Nothing so insubstantial!

Thinking how such thoughts of spells and magic would horrify sister Annora, Frey smiled a wry smile and took another mouthful of wine. It did help. It took away her fears. It made her feel stronger, with a growing defiance that gave her courage. Was she, Wulfnoth's daughter, intending to bow meekly to her fate, her spirit crushed by hopelessness? No, never! She must stand firm and proud, her head high.

She straightened to square her shoulders, taking a deep breath of the spring air. Who did he think he was, this fitzHugh of *Treeforthe* or

however one was supposed to pronounce that
heathenish Welsh word? For all his titles, his
trappings of wealth and power, he was merely a
man, nothing but a Norman. A cursed *Norman*!
Wulfnoth her father would be tearing out his hair
in heaven—or Valhalla, a more likely place for an
old warrior such as he. She was still his true
daughter, his beloved, fiery Frey with strong Saxon
blood flowing hot in her veins. No Norman upstart
would ever overcome Wulfnoth's daughter, whatever ruses he employed.

Buoyed up by the wine, Frey decided that there
would be no more tears. This situation required use
of native Saxon cunning.

"Drinking alone, my lady?" Blaize enquired
from behind her, startling her so much that she
whirled and, although the goblet was nearly
empty, slopped wine onto her hand. Fortunately
she retained enough wits to hold the cup away from
her so that the drops missed her beautiful green
velvet gown.

A gown that Blaize had ordered to be made for
her, she thought. She was the wife of a wealthy
man. There would be more clothes, and jewels,
luxuries by the cartful, if she pleased him. Wasn't
that what Edith had held out as a fine reward for
wifely duties? How envious Edith must be,
knowing that the sister-in-law she had called witch
was now Lady fitzHugh. And if Frey gave her new
lord a son and heir he would be even more
generous.

Dear God, what was she thinking. A child? . . .
Her head reeled in panic at the thought. No, never!
Saxon cunning. Saxon cunning!

She regarded him through her lashes, slyly
teasing him. "Who else was I to drink with, since
my lord chose to absent himself?" She held out the
goblet invitingly, surprised by her unexpected

talent for mummery: with the aid of the wine she was playing the flirt with alarming ease. "Come, taste it. It's sweet."

Looking wary, as if he didn't trust the sudden change in her manner, he stepped slowly toward her, a tall figure framed in spring blossoms, with dark eyes that sought to read her mind. "You've recovered from your distress, I see."

"Of course." She widened her eyes at him, enjoying herself as she fluttered her lashes coyly. "It was no more than a bride's natural nervousness—a reaction to the day's surprises. You will allow me a little maidenly apprehension, I trust. Come, my lord, drink a toast with me. Or do you fear that I might have drugged it? See—" She put the goblet to her lips and drank deeply once more before offering the last mouthful to him.

Blaize laid hold of her wrist with his right hand, taking the goblet from her with his left. The contact with his warm fingers sent a shock of vibrant pleasure through her, waking all her nerves to him despite her efforts to control the response. Watching her over the cup, he turned it deliberately so that his lips touched the place where hers had rested.

The overt intimacy of the action sent a little shiver through Frey as she found herself mesmerized by the sight of him so close. She watched his brown throat ripple as he swallowed the wine, then he tossed the goblet onto the grass and in the same motion jerked her forward, his arms closing about her waist, his eyes deep and alight with desire.

"I know a sweeter wine," he muttered, lowering his head until his nearness blotted out the bright sky and made her sight blur. Feeling dizzy, she closed her eyes as his mouth found hers, fastening hard and hot on her parted lips.

The wine Frey had taken robbed her of the strength and the will to resist her husband's ardor. But if she did not resist neither did she respond, not at first. She was numb, incapable of feeling anything, or so she believed; but as his kiss deepened and his arms pressed her closer to the strong length of his body she felt the familiar jolt inside her, waking all her senses to the scent, the touch, the feel of him.

Somewhere deep inside her a small voice protested, but it was too far off to be heeded. The wine had buried all her inhibitions. Her hands lifted of their own accord to fasten behind his neck, her fingers driving into the soft thickness of his hair. She was answering instinctive needs as she met the hungry working of his mouth with an equal passion, lost in mounting fever as she felt his tongue slide between her teeth, pillaging her warm secrets. Neither of them was aware of anything but a mutual desire for the other.

At last he broke that drowning kiss, all but wrenching his mouth free to draw a huge gasping breath. "Aelfreya!" her name breathed out of him as he stared down at her with eyes so wide and dark that she felt she could plunge into them and lose herself.

She hung in his arms, staring up into his face as she had in so many passionate dreams, wanting him to kiss her again, wanting him to claim her. The depths of her body ran molten with desire for him, making her forget all maidenly modesty. She had never known she could feel such emotions.

Saxon . . . Norman . . . none of that enmity mattered. At that moment she was only a woman. A bride. And she wanted this man who was her husband.

Her willingness shone in her eyes and in the softly swollen mouth that begged for further

attentions. Her body leaned pliant against him,
holding nothing back. The message of body
language was unmistakable. Catching his breath on
a wordless oath, Blaize bent and swept an arm
behind her knees, tossing her off her feet and up
into his arms. He lifted her with ease, as if she were
featherlight, and carried her with long, loping
strides toward the house, staring down at her with
vivid dark eyes.

Frey looped her arms about his neck, made
dizzy by the swirl of pink blossoms against a sunset
sky. Fully aware of what must come—even eager
for it—she hid her burning face in the curve of his
throat, rejoicing in his strength and the firm
muscles of the arms and body that cradled her so
possessively.

They reached the cold passage and then the
dark stairs, up which he bore her with lithe
pantherish strides, climbing two treads at a time,
striding at last into the quiet privacy of the bedchamber where he set her on her feet and gathered
her once more into his embrace. Bending his dark
head to hers he possessed her mouth again, this
time with an urgent determination that brooked no
denial.

She entwined her arms about his neck,
rapturously returning his kisses, but as his hands
began to stroke and caress her she realized that she
was feeling increasingly light-headed, as if she were
about to float off the floor. It reminded her of the
way she had felt in the first hours of the fever
which had struck her after she got the thorn in her
foot. Chills swept over her brain and stroked coldly
across her flesh. But she tried to ignore those unpleasant symptoms; she wanted the lovemaking to
continue. Now that it had begun she wished this
first time to be over before the effects of the wine
wore off.

Blaize's hands were moving ever more urgently on her, molding the contours of her breasts, sliding caressingly round her waist to explore every curve of her. She felt him tearing at the side lacings of her velvet gown, while all the time his eager mouth continued to caress hers in mounting fever.

Shaking off the strange, dizzy feeling that had assailed her, she found herself laughing at his fumbling haste. "Blaize, you'll tear my gown!"

"Then take it off for me," he ordered gruffly. "Take it off. I'm impatient, Frey."

"I know it, lord!" She drew away, touching his face with soft fingers, blinking to try to clear the mist from her mind, saying like a child, "You have never called me Frey before."

"Please!" he begged her. "Please!"

But as she bent to lift the heavy skirts she found her head swimming. She staggered off-balance. The chill swept her again, this time breaking cold sweat out on her skin. She felt Blaize take hold of her, steadying her as she swayed into him.

"Frey!" he said anxiously as she laid a hand to her burning head, feeling a deathly cold in her flesh and a churning in her stomach. She was unaware that her face had grown pale as parchment, or that she was shivering with ague. Her legs wouldn't hold her.

"Frey!" The voice seemed to come through white clouds that closed round to enfold her as she collapsed against Blaize, nausea boiling inside her. Then she was being lifted, placed on soft furs. A cool hand came on her heated brow.

"God's blood!" The curse bit through to her swooning mind. Next second he was gone, his boots thumping on the stairs as he called for someone named Hilda.

VII

A woman came and tended Frey, who recalled
her stomach voiding some hot, bitter fluid,
again and again until she was aching. She had no
strength to help herself. Sweat poured from her and
she felt a cold cloth pressed to her brow. Eventually, Frey realized that the Hilda whom Blaize had
summoned was the same rosy-cheeked maidservant
who had earlier shown her the bedchamber.

When the worst of the sickness had passed, the
maid helped Frey to remove her sweat-damp
clothes; then Hilda made her lie down again while
she wrapped the covers round her young mistress's
shuddering body. The maid kept saying worriedly,
"Oh, my lady! Oh, my lady! We meant no harm. If
I'd known this would happen I'd never have—" As
she smoothed the fur coverlet she slid a sidelong
look at Frey's pallid face, asking tenatively,
"Did . . . did Lord fitzHugh drink any of the wine?"

"A sip," Frey managed through her shivering,
overcome by a sudden immense lassitude. "A sip
only. But what do you mean? The wine . . . What
was wrong with the wine?"

Hilda was almost in tears now, wringing her
hands and rocking back and forth, her mouth
trembling. "God forgive me, but it was well-meant,
my lady. I swear it was well-meant! We intended to

150

be of service, not to harm you. Why, when I was wed, a philtre did wonders for me and my Robin."

Alerted despite her desire to slide into sleep, Frey forced her heavy eyelids to open. "Philtre? What philtre?"

"A love potion, my lady," Hilda admitted wretchedly. "It was in the wine. It was supposed to help you and your lord overcome your shyness on this first night. I never dreamed it would make you ill. But then maybe your stomach's more delicate than others, you being a highborn lady and all."

Highborn lady?! If Frey had not felt so ill she might have laughed hysterically. As it was, she thought only that life was fraught with ironies. Then she let her eyelids droop as they wished, sleep taking her into deep, comfortable depths of healing.

She woke at last to the sound of merry crowds beyond the shutters at her window. Evidently the night had passed and the day was well advanced. Pedlars called their wares about the marketplace outside the house, a pipe and drum played a gay jig, and right beneath her window a minstrel plucked a lute to accompany his lilting tenor as he sang a sweet but slyly suggestive love ditty concerning a pair of newlyweds. Nor was he there by accident, it seemed. Hardly had he begun a third verse of his song than footsteps pounded in the passage below and a man's voice sternly bade the singer:

"Be off with you, wretched fellow! If you do not cease this disturbance my lord will fetch a stick to you. Do you hanker to spend the rest of this day in the castle dungeons?"

The lute plucked a final trill, then the minstrel retorted, "Am I disturbing them, good steward? What—are they still abed? Tired from playing games all night, eh?"

A roar of laughter greeted this ribaldry, the

crowd enjoying the free show. Evidently the
minstrel was playing up to his audience.

"Off!" the steward roared.

Laughing, the minstrel departed, amid hoots
and catcalls from the onlookers. The steward
slammed the door. But only a short while later the
lute struck up again a little farther away, this time
with a joking lament about the singer's love of
gambling.

It was Easter Monday, Frey realized. The sounds
she could hear—the voices, the crying of wares, the
merriment and the music—were the sounds of a fair
taking place in the market square.

Unfortunately she was in no condition to share
with the folk of York their delight in the holiday.
She felt as if she had been pounded under the
hooves of a hundred horses. Her head ached, her
stomach was tender, her limbs weak and all her
muscles sore.

When she opened her eyes she found the room
in shadow. On three sides of the bed the hangings
had been drawn across to screen her, though on her
right they were still hooked back. Daylight filtered
in between the closed shutters, allowing her to see
Hilda sitting on the floor, her head and arms resting
on the bed. The maid appeared to be sound asleep.
She must have been there all night.

There was no sign of Blaize. He had slept elsewhere, evidently, leaving the maid to keep her
faithful vigil. Had he been angry? Frey couldn't
recall exactly what had happened. The previous
evening was vague as a poorly remembered dream.

As she stirred, a shaft of pain shot through her
head, making her give a stifled moan that roused
Hilda. The maid shot to her feet, looking anxious as
she remembered her duty and gasped, "Oh, my
lady! Are you awake? How do you feel this
morning?"

"As though I'd been trampled," Frey admitted wryly. "But I believe I shall live. Hilda . . . You are Hilda, are you not?"

The maid nodded vigorously, dropping a curtsey. "Yes, my lady. Yes, that's me."

"Then, Hilda, tell me . . . does my memory hold true? Did you say you had mixed a love-philtre in with the wine?"

"It wasn't meant to make you ill!" Hilda cried, her rosy face turning pale with distress and alarm.

Sighing, Frey closed her eyes. "No, I don't suppose it was. Don't fret about it, Hilda, I'm not going to be angry with you." But the effects of the potion proved that the maid was no skilled herbalist. The draught had wreaked a poisonous effect on Frey. She laid a hand to her head, trying to cool the pain there. "What was in the mixture, Hilda?"

"I don't know," the maid replied. "Oh, lady . . . have you a headache? Shall I bring a tincture?"

Frey managed a pale smile. "No more potions, I think, not for a while. Maybe some bread and milk, with honey, to soothe my stomach."

"I'll get it at once." Bobbing a curtsey, Hilda departed.

Had it not been for the noise of the market, Frey might have drifted back to sleep, but the clamor of crowds and calling of wares beat at her aching brain.

A few moments later she heard swift, heavy footsteps on the stairs, coming into the room. A hand unhooked the bed curtains near the door and Blaize was there, peering at her in the faint light. Hilda must have told him his wife was awake at last.

Though he was less richly attired than he had been for the wedding still he was a virtual stranger and the sight of him brought back her apprehension. It didn't help that he was frowning blackly, as if annoyed with her.

Frey couldn't remember what she had done to make him angry. Apart from the fact that she had taken too much wine and become ill at some point, she couldn't remember much at all about the previous evening.

"Are you better?" he asked.

"A little," she answered, dampening her dry lips.

Impatiently, he strode across the room to unbar the shutters and throw them wide. Sunlight and fresh air streamed in, making Frey wince and throw an arm across her aching eyes, but there also arose a hearty cheer from outside, as if the crowd had been waiting for some sign of life from the house where the bridal pair had spent their supposedly lusty wedding night.

"Hades!" Blaize muttered to himself and the light dimmed again as he pushed the shutters closed until only a sliver of light came in. In response to what they took as bashfulness, the crowd laughed and called lewdly.

His boots sounding loudly on the floorboards, Blaize strode back to the bed and stood glowering at Frey, arms akimbo. "One would think these yokels had never experienced a wedding before ours," he said testily. "So, my lady, perhaps you'll be a little more temperate in future—at least until you accustom yourself to good rich wine after the watered-down vinegar you've been used to at Ketilfiord. God's teeth! Was the thought of marriage to me so repellent that you had to stupefy yourself before you could face it?"

The harshness in his voice struck at the pain in her head, making her moan and press a hand to her brow. "Please speak more softly," she begged. "Do you wish the 'yokels' to have even more to amuse them? We shall be the talk of the taverns."

He leaned on the bedpost, bending toward her with furious eyes, though he did lower his voice—to a deep, menacing undertone. "Answer me, lady! Did you deliberately intoxicate yourself?"

"No!"

"No? Then why did you drink a whole jugful of wine?"

Was that what she had done? Unfortunately she didn't remember any of it with much clarity. "Maybe I was afraid."

"Afraid of what?" he demanded.

If he didn't know, she couldn't explain. She could hardly think with the headache pounding like a drum, pulsing inside her brain, making her eyes water as light struck them. She turned her head to one side, an arm across her stinging eyes, and wished he would go away.

After a moment he did leave, his boots striking angrily on floorboards and stairs.

Shortly afterwards, Hilda brought some sweetened bread and milk. The food helped to settle Frey's stomach and after a while, despite the raucous noise from the market, she slept again.

The second time she woke, the sun had moved from the front of the house, but still the market fair went on in a bright afternoon. Balancing her head carefully against a debilitating giddiness, Frey slipped her robe on and carefully climbed from the bed. Her bare feet made no sound on the floor as, leaning on the wall, she crept to the window to open the shutter a little and peer out.

The scent of hot pies made her stomach heave as she scanned the jostling crowds. Here a dancing bear pirouetted in ungainly fashion; there a pair of tumblers twisted their bodies for the delight of the crowd. The minstrel was still at work, catching tossed pennies in his cap and bowing with all the grace of a lord. Frey caught sight of a puppet show,

and a stall where a man demonstrated marionettes
that danced as he pulled the wires attached to their
wooden limbs.

Coming from the countryside, Frey had seldom
seen such a market, full of wonders, where all
manner of entertainment was to be seen and all
manner of goods could be bought, from freshly
brewed ale to wooden tops, leatherware, pins and
lace, bronze bowls and silk ribbons.

Directly below her, almost at the doorway of
the earl's house, a manservant stood patiently
holding the reins of a dappled gray palfrey,
apparently waiting for his mistress to return. Even
as Frey wondered where the lady who owned that
horse could be, a slender figure emerged from the
passage doorway below.

The lady was not alone. Blaize was with her.

Above the noise of the fair Frey could not
clearly hear what they were saying, but from the
timbre of their voices she knew they were speaking
French, so even had she been able to hear she would
not have understood. To compensate, she strained
her eyes to gather every clue available as to the
identity of this lissome visitor.

The woman was finely dressed in a yellow
mantle edged with sable, with a matching yellow
veil over golden hair, held by a silver circlet. Who
could she be? Frey wondered, and why was she
visiting with Blaize? Then as the woman turned to
look up at Blaize and offer her hand in farewell,
Frey caught sight of her face.

With an involuntary gasp of dismay, she drew
back behind the shutters, throwing a hand to her
mouth to contain any sound she might have made.
The lady who had been calling on Blaize was
Melissande, the beautiful lady-in-waiting to the
Countess of Chester—the lady who had pinched
Frey so spitefully while helping her attire herself

for the wedding—the lady whose blue eyes had been cold as icicles, frosted with hatred.

What had brought her here? Frey wondered, a stab of jealous suspicion smiting her. She remembered the courtly way Blaize had bowed over that fair hand—had he lifted it to his lips?

Realizing that she didn't feel well at all, Frey stumbled back to bed, still wearing her robe as she pulled the blankets around her, for warmth and for comfort. Fresh tears welled in her eyes, squeezing out to dampen her lashes as she thought of those two together. Melissande and Blaize. Blaize and beautiful blue-eyed Melissande . . .

In the dimly lit room with the shutters closed and the sounds of the fair continuing outside, Frey lay disconsolate on her bed, still shivering from the effects of the poisoning. But her physical discomfort was as nothing compared with the torment of wondering what ties bound Blaize with the countess's lovely lady-in-waiting. Again and again Frey remembered how she had clearly sensed Melissande's hostility as the ladies prepared her for her wedding that morning. Indeed, Melissande had scarely taken trouble to conceal her dislike of the bride. And now Frey fancied she had discovered the reason.

Could it be true that the lady Melissande believed she had some prior claim to Blaize's affection? Had Blaize given her reason to harbor romantic hopes?

Frey did not want to believe it. Besides, the evidence of an alliance between the two was very slim. Perhaps her suspicions were unwarranted. After all, if Blaize had wanted the lady Melissande he could have had her.

Or could he?

When it came to matrimony there were limits beyond which even an earl's bastard son—a son who could never be a full heir—might not reach. Since Melissande was a companion of the countess of Chester, it followed that she herself must be nobly born, her pedigree impeccable; most probably she was possessed of such vast dowry that the only suitable match would be with some royal prince or duke, not the by-blow of some illicit passion, however well-regarded by his noble father.

Was it, then, a case of unrequited love, a passion forbidden by the laws of inheritance and seemliness? Denied the woman he really loved, had Blaize hardened his heart and deliberately chosen a wife who was in no way out of reach? Had he married Aelfreya of Ketilfiord, a dowerless Saxon, out of pique and hurt pride?

No, there was more to it than that. He had gone to great trouble, using his father's influence and his own guile, to secure Frey for his wife. He must have wanted her very badly.

Wanted her, she thought bitterly—yes, that was the truth of it. He had made no secret of his physical desire for her. If only it had been as simple as it seemed, she might have learned to be happy with her lot; but with Blaize nothing was ever quite that straightforward. If he wanted her it was only because she had stung his pride, evaded and defied him, and in doing so had flung down a challenge that his manhood could not resist.

She guessed that no woman had ever dared do that before—not to the son of Hugh d'Avranches, feared lord of the palatinate earldom of Chester. Perhaps not even the highborn lady Melisande had been able to deny him.

Where had they met? she wondered. Since Melissande apparently spoke not a word of English, presumably she and Blaize had first encountered one another in Normandy.

Dear God! a sudden incredible thought struck in

Frey's mind like the thrust of an ice-cold blade: was Melissande the mother of Blaize's daughter Guenevere, now growing up in the court of Duke Robert of Normandy? It was all too possible.

In such an extremity, the lady would be cloistered in secret until the child was born. The baby would be given to a wet-nurse to suckle, separated from its noble mother forever. After a suitable period of time the lady would emerge from seclusion and perhaps be sent far away from places where she was known—say to England, to the service of a countess—so that any whisper of scandal might die away and leave her free to attain a suitable husband who need never know of her former disgrace.

The child, meanwhile, would be given an appropriate foster home and an education in keeping with his or her birth. Probably also that child would be openly acknowledged by its father, as the earl had acknowledged Blaize and as Blaize now acknowledged Guenevere. The pieces of this theory fit with terrible smoothness.

But Melissande was denied him, now and forever, however much he loved her and however fervently she returned his feelings. Frey could find it in herself to pity the ill-fated pair, except that she seemed to have become entangled in their despair, her own fate bound up with theirs. Now she wished she had never laid eyes on Blaize of Bayonne, nor slapped his face, nor acted the hoyden, thus provoking in him a desire to tame her to his will. With that in mind, as seemed all too obvious now, he had prevented her betrothal to the merchant Geronimus, engineered her incarceration in the nunnery and then organized this marriage. It had all happened as a result of his cool calculation. Of that she was convinced.

Unfortunately she was equally, and dismally,

sure that once he had achieved his object he would very soon tire of this "ignorant" Saxon who had nothing to commend her—no dowry, no high connections, no fashionable golden hair and blue eyes.

All Frey had was her pride, and if as a consequence of his heartless maneuvering he achieved his object he would rob her of that, too. She must resist him by all means at her command.

Blaize's footsteps on the stairs alerted Frey to his imminent arrival. She huddled closer into her blankets, thanking heaven that at least her headache was almost gone and by now her tears had dried. If she looked pale no one would wonder at it. But she felt dead inside, lost and desolate. If Blaize still cared for Melissande, this marriage was nothing but an empty sham.

The latch clicked and Blaize came into the room. He appeared to be in a more reasonable mood than he had displayed earlier, though he still frowned at her, his eyes dark and brooding as he paused by the bed. "I trust your head is clearer now," he said, a thumb hooking in his belt. "Faith! I've been inebriated myself at times, but never to such effect."

Frey considered informing him that it was not so much the wine itself that had made her ill; it was more the love-potion which Hilda had so helpfully added. But she guessed that Blaize would be furious if he knew the truth of it; he would probably regard the use of an aphrodisiac as an insult to his manhood, and Frey had no desire to bring trouble on the head of the well-meaning Hilda. The maid was genuinely contrite and had already been punished adequately by the fright she had had when Frey fell ill.

Instead of answering him directly, she said in a small, colorless voice, "You had a visitor, my lord."

Was it imagination or was there the slightest

flicker of guilt in eyes that were suddenly veiled against her as his frown deepened? "Who told you that?"

"I got up to look at the fair and I saw her, from the window," Frey told him truthfully. "It was the lady Melissande, was it not? One of the countess's ladies?"

"She came enquiring after your welfare," Blaize said in a dismissive tone that seemed to make the incident trivial. "It's kind of the countess to be concerned for you."

"Indeed," Frey sighed, wondering if she could believe him. "But how did they know I was ill?"

"Why . . . I told them, last night when I went to the Abbey."

"You went to the Abbey? You saw the countess?"

He flung out an impatient hand, as if irritated to have her question the obvious. "Of course I did. It was only courteous to thank Countess Arlette for her help with the wedding."

It also provided a perfect excuse for him to go and see Melissande, Frey thought dully. But as she searched his tanned face from under her lashes she found no sign of guile in him.

"Why did you not send the lady Melissande up to see me when she was here?" she asked.

"Hilda said you were sleeping," the answer came pat, sounding convincing enough though Frey in her present suspicious state of mind could not help but think that it made a convenient excuse. "And besides," Blaize added, "the lady Melissande speaks no English, and since you yourself have no French or Latin—" The sentence trailed off as he peered more closely at her in the ill-lit room, bending over the bed and finally sitting beside her, much to her dismay. She tried to make herself as small as possible, shrinking beneath the blankets, away from him.

"You are still too pale," he observed, a warm palm resting on her brow as if to estimate her temperature. "You were, indeed, very ill. At moments Hilda feared for your life, so she tells me. Why were you so afraid of me that you had to numb your mind with wine?"

His nearness made her breathing unsteady and in response to that gentle hand on her forehead she could feel hot color creeping into her face. His touch did seem to soothe her headache, strangely enough, though at the same time it set up responsive signals that coursed along her nerves, bringing both pleasure and panic.

Looking at him was painful. He was so handsome, and he appeared to be truly concerned for her. Perhaps in a way he felt guilty for being responsible for her illness.

Briefly she mourned for what might have been if he had remained simply a dark knight named Blaize of Bayonne. But that sweet dream was gone forever. She recalled the titles resounding across the Abbey courtyard, declaimed by Gilbert of York: "Blaize fitzHugh, seigneur de Bayonne, castellan de Triffordd." That was the truth of it: he was the earl of Chester's cherished son. And he was in love with another woman.

She lowered her eyes, plucking at the fur coverlet, as she made excuses for her behavior. "I had not guessed you were so highly placed, my lord. I'm a simple country maid. To be taken from my home and my family, and then from obscurity at the Abbey, without enough time to prepare myself for such unexpected elevation—"

His sharp laugh cut her off as he sat back, removing his hand from her brow. "Oh, come, Aelfreya. Is that what you would have me believe—that you consider yourself a 'simple country maid'? Hah! Once it was *'Wulfnoth's daughter, with the blood of Danish kings in my veins'*—do you not recall declaring those facts to me, with your eyes ablaze?"

"Too well," she said dully. "I said too much—behaved very badly, as I realize now. Had I known who you really were—"

"I am myself," he said, his expression softening as he reached to take her hand between his own warm ones and lowered his voice to a deep, intimate undertone. "Here in this room, I'm no more than your wedded husband." His brow creased in a frown as he chafed her hand to warm it. "But you're cold! Here—" Gathering up the fur coverlet, he lifted her with an arm beneath her shoulders and laid the fur around her, tucking it in with great care, as old Ula might have done.

Then the movements slowed as he glanced down at her breasts, where soft curves were exposed by the movement of her robe. Fresh awareness flowed between them and his eyes met hers, dark and opaque with a sudden desire he could not hide. Frey's stomach began to churn, so that for a moment she feared a return of her nausea. But this disturbance was different; it set her blood to pounding headily in her throat and dried her lips so that she automatically moistened them with the tip of her tongue. Blaize's eyelids flickered and all at once his glowing brown gaze was resting on a mouth that, despite all her efforts to prevent it, throbbed in response.

A panicky pulse began to flutter in her temple as he took her face between warm hands and bent over her, watching her mouth all the time. She closed her eyes, beating back the fright that had seized her, feeling too weak to resist him as his mouth covered hers with a soft, warm pressure that woke ripples all through her body. Instinct

made her want to lift her arms and wrap them
about him, to touch him with her hands and
explore the texture of his skin, but she lay limp,
hampered by the covers that bound her limbs like
those of a swaddled infant.

The kiss lasted only a moment, for which she
was both glad and sorry. She knew a bittersweet
pleasure from the soft pressure of his underlip but
she kept her eyes tightly closed as he drew away
just a few inches, his breath coming swift and
warm, fanning her cheek. He was looking at her
intently, she could sense it, even though she dared
not open her eyes to show him the confusion of her
own emotions.

To him, it must have seemed that he had elicited
no response at all. He caught his breath in anger.
The hands that held her face hardened, his finger-
tips pressed to her skull. He said hoarsely, "You
cannot be unmoved! You responded gladly enough
last night! Or will you claim that your passion came
only through the wine? Great God!" His arms swept
round her, lifting her and pulling her half across
his lap as he kissed her again, his mouth hard now,
hot and purposeful as he sought to force a flicker of
emotion from her.

The response was there, heady and sweet despite her remaining weakness, flowing like wine in
her blood. She steeled herself against it, resisting it
with all her strength. But beneath his onslaught her
lips parted and allowed his invasion, the hot thrust
of his tongue exploring her underlip and her teeth,
probing deeper in anticipation of a more intimate
exploration to come. Sensing it, she felt a warm
fluidity stir in her womb, her body preparing itself
for him without her will or permission.

Her physical self had turned traitor. Even as her
body trembled and her loins moistened so her skin
tingled under his touch, coming alive with nervous

pleasure as his hand stroked in her hair, round her ear. His fingers traced the curve of her jaw and smoothed down her throat to run along her collarbone and edge beneath her robe. In anticipation, her breasts were tingling, their tips hardened and thrusting against the thin fabric that covered them.

Mingled excitement and terror combined to bring a return of her nausea. Her head whirled with it and she feared she might swoon if the torment went on. Frantic, she clamped her hand around his wrist, preventing further intimacies as she wrenched her mouth from his and buried her face against the velvet of his tunic, gasping, pleading, "Sir! Please! I am not well!"

That same errant hand easily broke her feeble grip and came strongly under her chin, lifting her face in all its freckled pallor, marked with the sweep of long, copper-gold lashes against ashen cheeks. Not even he could fail to see the marks of illness that still lingered. "Look at me!" he ordered.

Blinking, Frey slowly opened her eyes, knowing that he must read her fear and her vulnerability, but at that moment she wished him to feel guilt, perhaps pity—anything that would persuade him to delay his assertion of his marital rights. In returning his gaze she sought to read the thoughts behind the frowning face that stared down at her, but his eyes were shuttered against her, revealing only a growing irritation.

After a moment he brusquely laid her back against the pillows and got jerkily to his feet, sweeping a hand through his hair.

"You will not be able to plead weakness forever," he growled. "But I promised you my protection and I shall not force myself upon you." He leaned over her, his eyes flashing as he added through bared teeth. "*Not yet!*"

Despite the implied threat, Frey felt weak with

relief and a little more color flowed into her cheeks.
"I'm . . . grateful, sir," she managed. "In due time,
when I feel better, of course I shall not deny you.
You are my husband. I took the vows in full
knowledge—"

"Aye, so you did!" he broke in. "And I shall
hold you to them, never fear. How long do you
expect this 'due time' will be?"

Faced with that agate stare, Frey felt her heart
quail as the blood once again receded from her head
and left her skin like freckled ash with deep blue
shadows under tawny eyes. "A few days, perhaps."
She would have liked to make it weeks, or months,
but a few days was the most she dared claim.

Even that, it seemed, was too long for Blaize's
liking. His mouth twisted in disgust. "A few days?
Faith! This was not how I had it planned." He
swung away as if to leave but swung back,
glowering, as a thought occurred to him. "From
now on I'll make sure you have only Adam's ale to
drink, lady. I'll have you well—and I'll have you
sober." With movements that were deliberately
menacing in their slowness, he laid a hand against
the bedpost and again leaned over to look into
Frey's eyes, adding in a fierce undertone that was
both a promise and a threat, "But I will have you,
wife! This is no saintly marriage between celibates!"

He slammed the door so fiercely behind him
that Frey imagined the entire house shook from the
impact. Trembling, she shivered into the blankets.
She did still feel unwell, it was true, but also she was
terrified of what his kisses might lead to. His arms
seemed to rob her of all pride, all sense, his touch
drew irresistible responses from her body, and
worst of all was the fact that when he was tender
with her it was all too easy for her to set aside her
doubts and foolishly believe that he might care.
That was a delusion, of course, but oh! the thought

was sweet. She very much wanted him to care. It
would make this marriage bearable.

But what, she wondered suddenly, had he
meant about her response—her passion—last night?
She vaguely recalled drinking the wine, then
walking in the garden and looking at the herb beds,
but after that her memories were misted. Struggle
as she might, she could not remember what had
happened.

She could not have responded to him! And if she
had it must have been in the drunken stupor
induced by the poisoned wine. It could not have
been real.

When Hilda brought her supper, Frey found
she could eat very little of it. Her muscles still ached,
her stomach remained sore and her head was
pounding. When she pleaded illness to Blaize she
had not been dissembling. Whatever that philtre
had contained, its effects had been more noxious
than she had imagined.

Eventually, she drifted again into an uneasy
sleep full of sensual dreams of Blaize; part of her,
even in sleep, anticipated his arrival in the bedchamber. Surely he would come. They were newly
wed. Where else would he sleep but in his wife's
bed?

But Blaize did not come. When next she woke,
morning light misted in around the shutters at the
window, though all Frey could see were the thick
hangings that surrounded her bed. Someone—presumably the faithful Hilda—had been in while she
slept and hooked the curtains across. She heard the
sounds of the city about its normal business, voices
calling, hooves clopping, carts trundling on cobbles
and sloshing in mud, children at play, and a pedlar
with a loud, strident bell and a discernible lisp,
calling, "Eelth for thale! Freth eelth!"

Aware of a lingering malaise, chiefly a certain

heaviness in her head, Frey tested her limbs to see
how they responded. She concluded that she was
well on the mend and should probably get up.

She had thrown back the blankets and was
about to rise from the bed when the latch clicked
and the rosy-cheeked Hilda appeared with a tray.
She gave Frey an assessing, worried look born of a
sense of guilt, Frey guessed.

"How are you today, my lady?"

"About to get dressed, if you will help me,"
Frey said.

"But are you well enough?"

"We shall see when I try it." She glanced at the
tray, which held a mug of weak ale and a thick slice
of wheaten bread smeared with butter and honey.
In response to the sight of food, her stomach
gurgled in hunger, no longer sore but eager to be
filled. "But perhaps I'll breakfast first," she added
as she drew the blankets round her again and
allowed the maid to set the tray across her knees.

The house itself felt still and it occurred to Frey
to wonder where Blaize might be. He had not come
to his bed. Had he slept again in the solar?

Gulping a draft of the refreshingly sour ale, she
clasped her hands round the mug and asked,
"Where is my lord?"

Hilda was making herself useful, straightening
the bed covers, unhooking the hangings and
opening the shutters to let in the morning sun. She
glanced over her shoulder to reply, "He came in an
hour since, though only to say that he was going to
the Abbey, my lady. He will be back before midday, I expect."

"Came in?" Frey repeated. "Came in from
where? It's early yet! Where has he been so early in
the day?"

Hilda turned from the window and as she
moved back closer to the bed Frey saw the maid's

cheery face downcast, her gapped teeth caught in her lower lip. "He . . . he did not come home last night, my lady."

The news struck Frey like a physical blow. "Not come home?" she echoed stupidly. "Then where did he . . . where did he pass the night?"

"It wasn't my place to enquire, but I expect he slept at the castle," was Hilda's guess. "The countess's escort is biding there. Lord fitzHugh would have business with his knights—and probably with Lord Gilbert, the king's castellan."

"Yes, of course." That was, Frey told herself, the most rational explanation, but she was disturbed to know that Blaize had been absent all night. On the edge of her mind she found memories of Melissande lurking. Even a lady-in-waiting to a countess could find ways of meeting a lover in secret. Minstrels' songs were full of such amorous trysts.

"Hilda, I will get up," she decided. "I can't lie abed forever."

"But are you sure, my lady?" the maid said anxiously. "You were very sick. Lord fitzHugh did say a few days—"

"Yes, that's what I told him. But I must make a start on recovery. Besides, my lord might wonder, if I make no effort, whether it was more than wine that sickened me."

The allusion made Hilda's apple cheeks appear to wither and her eyes grew round with fright.

"You haven't mentioned the love-philtre to him, have you?" Frey asked.

"I daren't do that, my lady," the maid said fervently, wringing her hands in her apron. "To tell the truth, I've been afraid that *you* might tell him of it. I'm grateful that you haven't. If I hadn't been so worried I'd never have said anything about it even to you. I see now it was a foolish thing to do. I deserve to be punished for it. But," the denial broke out of her in an anguished cry, "you were never meant to drink it all yourself!"

"I know," Frey sighed. "Well, never mind, Hilda. Comfort yourself. What's done is done. Fortunately I took no lasting harm."

"For which God must be praised! A lady's constitution isn't meant to weather such assaults."

Frey smiled wryly to herself. "I fancy my constitution is stronger than you think, Hilda. I'm a Saxon, not a thin-bred Norman with weakly blood. But there is one thing that mystifies me—I wish I knew what herbs and balms you put in that potion."

"Me?!" Hilda threw her hands to her face, her mouth agape and her eyes popping in horror. "Oh, it wasn't me who mixed the ingredients, my lady. I don't know anything about magic and medicine!"

"Then if *you* didn't make it, where did the philtre come from?" Frey asked in surprise.

"Why . . . from the apothecary, my lady. It was in one of his small green bottles, sealed with wax."

This news made Frey frown. A professional should never have made the mistakes that had made her ill. She herself would have had more skill than that. "Then the man must be a charlatan."

"Oh, no, my lady," Hilda denied at once, astounded by the charge. "People come from all over the kingdom to consult him. Why, when the king himself visited York this same physician prescribed him a remedy and was rewarded in gold."

It was all very curious, Frey thought. "Perhaps you should return to this apothecary and require of him his recipe. He made a mistake in the brewing somewhere. And if I knew the ingredients, I might prepare an antidote. My insides are still sore."

"But he wouldn't tell you!" Hilda exclaimed. "He guards his secrets jealously. He'd be out of business if he went about telling everyone how he mixed his remedies."

"Perhaps so," Frey said, though it seemed to her that the man should be put out of business anyway. She herself knew several recipes for love-potions and though some of them tasted foul none would have the disastrous effect that this apothecary's mixture had had on her. But she supposed the excess of rich wine on an empty stomach might have added to the consequences, too.

She set the subject aside, not wanting to distress Hilda further.

Having removed the empty breakfast tray, the maid drew back the covers and Frey, slowly and gingerly, eased her legs over the edge of the bed and paused a moment until the giddiness caused by the effort had abated. Evidently she was not as strong as she believed.

After a few moments, she got unsteadily to her feet and made her way across the floorboards to the washstand, where Hilda poured cold water into a polished bronze bowl for her. The herbs and rushes beneath her bare feet gave off a sweet aroma that reminded her of the bower at Ketilfiord, but she thrust aside the wave of longing and homesickness that tugged behind her eyes.

Just keeping upright required all her concentration and as she bent to wash her face her head clouded with dizziness, though the chill of the water revived her a little.

"What shall you wear today, my lady?" Hilda enquired.

"Anything." Frey couldn't think about clothes, not right at that moment. Besides, she didn't have much of a selection. "You choose something for me."

She groped for the towel and pressed it to her face, finding it softer than the unbleached linen she was used to. The luxuries that now surrounded her continued to take her by surprise. "I am Lady fitzHugh," she said to herself. "I am daughter-in-

law to the Earl of Chester." It still seemed like a bad
dream. Perhaps she would wake up and find that it
was untrue.

Not until she turned from the washstand did
she realize that Hilda had made a mistake over the
chests: instead of Frey's own battered clothespress,
the maid had opened one of the larger, more ornate
dressing chests.

"That's not mine," Frey said. "It must belong to
my lord. The other one, Hilda, the smallest chest
is—" The sentence trailed off in surprise; across the
bed Hilda had tossed a chemise of cobwebby muslin
together with a shift of fine cream linen, and the
garment the maid was shaking out, stroking and
admiring it as she did so, was no male tunic, nor
any article of clothing that Blaize would have worn.
It was a kirtle of finest wool, dyed in a soft red and
trimmed down the sleeves, round the shoulders and
on the flowing skirt with row upon row of minute
pearls—a most desirable item but, alas, not one of
Frey's. Her mind refused to grasp the inferences.
"There's some mistake," she said, a hand to her
aching head. "Those things don't belong to me,
Hilda."

"Oh, yes they do, my lady," the maid assured
her.

"They do? All of them?"

Hilda nodded happily, her eyes bright as she
shared her mistress's pleasure in the wardrobe.
"All of them. Lord fitzHugh sent orders ahead for a
trousseau to be prepared for you. All the seam-
stresses in the city have been busy for weeks. Didn't
you know? Perhaps it was intended as a surprise—a
wedding gift."

Still holding the damp towel, Frey walked
dazedly across to stare at the clothes packed neatly
in that magnificent oak chest among layers of sweet
herbs and flowers that would both add a subtle
scent to the fabrics and keep away the moths and

silverfish. From what she could see as she fingered through the garments in wonderment and growing delight, they were all equally as grand and costly as the red kirtle—clothes in velvets, silks and fine soft wools embroidered with bright silks, decked with jewels and trimmed with furs—tunics, robes, cloaks and undergarments, along with veils and shifts of sheerest muslin, and accessories like girdles of soft leather and gaily colored kerchiefs. Frey had never hoped to own such beautiful things.

"For me?" she breathed.

"But of course, my lady," Hilda replied. "You're Lady fitzHugh now—a baron's wife. You must dress as befits your station. Will the red do for today?"

Frey glanced again at the pearl-strewn gown, sighing, "Indeed, yes. Yes, it will do very well."

The lavish generosity of the gift overwhelmed her—except that on second thought she divined that of course Blaize fitzHugh would not want his wife to disgrace him. He had ordered the clothes more for his own sake than for hers. By comparison, her own clothes were fit for a goosegirl—just as the countess's maid had implied. Ketilfiord could never have provided such fabrics and such trimmings.

But she refused to feel shame because neither her father or her brother had been able to give her costly garments. Both of them would have done so had they not been reduced to near-beggary by Norman treachery. For all their property they had loved her— Wulfnoth without restraint and Reynold in his own less obvious way—which was more than she could say for Blaize fitzHugh. To her, love was the most precious gift of all, and one that not all her new husband's wealth could buy either for her or from her.

Even so, she was woman enough to look forward to wearing garments finer than she had ever owned before. When she saw Blaize, she promised herself, she would thank him sincerely, however double-edged his motives.

VIII

Frey still felt slightly dizzy and queasy when Hilda had helped her dress in the pearl-trimmed gown, and when she went down the dark stairs she had to hold on to the wall for support. To counteract the lingering weakness, she asked Hilda to prepare an infusion of fresh thyme from the garden, giving the maid clear instructions as to the preparation of the remedy, which she sipped as she sat by the fire in the solar.

She was determined to feel better before Blaize came back.

Whatever business the lord fitzHugh might be conducting at the Abbey, it kept him away from the house on the marketplace for hours. He did not even appear for the midday meal. Frey dined alone, then decided to take some air in the garden, warmly wrapped in a mantle lined with soft red foxfur, for though the day was mild she felt cold.

One of the manservants brought a bench for her to sit on beneath the blossoming trees. She watched the birds and breathed deeply of the herb-scented air, trying to overcome the lingering weakness that plagued her.

Noticing that her hands were very pale, she guessed that her face must be without color too. It was a wonder that particular apothecary had

174

customers left—he must have killed most of them off by now. No amount of wine could have such lasting effects, surely. If she didn't appear to recover soon, Blaize's suspicions would be aroused and Hilda would feel the full blast of his temper.

Hoping to allay his doubts, Frey left the bench and knelt by the herb bed, leaning to pull a few leaves of rue to rub on her cheeks. The plant contained an irritant that would bring some color to her face and, she hoped, make her look more healthy.

But as she put the leaves to her cheek a hand caught her wrist and whipped it away. The rue went scattering from her numb fingers. Startled, Frey looked up into her husband's flashing brown eyes and frowning countenance.

"More tricks?" he rasped.

Being careful to keep her head balanced on her shoulders, so as not to set off waves of dizziness, Frey stood up, blinking foolishly at him. "Tricks?"

"Rue reddens the face!" he informed her furiously. "Even I know that it's an artifice used by vain maidens in hope of improving their appearance. But since I doubt you were thinking of making yourself more attractive for me, for what reason were you employing the device?"

"No reason," Frey insisted, not having the wit to think of an answer.

"Don't lie to me! Were you trying to make yourself look flushed, to persuade me you still suffer from fever? Or were you about to eat the leaves, to make yourself sick again? What other tricks have you been using? I know your skill with herbs!"

The accusations astounded her. "Sir!" She pulled ineffectually against the hard fingers bruising her wrist. "You mistake me."

"I think not," he grated. "You will poison

yourself before you let me come near. Is that how
much you hate me? But there'll be no more of it.
From now on, I'll set a watch on everything you eat
and drink. You'll stay in your chamber until you've
recovered from these noxious remedies you've been
taking."

"I've taken nothing!" she denied. "Only some
thyme to soothe my stomach. I swear it!" Terrified
of the fury burning in his eyes, she tried to pry his
fingers from her wrist, but they were immovable
as a manacle.

Blaize cursed as her nails scored his flesh. He
captured her free hand and swung her round
against the trunk of a tree, leaning close to say
angrily, "Nails. Teeth. You stoop to using any
weapon against me. Be still before you tempt me to
retaliate in kind."

Frey stared into snapping dark eyes, knowing
him capable of carrying out that threat. He was her
husband and she was now his possession, his
chattel. If he chose, he could take her out to the
market square and give her a public thrashing. No
one would interfere to prevent him.

As if he read her thoughts, Blaize bared his
strong white teeth and growled wordlessly,
releasing her abruptly and stepping away from her
with his dark face set. "God knows I expected no
gratitude," he said with disgust, "but neither did I
count on open hostility. We must both take a few
days to think. Since you hate me so much, I'll not
trouble you in the meantime."

Being confined to her room suited Frey well
enough, especially since her husband kept his word
and stayed away. But slowly she began to wonder
what he was doing in the meantime. Was he
visiting the Abbey, finding excuses to meet with
Melissande?

The depth of his distrust of her was demonstrated when, in place of Hilda, an older woman appeared to act as Frey's body-servant—an uncommunicative, hard-faced harridan who said that her name was Dame Alice. Unlike the cheery Hilda, her manner was distinctly unfriendly; she could hardly bring herself to look straight at Frey as she fetched and carried.

Frey found a partial explanation for the woman's attitude when one day she noticed Dame Alice covertly making the sign against the evil eye. Evidently rumors of witchcraft had spread abroad—a red-haired woman with great skill in herbal medicine might also practice magic. Presumably poor Hilda had been dismissed for acting as an accomplice and aiding Frey to obtain the "noxious remedies" which had supposedly made her ill. Really, it was almost laughable.

Frey was allowed one visitor—a priest named father William who came daily to pray with her and to begin instructing her in French. Frey wondered if he had also been sent to watch for signs of witchery. But she greeted him civilly and within a few days fancied she had convinced him she was not an agent of dark forces.

Being obliged to learn French, however, irked her; French was the language of the Norman conquerors, the enemies of her people; her Saxon tongue halted and stumbled over alien sounds. But the lessons did give her something to occupy her mind during her enforced idleness as her recuperation continued, besides which, she told herself, having an understanding of their language would mean that in future no Norman, male or female, would be able to gossip about her to her face while she stood bewildered and ignorant. The memory of her humiliation at the hands of the countess's ladies, on the morning of her wedding day, remained vivid and galling.

Father William, Frey's tutor, was a big, quiet,
gentle man who believed good of everyone, probably because his own nature was almost saintly. In
his company she soon learned to relax as with an
old friend, and despite herself she began to make
good progress with her lessons in spoken French.
She also gradually recovered her health and began
to put back some of the weight she had lost during
the unhappy months of her sojourn at the Abbey.

To her surprise and pleasure, Frey discovered
that she had a quick mind, a retentive memory and
a decided talent for language. As her proficiency
grew, she began to look forward to her lessons. She
now regretted those lost opportunities in her youth.
If she had paid heed when the village priest came to
tutor Reynold, she might by now also be proficient
in Latin, as Emma was.

Emma . . . Frey wondered if she would ever see
her sister again. Did Blaize ever see Emma on some
of those long visits to the Abbey that kept him
away most of the day?

Her mind kept returning to the same visions—of
Blaize and what business occupied him during the
long hours of the April days. His duties must keep
him bound between castle and Abbey, since his
overt purpose was to fullfill his role as the
countess's escort. She was after all his father's wife
and under his protection on her journey from the
king's court back to her husband's domain in
Chester. Of course he went to see the countess.

But Frey knew that inevitably Melissande
would be present, too. She was ever more certain
that the beautiful lady-in-waiting was the real
magnet that drew him. To sigh for each other in
secret and without hope of physical union, with
languishing looks across a roomful of oblivious
people, was the very essence of the ideal of courtly

love. What man could resist such a lure? It would be
all the more poignant if he had once possessed the
lady who was now denied him—and if, as seemed
likely, she had borne to him a daughter named
Guenevere.

"You have a quick mind, my lady," father
William remarked one day. "I trust you use it only
for good."

"As far as my wilful nature will allow," Frey
replied with a wry, self-deriding smile, dragging
herself out of her dark musings on the subject of
Blaize and Melissande. "But since you've spoken
with my husband, you probably know all about
that. My lord considers me wild and capricious."

The priest looked at her, his eyes sparkling with
humor, his mouth trying not to give in to a grin. "I
know."

He looked so impish that a bubble of answering
laughter rose inside Frey and would not be held
back. She let it free to ring in gay peals around the
bedchamber, and the preist laughed with her.

She had found a friend—a friend who might
almost be called a conspirator, taking her side
against the forces of fate that bedevilled her. The
feeling was so good, the release from tension so
welcome, that Frey laughed until her chest ached
and she had to wipe away tears with her fingers.

She was still laughing when the door opened
and Blaize stepped in unexpectedly; he seldom came
home in the middle of the day. After a moment, as
she recognized the taut bleakness in his face her
laughter died. She pulled a kerchief from her sleeve
and dabbed at her eyes, taking deep breaths to calm
herself while a silence spread through the room.

Still smiling, father William rose from his stool,
spreading his hands at Blaize. "Ah, come, my lord,"
he entreated. "Don't look so bearish. Your lady is
recovering well. And she will soon be fluent in

French. She has a quick intelligence."

"I know that!" Blaize growled, as if he resented
the priest's interference. "But is she learning so fast
that you are teaching her jests now?"

The priest's smile faded and he solemnly folded
his hands inside the long sleeves of his robe,
inclining his tonsured head. "No, my lord. But if
laughter were a sin then the world would be a
sorry place. By your leave—" He bowed politely to
Frey. "Until tomorrow, my lady."

"Best say your farewells," Blaize amended in a
hard voice, making a dismissive gesture with his
hand. "This has been the last lesson. My lady and I
will be leaving York tomorrow."

"Leaving?" Frey gasped, getting slowly to her
feet with the kerchief fluttering from her hand.
"Tomorrow?"

Her husband gave her a hard-lipped look. "I've
already overstayed because of your illness," was his
explanation. "Now my duties demand that I move
on."

"Then I'll wish you both God's speed," father
William replied. Giving Frey an encouraging smile,
he sketched the sign of the Cross and spoke a
blessing over her before making a final bow and
heading for the door.

"Father—" she managed, stopping him. "Thank
you. Thank you for—" She could not articulate her
deepest feelings of gratitude—for his friendship, for
understanding, for uncritical companionship, for
human warmth in her loneliness, as well as for his
teaching. She knew she would miss seeing him
every day. Helplessly, she finished, "—for everything."

His smile said he understood entirely. "God be
with you, my child." Then he turned to Blaize,
saying, "A word with you, my lord?"

"Aye, if you must," Blaize grudged. "Come
down to the solar."

The door closed behind both of them and Frey, saddened and sighing to herself, went to look across the marketplace, which was quiet now, with afternoon shadows lenghtening. From the main room below she could hear the murmur of male voices as Blaize and the priest conversed.

Leaving tomorrow, she thought with dull dismay. Leaving York and going to . . . what?

She was glad that father William's request to speak with him had caused Blaize to leave her alone for the moment, allowing her time to compose herself. This time when they travelled on they would be leaving behind everything she knew—every person and every place she had come to know and trust. Never before had she been farther from home than York, but now her destiny would take her on a long journey into unfamiliar territory. The distance involved was hard to grasp. There seemed no likelihood of her ever seeing her family again.

Once on that journey, she thought, she would have no one to lean on. Except Blaize. Her husband. Her torment.

When she heard him climbing the stairs, she turned to face him, gathering composure round her like a cloak though inside she felt numb with apprehension, conscious of her youth and inexperience. The door swung back and he was there, tall and lean, his strong body clad as usual in dark garments—a deep blue tunic this time, trimmed at the shoulders with black bear fur above which his face was set in frowning, angular lines, topped by that flowing browlock of dark hair.

As always the sight of him smote her to the heart and filled her with yearning sorrow—Blaize . . . the handsome knight—until she recalled that such soft feelings were one-sided. Every time she saw him now he was hard, grim, unreachable: the mighty Lord fitzHugh of Triffordd, who in some other incarnation had been Blaize of Bayonne.

For a moment they exchanged glances across the room with the bed between them, he challenging, she outwardly poised despite her inner turmoil. Then deliberately he turned and pressed home the peg that prevented the latch from lifting, effectively locking the door.

Divining his intentions, Frey felt her heart start to thud, slow and heavy at first behind her breast. Hoping to break the tension, she dipped a curtsey, murmuring the Norman greeting of, "*Mon seigneur.*"

He muttered something in reply, using the same language, but he spoke so fast and low that she did not catch the words; she fancied they were, anyway, outside the few she had so far learned.

"What's that?" she asked. "What does it mean?"

"It's of no importance," Blaize said, watching her with veiled eyes. "So, my lady, does this imply that you intend to be an obedient wife to me from now on? Father William has just finished enjoining me to use you with kindness. It seems you've worked your spell on him, too—on a priest!"

"Father William is a good man," she replied. "I learned to think of him as a friend, at a time when I have been sorely in need of friendship."

"So I surmised." He began to walk slowly toward her, coming around the end of the bed. Frey felt a pulse jump in her throat and begin to thud with mounting frequency. One hand came up to cover that telltale throbbing while the other crept behind her and spread against the cold wall as if for support.

"What time do you intend that we shall leave tomorrow?" she asked through a sudden hoarse constriction in her throat.

"At first light. You must be sure to rest well tonight."

Hotly aware that they were alone in the chamber, with the bed waiting not many feet away, Frey cleared her throat and chattered, "Shall we travel with the countess?"

Blaize paused two feet away from her, almost overpowering her with his breadth and his height, the vibrance of his dark presence, and the slight frown that gathered between his brows as he saw and interpreted the apprehension in her eyes. "Countess Arlette left York three days ago," he said. "I charged Lord de L'Isle with the responsibility of escorting her, since I was obliged to remain here until you were well enough to travel. But if we ride hard we may catch up with her before Chester. She will not travel fast with so large a train."

Frey's mouth felt dry. She moistened her lips, saying, "I shall enjoy that. I've always loved to ride."

"I know that!" She almost believed there was pain in his voice as his hands shot out to fasten on her shoulders and shake her a little as if in exasperation. "Why are you so afraid of me?" he asked. "Why, Frey?"

Unable to find words to express her fear, she shook her head, staring up at him wide-eyed. Beads of sweat broke out on her upper lip as the mist across her memory parted and allowed her glimpses of what had occurred in the garden on their wedding evening—his arms around her, her own hands tangled in his hair to hold his head down as he kissed her; she recalled the urgency of wanting him as eagerly as he wanted her, then being swept up into his arms, carried effortlessly to the bedchamber, hearing him call her Frey for the first time . . .

That was where Saxon cunning had led her—into a betrayal of everything she had been brought up to believe, because her stupid senses responded mindlessly to this particular Norman invader. Yet even as the angry thoughts built in her mind she knew they were only a smoke screen for the deeper reason for her fear: she could not forget hearing Edith cry and moan in distaste and pain whenever Reynold asserted his husbandly rights.

"Do not be afraid," Blaize commanded, pulling her into his arms.

A little moan of fright was lost in his mouth as he bent to her but she knew she could not deny him any longer. They were truly wed, before God and under the law of the land. She was his possession to use as he pleased.

Then so be it, she thought. He had the right, let him use her as he would. She would not cry out or make protest; she was of a stronger mettle than Edith. But neither would she offer help or encouragement. Her body might belong to him but she would make sure that her mind and heart remained her own. She would bury her feelings, leave her true self behind in Yorkshire and go on with this man who had rearranged her life; she would be his wife in all ways, except that she would deny him the satisfaction of caring for him. Since all he wanted was the possession of her, an empty shell of a woman would presumably be enough to satisfy him.

Abruptly he put her away from him, his hands on her shoulders as he stared down into her face, his gaze flickering with questions. Deep in those brown eyes there burned a flame of desire, fanned by a determination that tightened his lips and drew his brows together.

In a stern, quiet voice that brooked no argument, he said, "I'm in no mood for fumbling. Go to the bed. Draw the bed curtain. Hide behind it if you must. Then undress yourself and get into bed." Taking his hands from her shoulders, he straightened and drew a breath. "Do it now, Aelfreya. I've already waited too long. The time has come for you to fulfill your wifely vow."

Frey made no reply. She had no choice but to obey him. With a dignity that cost her dear, she turned and walked softly away, her head high, every muscle tensed against the trembling that had invaded her being. Quietly she hooked the side curtain, the side nearest to the window, across between the posts of the bed. Then without looking at Blaize she enclosed the bed end, too, finally moving out of her husband's sight.

For the briefest moment she contemplated running away, but if she tried to remove the peg that barred the latch Blaize would hear her and stop her. Besides, what good would running away do, except to arouse his anger? She was his wife. She would lie and endure his lust, since that was the fate of wives.

As she undid the lacings of her gown and slid it over her head, the light in the room faded. Blaize was closing the shutters, leaving an intimate dusk. Frey heard the bar scrape home into its brackets, fastening the shutters and deadening the sounds from outside, ensuring too that any sound made in the room would be muffled from the ears of any passerby in the street.

Did he expect her to cry out? she wondered, her head whirling as a hot flush of terror assailed her. Did he think she might sceam in pain? The thought made her hurry with the rest of her clothes, dropping them to the floor before she scrambled under the cool caress of expensive linen sheets, woollen blankets and that soft fur cover to lie stiff and shivering inwardly.

"Are you ready, Aelfreya?" Blaize's voice came softly from behind the curtain. She saw his hands

reach for the hooks, tearing down that flimsy
barrier between them, and after one startled glance
that told her—shockingly—that he was naked, she
closed her eyes tightly, willing herself to lie still.

A gruff sound escaped him as he leaned to take
hold of the covers and in one swift motion tossed
them back. Frey felt the cool air on every inch of
her skin, knew that her husband's eyes were
feasting on her. Her every instinct demanded that
she cover herself, but she steeled herself not to
move. The hands by her sides clenched into fists as
a flush of self-awareness stole up from her toes,
imbuing her whole body with its heat before
rushing to bring blood up her throat and into her
face.

"God's blood!" Blaize said under his breath in a
voice that shook.

His hand touched her breast, caressing the
sensate tip that was already engorged in response to
its exposure. Frey caught her breath, her teeth
clamping on her lower lip as she forced herself not
to brush him off. Her virgin modesty rebelled at
her own inaction, but she had determined to let
him have his way without help or hindrance. Her
innate stubbornness came to her aid.

Gently, with a touch that was almost tremulous,
Blaize explored her body, the hollow of her waist,
the line of her thighs, the curve of her hip. In
response to the tender caress of his fingers her skin
caught fire, sending trills of pleasure across every
nerve-ending. Her breasts seemed to swell under
his hands, the nipples straining against the flesh
that enclosed them, and when she felt his lips softly
close around one of those peaks a soft cry escaped
her, bitten off as she sank her teeth again into her
lip. She must not make a sound! She must not move!

But though she contained her growing arousal
behind a show of indifference, and though her fear

of lovemaking kept her rigid as a plank, the center of her body began to run liquid, melting with desire as he parted her thighs and she felt him lift himself over her. His mouth covered hers, his tongue snaking between her lips as she felt his tumescence touch her. Waves of need rolled over her, mingled with an overpowering fright that made her cry out, though the sound was no more than a squeak, lost in the hot mouth that enveloped hers as the last of Blaize's control snapped and with a groan he sank fully into her, thrusting inside her in mindless need.

Only later did Frey realize that there was no pain, not for her. A suffusion of pleasure swamped everything else as their bodies commingled, lifting her on a wave that soared skyward and crashed at last on some foreign shore she had never dreamed existed. That tidal wave of fierce pleasure left her exhausted, limp and fulfilled as Blaize rode to his own orgasm, his whole frame stiffening as he achieved the long-awaited consummation of their marriage.

As he broke contact with her he rolled aside and lay on his back, breathing hard. The heat of his body came like a fire beside her but Frey remained still, as she had remained throughout. Though the force of their joining had shattered all her preconceptions and though she was secretly elated that she, and she alone, had given Blaize his surcease, the stubborn Saxon within her remained aloof. Her body might be throbbing with sweet fulfillment, her heart pounding and her senses all alert to him, but outwardly she appeared unmoved, merely a little flushed and dewed from being the object of her husband's amorous intentions.

So it must have seemed to Blaize.

"Perhaps I should have brought a jug of wine!" he said in a low, angry voice. "Perhaps you need to be drunk before you respond."

"I shall never respond to you," Frey replied, viciously pleased to think that her dissembling had fooled him. "Never!"

"You lie! Or have you forgotten?" He threw himself to his knees beside her, a hard hand shaking her shoulder. "Because on the day we were wed you did respond, lady! You were as eager as I. If wine is the key to—"

Frey's eyes flew open. Now she too was growing angry. She must rid him of the dangerous notion that she had ever freely responded to his advances. "It was not the wine!" she cried.

"What?" He leaned over her and laid his hands on either side of her face, turning it up to his. "What?" The expression on his face was darker, bleaker than she had ever seen it. "Not the wine? Then what was it that made you cling to me so sweetly? Tell me! Let me repeat the circumstances!"

Taking a deep, unsteady breath, no longer caring about the consequences, she threw the truth at him. "It was a love philtre! It was in the jug of wine! *That's* why I responded. *That's* why I was so sick!"

He released her as if she had burned him. He moved back, staring at her with eyes like cold fires.

"Oh, yes, my lord—a love philtre!" Frey repeated the words clearly, rejoicing in the hurt she was inflicting. "Hilda thought it would help us, but instead it made me ill." A bitter sound somewhere between laughter and a sob shook out of her. "A love philtre for us. Well, laugh, my lord, laugh! Isn't it the greatest jest you've ever heard?"

Muttering a wordless oath, Blaize began to throw on his clothes, his back turned to Frey. When he was fully dressed he raked a hand through his hair to give it some semblance of tidiness and strode for the door. He jerked the little locking peg out from behind the latch and snatched the door open, throwing it to crash back on its hinges as he thudded down the stairs calling for the steward, John.

Pulling her nightgown around her, Frey went to shut the door and then sat on the bed, wondering what mischief she had inadvertently started. She hoped she would not get poor Hilda into too much trouble.

Even with the door closed, she could hear Blaize angrily questioning the servants in the solar, though apparently eliciting no satisfactory answers. His voice grew louder and louder, then quieted and fell eventually to normal pitch as his temper subsided and reason resurfaced. After a while he returned, scowling.

"They say they know nothing about it," he told Frey with a gesture of anger and frustration.

"Not even Hilda?" Frey asked.

"Hilda is no longer in York," he informed her, "which seems fortuitous, since you seek to lay the blame for this trouble on her. If I discover that you've been lying to me, lady—"

"I'm telling you the truth," Frey said flatly. "Why should I lie to you, sir? And if Hilda is gone that is no fault of mine since you yourself dismissed her from our service, in order to rob me of yet another friend."

He gave her a sour look but refused to rise to that jibe. "Whatever my reasons, her leaving means that you have no way of proving that there was anything in the wine that night."

"You have my word for it."

Not bothering to deny the charge, Frey lifted her chin proudly to look him in the eye. "Does not your own intelligence tell you that plain wine, however rich, would not have made me so ill—near to death's door, as you told me once? There was something in the wine, though exactly what it was I do not know, except that it was some kind of aphrodisiac, intended as a kindness."

"A *kindness!*" The word exploded from him and he threw out his arms in angry disbelief. "Is that what Hilda said? God's teeth, did she think me incapable of consummating a marriage without the help of some old wives' potion?!"

Frey had known he would take it as a personal affront; it was typical of the man's arrogance to do so. "Perhaps it was not your manhood Hilda was considering so much as *my* maidenly fears!" she exclaimed. "She's wed herself. She knows how a woman feels at such a time. But she did not know that I would drink so much of the wine, nor that the philtre would make me ill. If anyone is to blame, it's the apothecary, for being careless in his recipe and his mixing."

Blaize's frown bit deeper, pulling his brows together. "The apothecary?" he repeated in a quieter, puzzled tone. "It was not a homemade brew concocted by Hilda herself, then?"

"It seems not. My lord . . . I beg you not to think of sending for Hilda and punishing her. She meant well."

He glowered at her under a suddenly thunderous frown. "If she were here, I'd teach her never to interfere in the personal affairs of her betters again. As it is—" He gestured impatiently. "Enough of this for now. Get dressed. Put on your cloak."

The sudden switch of subjects disconcerted Frey. "My cloak? Why, where are we going?"

"I assume you will wish to take leave of your sister," he said, much to her surprise. "I shall take you to the Abbey."

"Oh . . . Thank you!" Her gratitude was unfeigned, her eyes shining with pleasure. "Thank you, my lord. I was afraid that you had forgotten . . . that you intended to leave without allowing . . . I mean—"

As she floundered, not saying at all what she meant, she saw his face go still as stone and when he spoke his voice held no expression. "I know very well what you mean, my lady. You think me devoid of human understanding. Well, put on some clothes, groom yourself. Quickly, or the nuns will be abed before we get there."

Later, as they rode together through the city, Blaize astride his stallion and Frey again seated sidesaddle on the elegant little palfrey, she tried to make conversation. His offer to take her to bid farewell to Emma had taken her by surprise and she was beginning to wonder if she might have misjudged him in some ways. But her efforts at congeniality met with no reward. Blaize remained terse, occupied with brooding thoughts, and when they arrived at the gatehouse of the Abbey it became clear that he did not intend to accompany her inside.

"Will you wait for me, my lord?" she asked, puzzled.

"No," Blaize returned, his mind elsewhere. "I have things I must do. I shall return for you later."

Though Frey was thankful that she might see her sister alone to make her farewells, her heart was heavy as she watched her husband ride away. By telling him about the love philtre she had damaged his pride, she guessed. Would there never be a time of peace between them?

By pulling on the silk rope to make the bronze bell clang, she summoned the gateward of the Abbey—a shuffling old man wrapped in a rough cloak against the chill of the spring evening. When she asked for the novice Emma of Ketilfiord, the gateward conducted her to the outer parlor and bade her wait there.

Left alone, Frey surveyed the bare, white-washed room where not long ago Reynold had waited to tell her of the marriage offer; where she and her family had gathered the morning before the wedding. Frey felt immeasurably older than the girl she had been then—a frightened girl who had blanked her mind to thoughts of a future she could not picture in detail. Now, though she was still apprehensive, she had learned to accept what fate brought and she could picture her future all too clearly: it held only sorrow and disillusionment.

After a while, the door opened silently and Emma appeared, pale but smiling, gray as a ghost in her novice's robe with her misty, shortsighted eyes lit by spiritual certainty. With her came the more worldly, more approachable Constance, trying to hide tears that would not be stemmed. Frey embraced her sister and then her friend warmly, then the three moved apart to study one another gravely.

"We heard you'd been ill," Emma said with concern. "You do have shadows under your eyes. How is it with you now, sister?"

"I'm well," Frey assured her. "It was nothing. A little sickness in the stomach, that's all."

"Then all is well?"

"Yes. Yes, all is very well with me," Frey lied brightly. "Dear sister . . . and Constance, my friend . . . I'm come to say goodbye to you both. My lord and I leave for the west in the morning."

"We'd heard," Constance said, her eyes brimming again as her lips trembled. "Oh, Frey . . . I hope you will be happy."

"Of course she will!" Emma said briskly, making Constance turn away with a fist pressed to her mouth. "So, Frey, you're following the countess to Chester. You'll see the earl's court, and all the nobility there. You'll be one of them! How excited you must be."

"Oh, I am."

Once Emma would have pounced on the insincerity in her voice, but now she either failed to notice it or chose to ignore it. Both of them knew that Frey had no choice in her own fate; she must go with her husband wherever he went.

"Didn't I tell you God's purpose would be made clear one day?" Emma asked. "You've been greatly blessed, sister. You've been granted your heart's desire. I hope you give thanks every day."

"Indeed," Frey said.

Emma smiled on her, sweetly and benevolently. "I knew you were in love with him from the very first. Now I can say goodbye and know you will be happy, as I am happy. We are both fortunate women, Frey. But I must go. I have to see the holy mother before I go to bed." Her face glowed with contentment as she leaned to kiss Frey's cheek. "Farewell, dearest sister. I shall pray every day for your continued happiness. Write to me if you will. No doubt there will be a priest at Triffordd who will set down the words for you." Going to the door, she paused to glance round and say, "And I'll pray that God will grant you and Lord Blaize the gift of a son. God be with you, Frey."

"And with you," Frey said as the door closed.

So Emma was happy; that was a comfort. Frey was glad she had not poured out her troubles to worry her sister. Emma had the life she had been made for; Reynold had his heirs and his security at Ketilfiord. Frey must be thankful that at least her family had what they wanted.

In the silence she turned to find Constance watching her with tears brimming over. "Your sister's too much with the angels to understand, isn't she, Frey?" the sad young woman asked. "*Are* you in love with your fine husband? *Are* you happy?"

"I'm content," Frey amended quietly. "Isn't that the best we can hope for?"

"No!" The passionate cry was almost a sacrilege in that place and even Constance looked dismayed as echoes wakened in the bare room. Wide-eyed, she glanced again at Frey and shivered. "Or perhaps you're right. Perhaps it's better not to love too well. Love hurts, Frey. I've learned that every day since I lost Colin. So beware! Don't grow to love your rich Norman lord, handsome though he is. He'll leave you some day."

Frey flinched as though she had been struck, drawing her cloak more closely round her as she said stiffly, "What's this—clairvoyance? Do you claim to foretell the future now, Constance?"

"It's not what *I* say, it's what *they* were saying."

"They?"

"The ladies' companions to the countess of Chester."

"How could you know what they were saying?" Frey demanded, her voice hoarse with a scorn born of fear. She didn't really want to hear what Constance was trying to tell her. "They all spoke French. They had no English."

Constance stared at her in misery. "I too know French, Frey. Didn't I ever tell you that I was made to learn it? The old man to whom I was betrothed insisted that I be educated in Norman ways. He had many Norman friends. But that doesn't matter now. Frey . . . I was in the garden one day, about a week ago, when I heard those ladies laughing and gossiping in the cloisters."

She stopped and seemed unable to go on until Frey prompted sharply, "Well? What malicious untruths were they exchanging?"

"They said . . . They said that Lord fitzHugh

married you on a whim, because he could not have the lady he really wanted. They were laying wagers on how long this marriage will last before he tires of the game and finds some excuse to discard you. A year was the longest any of them would lay money on."

Feeling cold, as though blood were draining from all her extremities, Frey stared at her friend, not wanting to believe this news. Unfortunately, it was all too easy to believe. Constance was unhappy, that she knew, but surely she was not unhappy enough, nor cruel enough, to invent such a story.

Besides, it only helped to confirm what Frey herself had already suspected.

"Forgive me," Constance begged through streaming tears. "But I thought you should be warned."

"Perhaps I already knew," Frey said as if to herself. "Tell me, did they mention the name of this lady, this . . . light o' love whom he could not have?"

"No." Constance's lip trembled as she spoke, "No, they did not name her, but their secret smiles and glances went to one of their companions. A fair lady, with—"

"Melissande!" Frey muttered under her breath, feeling as though her heart had died inside her.

"What?" Constance said.

"Nothing. Nothing."

"Perhaps—" Constance ventured. "Perhaps, in due time, if your marriage should end, your husband will send you back here. We could be together again, as we were before."

Together like before, trapped here in the Abbey without hope of escape? Suddenly Frey knew that anything was preferable to that.

"Oh, Frey—" Constance choked. "I shall miss you so!"

She flung herself at Frey, kissed her, and fled from the parlor, leaving the door open. Evening shadows lay long across the courtyard, with a single square of pale sunlight slanting to lay itself against the door of the apartments where the Countess of Chester had stayed. The sight of that door brought memories flooding back to Frey.

After the treatment she had had at the hands of those fine ladies, she could readily believe Constance's story of their spiteful gossip. But why should she care if the ladies had taken wagers on her future? Frey herself had guessed all along that Lord fitzHugh's lust for his little Saxon bride could be only a temporary aberration.

It was just that she had entertained tiny, foolish hopes that were all extinguished now. If Blaize cared for Melissande, then indeed the future looked bleak for Aelfreya of Ketilfiord.

When Blaize arrived to escort her back to the earl's house he was in a foul temper which he barely troubled to curb. What little he said to her was spoken brusquely and impatiently, though after a while she realized that his anger was not, this time, aimed directly at her; it had some other cause. He did not say where he had been, or why, nor did she dare to enquire when his fierce mood locked her out.

They returned to the house on the marketplace and ate supper together in the solar in virtual silence.

From the corner of her eye, Frey watched her wedded lord apprehensively, wondering what was irritating him that night. Remembering Emma's naive comment about her being in love Frey pulled her mouth awry. How could one love a man one did not know? If she had ever been in love it had been with a dream that had the same face and figure as the man beside her, that was all. Blaize of Bayonne, her handsome, smiling knight, had existed only in her girlish imagination.

In reality, Lord fitzHugh of Triffordd was a complex man suffering from a frustration that drove him to incomprehensible actions. For reasons Frey could only guess at, the highborn lady Melissande, whom he loved and who returned his love, was denied him; so he had taken to wife an insignificant Saxon. Why? Was it in obedience to his father the earl because, without Melissande, Blaize no longer cared what he did with his life?

"Well, go!" he growled suddenly, turning on her. "Pray do not sit there so pale and apprehensive. I shall sleep in here tonight—again. I'm becoming accustomed to it."

Frey stood up, hovering uncertainly, wondering if he really meant to leave her to sleep alone.

As if reading her thoughts, he gave her a glance of bitter disgust and added, "I'm in no mood for more argument with you tonight, lady. Go to your bed and sleep without fear. But do not think I'm finished with you yet. We have the rest of our lives still to come."

IX

Lord Blaize fitzHugh, with his wife, his escort of knights and foot soldiers, and with his pack train of laden mules and horses, left the city of York at first light on a chill April morning in the year 1093. At first the long skein of the procession passed between fields touched with dawn frost, where peasants bent at their weeding and hoeing among the tender young corn; then slowly the land climbed to undulating hills, the road winding away among open woodland.

Frey rode uncomfortably but decorously, perched sidesaddle as befitted a fine Norman lady, with her knee hooked round the pommel of her saddle and the long skirts of her cloak trailing almost to the ground. At a last vantage point on the climbing road, aware of the view opening out behind her, she checked her pony and paused to take a final look back.

From this distance, a veil of smoke from several hundred roofs misted the city and its wooden castle. Frey could not see the Abbey where she had had that last brief meeting with Emma and Constance; it lay on the far side of York. And further still, the thought came sorrowful and inescapable, somewhere miles away among the blue hills lying along the horizon, lay Ketilfiord, Wulfnoth's vill, with

Reynold and Edith, Ula and the babies.

Knowing she was unlikely to see her home or her family ever again, Frey tried to control a ball of tears that knotted in her throat and swelled behind her eyes, but the moisture blurred her sight and a warm trickle ran down beside her nose.

Surreptitiously she wiped the tear away, keeping her head bent inside the wide hood of her cloak, not wishing to display weakness in front of her husband.

Behind her, the man leading the first packhorse coughed harshly, his breath a faint cloud in the morning air. Then Blaize, who had drawn his stallion alongside Frey, said, "It's time to move on, my lady."

"Aye," Frey whispered. "I know it."

His hand came out to rest on her wrist, drawing her attention to his shuttered face. She knew he must be aware of her distress; the bright dew of her eyes betrayed her. But he did not scoff at her, as she had feared. Behind his grave expression he seemed to understand. He said, "We must look forward, not back."

"Yes, my lord." Giving herself up to whatever fate waited, she turned her face to the west, setting her back toward everything she had known and loved for all her twenty years. She took a deep breath and brushed a heel against the palfrey's flank. The animal obediently resumed its steady pace.

As the slow journey continued, Frey rode a little behind and to one side of Blaize's stallion. They moved ever deeper into dew-glittering woodland where the trees had been cropped back from the road to deter robbers who might have attempted an ambush. Ahead of Frey and her husband, two knights led a party of a score of men-at-arms, and behind came the string of packhorses, followed by

more foot soldiers forming a rearguard. Lord
fitzHugh of Triffordd no longer travelled alone as
he had in those early days when he had been Blaize
of Bayonne.

Frey was well wrapped in a weatherproof cloak
woven from the lanolin-rich wool of English sheep;
it was lined with rich black beaver fur, fashioned
with wide sleeves and a warm, voluminous hood.
Blaize wore a similar garment, but while Frey kept
her hood raised to warm her ears her husband
went   bareheaded   with   the   pale   April   sun
illumining his brown cheek and thick dark hair. He
had hardly spoken to Frey all morning, though she
was aware of him beside her, of the breadth of
shoulder under the flowing travel cloak, and the
strong hands, gauntleted now, that lightly held the
reins of the stallion.

Memories of those hands touching her body,
caressing with eager intimacy, waking chills and
delight across her flesh, rose up to choke her throat.
She must not think of it. That way lay confusion.
She must set her mind to other things.

Look forward, Blaize had advised. Resolutely,
Frey decided to do just that. Regrets were vain, and
much too tardy. She would set them aside and
consider the future that lay before her.

Immediately ahead lay this journey, which
would probably take six days to cross the center of
England with its high backbone chain of hills called
the Pennines. After that, Blaize had intimated that
they would sojourn briefly in the city of Chester, at
the court of his father, Earl Hugh, before travelling
on even further west, toward the castle of
Triffordd, which lay somewhere in the disputed
territory that formed the Welsh marches.

The Welsh marches!

The phrase struck Frey with the force of a
familiar voice heard unexpectedly when its owner

is thought to be leagues away. How could she have forgotten what it meant?

The Welsh marches!

That was where Nicol was!

It was as though a shutter had opened in a dark room and let in a shaft of sunlight. With a resurgence of hope that brought the blood flooding to warm her face, Frey remembered that this journey might lead to a reunion with her childhood sweetheart.

Since Blaize had reentered her life, appearing as if by magic as her bridegroom in the Abbey court-yard, she had given hardly a thought to Nicol; yet it was mainly because of him that she had agreed to the marriage when it was first mooted. Of course she had not known at the time who her bridegroom was to be, but the identity of her husband made no difference to her hopes of seeing Nicol again.

Surely, somewhere along the way, she and Nicol of Linscote were destined to meet once more. He was bound in the service of Earl Hugh, she reminded herself. Of course they must meet.

If nothing else, it would be good to have one friendly face amid a sea of strangers. To Frey at that moment, journeying ever further into unknown territory, the whole future seemed to be filled with strangers—people and places unknown to her, and possibilities she found hard to envisage. She felt very insecure.

Of course, there was Blaize, her husband . . . Letting her eyes dwell on his dark head and the straight back draped with his thick cloak, she found a heavy sadness in her breast. Yes, she and Blaize were wed, but even so he, too, was a stranger to her. Lord fitzHugh of Triffordd. Had she ever really known him?

As if he felt her gaze on him he glanced around and, reading some of her thoughts in her pale face, he checked the stallion and waited until her palfrey drew level. "Must we ride in silence?" he asked. "There must be things you wish to know, questions you would like to ask. Shall I tell you something about Triffordd?"

Frey blamed him for her predicament. He was the sole cause of her present unhappiness. Determined not to show any interest in the life he could offer, she shrugged and replied indifferently, "As you will, my lord."

Momentarily, temper flickered behind his eyes and tightened his mouth, but he controlled it and set his gaze to the track ahead as they rode on. "The castle lies some two or three days from Chester, quite near to the seacoast, on a hill above the village of Triffordd, which lies in a fertile valley. Inland there are thick forests and bleak, rocky mountains—a wild country, often wet with rains, and peopled by tribes of savage Welshmen who still defy the king by force of arms. That is why the king needs marcher lords like me—to hold and secure the territory we are slowly gaining. One day soon, Wales will fall to us."

He had warmed to his theme and spoke with the utmost confidence and arrogance, dismissing the puny rebels who opposed the Normans' inexorable push westward. "Those ill-disciplined tribes are incabable of concerted effort. The land is rent by petty squabbels among petty princes, few of whom can call on enough men to fight a real battle, face to face like soldiers who have pride in their craft. They content themselves with skirmishes and cowardly ambush. Like wasps who sting and retreat. They're more nuisance than threat."

Pausing, he sent her a sidelong glance as if to gauge her reaction to this talk of blood and war. "But you may feel safe at Triffordd, my lady. The Welsh have learned not to try my patience by frontal assault on my stronghold. The castle is well-

nigh impregnable. I keep a large garrison there and
patrols go out regularly to ensure our continued
security. Our main purpose is to hold the road to the
coast in the name of the earl. But if real danger
should threaten, I'll have you escorted to the protection of Chester. You need have no fears for your
personal safety."

"I understand," Frey said tonelessly.

"Unless—" he added with another look from the
corner of his eye. "Unless you would prefer to
remain at the earl's court, in Chester, taking your
place among the countess's ladies while I'm
occupied with the Welsh?"

For the first time in minutes Frey looked at him
squarely, her eyes wide with dismay. "Stay in
Chester? Oh, no!"

"You might prefer it. Triffordd has few
luxuries."

"No!" To remain at the earl's court . . . Oh, that
she could not do! She had to go to Wales; only in
Wales could she hope to find Nicol.

Besides, the thought of playing lady-in-waiting
to countess Arlette horrified her. To be left alone
among those noble, spiteful ladies would not please
her at all, especially when it meant being constantly
thrown into the company of the fair and jealous
Melissande. No, indeed! To Frey, the thought of a
garrison castle in the wilds of Wales, however
fraught with difficulties and dangers, was infinitely
preferable to a soft life in the company of
Melissande.

Blaize must have read some of these thoughts in
her face; a little frown quirked between his brows
as he said, "Are you willing, then, to endure the
hardships of a military garrison?"

Aware that her swift refusal of the idea—and
her thoughtless vehemence—had roused his
curiosity, she lowered her eyes demurely, murmuring, "If you can endure it, then so must I. I am

your wife, my lord. A wife's place is beside her husband, is it not?"

"Aye, so it is, in an ideal world," he said with heavy irony. "But unless my memory misleads me this is the first time you've displayed a desire to fulfill that role."

When she made no reply he took a deep breath and went on, "So! Triffordd it shall be, for both of us. You will like it there. It is not so different from Ketilfiord—life in the village runs by the seasons, from Candlemas, through haying, to harvest. Triffordd means 'three roads' in the Welsh tongue, so I'm told. One road leads to the west along the coast, another one points back to England, and the third— a less well-defined track, overgrown in places— twines through the forests toward the mountains. That's where the Welsh lurk, hiding among trees and rocky fastnesses like the scoundrels they are."

Apparently realizing that for all his efforts to interest her she still failed to show any response, he ended the one-sided conversation by adding something deliberately in Norman French.

The words piqued Frey's curiosity. Determined as she was to continue to appear indifferent to anything he might say or do, the sentence he had spoken made her puzzle for a moment, searching her memory of those lessons with the kindly priest.

"Ah," she realized, pleased with herself. "You said . . . 'it's a beautiful place.' "

Blaize's mouth stretched in a smile that applauded her prowess with his language, though his dark eyes remained bleak and watchful. "I said it *can be* a beautiful place."

"Oh—yes, of course. I have yet to master all the tenses."

"Perhaps we should continue the lessons," he suggested. "It will help to while away the time on our journey."

And so, as their journey continued he began to teach her the French names of things they saw along the way—trees, flowers, birds, small animals—and instructed her to put these words into sentences. The exercise made both of them set aside their personal differences and as the mood relaxed Frey fancied that her eagerness to learn, and her diligence in accomplishing the task, were winning her lord's approval.

Of course, he could not know that the main reason she was anxious to become fluent was in order not to disgrace herself and show herself up for an ignorant countrywoman at the earl's court—and if she could understand his language then she might also protect herself from the spite of highborn ladies. Ladies like Melissande.

That noon they reached a manor where they rested the horses while the lord gave them food and drink in his hall, obviously flattered that baron fitzHugh should honor his dwelling, however briefly. Then they rode on and the French lessons continued as they rode deeper and deeper into thickening woodland.

Toward evening, as the sun went down behind dark hills ahead of them, it began to rain with a steady misting drizzle that looked set for the night. Blaize increased the pace so that his party reached another manor before they were entirely soaked. Frey spent the night on a straw pallet in a roomy cottage along with the lord's four young daughters, while Blaize and the other men took rest in the hall.

On a cool, cloudy morning the journey continued.

Perched again on that detested sidesaddle, with aching limbs and a sore behind, Frey wondered if she would ever rid herself of the stiffness this long ride was inducing. She thought back to the

merriment that had filled the bower cottage the
previous evening, and to the girls' open envy of her.
"Your lord is so handsome," the oldest of the sisters
had sighed. "How lucky you are, my lady. I wish a
rich baron would come and carry *me* away."

Frey recalled that she had had the same dream
herself—a dream of a prince riding out of the west,
astride a fine stallion, coming to whisk her into a
romantic future filled with the pleasures of love,
fidelity, companionship for life. How naive she had
been. Love . . . precious little room for that emotion
existed in this world, as she had cause to know
now. As for fidelity . . . her handsome husband
might be carrying her off to his castle in the west,
but in his heart he yearned for another woman, not
for his young wife. He might want Frey physically,
to assuage his body's needs, but that was not the
same. And companionship? She doubted she could
ever attain that with Blaize fitzHugh.

Was Blaize thinking of Melissande now? Was he
eager to reach Chester and a reunion with his lady-
love? The questions ran on, tormenting her and
causing her to sink into a moody depression.

Blaize, drawing alongside her, addressed her in
French, but that morning Frey could not seem to
concentrate on lessons; her mind was too full of
other things.

She asked, "Where did you learn English, my
lord?"

He hesitated, a sidelong glance assessing her
profile. "At my mother's knee."

Astonished, Frey looked fully at him, the heavy
hood falling from her veiled head. "Your mother?
Do you mean . . . would you have me believe that
your mother was Saxon?"

"Whether you believe it or not, it's true," he
affirmed, a corner of his mouth twisting in sardonic

humor. "So you see, my lady, when you named me a Norman dog you were only part right."

He was half-Saxon! An Englishwoman had borne a son, out of wedlock, to the Norman lord Hugh of Chester. Frey could hardly believe it. Then as her surprise faded she found a hundred questions swirling in her mind. She had forgotten that she had planned to feign total indifference. This time, Blaize had captured her whole attention.

"But who was she?" she wanted to know.

"Her name was Hwaisa," he replied. "She was of gentle birth—a lady-in-waiting attendant on the lady Margaret, who was sister to Prince Edgar of England."

Frey's eyes grew round with wonder and amazement. Such names were among the noblest in the land. Prince Edgar, whose lineage went back to King Alfred the Great, might have inherited the throne of England on the death of King Harold at Hastings, but in 1066 he had been no more than a boy. He had lived most of his life under the protection of William of Normandy and had chosen to remain under the patronage of the Conqueror sooner than struggle against the tide of history.

"My father met my mother when the lady Margaret paid a visit to her brother in Normandy," Blaize was saying, as if he were anxious to tell it all now that he had begun. "They were both very young. Youth had its way with them."

"Then why didn't he marry her?" Frey asked. "If she was a highborn lady—"

"She was, but not of high enough station to be the wife of Hugh d'Avranches. His father had other plans in mind."

"Yes, of course," Frey muttered, pulling her mouth awry. It was ever the same: in this world everything hinged on power, inheritance, dowry; the right marriage, the increase of property. It must have been so with Melissande—her father had presumably made plans for her which had precluded a match with Blaize of Bayonne.

Misinterpreting her expression, Blaize said swiftly, "Do not mistake me. I believe there was love between them, even though it was doomed from the start. They had to part. My mother returned to England—to her father's home, in Essex. I was born six months later."

"But—" Frey hesitated, eager to know it all but not wishing to offend him by probing too deeply into such a personal matter. "When did the earl acknowledge you as a true son of his blood?"

Blaize slanted an eyebrow at her. "He acknowledged me from the beginning. It was no secret, nor any shame to him. He paid for my education, and when I was ten years old he had me sent to Normandy to be trained for knighthood."

So even though his blood was half Saxon, she thought, he had been raised in the ways of Normans. He might as well be wholly Norman. And during his stay in Normandy he had met Melissande.

Curiosity in full flight now, wondering if he might reveal something of his relationship with Melissande, she prompted. "And then? What came next?"

"Then, when I was sixteen—" He looked away as the stallion shifted restlessly, dancing a little away and back again before it settled. Watching its black mane toss, Blaize added, "At that time it suited the earl my father to confirm an alliance in France. He married me to the heiress of Bayonne."

Married? Frey thought numbly, all her preconceptions scattering into a million tiny shards of bafflement. Blaize had been married—to the heiress of Bayonne? Then where had Melissande entered the picture?

Fortunately Blaize was concentrating on calming the skittish stallion; he failed to see the color that ebbed and flowed on her face as her thoughts chased in circles.

"And for that," he said, "I'm grateful to my father. Until then I had little beyond his charity. Bayonne gave me lands of my own and a position of honor in the world."

"I see." She could say no more; if she did he would hear the croak that had got into her voice. A strange emotion had caught at her to hear him speak of being married, though to judge by the calm tone of his voice it had been no love-match.

No, the marriage had been a convenience, as were so many in these days. Love had come later, when he met Melissande. But Frey doubted that he would care to talk about that.

Blaize looked at her across his shoulder, his eyes narrowed. "Are all your questions done, my lady?"

Clearing the obstruction from her throat, she kept her chin high and her gaze on the mounted guard some distance ahead. She had resumed her mantle of indifference. "Unless you wish to tell me more, my lord."

She heard him catch his breath in anger and suddenly he leaned to grasp her shoulder. As she glanced at him in surprise, tensing to fend off what seemed to be an attack, he dragged her cloak's hood up over her head, saying tightly, "It's going to rain. Protect yourself. I'll not have you falling sick again."

They rode on in silence as the gray clouds began to weep a gentle, misting rain that eventually made Blaize raise his own hood, hiding all but his profile from her. She watched him from the warm shelter of beaver-lined wool, troubled. Of course she was still curious. He had never spoken about himself before. Now that he had begun she was anxious to know everything, though she didn't want him to guess the depth of her interest in his personal life.

Eventually, goaded by her curiosity and by his silence, she asked, "What became of your wife?"

"She died," Blaize said tersely, not even glancing at her. "A year ago. At Eastertide."

Again silence. Again her mind full of questions.

So his wife had been alive when he first came to Ketilfiord, she calculated, but she had died before last midsummer—last midsummer when, on the day of Frey's planned betrothal to Geronimus, Blaize had returned to Ketilfiord so unexpectedly. That same night the Vikings had descended, and later Blaize had made advances to Frey in the woods and elsewhere. She remembered it with shameful clarity.

But what had been his real motives—his real feelings? Grief over his wife? Frustration because Melissande was denied him? Had he cared for his wife enough to grieve for her? How long had he known and wanted Melissande? Why hadn't he married her when his wife's death freed him? Why . . . how . . . what . . . ?

"Did you regret her death?" she asked.

"I'm sorry when any human being dies untimely," he replied, with little or no emotion in his voice. "But we are all of us mortal."

"Then you didn't—" She stopped herself, realizing that the question and the impulse behind it were naive—based on some sort of stupid wishful thinking. Of course Blaize hadn't loved his heiress. He had married her solely because it suited his father to "confirm an alliance" and it gave Blaize lands and position of his own—he had admitted as much, quite coldly, only a few heartbeats ago.

He reached out to grasp her rein firmly in a strong gloved hand, halting both palfrey and stallion as he glared fiercely at Frey from the shadows of his hood, saying savagely, "Did I have tender feelings for her? Is that what you want to know? Do you really care how it was, my lady? Can you begin to comprehend?

"I was sixteen—a green boy. And she a woman twice my age and more, twice widowed by wars. Oh, I did what was expected of me. We both did. Ellamine knew her duty well enough. But it gave neither of us any joy. She bore my child and then, much to her relief, my duty called me away to serve the earl my father. I never saw Ellamine again—her, or my daughter."

Then Melissande was not the mother of his child! Some stray part of her found time to thank God for that, at least.

Shaken by the violent passion in him, that seemed to stem from deep pain, she muttered, "I'm sorry."

"Sorry?" he rasped. "Why are you sorry? I did my duty by her. Isn't that what we all should do?"

"But there should be more!" Frey cried, driven by agitation to expose something of her real feelings. "Duty is such a cold word. Where does the heart come in? Why do we have hopes and dreams, my lord? Or do you have no time for such idle fripperies?"

The bronchitic cough of the leading packman warned them that he had almost caught up with them. Not wanting their argument to be overheard, Blaize sent a flashing glance over his shoulder at the man and drew a little away from Frey, touching spur to his mount so that they moved again. Frey followed, a pace behind his shoulder.

"A soldier has no time to indulge in dreams, my lady," he said in a low tight voice that only just carried to her ears. "Such things are for maidens and callow youths. A soldier has appetites—hunger, thirst, the need of sleep when he's weary, the need of comfort after onerous duties—aye, and the need

of a woman when his body burns." He glanced back
to give her a hooded look, reminding her that she
was now the woman who must fulfill that need in
him.

As she read the message in his eyes her stomach
lurched. Soon he would wish to lie with her again.
The thought dismayed her and yet there was some
traitorous part of her that looked forward to that
moment with carnal delight.

It suited him to pretend to be unfeeling, Frey
thought, but he might not be so sanguine with
Melissande. Evidently Melissande was the only
woman who had been able to penetrate this
soldier's armor. Yet he was not all harshness,
whatever he might say: Frey herself recalled a day
when he had tossed young Wulfnoth in his arms
and laughed at the baby's squeal of delight. But his
laughter had died and he had seemed saddened
when Edith reminded him of his own daughter, far
away in Normandy.

Unfortunately, in the months that had passed
since then Blaize appeared to have armored his
heart completely against such shafts. Why? Because
after years of hoping for Melissande he had, for
some reason, been unable to attain her hand when
at last his wife's death freed him? That seemed the
most likely answer. Because he was hurt and had
lost all hope of happiness, he had shut himself off
from feelings and married Frey in an attempt to
break her proud spirit and prove to her which of
them was master.

The real, caring Blaize existed somewhere deep
down inside the hardened soldier, but Frey was
sadly sure that she was not the woman who could
reach him.

The journey continued, over hill and dale,
through valleys where fields and habitations

spread, where they were afforded hospitality and
shelter. They passed through deep woods dripping
with rain, where in places a peasant family had
cleared a patch of trees, cultivated the ground and
built a house, or maybe two—the beginnings of
another settlement. Mists rose as the sun broke
through with increasing power, and spring sent a
haze of green along winter-bare branches.

Blaize had resorted to more French lessons,
which kept him in communication with Frey and
even, on occasion, brought an almost companion-
able feeling between them. If their relationship
could have stayed at that level Frey might have
been content, but she knew that sooner or later he
was going to feel that "need of a woman" again. So
far their circumstances had prevented any
intimacy, but she knew the time must soon come.

She faced the prospect with ambivalence, part
of her recoiling while another part secretly
anticipated their union with pleasure. Although she
tried to force her mind to thoughts of Nicol, as a
defense against hurt that Blaize could inflict, she
was becoming afraid that if Blaize made love to her
again she might not be able to conceal the fact that
her feelings for him were growing more tender
with every day.

On the third morning as they rode away from
the manor where they had spent the night, Frey
saw deeper forests ahead, sweeping up steep hill-
sides with, in the distance, higher, barer mountains
like dark humps against the horizon.

"The Pennines," Blaize informed her. "While
we cross those heights we must shift for ourselves.
There are no villages on the moors."

When they entered the thick forests the party
rode more closely together, the knights and men
only just ahead of their lord and his lady, while the

guards in the rear rode flanking the train of pack-horses. Around them hung a feeling of impending danger; they were moving well beyond the bounds of the king's peace. Frey had heard tell that the forests were the haunt of outlaws and robbers.

So far beyond habitations the trees crowded close to the track. Frey sensed an extra watchfulness about the guards, and Blaize had pushed his cloak aside so that his sword was ready to hand and would not be impeded by the heavy, fur-lined fabric. She found herself instinctively riding closer to her husband than usual, seeking his protection; she had heard him speaking with his knights—Sir Simon and Sir Henry—and she had caught the word "brigands" even though they spoke in French.

They rode as fast as the horses' welfare would allow, through deep gorges where streams rushed around them, up steep ascents where shadows thickened beneath trees, on for several hours, pausing at noontide to eat a cold meal and rest the horses, then pushing on. At last the trees began to thin and the dark hills rose closer to hand, brown and treeless.

As they travelled deeper into the folded hills, the tension relaxed. Robbers stayed close to well-frequented ways where there was ample opportunity for prey, and ample cover in which to hide. Here on the open, windy moors even a hare could be spied moving some distance away. What few trees grew were isolated specimens, stunted and twisted into weird shapes that made Frey wonder what sort of country she was heading for. Dead brown heather covered the hills like fur, relieved here and there by craggy outcrops of gray rock, and clumps of green where long, coarse grasses grew by rushing streams.

By the time the sun began to set amid a welter of tumbled golden cloud that spread a glow across sky and land, Frey ached in every muscle. She had never ridden so many hours at a time and she had begun to wonder if her right leg would ever straighten itself again; it seemed to be set permanently around the pommel of the sidesaddle.

Then as they rode down a deep decline to a valley where trees clustered along the banks of a riverlet, Sir Henry drew back to speak to Blaize. Evidently they were discussing whether this was a suitable place to spend the night. They agreed it was probably the best position for several miles, so at a clearing by the river the party stopped.

Even Blaize stepped a little stiffly from his stallion and several of the men-at-arms groaned audibly, complaining about the pain in their muscles as they dismounted. With an effort, Frey dislodged her knee from the pommel and all but fell into her husband's waiting arms, clutching at him. The shock of that close contact with his warm solidity set her head whirling in the moment before Blaize eased her to the ground. Groaning, she forced her locked leg muscles to obey her will and hold her upright. She eased her aching back and bent to slap life into her calf, keeping her head bent so that he shouldn't see the flush of awareness that stained her cheeks.

Blaize's voice came dryly from regions over her head, saying, "Are you tired, my lady? I thought you enjoyed riding."

"So did I!" she replied with a heartfelt sigh. "This day may have cured me of the fancy."

Straightening, she looked up through her lashes into dark eyes gleaming with humor above a mouth that twitched on the edge of a smile—not mocking but approving her fortitude and sharing the experience of bone-weariness. How strong and handsome he looked, she thought with an emotion very like pain. The cloak draped his tall frame, with the hood thrown back so that his tousled hair was outlined against the golden sky.

The laughing light in his eyes made Frey smile ruefully at him and as she did so she saw the change that came over his expression. The teasing gleam died and he was suddenly intent, his lashes flickering as he searched every feature of her face and let his ravenous gaze rest on her mouth.

Emotion rose up and choked her, so that she hung there, mesmerized by the hunger she read in his eyes. He made a move as if to take her in his arms and she caught her breath, stiffening to repulse him, but before he could touch her Blaize checked himself, remembering that they were not alone. A moment later he swung away, giving orders to his men as they started to make camp.

Sir Simon came up to Frey, fair and smiling, offering her a goblet full of watered wine, from which she drank gratefully, feeling the liquid soothe her parched throat. She emptied the goblet and set it down on a stone as she set out to stretch the cramp from her legs. Behind her, Blaize and the two knights checked the horses, one of which seemed to be lame, while the other men set about lighting a fire and erecting tents of hide.

Tents, Frey thought. Then tonight, presumably, she and Blaize would have a semblance of privacy. That thought must have been in his mind all day: tonight the soldier would expect his wife to serve his appetites—to answer his "need of a woman."

Disconcerted by the conflict of emotion such thoughts inspired, Frey moved away from the camp. Hearing the men's voices dwindle behind her, she strolled beside the broad stream easing her shoulders and her neck, getting rid of the stiffness in her muscles. Slowly the water's bubbling erased all other sounds. The stream ran clear and cold, chuckling over a bed of rounded stones, reflecting the last of the sunlight that fanned out overhead. On either hand the hills rose steeply, clad in pine trees whose spiny tops looked dark against the paling sky.

Hearing a cry—it must have been a small animal, for surely it couldn't have come from a child's throat, not in such an isolated place—Frey looked toward the sound, up the hillside to where a cave lay, fronted by an apron of more level ground where a growth of nettles clustered thickly in the shelter of a big boulder. The nature of the sound gave Frey a moment's puzzlement before she dismissed it as the call of a stoat or weasel. But the nettles gave her an idea—they would make a good expectorant medicine for the packman, whose loud loose cough had punctuated their journey all the way from York.

Wincing at the protesting pains in her legs, she began to climb the steep rise, grasping at tufts of grass and small rocks, making for the shoulder of hillside where the great boulder sat and the nettles grew. At last she reached the ledge, perhaps twenty feet above the stream. Her gloved hands tore at the stems of the nettles, pulling a bunch free.

But her exclamation of satisfaction died as she heard a sound from somewhere in the cave that gaped dark at the back of the ledge. She froze, peering into that black maw, remembering tales of wildcats, or even wolves, not to mention brigands . . . Keeping her eyes fixed on that darkness, she began to edge backwards.

"Hold!" The stern young voice spoke from beside her, stopping her.

Startled, Frey glanced round to see a lad no more than ten or eleven summers old standing there, dressed in ragged garments, his shoes held on his feet by cloth bindings, his face and hands covered with dirt. But the hard light in his eyes bespoke an unchildlike threat, and his knife in his hand had been honed to keen sharpness.

He was holding that knife pointed directly at her breast.

The startled Frey fancied he had materialized from the earth; then she realized that he must have been hiding behind the boulder. Perhaps he had been lurking in the cave when she approached. If so, how many more were with him? Had she stumbled on a brigands' hideaway?

"Give me your cloak," the lad instructed, hardening his young voice to a growl, though behind the grim look on his face Frey discerned the faintest flicker of uncertainty. "Your cloak, lady!" he repeated when she hesitated, and he snatched at the cloak, tugging at it as if to demonstrate what he wanted in case she did not understand Saxon English. He took her for a Norman, apparently.

At the same moment, a thin voice from the cave called, "Will! Will!" It was a child's voice, sounding weak and ill.

Frey saw the youth's determination waver. Evidently he was not yet toughened to his life of thievery; some extremity had driven him into outlawry, but his present concern lay in that cave. Now he was torn between answering the call and continuing his demands for her cloak. He must also be remembering that she could not be alone on the moors, that others would be nearby and would come looking for her before long. All these things she read in his face as his glance flicked to the cave and back again.

"Who are you protecting?" Frey asked. "A child? A sister, or is it a brother?"

The lad's eyes narrowed, his face wary, then grudgingly he said, "My brother."

"Is he ill?"

Again the hesitation, then: "He's hungry. Our

food ran out three days since. And he's cold—that's why I need your cloak."

"And are you alone—just the two of you?" Apparently that was the case; to her relief they were not part of an outlaw band. "Then let me help," she suggested and, seeing that he still doubted her, "Will, I'm Saxon, too. Let me help you!"

The child in the cave cried again, fearfully, "Will! Where are you?" and as the youth's glance again flickered away from her Frey scooped up her skirts and began to make for the cave.

In the jumble of rocks behind the opening she found a small boy of perhaps four summers, slumped in exhaustion. He was stick-thin, his face pallid under its coating of filth, with blue shadows under eyes haunted by fear as he stared at her from beneath a mop of matted hair. Beside him lay the skinned and dismembered body of a hare, which the child had been trying to eat raw. His mouth and hands were sticky with dried blood.

"Dear God—" Frey sighed, turning to the youth Will. "What are the two of you doing here?"

He stared at her sullenly, still suspecting her motives.

"Please, Will," she begged him. "I mean you no harm. That I swear on the soul of my father Wulfnoth, thane of Ketilfiord—a stout Saxon who fought with King Harold. Listen to me . . . unless you let me help, your brother will soon be very ill. Is that what you want? Tell me where you come from. Where is your mother?"

As she returned his look steadily she saw the defiance drain out of him. He too was thin and hungry, in need of a friend. "Mam's dead," he said. "Our father, too. Because he spoke against the Normans, Lord Robert had his tongue cut out, and then they flogged him until he was dead. They made us watch."

"Oh, Will—" Frey hurt for the lad's pain.

"Then Tam was caught stealing eggs and Lord Robert was going to have him thrashed with briars. I got him loose. We ran away." His mouth tightened stubbornly, despite the bright tears in his eyes. "And we're not going back! They'd flog us both. It'd kill Tam. Better to take our chances out here."

"Yes, I understand," Frey said. "But April is hardly the best time to try living off the land."

"We'll join a robber band," Will replied. "Anything's better than going back to slavery for the Normans."

"They're not all so bad," she argued, thinking of her own wedded lord: Blaize might be hard at times but he was not cruel. "But your Lord Robert sounds like a monster. You can't go back to him."

Aware that any moment someone might come looking for her, she thought swiftly for an answer. She couldn't take the pair back to camp with her; unfortunately she couldn't be sure that Blaize would feel the same as she did. Under Norman law these two boys were proven thieves and runaways; they should by rights be returned to their home village for whatever punishment their lord wished to mete out. Blaize might insist that they go back.

Even a life of outlawry was preferable to that. At least the outlaws were free men. Many good Saxons had taken to the forests sooner than serve Norman overlords. With them, Will and his little brother might have a chance of growing up with some self-respect.

"Listen, Will," she went on. "I'm with a party bound for Chester. We're camping back along the stream. Tonight after supper I'll make up a bundle for you—some food and blankets, whatever I can find. I'll leave it near the stream, this side of the clearing. It will keep you going for a while."

His green eyes studied her solemnly. "Why should you help us?"

"Because I'm Saxon, too. I know how you feel about the Normans. And though I'm married to one of them, and travelling with a whole party of them, I won't betray you. I swear it, Will."

At that moment a distant voice—Blaize's voice—came drifting on the breeze, calling her name. Frey glanced round in alarm, but the cave was hidden from most of the valley by a shoulder of hillside and she calculated it would be a short while before Blaize came in sight.

"It's my husband," Frey said hurriedly. "I must go, Will. Trust me. If my husband finds you—"

"All right, then go!" His look was full of defiance and menace. "But if you betray me, lady, I swear I'll cut your heart out!"

It was mostly bravado, Frey guessed, though the threat sounded sincere enough. But since she had no intention of betraying him she had no qualms.

She hurried back to the nettle patch, hearing Blaize call her again. This time his voice was much nearer.

A scuffle by the cave caught her eye. Will was dragging his young brother out of hiding, evidently intent on getting away before Blaize could arrive. He didn't entirely trust Frey. On the moors the boys might hide until they were sure no hunt was afoot. But Tam was reluctant to move. Tears poured down his face. He hardly had the energy to walk.

"Aelfreya!" Blaize's voice called again from along the vale and as she glanced round he came striding along by the stream below, his long cloak flowing about him. "Aelfreya, be careful!"

She was, she realized, very near to the edge of the drop. Another step and she would have slipped, so intent had she been on watching the boys and praying that they would get out of sight. From where he walked below her, Blaize couldn't see them, but even so they were perilously close to discovery.

Even as she hovered, heart in mouth, little Tam slipped and caught his leg on a rock. He gave a sharp, bitten-off scream of pain. Will froze, his eyes huge in his dirty face as he glanced back at her. Frey saw Blaize's attention sharpen on the craggy hillside above her. Another moment and he would start to climb.

Another moment and he would see the boys!

𝔛

If she was to protect the two runaway Saxon boys, Frey had to do something. She acted instinctively. Letting out a cry of alarm to distract her husband, she pretended to slip. She threw up her arms and let her feet go from under her, over the edge of the drop. The ground seemed to open beneath her. The nettles scattered from her hand as she fell. She was tossed and battered on the uneven slope of the hill, rolling dizzyingly until her fall was halted by an obstacle that proved to be Blaize's body, thrown down to save her, with hands that reached for her and gathered her into the safety of his embrace.

There on the hillside, wrapped tightly in his arms, she gasped, "It was a hawk. A hawk startled me. Did you hear it cry? It came swooping at me. Did you see it?"

"I saw only you," he said, his voice not quite steady. "There may be a nest nearby—probably with eggs in it. The hawk must have thought you were an enemy after its brood. Are you hurt?"

Shutting her eyes—shutting out the sight of that agonized look on his face, which she refused to believe could be real—she mentally reviewed her limbs and body. She was shocked, her heart still thudding from the fright, but the thick cloak had cushioned the worst of the fall. And, thank God, her ruse had worked. Blaize believed her story of the hawk; Will and Tam were safe.

"No," she answered eventually. "No, I think not."

"Are you sure?" He scrambled to his feet, helping her up. "Be careful, it's steep. Take my hand and let me guide you."

The hill seemed much steeper going down. Step by step, with her husband's help, Frey inched down to more level ground by the stream, where she found her hands held tightly as Blaize looked her up and down with what appeared to be real concern.

His glance lighted on her cheek, where she became aware of a patch of sore, stinging flesh. Lifting his hand, Blaize touched the place with fingers that shook. "Your face—"

"It's nettled," Frey said, recognizing the sensation. Unable to stop herself, she twisted her head away from his disturbing touch and saw his face darken as his hand fell away from her. "I was gathering nettles," she told him. "To make medicine."

"Medicine?" he repeated blankly. "For what purpose?"

Wondering if he suspected her of further witchery, she looked him straight in the eye. "For the packman's cough."

He stared at her as if he didn't believe he had heard correctly; then an unsteady laugh shook out of him. "The packman's cough? Dear God!" He took her face between his hands, his expression veering between exasperation and amusement. "Frey, you continue to—" The words cut off as with a smothered groan he bent and kissed her, his arms sliding round her to press her close although the thickness of their cloaks separated them. His mouth

possessed hers hungrily, awakening feelings whose
power she had almost forgotten.

Her lips parted under his without her willing it.
Too clearly she remembered the ecstasy only Blaize
could bring. In another moment she might have
thrown aside all her misgivings and clasped him to
her, uncaring of the consequences to her pride.

"Hades!" He tore free of her, wrenching at the
brooches that held his cloak. He flipped the
garment off, spreading it wide so that it settled on
the grass; then he turned back to Frey and reached
for the ties that enclosed her in fur-lined wool.

Frey fended off his groping hands, his rough
haste bringing panic to beat at her mind and dismay her. "My lord!"

"Why not!" His glare was savage as he threw
off her hold and fumbled again with the fastenings
of her cloak, all but tearing it from her to toss it
aside in a crumpled heap as he pulled her back into
his embrace. "You'll not deny me," he growled at
her. "Not this time."

His hands and arms forced her body close in to
his. Fierce dark eyes burned down at her as she
hung unresisting in his clasp; then he bent his head
and buried his face against her throat, his mouth
hot and damp on her skin.

Overhead, dark clouds drove across the sky as
the sun sank further below the horizon. Frey saw
the clouds, but what she was mostly aware of were
the tremors that had started inside her, threatening
to sweep her away on the tide. Too well she
remembered how sweet the fulfillment had been
that day in York when he made her his true wife.
Once experienced, such feelings could never be forgotten; some passionate part of her would always
long for a repetition of the moment.

But oh! how she wished that he would take her
with love, not simply to soothe the driving need of

his body!

"My lord," she managed thickly. "I will not deny you. But must we lie out here under the open sky, without even the shade of a tree to guard us? What if your men come seeking us?"

He became still, as if thinking about it, then he held her away from him to study her face before he glanced at their surroundings, looking for a more suitable place.

"The cave," he muttered. "Come with me to the cave."

Laying hold of her wrist, he bent and scooped up both their cloaks and began to walk up the slope. Frey hung back, saying frantically, "No, not the cave!" She was afraid that some sign of the boys might remain to alert her husband's suspicions. On no account must she draw his attention to those lads.

Blaize glanced round at her, his face dark with angry blood. "What's this? More trickery? I need you. You understand that, surely? You know how it's done. Do not try my patience, lady." His hand tightened, stopping the flow of blood to her hand as he jerked her forward. "Come!"

Frey was half dragged up the hill, protesting at his brutal grip on her wrist, stumbling and tripping over grass and her long skirts, all the time fearing that in the cave he would see some clue that might lead him to suspect that she was trying to hide something.

But to her relief there was nothing left in the cave. Will had taken everything, including the raw pieces of hare meat, and all that remained were some smears of blood and a few tufts of fur which, fortunately, Blaize failed to see. Blaize had other things on his mind.

Leading her to the back of the cave, he kicked aside the scatter of small rocks and leaves and bent to lay both of their cloaks on the floor before turning to Frey, his jaw set and his brow dark. He expected further resistance, that was clear.

But Frey was so relieved that the boys had got away that nothing else mattered. If she could distract Blaize for a little longer, Will and Tam could make good their escape. Besides, an errant part of her was still aquiver with expectation. Her heart felt unsteady and her body seemed to be tingling, making her aware of her breasts and loins. And so she held out her arms to Blaize, her eyes fixed on the lacings of his tunic; she dared not meet his gaze, not right then; she was half ashamed of the feelings warring inside her. He must not guess she was anything more than a wife willing to do an unpleasant duty.

He stepped closer, a hand beneath her chin forcing her face up. Frey closed her eyes, guarding her thoughts from his penetrating gaze, and felt the shudder that ran through him as with a muttered oath he gathered her into his arms and bent his mouth to hers with an insistent pressure that drew answering tremors from the depths of her being.

Not breaking that kiss, he bent and swept an arm behind her knees, lifting her bodily into his arms. Then he knelt with her and laid her on the cloaks, whose thickness masked the uneven rock beneath. The bed was nearly as soft as her own at Ketilfiord, though in the bower there she had never felt a hard male body beside her own, pulsing with life and vibrant desire.

He was breathing heavily, distracted by his lust for her. Without further preamble, his hand slid down her body to claw in her skirts and lift them. Cool air caressed her skin and Frey, torn between desire and despair, shivered convulsively, unable to prevent herself from stiffening as his fingers brushed the silk of her naked thigh and arrogantly plunged to find the moist center of her body. Having satisfied himself that the way was open, he began to tug at the lacings of his breeches.

He took her with little finesse, forcing her thighs apart with his knee before thrusting into her impatiently. His haste destroyed any pleasure she might have experienced. She was merely a vessel he was using for his own gratification.

"A soldier has appetites," he had said. "Hunger, thirst, the need of sleep and comfort—and the need of a woman when his body burns." At least the first time he had made love to her he had made some show of delicacy. Here in the cave he was rutting with the mindless urge of an animal, simply because his lust demanded relief, with no regard for her sensibilities.

She lay with her eyes screwed shut, every muscle tense as a bowstring. And from between her closed eyelids tears squeezed out to trickle hotly down her temples and into her hair.

At last the thrusting motion of his body ceased and, as he lay breathing heavily with all his weight on her, he finally took note of her again. Seeing her tears, he shifted his body from her though his hands came up to cup her head with hard fingers as he stared down at her, commanding, "Open your eyes! Look at me, lady!"

Frey did so, showing him the misery behind the glitter of her tears, through which his hard face shimmered as if seen in a stream.

"God's teeth!" He withdrew from her in one whirl of motion, and got to his feet, his back turned to her as he hastily refastened his breeches. Frey too sat up, straightening her skirts, feeling soiled and achy. How she longed for a hot tub to soothe away the effects of the journey and now her husband's ungentle ministrations. This marriage seemed to be one long tale of indignity.

"You act like some untried virgin," Blaize muttered through clenched teeth. "Other men have had you. Why then do you reject me?" He swung round to look at her, his face charged with bitter anger. "At least I married you before I—"

Seeing the shock that widened her eyes to swimming pools of tawny gold, he stopped as though lightning had struck him. A look of disbelieving horror spread over his face.

In the act of getting up, Frey had paused on her knees, stricken by the injustice of what he was implying. "Other men?" she managed, her voice shaking. "How sweet to know you hold such a good opinion of me, my lord. You made me a lady but still you think me a strumpet."

His face had darkened again with rage. "And are you not?" he growled. "Such maidenly outrage at a poor choice of words! I take back 'men.' Make it 'man'—if indeed he was the only one, if indeed he may be called a man who ruts unwed in the woods with a neighbor's sister, however willing and provocative she might be."

Each word struck Frey like a blow, but with a mighty effort she kept her voice under control. "Provocative, perhaps," she said unsteadily. "I was young and wild in those days and did not understand how my behavior might have been misconstrued. I was ignorant of such things. But willing . . . No, never that!"

"Don't lie to me! I had proof enough in York that you are no virgin. Where was the blood to stain the sheet? Where was the pain of a ruptured maidenhood? Do you think me an untried boy not to know the difference? I was not the first to walk that road, lady."

She stared at him, pale-faced, her lips trembling, not knowing how to defend herself. He was wrong, but how could she prove it now?

Eventually, in a voice so strained it hardly sounded like her own, she managed, "Beyond a few fumbled kisses Nicol of Linscote knew nothing of me. And he was the only man to come close to me, before you. He loved me. He would not have used me as you have, sir. Not Nicol."

"If you believe that," Blaize said roughly, scorn twisting his lips, "then you're either a fool or he's not natural." As if tired of the discussion, he got to his feet in one lithe motion and stood towering over her. "Well, get up! Don't sit there like a whipped pup mourning for your lost love. We shall be missed. Do you want them to come and find us like this?"

A bitter laugh shook out of Frey, half strangled by her distress. "Oh, no, sir. The saints forfend that Lord fitzHugh be discovered with a weeping wife."

With a muttered curse he bent and laid hold of her wrist, dragging her to her feet. "My wife you are and my wife you'll be," he vowed grimly. "You'll put aside thoughts of Nicol of Linscote. We are wed, the knot tied, the contracts exchanged, and in front of many witnesses. There'll be no going back now—not for either of us."

As darkness fell, Frey and her husband, with the two knights Simon and Henry, sat around a fire where chunks of venison were roasting on sticks. The men had caught the deer earlier; since they were within the outer bounds of Earl Hugh of Chester's wide territory, the earl's son was entitled to take deer if he pleased. There was bread, too, flat unleavened cakes baked under stones in the fires, and wine and ale in plenty. In all, a goodly feast for hungry travellers.

At Frey's request, Blaize had sent one of his men to collect nettles for boiling. He hadn't scoffed at her; in a curious way he seemed to feel guilty and

anxious to make reparation for what had happened
in the cave. Not that that made Frey feel better. The
incident had left her feelings numbed—she didn't
hate Blaize, she simply felt indifferent.

She had mixed the medicine as she had learned
from old Ula, and the packman had seemed grateful
for the potion. Perhaps it had helped him; his cough
came less often as he and his fellows ate their own
supper under the trees some distance away.

As a distraction from her personal unhappiness,
Frey fixed her mind on thoughts of secretly aiding
the two runaway Saxon boys. She ate as little as she
could, secreting the rest of what she was given
under her skirts. It must have appeared that she
had a good appetite that night.

She wondered if Will and little Tam were
nearby. The scent of roasting meat and baking
bread must be gnawing at their stomachs. She felt
guilty sitting here in comfort, most of her bodily
needs being satisfied, when those two young boys
were out on the moors alone. They had nothing and
she now had everything she might desire, in
material ways at least. She wished she could do
more to help the lads. If only she dared confide in
Blaize.

But he was talking with Simon and Henry,
scarcely acknowledging her presence. Since they
returned from the cave he had avoided contact with
her. She was dreading the moment when they must
retire to the tent which had been erected for them.

Eventually she made an excuse to leave the fire
and, under cover of red-licked shadows, managed
to steal away with the food she had been gathering.
From the tent she took one of the blankets and
bundled the food up in it, concealed the bundle
under her cloak and made into the woods on the
pretext of relieving herself.

Once out of the circle of firelight she let out a

breath of relief and, making for the stream, placed
the bundle on the bank near a rock, far enough
away from the camp for Will to take it without
much danger. The moon was rising over the hills, a
sliver of light by which Will should easily find her
gift. Praying that it would help, in some small
measure, Frey returned to the camp.

Later that night she lay inside a tent made of
hide and listened to her husband breathing beside
her. They had blankets as well as their cloaks for
warmth, while their mattress was of rich furs
spread on the grass beneath their tent. With the
flap closed, most of the April night's chill was
excluded.

She was grateful that Blaize had allowed her a
period of privacy in which to prepare for bed,
though all she had removed was her outer kirtle,
keeping on her shift and long undertunic. She had
been warmly bundled in her cloak and pretending
sleep by the time Blaize had left off his conversation
with the knights and come to join his wife. He had
not spoken to her, nor made any attempt to touch
her.

Though she was tinglingly aware of him,
another part of her mind was searching the darkness outside, thinking of Will and young Tam.
Were they nearby? Would Will find the bundle she
had left? Would it keep them going until they
found other help, or would it only prolong the
agony of dying of starvation? How she hated the
unknown Lord Robert, the Norman whose cruelties
had robbed the boys of their father and forced them
to flee from their home. And how she wished she
could have gathered the pair under her protection,
especially little Tam. He reminded her of her
nephew Wulfnoth.

But her senses could gather no clue to the boys'

whereabouts. She heard the wind buffeting across the moors, sighing in the trees that filled the sheltered valley where the camp was set; she heard an owl hoot mournfully as it floated in the moonlight alert for prey; she heard the guards conversing, low-voiced, and the packman still coughing despite the nettle medicine . . .

The night was suddenly rent by a loud, wordless bellow that came from not far away, followed by alarums from the men on guard and a stirring among the sleeping retainers. As Frey sat up, her heart thumping heavily in her throat, Blaize threw aside his covers and got up to unlace the tent flap and peer out. Frey had an impression of running men, a disturbance somewhere beyond the camp. She heard the distinct sound of a sword being drawn from its metalled scabbard.

"Hades!" Blaize reached behind him in the darkness, his hand finding his ready sword; then he ducked from the tent and was gone.

Scrambling to the flap, Frey peered out. The fire had been kept well-fed to frighten off any stray wolves and now by its light Frey saw her husband standing straddled with his back to her, fists on his hips as a cluster of men-at-arms dragged something into the camp. As the confusion of bodies parted, Frey saw that one of the guards had captured a prisoner. He was holding the slight, struggling figure of the boy Will by the scruff of the neck.

Grabbing up her cloak, Frey dragged it round her shoulders as she left the tent and ran to protect the boy.

The guard was saying that he had been making a patrol of the camp when he caught the lad sneaking about in the dark. Thieving, so it appeared. As evidence, the man tossed down a bundled blanket, which unwrapped to let fall its small store of food.

"I caught him red-handed, my lord. What shall I—?"

A high wailing interrupted him as another of the men appeared from the shadows dangling little Tam by the back of his tunic. The child was crying, sobbing in fear and terror, but the man only laughed, saying, "And what about this? A robber chief, a man to be much feared by the look of him, my lord." He carelessly dropped the boy to the ground almost at Blaize's feet and held him there by means of a booted foot heavy on the weeping child's back.

Fury at such unkindness to two helpless youngsters sent Frey forward. "Craven bullies!" her voice cut sharply across the scene. The guard holding Tam down looked surprised and stepped back as she came near. She scooped the sobbing child up into her arms, whispering words of comfort to him as she hurried to Will's aid. His captor, too, drew back, astonished, as his lady threw an arm about the ragged urchin and drew him close to her side.

With Will half under her cloak and little Tam clinging his filthy arms round her neck, Frey turned to face her husband. He was a dark, featureless figure backed by streaming red firelight that glinted on the sword in his hand. How terrifying he must have looked to Will and Tam; Frey herself knew a momentary tremor of apprehension before her need to protect the boys came to her aid and she straightened her spine, lifting her head defiantly.

"These are not thieves, my lord. I myself left that bundle for them."

She heard Blaize catch his breath in disbelief before he queried, "*You* did?"

"Yes, my lord," she confirmed, speaking clearly with her chin jutting. "I encountered the lads earlier and offered my help."

"You encountered them when?"

"Soon after we stopped to make camp. They were hiding in the cave."

She sensed rather than saw the gathering frown on his brow as he reviewed this news and assessed its implications. "The cave?" It was spoken so low that the words hardly reached her, but she guessed that he was beginning to understand what must have happened.

All Frey knew was that she must at all costs prevent him from sending the boys back to the vicious mercies of Lord Robert. She must use all her powers of persuasion.

Knowing that she must make a brave sight in the firelight, her red hair falling in loose braids over her shoulders, the cloak flowing over her undergown, the two children in her embrace, she fell to her knees and lifted her pale face, summoning a ringing voice to plead passionately with Blaize: "My lord . . . they are nothing but pitiful children, alone and defenseless, driven out of their homes, their father slain because he dared to speak out against injustice, their mother dead. Their only sin was that this babe—" She stroked Tam's matted hair before again hugging the child to her, "This babe stole some eggs, because he was hungry. His lord would have had him flogged with briars until he bled half to death. And so his brave brother rescued him and they ran away. My lord . . . they have learned to fear Norman cruelty, and with good reason. All that awaits them is a life of outlawry, unless some Christian soul takes pity on them.

"My lord . . . I have cause to know that not all Normans use my people so harshly. Prove it to these poor lads, too. Let me take them into my service. I know they will repay your charity a thousandfold with their loyalty and their steadfastness."

When her impassioned speech ended, Blaize

was silent for a while, his arms folded and his cheek resting on the flat blade of his sword. Then gently, quietly, he began to question Will about the circumstances which had brought him to the moors. Encouraged by Frey, the boy answered all Blaize's questions.

The story which emerged told of such inhuman cruelty on the part of Lord Robert that even the men-at-arms began to mutter, while Sir Simon and Sir Henry eventually joined their voices to demand that retribution descend on the man.

"I shall see to it, never fear," Blaize replied, his voice dark with disgust. "I know the man. He holds his fief from my father. When the earl hears of this, Lord Robert shall be punished. As for these lads—" He turned again to Frey. "They shall join our company. I shall decide their future when we reach Chester. Meantime, Simon, I charge you with their care. See that they are fed."

"Aye, my lord." Sir Simon sounded as though he would relish the task. He bent to take little Tam out of Frey's arms, and with an arm about Will's shoulder he moved back to the tent he was sharing with Sir Henry.

Blaize bent to help Frey to her feet, his hand firm and warm under her elbow. "Why did you not tell me of these lads before?" he asked in an undertone.

"I dared not," she said.

"Do you think me as heartless as their lord Robert?"

"You are a Norman," Frey replied.

"Ah yes." His voice had gone dry, tinged with bitterness. "And for that sin you will never forgive me, is that not so? Come, my lady, the excitement is past for now. You need your sleep."

It was a much relieved Frey who lay again beneath the tent's shelter, the breath of a breeze caressing her face from some slight gap in the hide. Now that the boys were safe she could relax. Beside her, Blaize seemed already to be asleep.

Her own mind remained active, busy with memories of the day and puzzling over the contradictions she found in Blaize. At times he was the hardened soldier, gruff and brutal, yet at other moments he was capable of great sensitivity; she was grateful to him for his understanding and kindness toward Will and Tam. If only he would display the same concern to her, how different everything might be.

Maddeningly, she kept remembering, though still only hazily, how it had been on the evening of their wedding day. In the garden of the earl's house, Blaize's kisses had roused her to a pitch of fever that had matched his. And on the day when he had made her truly his wife only her mulish stubbornness and her pride had prevented her from returning his caresses with equal passion. If only he would be kind and gentle with her, perhaps she might rediscover those feelings. Or had her lack of response convinced him that no purpose would be served by attempts at tenderness?

Restless, she turned over, facing toward the sleeping Blaize, and huddled into herself, searching for oblivion in sleep.

"Are you awake?" Blaize asked softly, surprising her; she had thought he was deeply asleep, so still had he been lying.

After a moment when she wondered if she should herself feign sleep, she said, "Yes."

His voice came deep and regretful, lowered to a caressing bass in the darkness. "Do you truly consider me nothing but an enemy—a hated Norman?"

Frey hesitated, then answered truthfully. "Life is not so simple, is it? There is good and bad in all of us, Norman and Saxon, man and woman, great lord and wretched outlaw."

"Indeed, that is so." He fell silent for a while and Frey wondered if this time he had really gone to sleep; but his voice came again, soft and intimate. "Tell me, Aelfreya . . . is it true, what you told me in the cave? You have never known intimacy with another man?"

The question brought a choking lump of distress to her throat. However hard she pleaded innocence, would he ever believe her? He was right, there had been no evidence of virginity such as she had been led to expect. She remembered her own surprise when their first conjoining had brought no pain nor show of blood.

"It is the truth," she managed in a hoarse whisper. "But how can I ever prove it?"

"I need no proof," he said. "I know it's the truth. I've been a fool not to know it before. In Ketilfiord, you were given to riding astride, were you not?"

"Since childhood," she agreed, puzzled. "But . . . can that affect such things?"

"Indeed it can. Why do you think great ladies take such care only to go sidesaddle, especially before they marry? The maidenhead can be stretched by such exercise, so that it loses it's tautness and ceases to provide a barrier."

"It can?" How astounding that it should take a man to explain this to her. She had never thought she would be able to discuss such things with Blaize, but his matter-of-factness swamped any tendency in her to squirm with embarrassment. "Then . . . you do believe that I have never—"

"I believe it, Aelfreya," he replied, much to her relief. "I should have understood it before. You are inexperienced in the ways of love. And is this, then, why you're afraid of me?" Without giving her a chance to find words, he answered the question himself, impatiently, "Yes, of course it is. It explains much that has been puzzling me. Aelfreya . . . forgive my blindness."

Recognizing the note of genuine regret in his voice, her frozen heart thawed a little toward him, though she was afraid to speak for fear he would hear the emotion in her voice. This was a Blaize of whom, so far, she had been vouchsafed only the briefest of glimpses. The moment was unbearably sweet.

She heard a rustle, as if he were propping himself up on his elbow. "Aelfreya—" he said again, anxious now. "Did you hear me?"

Still choked with a strange emotion, she made a little murmur of assent.

"And do you forgive me?"

Again she wordlessly confirmed it: "Mn hmn."

He moved in the darkness, making her open her eyes wide, though she could see nothing. "We might be warmer if you let me hold you," he said. "Are you warm enough? I'm not. My hands are cold. Feel them."

His hand brushed her shoulder through the thickness of her cloak and she reached out her own hand to clasp it, partly to prevent its exploring further than she wished. But as she touched his skin she felt how cold it was—this was no lying ruse to pave the way for further intimacy.

For some reason she felt grateful to him, and affectionate. He had, after all, been very kind to the two boys Will and Tam and now he was trying hard to make reparation for his harsh treatment of her earlier—there could be no other explanation for the unexpected vulnerability she sensed in him. Would it be so hard for her, in return, to soften her own attitude toward him, just a little?

She pressed his hand between her own, drawing it to her cheek to warm it. In this mood, Blaize was as appealing as a little lost boy.

Except that he was not a boy. Frey could not forget the fully mature and virile body attached to the hand she held. She recalled the muscular strength of him, the touch of his hands on her body, the heat of his naked flesh against hers—and the lunging, merciless thrust of his manhood inside her, taking her in lust rather than in love, as it had been in the cave. Her head whirled with fright, the memory causing the muscles of her stomach and thighs to clench as if to repel a further invasion. If he tried to make love to her again she might not be able to lie still under the onslaught. She might fight him off.

"Ah, you're blessedly warm," he sighed, and shifted position again, making her stiffen as his free hand came cool against her other cheek. "Aelfreya," he whispered from only inches away. "I want to hold you. Just to hold you. I swear I'll ask for nothing more. Not tonight. We are both tired. Let me lie with my arms about you."

His nearness confused her and she wished she could read his face. His breath was a warm zephyr caressing her cheek in the darkness. "My lord—" she managed, and caught her breath as his lips stopped the words, soft and gentle on hers.

"Call me by name," he murmured. "Say my name, Frey."

Mesmerized by his husky voice in the utter blackness of the night, and by the touch of his hands and the faint warm breath on her face, she whispered, "Blaize."

"Aye, Blaize," he agreed, as if the sound of his name on her lips was pleasing to him. "Your wedded husband, sweet lady. And this night I have a yearning to hold my wife warm in my arms."

As he spoke he was lifting the cloak that covered her, slipping beneath it with her. Hands on her shoulders encouraged her to turn over so that she had her back to him, her head on his enfolding arm, her body curled as he fitted himself around her, his knees bent behind her thighs. Holding her close and warm against him, he sighed contentedly. "That feels good. Thank you. Now sleep, my lady. Sleep sweet and safe."

For a few minutes Frey lay tensely, fully alert—fully expecting moves toward further intimacy. But Blaize lay still and soon his even breathing told her he was asleep, with his arms loosely around her and his body curved protectively to hers. He slept. He had kept his word. Oh, Blaize . . .

Relaxing, Frey could only agree with him that the sensations of lying close with him did indeed feel good. Very good. She went to sleep in a warm glow of contentment such as she had expected never to find again.

Birdsong woke her—birdsong and the quiet murmuring of male voices, underlaid by the iced rippling of the stream. A fire hissed as someone tossed the dregs of an ale cup onto the embers.

But that was outside, in the chill air of an April morning on the high moors. Here in the tent, enclosed in friendly half-light, Frey was still somnolent, reluctant to bestir herself to resume the endless journey to Chester. She felt too warm, too safe, breathing in the scent of her husband's body, her head resting on the rise and fall of his naked breast, his curling chest hair faintly rough and sensual against her cheek.

Somehow she had turned toward him in the night, as if welcoming the warm embrace of his arms, and now her own slender arms were wound about his torso. She discovered herself to be lying half across him, her head resting on his chest, her legs entangled with his, almost every contour of his body distinctly revealed to the inquisitive nerves which pulsed in her own flesh. Disturbed by that

intimate entwining—and by the instinctive pleasure
she was taking in it while half asleep—she readied
her muscles to pull free. But as soon as she moved
Blaize's arms tightened about her, pinning her
where she was.

A hot flush coursed along Frey's veins as she
wondered if he had been aware of her unconscious
response to him—her body melting and molding
against his. She guessed that he was sharing the
sensual pleasure of being so close. She had thought
he was sleeping, but evidently he had been awake,
and totally aware.

"Be still," he breathed. "Let them think we're
still sleeping. This is much too sweet to end."

He was right, the moment was poignant with
nuances of togetherness. Frey allowed herself to
relax, becoming pliant and receptive to all the tiny
messages that flowed limb to limb, muscle to
muscle, flesh to flesh between them. She had never
felt so close to anyone in her life before.

Cautiously she opened her eyes. Faint light filled
the tent and to her relief she realized that Blaize
was not, after all, completely naked: his linen shirt
had come unlaced at the front where her head lay,
that was all; he still wore the loose linen breeches
that covered men from waist to knee.

Softly, so as not to make a sound that might be
heard by anyone outside their warm nest, he rolled
over until he was gazing down at her, his
expression veiled by shadow. He smoothed stray
locks of hair from her brow, traced with long slow
fingers the line of her cheek, the shape of her
trembling lips. As he bent over her, Frey felt her
lips tingle and fill with blood, making her lift her
face and offer her mouth willingly to receive an
accolade of gentle kisses.

She had always been stirred by his kisses, it was
true, but now her blood seemed to catch fire. Her
hands slid up the front of his loose shirt, her finger-

tips making tingling contact with his flesh before she fastened them behind his neck and found herself being swept away on a tide of longing, drowning in the fascination he had always exerted on her.

He spread one warm hand against her throat, his palm gently molding that tender white column, his thumb braced under her chin as if to keep her mouth upturned beneath his. Then slowly that hand stroked down from her throat to her shoulder, edging inside her shift, making her shiver with anticipation in the unbearable moments before shafts of pleasure shot through her from that sensate tip as she gasped aloud and felt her open mouth claimed with eager passion.

His kisses grew deeper and his hands began to stroke her through her clothing—her arms, her shoulders, her ribs—as if he would discover the outline of every curve of her. His mouth became ever more feverish as he sought a way inside her clothes, where flesh might answer to flesh.

Frey found herself helping him, lifting herself so that her shift and undertunic could slide off over her head and the cool air caressed the white length of her body. Blaize knelt beside her, his gaze feasting on her, his hands stroking over her to explore every curve and hollow, his lips and tongue teasing her breasts until she felt she might burst with the delight of it. Unable to hold back, she reached out for him, her eager fingers tearing at his shirt and at his breeches until he, too, was naked.

With a low groan in his throat he lifted himself to lie on top of her and she felt her entire body flush with shock—and with an undeniable sense of satisfaction—as she realized how ready he was to claim her. The thrust of his manhood against her thigh came hard and throbbing, seeking an entry, but this time in a tentative, pleading way, not forcing but enjoining her cooperation for their mutual pleasure.

She was all responsiveness as a flush of pleasure
loosened her body, making her alive to every
contour of him as she opened her thighs to receive
him. The sensation of his entry brought a tiny
moan from her, though Blaize silenced her with his
mouth, the slow movements of his body drawing
her ever deeper into realms where feeling was all
and her only wish was for him never to end that
luxurious, languorous ride. Waves of irrepressible
desire began to shudder through her and for the
first time she found herself driven to move with
him, arching her hips to his to intensify the joining.
She was beyond thought now, beyond anything but
the need to keep those waves crashing, growing
ever more intense as their movements quickened
and their two bodies combined in a harmony of
motion and feeling.

Frey felt that she was climbing, being lifted up
some tall mountain where every peak became a
plateau which revealed a higher peak, up and up
through layers of cloud, until suddenly they burst
through into sunlight. The final peak swept her to a
release that held her suspended for long, shattering
moments before the gentle slide down on the other
side, where the real world lay waiting.

Afterwards, for a little while, Frey allowed
herself to indulge in the sweetness of lying with her
husband, both of them quiet now, their breathing
slowly returning to its normal peaceful measure. A
warm feeling of gratitude and affection stole over
her, making her nestle more closely in Blaize's
arms. Oh, if only he could always be tender and
considerate like this!

"Ah," he breathed in her ear, his voice vibrant
with laughter. "Now I know how to tame the
wildcat. I must start my persuasion while she is yet
asleep."

He was mocking her—the thought struck like ice through the glow of her euphoria. Had his tenderness been all pretense, then, intended only to persuade her to allow him his way without a struggle? What a fool she was to have been misled. Her own response had been genuine, rising from secret wells of affection that she was only now starting to explore. But now she remembered that Blaize cared nothing for her. His earlier behavior had proved that. The only woman he loved was Melissande. How could Frey have forgotten Melissande?

His mockery, and her own naivety, stung her, leaving her cold, sickened and disgusted with herself.

Then one of the men outside laughed at something a companion said. All at once she was horribly conscious of the proximity of those men outside, who were chatting in low voices and probably debating whether to rouse their lord and his bride. They sounded amused. Did they know what had been going on in the tent?

Shame and embarrassment suffused Frey in their disconcerting glow, rousing her temper. How easily she had been seduced: that was what it had been—a coolly calculated seduction for his own gratification, while she was half asleep and unable to find the wits to resist or even feign indifference. What had Blaize assumed from her willingness? Did he guess that she was beginning to feel very tender toward him at times? What a triumph that would be for him. Would he boast to Melissande that his silly Saxon wife had been unable to resist falling in love with him? Frey must disperse that impression at once.

Clearly, coldly, and very quietly for his ears alone, she said, "Even a Saxon wildcat may feel gratitude for one who protects the young of her species. Your kindness to young Will and Tam deserved a reward, my lord."

She felt him stiffen as if she had run him through. "A reward? God's wounds!" The whispered curse bit out of him as he jerked away from her, disentangling himself from her embrace. "Is that why—?"

"*Mon seigneur!*" a voice called from just outside the tent, making Frey stiffen and drag some covering over her, while Blaize glanced round. "*Mon seigneur, c'est tard!*"

"Hades!" Blaize muttered under his breath, reaching for his clothes. "I know it's late. Mayhap you should have roused me sooner." He raised his voice to reply in French, saying that he would be out shortly. It sounded as though the man moved away.

Sighing heavily, Blaize looked down at Frey, his dark eyes shadowed by bitter anger. "Is there to be no end to this war between us? What must I do to earn a surcease?"

"Turn back time," Frey said dully, turning her face away from him. "Undo everything that has happened."

"I begin to wish that were possible," he said darkly. "I have tried to be patient, but even a saint would be sorely tried by—"

"Then perhaps—" she interrupted, lifting herself on an elbow, her cloak gathered to cover her to the chin. "Perhaps you should leave me at Chester, with the countess."

He was almost fully dressed now, kneeling on one knee beside her as he fastened his belt, though he paused to stare down at her with a suspicious frown creasing between his brows. "Leave you at Chester? Why should I do that?"

"Because . . . because we should be happier apart, my lord. You must know that. Besides, I'd

only be in your way at Triffordd—a briar in your
flesh—a distraction when you need your wits to
fight the Welsh. I know nothing of military
garrisons."

Anything, she thought, was better than being
alone with him night after night and having to
submit to his lust while trying not to reveal how
her heart was aching. She would end up welcoming
even the sham of love, letting herself believe that it
might be real and all the time trying to forget that
in reality all she could ever be was a substitute for
Melissande. Such self-deceit would kill her, in the
end; it would rob her of her last shreds of pride.

"Leave you behind?" Blaize growled. "What,
leave you to applaud your own cleverness in
gaining my name and my protection while
avoiding paying the rights and dues which you
freely promised to me when we spoke our wedding
vows? Leave you—to moon in your chaste bed over
Nicol of Linscote?"

"And why not?" she cried. "At least Nicol cared
for me!" She wanted to scorch him now, to wound
as she had been wounded. Of course he wouldn't
leave her behind in Chester; she had never really
thought he would.

Blaize's face hardened. He grabbed up his cloak,
trailing it over one shoulder as he stared coldly
down at her. "By all the saints, lady," he said
through his teeth, "if that's what you wish, so shall
it be!"

Startled, she looked at him with wide tawny
eyes in a pale face. *What* had he said? Did he mean
it?

Her expression made him smile bitterly to
himself. "Aye, you heard me right—you may stay
at Chester for all I care. You may shut yourself up in
another nunnery and share the life of chastity with
other dried-up, bloodless women." He bent closer,

baring his teeth in a snarl that showed white in a
dark face with glimmering eyes. "But do not expect
me to share your abstinence. There are women—
women in plenty—who do not require a man to beg
and plead for favors. Women who face the world as
it is, not as they wish it to be—as you will have to
face, later or sooner, that Nicol of Linscote is lost to
you for ever. He was disinherited. Or had you
forgotten that?"

Clutching her own cloak to her breast, Frey
stared up at him, seeing the broad chest heave
beneath the unlaced shirt, the dark face above it
holding eyes that gleamed hatred at her—hatred,
and a strange cold satisfaction that made her catch
her breath.

Dreadful suspicions filled her mind. Nicol had
been in the service of Earl Hugh, and Blaize was Earl
Hugh's acknowledged son. He could do anything.
Anything. Hadn't he once said so?

"*You* were responsible for that!" she gasped as a
cold wave of comprehension cleared the cobwebs
from her brain. "*You* organized it! You had Nicol
disinherited—to keep us apart forever!"

Blaize watched her for a moment, his mouth
turned almost ugly with contempt. "I should have
left you to that fat merchant," he said, grabbed up
the rest of his clothes and ducked out of the tent.

XI

That day Blaize elected to ride with Sir Simon but he sent Sir Henry back to accompany Frey. Young Tam rode not far behind her, atop the bundles lashed to the leading packhorse, while Will walked beside him, acting apprentice packman. As the journey resumed, Frey kept glancing back to check on the boys. Tam seemed happy enough to be back in the care of adults, though Will's young face remained dark with suspicion; Frey guessed that he still feared he might be delivered back to the hated lord Robert.

Sir Henry, riding alongside her, was a thin young man with lank brown hair, a pleasant, plain countenance and a shy manner. He came from Normandy and had little English, as she soon discovered. At first the young knight seemed ill at ease in her company, but she did her best to be friendly and before the morning was over they were managing a sort of conversation in simple French sentences.

So the journey continued. The way was tortuous, through deep gorges and over high, empty plains of heather where nothing was to be seen but hares and birds.

Slowly, Sir Henry learned to relax. Frey's willingness to try out her French and learn from him flattered him and with much gesturing and misunderstanding he increased her vocabulary, often laughing shyly with her over her mistakes. Apart from the pain inside whenever she thought about Blaize, the day passed pleasantly enough.

That night they camped again in a shallow valley and while the men erected tents and prepared a fire for supper Will and Tam were given small chores to do. The leading packman, whose cough had been noticeably less harsh that day, seemed to have taken the boys into his care and even Will seemed to be responding to a kindness of which he had experienced too little during his short life.

As the older boy went about his chores of fetching water and breaking kindling, Frey noticed that often his narrow eyes fixed on Blaize, as if he went in fear of the dark Norman lord who was now his master. She sought a chance to speak to the lad, on the edge of the camp.

"You need have no fears of Lord FitzHugh," she assured him. "He will keep his word. Not all Normans are like your lord Robert. Believe me, Will. Once I, too, hated all Normans simply because they *are* Normans, but there are good Normans and bad ones, and most are in between, just as we Saxons are."

Will said only, "Aye, lady," and moved on, but his look said that he still suspected her motives. He simply did not understand why she had helped him and his brother.

Frey guessed that, had it not been for Tam, Will might have tried to run away again, but little Tam's welfare kept him where he was. On the moors, alone, Will might survive; Tam would not. So for Tam's sake, Will was prepared to stay with Lord fitzHugh's train—at least for the present.

He was, she thought, like a pup that had known

nothing but kicks and cuffs. He didn't know quite
how to react to kindness and he didn't know how to
trust. But he would learn, given time.

As soon as supper was over, Frey retired to her
tent while Blaize sat talking with his men around
the fire. Although she was not asleep when he came
in, he did not speak to her or attempt to touch her.
Their quarrel of that morning remained a bitter
barrier between them.

Frey lay awake thinking, remembering. Her
feelings for Blaize were in confusion; sometimes she
thought she hated him, at other times she
experienced a strange warm tenderness. Had he
really arranged for Nicol to be disinherited? It
seemed all too likely; thus he disposed of his only
possible rival. And yet for all his seeming hardness
he could be kind at times. She recalled her conversation with Will, belatedly wondering at the
readiness with which the words had come to her,
assuring the lad of her confidence and trust in her
husband. She had spoken from her heart, unthink-
ingly.

And it was true: in many ways she knew she
could trust Blaize implicitly. He was honorable, just,
and truthful—at least to other people. It was only
toward herself that he showed a different
character. He had married her out of lust, hurt
pride and the disappointment brought by love
unrequited.

Frey's anguished wish went silently heaven-
ward through the windy night: Oh, if only
Melissande did not exist!

Blaize, moving from his blankets, roused her
from sleep the following morning, but when she
stirred and blinked at him he only said, "You can
try your charms on Sir Simon today, since it seems
you're happier in company other than mine." Then

he left her to dress.

And so, as they came down from the bleak heights of the Pennine moors, it was the fair and handsome Sir Simon with whom Frey rode and spoke her halting French. Simon did speak a little English, heavily accented but nevertheless comprehensible. The charming, golden-haired knight was far bolder than Sir Henry, sending many gleaming sidelong glances from bright blue eyes that told Frey he was not averse to a little flirtation with his lord's wife to enliven what was becoming a tedious journey. However, flirtation was all it was, practiced in a courtly manner which kept his charm exercised until such time as he found other ladies to enchant.

Frey smilingly fended off his exaggerated flattery, not wanting to appear to be giving him encouragement, thereby giving Blaize cause for censuring her. Even so, her drooping spirits revived like wilting flowers given water in the knowledge that Simon found her attractive enough to warrant flattery.

During the afternoon they left the hills behind and came to a fertile plain where villages abounded, each manor with its main hall and cluster of peasant houses surrounded by fields where men worked among the young crops, and copses where pigs rutted beneath the trees. Twice along the road they passed slow-moving trains of ox-carts heading away from Chester, laden with salt from the natural deposits that were one of the assets of the earldom. Salt was a costly commodity and a strong guard of Earl Hugh's crimson-cloaked soldiers rode escort on each of the strings of carts.

Knowing that the end of their journey was almost in sight, Frey found herself growing more and more tense with each passing mile. She had heard tales of great courts but until these last few weeks she had scarcely dreamed of attending one herself, and even since her marriage she had tried to avoid thinking of what it would mean. Now that the moment was at hand she found herself anticipating that she would be swamped and overawed by the grandeur of the earl's court, committing sins of gaucherie, being mocked by the grand lords and ladies for her simple country ways, found wanting in beauty and grooming . . .

When Blaize was back within sight of Melissande, the thought came like the slap of a whip, would he even want to look at the wife who did nothing but defy and irritate him?

And would he, as he had threatened, really leave Frey behind in Chester when he travelled on to his own domain in the Welsh marches? At last, on the sixth day of their journey, Lord fitzHugh's train wound out of sunlit woodland and Frey saw before her a broad stretch of strip-cultivated fields filling the fertile plain of a river estuary. But her eye was drawn beyond the fields to the massive sprawl of buildings that was the city of Chester. It was larger even than York, hazed by a pall of wood-smoke above which flew clouds of screaming gulls. Beyond it, in the distance, Frey saw the steely gleam of the sea.

She had travelled right across the waist of England, from sea to sea. Her old home at Ketilfiord seemed left behind forever, whole worlds away.

Inexorably, the train moved on, soldiers, knights and pack-animals following the rutted, much-trodden track toward one of the fortified gates of the city. On either side lay a jumble of rough dwellings built in the shadow of the great walls as if huddling there for shelter, and out of these rude hovels children came to stare and point at the newcomers, with dogs yapping round them.

Frey glanced behind her and saw Will walking

close behind the packman, one hand clasped round
Tam's fist as the little boy bestrode the packs and
stared wide-eyed about him. Having satisfied herself that the pair were safe, Frey turned back to
contemplation of what lay ahead. Her own eyes
were almost as wide with wonder as young Tam's.
She felt apprehensive and yet fascinated by what
she was witnessing, beginning to appreciate what it
might mean to be the wife of the mighty Lord fitz-
Hugh.

The old Roman walls, kept in good repair by the
earl's men, protected crowded streets of houses
built mainly of wood and wattle. In such a city, fire
was the greatest hazard. Many church towers rose
above the urban thatches and, dominating the city,
on a promontory overlooking the busy harbor and
the broad estuary of the river Dee, stood the pale
bulk of the great castle where the earl kept his
court.

Chester had a bustling, thriving air about it.
Where York had several times been razed by fire
and war in the strife which followed the Norman
Conquest, Chester had remained intact. Its earl was
supreme in his own lands; at a time when most
buildings, even royal dwellings, had been swiftly
erected from wood, he had built his castle in
stone—indeed was still building it, as Frey saw from
the huge blocks of masonry being carted through
the streets, and from the scaffolding around one
corner of the mighty keep, where masons and their
men perched precariously like tiny dolls against the
blue sky.

Frey had never seen such a castle. It loomed
enormous over the city, with high walls several feet
wide and many watchtowers. The portcullis in the
turreted gatehouse protected a vast courtyard with
wooden outbuildings crowding behind those great
walls, storing provisions and housing the garrison.

And to one side stood the massive three-storied keep, from where the sound of hammer and chisel on stone came melodically over the bustle of soldiery and servants in the courtyard below.

Somehow, Lord fitzHugh's train eased itself into the courtyard and began to disband. Trying to hide her own apprehension, Frey assigned the leading packman to continue his care of Will and Tam, at least for the present, and then, aware that Blaize was growing impatient with her fussing over the lads, she obediently followed where her husband led, her eyes round as she gazed on the wonders about her.

A flight of broad stone stairs climbed steeply up the outer wall of the keep, leading to a door behind which lay a room that was both guardhouse and weapon store; a guard came up to challenge Blaize but, recognizing him, changed the challenge into a salute and greeted him warmly in French, evidently welcoming him home.

But even as he spoke, the man's eyes slid to Frey and appraised her curiously. She guessed she must have been the subject of gossip and speculation—the dowerless Saxon wench whom the earl's son had married in a fit of madness.

Blaize made some reply to the man, then took Frey's elbow in a proprietary hand, hustling her away from the guard's inquisitive stare.

A shadowy archway in a far corner of the guardroom gave access to more stone stairs, cut like sections of cheese, twining tortuously and gloomily inside the thick wall of the keep. The way was lit by occasional slits through which Frey glimpsed the city spreading out below, though most of her mind was on what lay above; the sound of many people grew louder, voices calling and laughing, the scuff of feet on reeded stone, the music of a lyre someone was tuning, the yelp of a dog as it was stepped on or kicked out of the way . . . At last the enclosed stairs reached another archway, and beyond it Frey had her first sight of the bustling great hall—the main room where the life of the castle was conducted.

Its ceiling was high and vaulted, its stone ornately carved over pillars of fluted splendor, the stonework painted in bright colors with motifs picked out in gold leaf. Carved doors around the main hall evidently led to other, presumably private, chambers, and above them a gallery circled the room, where people strolled at their ease or sat in the embrasures of windows which let in light and air. At the far end of the great hall, a dais held the high table, backed by several high-backed chairs which were the focus for a crowd of people all eager for attention, and warmth was provided by log fires that burned in great fireplaces built into the walls at either side.

At first when Frey stepped into the hall she was astounded by the milling throng of nobles, knights, ladies, pages, servants and dogs—and by the rich mass of colors before her eyes. The walls were covered with thick hangings, tapestries worked with gold and silver and all the colors of the rainbow, showing pictures of heroic deeds and moral, religious subjects. In other places swords and shields, bright with decorations of enamel and gold, were displayed against the gray of granite. But what struck Frey most nearly was the noise! Such a hubbub of voices talking, laughing, singing, giving instructions . . .

"Blaize!" a hearty voice called over the rest. The crowd by the high table dais parted to reveal a bulky, dark-haired man in rich robes encrusted with gold embroidery. His belt fastened low under a weighty stomach and he wore a long moustache beneath which his smile was broad as he came to embrace Blaize, greeting him exuberantly and affectionately. Among the stream of words too rapid for her to translate, Frey caught the meaning of one phrase—"my son."

Frey felt her scalp tighten with a chill of disquiet. This man must be the Earl of Chester, Hugh d'Avranches, less formally known as Hugh the Wolf. He didn't look like a wolf, not at first sight, but underneath all that exuberance and *bonhomie* he was alert and watchful, his eyes missing nothing of what went on about him. In the midst of conducting his court business of seeing petitioners and consulting with his chancellor he had not missed the arrival of his son.

Nor was he, as Frey had expected, an elderly man, but still fully active, probably only some fifteen years older than his son. Frey remembered Blaize saying that both of his parents had been very young when he was conceived, but until now she hadn't really thought what that meant.

Now Blaize introduced his wife and the earl looked her up and down, critically but smilingly, before treating her to a suffocating embrace and kissing her enthusiastically on both cheeks, apparently delighted to welcome her as his daughter-in-law. Chucking her under the chin, he made some light remark to Blaize, then turned away and went back to his business at the high table.

Frey felt confused. Whatever she had been expecting from Hugh the Wolf, it wasn't such warmth and pleasantness. Had all the tales she had heard about him been false?

Blaize looked down sidelong at her, his mouth quirking ruefully as he explained, "My father says you're beautiful, but a little too thin to suit his taste."

"The last is true," she replied. "The first . . . is

flattery. I know well enough that beauty has never been one of my virtues. The earl—and everyone else at his court—must wonder why you took so much trouble to secure *me* as your bride when you could have wed any woman in the kingdom."

"Aye, you may be right," Blaize said in a tone that implied he was beginning to wonder the same thing himself.

A steward came up, bowing, and showed them to a door hidden behind one of the tapestries. It led into a side chamber large enough to contain a curtained bed against the side wall, a stand bearing a bowl and ewer, two stools and a space for two or three dressing chests. There were poles set into the walls above head height, for the hanging of clothes to air, and the shutters at the narrow window stood open to the mewing of gulls floating on a brisk breeze that brought the tang of the sea from the estuary.

As the steward departed, Frey stood in the center of the room feeling as though she were a hare that had walked into a glittering trap. Through her own foolishness she had led Blaize to threaten that he would leave her here. Would she ever escape the great castle of Chester?

"No doubt you'll welcome a chance to rest after our long journey," Blaize said. Seeing her glance go automatically—apprehensively—to the bed before resting on him questioningly, he afforded her a cold smile. "I meant alone. I have business to attend to. I'll have some food sent to you. Never fear, I shall not trouble you for favors you have no wish to give. And tomorrow I'll be gone—gone to Triffordd and the Welsh wars." He swept her a courtly, derisive bow. "By your leave, my lady," he murmured, and was gone.

Left alone, Frey paced the room restlessly. She had never felt so helpless, so ineffectual in guiding

her own destiny. Blaize couldn't mean to leave her
here. He couldn't!

The narrow window embrasure, open to the
breeze, looked onto a harbor crowded with ships,
both rivercraft and seagoing vessels, all meeting
here in the estuary. Men clambered about them,
loading and unloading cargo, tending to sails and
rigging. Bustling wharves were backed by sturdy
warehouses and the air was awhirl with white-
winged, crying gulls.

The estuary snaked away into the distance,
broadening northward into the silvery expanse of
the sea. Beyond a thickening evening haze away to
the west, Frey fancied she could pick out distant
hills, dark and blue. Was that Wales? she
wondered.

Hearing Blaize speak of the Welsh wars had
reminded her sharply of something Reynold had
said when he came to tell her the earl had found her
a husband. In her mind she saw again that bare
white room at the abbey of St. Winifred, and her
brother's thin face pinched with care as he tried to
persuade her to accept the match: *"Since fitzHugh is
a marcher lord he'll be away fighting . . . and if he
should perish under Welsh arrows—"*

She laid her hand against the cold stone of the
window embrasure as a wave of fear assailed her.
She had forgotten that aspect of it! Now that she
knew the identity of fitzHugh, the thought of his
perishing under a hail of Welsh arrows was
terrifying.

He couldn't really intend to leave her here while
he spent the best months of the year in the marches
of Wales, could he? To leave her here, where she
would spend every waking moment wondering if
danger threatened him, and every sleeping
moment locked in nightmare; here, among
strangers who despised her, strangers whose

language she had only just begun to learn; here, in a
terrible castle of stone where the very rhythm of
the day was foreign to her? Blaize had brought her
to this place. He was responsible for her. He
couldn't just abandon her.

Unable to make sense of the conflict of her
emotions, she was almost relieved to be interrupted
by the arrival of a servant with food, and then by
more servants bringing the familiar clothes chests
which had stood in the bedchamber of the house in
York.

Tonight, in this chamber closed off from the
rest of the castle by a sturdy door and those thick
tapestries, and on his last night before leaving for
dangerous duties at his own frontier castle, she and
her husband would be alone. The thought set her
aquiver with rolling spasms of heat and cold. She
didn't want him to leave her; she wanted him to
make sweet love to her as only he could. And yet
she detested her own weakness, for her increasingly tender feelings toward him were not returned.
Blaize might use her to still the fire in his loins, but
he would never love her. She was a fool to yearn for
what she knew was impossible.

Frey retreated to the bed while she had it to
herself and eventually she lay down and went to
sleep, worn out by the long journey and by the
many hours in the saddle.

She woke to find Blaize in the room, stripped to
the waist and splashing himself with water from
the bowl. She lay still, watching him through her
lashes, letting her eyes explore a broad naked back
rippling with muscle. His taut, lean hips were
covered in linen breeches that fitted to the knee and
below that his sturdy calves were stockinged in
white, cross-thonged with leather strapping,
ending in bronze-studded sandals. As he sluiced
himself down he turned toward her, displaying
more of that tall frame to his wife's fascinated gaze.

She knew that body well, knew how it felt against her, but she had never had the chance to study him so intimately before. A down of dark hair covered his forearms and smudged a triangle across his muscular chest, tapering in to his waist and the cord that tied the linen breeches. How fine he was, Frey thought, an unidentifiable ache tugging deep inside her.

The sight of him unclothed stirred her more than she would have dreamed. She found herself studying his body in detail, wanting to know more of him, and as he snatched up a towel to dry himself she thought of his hands: brown and strong, with long fingers. Capable hands, rough hands, hard hands—that could yet be so gentle on her flesh. She recalled how he had made slow, tender love to her that morning in the tent. The memory made her breathing unsteady. He had called her his sweet and his love—but men did speak such words when they wanted a woman's soothing for their flesh.

Seeming unaware of her scrutiny, Blaize reached for the robes which had been hung on a pole so that the creases would drop out. On another pole hung Frey's wedding outfit—the yellow undertunic and the gown of forest green velvet with its embroidery of flowers. She had never thanked him for it, she realized.

Covertly, still feigning sleep, she watched as her husband pulled on his own undertunic, this one an ankle-length robe of finest white linen with tight sleeves to his wrist. He fastened it at the throat with a gold brooch and reached for the fur-trimmed outer robe, of a rich golden ochre with bands of embroidery around shoulders, wide sleeves and hemline. With a golden girdle round his waist he transformed himself into Baron fitzHugh, the earl's son, lord of Bayonne, castellan of Triffordd. Incredible to recall that not many nights ago she had slept so peacefully, so happily, in the arms of such a man.

Taking up an ivory comb mounted in silver,
Blaize began to tidy his hair, gazing out of the
window to watch the swoop of a screaming gull.

"My lord—" Frey ventured through a thick
throat.

"My lady?" the answer came at once, cool and
incurious.

He had known she was awake all the time! Had
he enjoyed knowing she was watching him dress?
The thought made her scalp tighten and she sat up
on the bed, nervous now.

"My lord . . . I wish to go with you to
Triffordd."

Now, for the first time since she had woken, he
looked at her. His dark face was still, his brown
eyes unreadable. "Why?"

"It's my place to be with you."

"No, lady, that is not your reason," he said
steadily, putting his comb down on the washstand.
"You fear to remain here alone, I don't doubt. But
you will soon find friends among the other ladies.
Since you've been learning so quickly, the language
will not long be a barrier to you."

"But if you leave me here . . . what will
everyone think?"

He shrugged, as if it were no concern of his.
"What should they think? I assure you no one will
question my decision. Several of the marcher lords
leave their ladies here for safekeeping in their
absence. Ladies find the court here safer and more
congenial than facing the rigors of life and the ways
of rough soldiers on the marches. And," he added,
still in that insulting, careless tone, "no doubt you'll
soon acquire your share of admirers among the
young men. The beautiful Saxon lady fitzHugh will
cause quite a stir, I imagine."

Now she knew he was mocking her. "They're

more likely to laugh at my country ways and my freckled face," she said dully. "Blaize . . . I don't want to stay here!"

"What you want," he retorted, swinging to face her fully, "is of little account. You will do as I say. You will stay here. And I shall leave tomorrow. But tonight—" He came closer to lean over the bed with glinting eyes, making her cower away from him. "Tonight you will behave like an obedient wife, my lady. We are to be the chief guests at a celebration supper."

Her stomach sank and seemed to rise again to swamp her throat with bile. "A celebration?" she managed. "In honor of what?"

"It's an occasion for rejoicing," Blaize said bitterly, his lips twisting, "over the union of Blaize fitzHugh with the lady of his heart. And, by God, you'll play the part with all the deceit at your command. I'll not be made a laughingstock. Do you understand me?"

Blanching under the ferocity in his eyes and voice, Frey muttered, "Aye, my lord."

"Then prepare yourself," he ordered, and swept out, tall and imposing in his velvet robes.

She supposed she deserved his bitterness and sarcasm. *The lady of his heart*, indeed! If only that were true. But presumably it was what everyone at the earl's court believed and so she must play the part to the hilt. She guessed that she must not, by word, deed or glance, reveal the truth of their uneasy union, for if that were known he would truly become a laughingstock. Lord fitzHugh couldn't even control his own wife.

Oh, Blaize . . . she looked down at the hands trembling in her lap, conscious of an almost intolerable pain in her heart. She had never foreseen the anguish this marriage would bring. Her sweet girlish dream had turned bitter as rue.

"My lady?" the soft, almost timid voice made
Frey look up, startled, to see by the door a red-
cheeked woman dressed in a blue kerchief and
plain blue kirtle with an apron. It took a moment
for her to believe that that apple face really was
familiar—she had last seen its owner several weeks
ago, in York.

A surge of unwonted pleasure and relief rose
inside her, making her jump off the bed with a glad
cry of: "Hilda!"

Smiling in response to so warm a greeting, the
maid shyly bobbed a curtsey. "My lady. Well come
to the castle of Chester!"

'It's well come indeed, now that you're here,"
Frey said, feeling almost light-headed. "I never
thought to see you again. What are you doing here,
Hilda?"

"I'm to help you dress, if it pleases you."

"It pleases me greatly!" Frey exclaimed. "But
that was not what I meant. Hilda, how—"

"Please, my lady," the maid broke in hurriedly,
"we'd best hurry or you'll be late for supper. You
need to look well tonight. You're to be guest of
honor."

The reminder dampened Frey's spirits and
made her wrinkle her freckled nose. "I know," she
sighed. "You will have to instruct me on how to
behave, Hilda, for I've never supped with an earl
and countess before. I fear I might disgrace my
lord."

"No, never, my lady!"

Smiling at the maid's swift loyalty, Frey bade
her, "Come, unlace me, and tell me how you come
to be here in Chester."

"Why . . . I'm with the countess's household,"
Hilda replied in surprise, her fingers busy in the
side lacings of Frey's travelling kirtle.

"The countess?" Frey was astounded. "Is that why you were in York? You came with the countess?"

"Why, yes. I thought you knew that, my lady. I go everywhere with the countess. But, because of the wedding and all, I was lent to serve you at the earl's house in York."

"I see."

"And then," Hilda went on, "when Lord fitzHugh dismissed me, I went back to the service of the countess and her ladies."

"I didn't know," Frey sighed, shrugging out of her gown and going to wash her hands and face. That terrible day in York, when Blaize had accused her of poisoning herself to keep him at bay, came back in every hurtful detail, saddening her. With the towel in her hands she turned to say, "Hilda . . . I'm sorry for the trouble I brought you. Forgive me, please. To be suspected of aiding me to poison myself cannot have been pleasant for you."

"No, my lady, though I never blamed you for it. He jumped to conclusions because he was angry. I could see that."

"And I don't suppose he gave you much chance to deny the charges," Frey guessed.

Hilda pulled her mouth awry. "That he didn't, my lady, hard though I tried to defend myself—and you. He wouldn't listen to me. And it wasn't my place to trade arguments with a baron, especially when he was in such a fine temper—if you'll pardon my boldness."

"I'm well acquainted with his temper," Frey said sadly, hanging the towel back on its pole. "And I fear you may have to face more of it, Hilda, for in a moment of anger I told him about the philtre you put in the wine."

Hilda's rosy cheeks lost some of their color at this news, though "Oh" was all she said.

"Perhaps he's forgotten about it by now," Frey said hopefully.

"He's not one to forget a thing like that," Hilda replied, bracing herself as if to face the onslaught as she added briskly, "But don't you worry, my lady. If he speaks to me about it I'll tell him the truth."

"Yes, do that. I'm sure he'll understand." Frey wasn't quite as sure as she sounded, though surely by now Blaize's anger over the love potion must have cooled a little. It all seemed so very long ago. "Oh, I'm so glad you're here, Hilda," she added impulsively. "A friendly face makes such a difference."

While Hilda combed and braided her hair and helped her dress in the rich bridal clothes, Frey questioned her as to how she ought to conduct herself that evening. The answers only added to her confusion; there was so much to learn! Her nervousness was returning, making her palms damp and her heart race as she contemplated the ordeal before her. The feast was to be a celebration, with herself and Blaize as the target for all eyes. With so much hostility between them, how would they ever conceal it from the curiosity of the earl's court?

Frey was almost ready when a page came to inform Hilda that she was required to attend on Lord fitzHugh as soon as she had finished dressing his wife.

"I shall come in a moment," Hilda said, finishing organizing the folds of Frey's light veil before slipping a silver circlet round her brow to complete the toilette. As Frey stood up, the maid surveyed her critically, then smiled, "You're a picture, my lady. Lord fitzHugh will be the proudest man in the court tonight. Now, by your leave, I'll go and attend him."

"Yes, do so. And, Hilda—" Trying to convey everything with her voice and eyes, she ended simply, "Good luck."

Hilda departed with her shoulders squared, leaving Frey hoping that the matter of the love potion would not bring too much more trouble for the maid. Hilda must be regretting the day she was ever assigned to the service of Lady fitzHugh.

However, whatever transpired between Blaize and Hilda did not take long; within a very short time, it seemed, the door of Frey's chamber opened again and Blaize himself appeared, still garbed in the flowing ochre robe that made him look so tall and imperious. Behind him in the hall the noise was growing as people gathered for supper.

He shut the noise out, closing the door, looking Frey up and down critically and appreciatively, unable to conceal the glow of satisfaction in his dark eyes.

"At least you look like a bride," he commented grudgingly. "Can you play the part convincingly?"

"I hope so," Frey said, rubbing her damp palms together. "My lord . . . did you see Hilda?"

"Hilda?"

"I hope you haven't asked the countess to punish her for what happened in York. It was well meant, my lord. She never intended to do me harm."

Blaize shook his head, his brow furrowing and his eyes suddenly unfocused as dour thoughts moved behind them. "No trouble will come to Hilda, my lady. Set your mind at ease on that." His frown said that he planned trouble for someone else, however, but before Frey could fully interpret the expression on his face it changed, softening as his mind returned again to her. "Why have you braided your hair? I prefer it loose, as it was on our wedding day—as it was that midsummer night you fled from the Viking. Do you remember?"

She remembered it much too clearly, and when he looked at her in that way, with that languorous, lascivious amusement in his eyes, she knew he could very easily enchant her again. "I remember," she said quietly.

"Then come to me," he suggested, holding out his arms. "Begin to play the sweet willing wife now, before we go into the hall."

Slowly, obediently, she stepped forward, her eyes on his so that she read the faint derision in him as she stopped only inches away. She expected him to sweep his arms around her. Instead he looked her over deliberately, examining every inch of her curvaceous slenderness, her pale, natural beauty; then he took her face between his hands, holding it as if it were a delicate flower.

"Plain and countrified,. my lady?" he inquired in a charged undertone. "Indeed, that's a lie! You're the most beautiful woman in this castle. And you're mine!"

As if to demonstrate this fact, he kissed her upturned mouth with a sweet passion that made her breathless, her heart thudding so loud in her ears that she almost failed to hear the first notes of a trumpet fanfare from the hall. A tenuous hope took root in her heart. Dared she believe that he meant what he said—that he was proud of her, felt possessive about her?

The fanfare went on, silvery and piercing even through the solid oak door.

Blaize released her and stepped back, taking a deep breath before saying raggedly, "That's for us. The celebrations begin!"

As he opened the door to the chamber, the fanfare sounded louder. Servants parted the tapestries and Lord fitzHugh led his bride out into the great hall of Chester castle, where knights and ladies stood waiting by long tables down each side of the room. Applause greeted the recently wed pair and Frey was glad of the yellow torchlight that flared from the walls; it would hide most of her embarrassed blushes as it would conceal the sweetly bruised swell of lips so recently ravaged by her husband's attentions.

Across the end of the room, waiting behind the high table on the dais, stood the most important nobles of the earl's court. All of them were gorgeously attired, glinting with gold and jewels, and at the center of the table the earl and his countess waited to greet their guests of honor with kisses—for Frey these came hot and wet from Earl Hugh, coldly formal from his wife. Frey was placed on the earl's left, with Blaize at her side translating his father's jovial remarks to her. And so the feast began.

The meal went on for what seemed hours, dish after dish being paraded in by a stream of servants: savories and sweetmeats, roasts and stews, washed down by rivers of wine. Countess Arlette picked at her food and said very little, conversing only occasionally with the earl's chancellor, a dry stick of a man who sat to her right, and as the meal progressed the earl too forgot his attempts to entertain his new daughter-in-law, much to Frey's relief. She herself was so nervous she could eat hardly anything and, remembering her experience on her wedding night, she drank sparingly too. She must not disgrace herself tonight. She remained in a fever of hope fuelled by her recollection of the way Blaize had kissed her before they left their chamber. If all could be well between them, how happy she would be!

Beside her the earl became absorbed in eating, drinking, and shouting with laughter at the antics of his fool, the dancing bear that performed, the tumblers, and the men balancing swords. After the balancing, a minstrel stepped up with a lute and sang several songs, most of which the company seemed to know and some of which they joined in with, loudly and raucously.

A final course of food was announced by another blare of trumpets. This consisted of yet more wine and baskets of dainty tidbits to fill any spare corners that might have gone unstuffed by the rest of the fare. Central to the procession, two cooks in white aprons carried aloft on a golden platter what to Frey was a wonderous sight—an edifice of sugar and pastry artfully formed to resemble a wicker cage containing two birds entwined. The sight of this confection made the earl shout with laughter and bellow some remark that caused a general howl of merriment around the hall.

"They're turtledoves—lovebirds," Blaize informed Frey under his breath, by way of explanation.

"Ah," she responded, not daring to look at him.

Answering loud calls from some of the men in the main body of the hall, Blaize lifted his golden goblet in acknowledgment, smiling as if their comments pleased and amused him, though Frey saw that the smiles were not entirely truthful.

"What are they saying?" she asked.

"It's better that you don't know," he replied with a look that told her the remarks were ribald. Frey felt herself flush at the thought, which brought more approving hoots of laughter.

And then there was dancing.

Musicians up on the circular gallery played while couples formed intricate patterns on the floor below. Frey noticed some intimate fumbling and fondling between knights and ladies under the flare of torchlight and the influence of wine. The earl suggested that she and Blaize should join in the dance, but Blaize demurred on the ground that his bride was unacquainted with the steps.

However, after several similar measures the earl

grew insistent—he was determined to have the pleasure of watching his son dance with his new bride.

"He says you've been watching long enough to learn the steps," Blaize informed Frey. "I fear we must do as he wishes."

So she was led out to join the merry throng and was surprised to find herself enjoying the dance, parading on Blaize's hand or with his arm at her waist, turning with him, smiling at him. The steps were not difficult at all, once she overcame her shyness. The dancing was delightful.

In her heart the echo of her husband's passionate declaration still lingered—"*You're mine!*" —making her dare to hope that perhaps he meant it. Perhaps he did care for her a little, after all. Perhaps . . .

And that was when she caught a flash of jealous blue eyes and realized that Melissande was among the company.

The sight of the beautiful lady-in-waiting was sufficient to make Frey play her part of adoring bride with ever more abandon, solely to convince Melissande that she no longer had total control over Blaize's heart. She smiled flirtatiously up into her husband's dark eyes, brushing closer when the dance required her to pass him, and she was gratified to see that he appeared to be equally engrossed in her, as if he were fascinated by her, enchanted and made eager for the night by her enticing behavior. He too might be playing a part, in order to befool his father's court into believing that all was well between him and his Saxon bride, but more and more she allowed herself to believe that it was not all pretense.

Perhaps, after all, he had forgotten his love for the unattainable Melissande.

When they returned to the high table, the earl

demanded a dance with his son's wife and once
again Frey was led out to the floor. This occasion
was less agreeable; Earl Hugh was clumsy with
drink, his hands hot and errant, and he kept
making blurred remarks that were imcomprehen-
sible to Frey. The countess, still at the high table,
sipped her wine and looked bored; evidently she
was accustomed to her lord's brutish behavior.

There came a moment when the earl tripped
over the hem of his own robe and, releasing Frey in
his efforts to save himself, stumbled into another
couple, knocking them down. Earl Hugh sprawled
with them, bellowing with laughter, and one of the
dogs came dashing up, starting to bark in excitement.

Someone cursed and kicked the dog aside. It
vanished under a table with its tail between its legs,
while a crowd gathered round to help the lord of
the castle to his feet. In the uproar, Frey found
herself pushed aside and temporarily disregarded.
She saw that she was near the arched entry to one
of the shadowed, twisting stairways that led up to
the gallery. Hoping for a few moments of rest and a
chance to catch her breath in privacy, she slipped
away and climbed the winding stair.

She came out at a spot opposite the place where
the musicians still played despite the growing dis-
order of the party below. This side of the gallery
was mostly in shadow, light coming only from
torches in the hall below as Frey took shelter
behind the cool stone of a pillar, using it as a shield
as she mopped her brow and peered down into the
whirl of noise and color.

The evening was degenerating into a drunken
spree. One or two of the knights lay slumped across
the tables in a stupor. From this vantage point Frey
could see that once-white tableclothes were stained
with wine and food, and the scented rushes on the

floor had been kicked into heaps strewn with bones and pieces of offal. Dogs chewed on the bones, getting under the feet of the dancers. Yelping and barking joined the furore. The dancing grew ever wilder, the fumbling more overt. More than one couple embraced passionately in shadowed corners and one pair came up the stairs, not even seeing Frey as they went on to the upper story where the ladies' bower and the pages' quarters were located.

Below in the hall two men were arguing. One pushed the other. A fight broke out between them. No one took the least notice, except to stay clear of flying fists. It was disgraceful, Frey thought. Even at Ketilfiord, even on the wildest occasions when Wulfnoth had been alive, she had never seen behavior such as she now witnessed in the noble court of the Earl of Chester, second in power to the king. It convinced her, if she needed further convincing, that she had not the least wish to stay at the castle a moment longer than she had to.

She laid a hand to her head, which was beginning to pound, and as she did so she froze, her gaze riveted to the far corner of the hall, to an alcove where flickering torchlight barely reached. There, a pair of lovers were ensconced. Despite the shadows enfolding them, Frey recognized the couple at once: one was Melissande, unmistakable with her golden hair gilded by a faint glow of torchlight.

The other figure—the male half of the amorous couple—was Frey's husband.

XII

Stricken with despair, Frey watched the pair in the corner. They were oblivious to everything around them, aware only of themselves. The sight of them destroyed all Frey's foolish hopes. Of course Blaize hadn't forgotten Melissande. Men such as he did not forget their first true love, however long they lived, or whatever other women they might use to pass away a sad moment, or a lonely hour—or a loveless lifetime.

Their very attitudes were enough to announce their relationship to anyone who cared to look. Melissande had her back turned to Frey, her hair streaming free in golden waves, her head thrown back to look up straight into Blaize's eyes as he bent over her, intent on her alone. He was holding her hand close to his heart, his whole demeanor that of a tender lover pleading for favor—or perhaps for forgiveness. Evidently Melissande was proving stubborn; perhaps she was jealous, angry with him for playing the fond husband so well. Frey saw her shake her golden head and try to pull away, but Blaize restrained her, seeming to be increasing his pleading. He did not intend to let her go until he had extracted the promises for which he was so anxious—perhaps a tryst for later, when everyone was asleep.

Frey could read every nuance just as clearly as if she were close enough to hear their words. She felt physically sick, her stomach churning and nausea burning at the back of her throat. Not wishing to witness more of that intimate scene between the lovers, she turned blindly and stumbled back down the darkened steps, hardly knowing what she was doing.

The revellers in the hall presented a daunting barrier that would prevent her from easily reaching her room. If she tried to push by she was terrified that a hand might strike out and stop her, someone might cry, "Ha, the bride!" and force her back into the center of attention. She couldn't have borne that. She had to escape from the suffocation of that place.

She took the nearest available route—the stairway dwn to the guardroom.

The stair was in almost perfect darkness, so that Frey was obliged to feel her way, her fingers groping round the smooth curve of cold stone walls, her slippers seeking for the edge of each section of step. Through the slit windows she glimpsed the occasional twinkle of a lantern somewhere in the city, or the red flicker of a guard fire on the castle rampart, but most of the buildings lay dark, slumbering under their pall of smoke, bathed in lambent moonlight.

A surge of hoarse laughter from below made her pause by one of the window openings, her mind clearing of its anguished panic. Where did she think she was going? The guardroom lay between her and the outer stairs; if she tried to leave she would be stopped, or her passing reported at once to Blaize or his father. And even if she did gain the outer stair there were still the courtyard to cross, the gate and its portcullis to be outwitted, and beyond them the sprawling city itself, under

curfew with the watch on the alert, and then the
barred and guarded gates in the ancient Roman
walls . . .

Fist to mouth, she bit her knuckles hard as
punishment for her stupidity. This was not
Ketilfiord, where escape to cool woods could be
maneuvered with just a little cunning and stealth.
Here in the castle of Chester she was no better than
a prisoner. Lord fitzHugh's wife would never be
allowed to pass unescorted and unremarked.

Oh, fool, Frey! Did she really want to rouse
Blaize's anger over behavior that was sure to
embarrass him? Weren't there problems enough
between them?

Blaize! Blaize and Melissande . . . the memories
of seeing them together made her head feel tight
and brought tears stinging behind her eyes while a
scream of anguish gathered in her throat. There
was no mistake. No mistake! All evening she had
allowed herself to hope, like a fool. There was no
hope. Blaize didn't care for her. He had never cared;
he never *would* care. It was Melissande he loved. All
Frey could ever be was a poor substitute.

Leaning on the curve of the wall, she closed her
eyes and took a few deep breaths. What, after all,
had happened that was worse than before? She had
suspected for weeks that some deep tie of affection
bound Blaize to Melissande. Tonight she had simply
had it confirmed.

Yes, that was why it hurt so much: before, she
had only suspected, had cherished the tiny hope
that she might be wrong. But now she knew, for
sure, that her marriage was a sham and could never
by anything else.

Well, so be it. If it was fated thus, she would
find some way to live with it. Perhaps it wouldn't
hurt so much once Blaize had gone on to Triffordd
and left her to molder at the court—left her to the

mercies of the fair and jealous Melissande.

Feeling so battered that nothing else could harm her, she forced her heavy legs to carry her back up the stairs. In the great hall, as fortune willed it, she passed unremarked by the riotous merrymakers as she edged round close to the tapestried walls, found the door to her chamber and slipped inside. Softly she closed the door behind her, leaning on it in emotional exhaustion.

The room was softly lit by candles in sconces on the walls. Wax candles. Such riches! At Ketilfiord there had been only rushlights, dim and uncertain, but for all the wealth and luxury that surrounded her now she heartily wished herself back in that simple manor house with her family about her.

The very thought of it brought stinging tears to fill her eyes. She trailed across the room and sank down on the bed, her head in her hands.

After a while the door latch clicked and the noise from the hall sounded louder. Frey shot to her feet, hurriedly wiping the tears from her face with a kerchief as she heard Blaize exchange some last witticism with a man who slurred his words with drink. Then her husband came in, still clad in the rich robes that suited him so well.

Even in the dim candlelight, Frey say that his argument with Melissande had left its mark in the thinning of his lips and hard lines about his face. As he looked at her he forced a smile, though even that failed to lift the bleakness from his eyes.

"I've had my fill of merriment, too," he said. "Such feasts are not to my taste. I prefer to be alone with you, Aelfreya."

"Yes, my lord." She turned her shoulder to him, folding the damp kerchief and laying it on the nightstand, hoping to give her face time to lose some of the puffiness of weeping.

A low laugh escaped him as he stepped toward

her and caught her arm, spinning her to face him. "Shy, are we? Or pretending so? Ah, come, good wife. There is no longer need for coyness between us."

As he bent over her, she felt the sexual tension in him and saw the smoldering desire in his eyes. All too clearly she recognized the cause of his arousal, and she knew that it had nothing to do with her: he had been drinking all evening, and then he had been talking with Melissande, indulging in a lovers' tiff. It was Melissande who had roused him to the lust Frey sensed in him. Melissande must have sent him away. Now he expected his wife to assuage the hunger in his body which another woman had fired.

Involuntarily she winced and turned her face away from him. Blaize stopped short, his expression hardening as he straightened and stared down at her, a frown creasing between his brows.

"What's this?"

"I'm tired," she said, pulling free of his grasp.

For a moment longer he watched her in puzzled annoyance, then his mouth twisted as he realized her intent. "So the pretense is done with, is it? It *was* just pretense."

What else had he expected? she thought bitterly. Did he really think she could so easily forget all the pain that divided them? "Is that not what you asked of me?" she returned. "To play the bride and not disgrace you? I believe I carried out the request as well as could be expected. And you too were acting out a role, my lord, do not deny it. We both make convincing mummers."

He paused for a long moment, his eyes glowing, his brow darkened with a weary anger that had her quaking. His hands clasped and unclasped convulsively, as if he would have liked to have them at her throat; sensing the threat, she cowered away even further and saw the contempt that twisted his lips.

Jerking at the knot at his waist, he let the golden girdle fall to the floor as he said grimly, "To bed, wife. We've a long journey to make tomorrow."

For a moment she was distracted as she realized that he intended to undress in front of her. He was drawing the ochre robe over his head and hanging it on its pole, leaving himself in the long undertunic, breeches and stockings; then as he bent to sweep up the hem of the undertunic, the import of his words registered in her startled mind.

"We?" she repeated breathlessly, her hands to her throat. "We are *both* leaving tomorrow?"

He paused briefly to afford her a hard, unreadable look. "Aye, you heard me right. I've changed my plans. I've decided that you shall come to Triffordd with me after all."

"Oh," Frey said, unable to understand what had prompted this change of heart, or to articulate her relief. "Oh—"

"Is that relief or dismay?" he mocked, continuing to undress. Within seconds he had stripped himself of everything but his linen breeches, and in the candlelight his brown skin, shadowed with a light growth of hair, seemed to gleam with a vibrant, tactile life. He looked at her sidelong, asking sardonically, "Do you need some help with your clothes?"

Frey swallowed hard, clenching her hands until her nails bit into her flesh. Her palms were damp with nerves, but her fingers were tingling with the urge to stroke her husband's flesh. How fine he was—tall, well-shaped, taut of muscle under warm olive skin. Too well she remembered the delights of lying with him and feeling that strong body blend with her own. Part of her longed to repeat that ecstatic conjoining of flesh. Part of her longed to have the courage to undress in front of him and let his eyes enjoy their banquet before his hands and body took their fill.

But it was not her he wanted. He had come to her straight from Melissande, his blood stirred by Melissande, his senses full of the sight, sound and scent of the golden-haired woman he loved! He would close his eyes and pretend that it was Melissande, not Frey, he held in his arms. The knowledge was a torment.

"My lord—" she managed in a strangled voice.

He tilted his dark head sardonically, taunting her. "My lady?"

"Will you . . . Will you please blow out the candles?"

"And have you fumbling in the darkness?" he asked, all mocking consideration. "No, indeed. By all means let us use the lights while we have them. Why play the coy virgin, wife? I have already seen you naked." He remained where he was—between her and the candles—his dark-haired arms folded across his broad chest, waiting.

Stricken with hot waves of self-consciousness but knowing she had little choice but to obey, Frey turned her back to him, beginning to unfasten the side lacings of the velvet gown. It was true that he had seen her naked before, but that had been in the heat of lovemaking, when her natural modesty was swamped in her need of him. Being obliged to divest herself of her clothes in full sight of his cold, probing eyes was another matter entirely.

A shudder ran through her. Her whole body and all the veins in it seemed to be throbbing in time to the beat of one huge pulse and her face burned as she drew the gown over her head and felt it taken from her hands by her husband, who with every appearance of helpfulness hung it on its pole.

"Thank you," Frey croaked.

"My pleasure." He returned to his former stance with a face as immobile as carved oak.

Waiting again. Waiting for more.

Clad in her long-sleeved yellow undertunic, Frey began slowly to unbraid her hair, shaking it free to fall in long rippling strands about her shoulders and down her neck, combing it through with her fingers. Then still resolutely turned away from Blaize, reaching for the complicated back lacings of her undertunic.

Suddenly Blaize was right behind her, his hands on hers stopping their movement. Her heart jumped in alarm and started to race, beating suffocatingly in her throat, the pulse like a trapped bird.

"This requires my help," he observed, parting her hair at her nape, letting his fingers run voluptuously through the silken waterfall as he stroked it aside, over her shoulders, until the heavy locks fell in front of her in two long swaths.

He began to unlace the tunic very carefully, maddening Frey, his fingers deliberately brushing her spine through the muslin shift she wore next to her skin. The yellow undertunic parted down to her hips and his hands came on her shoulders, easing the linen free with such slow sensuality that her whole body responded irresistibly. She felt her breasts tauten, the nipples catching on the muslin of her shift, and at the center of her body, deep in her womb, something began to flow with desire.

"Are you cold?" he enquired softly as another irrepressible shiver ran through her.

It was not the cold that made her tremble but the touch of his long fingers, and the thought of his lovemaking, though she said, "A little."

"You'll be warmer in bed," he assured her; the assurance only made her tremble more, thinking of the method he would employ to warm her. Lust without love, carnality without caring.

She could not be so cold, she knew. Already her senses were beginning to take over from her mind, despite her willing herself to remain unmoved. But she would not respond, however skillfully he tried to rouse her. She would not. Not this time!

Under his sensually slow urging, the tunic was pushed from her arms, slid from her hips and left to slither about her feet. She stepped out of its folds, away from him, dressed only in her muslin shift as she turned to look at him with veiled eyes, her arms folded about herself.

Blaize drew a deep breath as he looked her up and down, savoring the sight she made in the sheer fabric undergarment. His eyes were glimmering with a strange light as he studied her face for endless moments, his expression implacable. Shaking, Frey waited for the final humiliation—the order to take off her shift and reveal herself completely to his eyes.

Without haste, he bent and swept up the yellow tunic, hung it up alongside the green velvet, and to her relief calmly turned to pinch out the candles one by one.

Frey let out the breath she had not known she was holding. The shutters at the window had been closed by the servants. Now the room was in total darkness, filled with the faint acrid tang of smoke from the extinguished candles, and with the vibrant, if invisible, presence of Blaize fitzHugh.

Out of that darkness his voice came mercilessly: "And the shift, if you please." After a moment of silence, he added in a threatening undertone, "Lady, if you refuse me I swear I'll tear it from you!"

Frey strained to see him in the darkness but could make out no shape but floating monsters produced by her own mind. She trembled, clutching the thin shift round her, knowing it was no protection against him, or against the surge of desire that had become an ache inside her. That ache betrayed her, denied everything she had ever believed or hoped for, but there was no ignoring it. Blaize fitzHugh had turned her into a wanton, made her want him even when she knew his real feelings were fixed on someone else. "Oh, why didn't you stay with Melissande?" she cried in despair. "These games might have amused her. They do not amuse *me*, sir!"

There was a silence so profound she could hear the blood singing in her own ears. Then: "Melissande?" His voice was ominously quiet, filled with nuances of threat. "Lady, I'll not deny this castle has its goodly share of indiscretions, but do you really expect me to add to the score? I find your suggestion insulting—and so would Lord Delmonde, were he not away in Normandy."

"Delamonde?" she managed. "Who—?"

"The lady Melissande's husband."

Melissande was married! she thought with a shock. Ah, but that explained so much! That explained why she was out of reach even for Blaize fitzHugh, the earl's son.

She cried out in fright as without more ado Blaize reached for her, his hands finding the arms she huddled to her breast. When she tensed to resist him he grasped both her wrists, pulling them down and away from her body, stepping so close to her that she could feel he was naked and aroused. In that instant of shock, she forgot about Melissande, about everything but the sensual power of the man to whom she was married.

His arms swept round her waist, pulling her full against him as he muttered, "You're my wife, Frey. My wife! Don't deny me now. I'm in sore need of you."

A hand behind her head held her still while his lips caressed her face, eagerly but gently, nibbling, coaxing. She hardened herself to resist, hating her body for its willingness to lean against him, plaint as a willow, but the feel of his skin against hers through nothing but the sheerest muslin, of his arms hard and urgent about her, his lips pressing kisses on her throat, her face, then finding her mouth . . . it was all too sweet for a lost and lonely woman to resist.

As he kissed her mouth a moan that was both protest and surrender shuddered out of her and a shock of heat ran through her. In that moment she was transformed from thinking, reasoning, resisting womanhood to willing wanton wife, compliant to his every demand, ignoring the last protests of pride and common sense. The small warning voices trailed away, smothered under the mounting beat in her blood as she twined her arms around her husband and let her hands enjoy the smooth warm contours of his body.

Catching his breath at her first touch, he did as he had threatened—he tore the gossamer shift from her. The thin threads parted easily under his urgent, ardent hands, and the shreds of the shift fell from her as he groaned in pleasure at his freedom to caress her with no more barriers between them. He eased her backwards to lie across the bed, rousing her with hands and mouth and body until once again she was aching, needing, arching herself in silent, mindless pleading for him to take her. Nothing mattered but that.

This time the consummation came simultaneously, overwhelming both of them as he sank into her and she heard herself cry aloud. Blaize too muttered something—a curse or a prayer, she couldn't tell—as the shudders of fulfillment coursed through his taut body.

She lay breathless under her husband's heavy, sated weight as he kissed her bruised and swollen mouth and murmured, "Forgive me, Frey. Forgive me."

Forgive him for what? she wondered. There was nothing to forgive. Only he could make her feel so much a woman, so fulfilled . . .

Then as if she had plunged into an icy pool she fell from pink clouds of euphoria and remembered the truth of things—the bleak mood he had been in when he entered the chamber; his cold, arrogant sensuality; all caused by his quarrel with Melissande . . .

Now in the secret darkness tears came welling to her eyes—and with them came bitterness. So he had won, after all. He had what he wanted. By feigning tenderness he had robbed her of every last shred of pride, made her respond to him with warmth, made her reach out for him and cry aloud in her ecstasy, but for him it was just a temporary relief for the hunger in his blood—a hunger of lust that Melissande had kindled in him. In the darkness who could tell one woman from another?

Suddenly his weight was unwelcome to her. She shifted under him and he lifted himself to lie beside her, sighing hugely. "I'm not so strong as I thought myself. I imagined I could lie naked beside you and do nothing. But the temptation was too great." He turned to her again, touching her hair and her cheek with tender fingers. "You make a fever in my blood. Forgive me, Frey."

"There's nothing to forgive, my lord," she answered quietly, calmly, the words echoing in the emptiness that filled her soul as tears dripped down her face into her hair. "I am your wife. You used me as was your right."

"Don't speak such words," he begged. He raised himself, leaning to kiss her cold lips while his fingers trembled across her face and paused, surprised, at the trail of salty wetness flowing across her skin. "Why are you crying? Did I hurt you?"

She shook her head. "No . . . No, you were gentle. For that I'm grateful."

"Grateful? Frey, I don't understand you. Things have not gone well between us, but they will improve from now on. I swear it. When we reach Triffordd—" He stopped himself, adding anxiously, "You will come with me to Triffordd, will you not?"

"Yes, my lord," she replied in that same colorless voice. "I shall come with you." But because she was hurt, because she wanted to lash out and wound him in return for wounds he had inflicted on her, she felt obliged to disabuse him of any mistaken impression he might have formed. "I shall come with you to the Welsh marches—for that is where I hope to find Nicol of Linscote."

He stiffened as though she had slapped him, said, "I see," and after a brief moment he moved away from her, as far as he could in the bed. After that there was silence in the room, with the sea sighing outside in the estuary and a lone gull crying like a lost soul in the night.

Frey hardly slept. All night long she was aware of Blaize tossing restlessly, shifting his position every few minutes as if unable to find comfort. Every time his arm or his foot brushed hers he withdrew as if he couldn't bear the contact and when at last he did sleep his dreams kept him shifting and muttering incoherently. She lay still, staring into the darkness dry-eyed now; her tears were all done, she felt nothing at all.

After hours that seemed like eons, a grayness crept between the shutters, bringing texture and shape out of the darkness. Blaize threw back the blankets and got up, feeling his way across the room and cursing as he scraped his shin on a stool in the shadows. As if he could not bear the half light any longer, he flung the shutters wide and let the dawn glow in.

Lying motionless, feeling empty, Frey watched him sluice himself down at the washstand before pulling on his usual breeches and stockings. He sat down to wind leather thongs over the stockings and put on his boots. Next he donned a fresh shirt and tunic, and his belt with its sheathed dagger. He ran a comb through his hair, straightened his tunic and glanced across at her, unsurprised to find her awake.

"I'll have them bring breakfast for you. Be ready to leave when I send for you."

Frey said nothing. The stony resentment inside her demanded that she not voice her usual obedient, "Yes, my lord." Though she must do as he bade her, she had to make a small stand against fate.

Her silence seemed to infuriate him. He took a stride toward the bed and stopped, looking down at something that had tangled round his boot; bending, he snatched up a piece of muslin, floating and white—the shift he had so eagerly torn from her in the throes of their lovemaking. He dropped it on the bed, affording her a bleak look.

"The Welsh marches are not the Isles of Paradise," he informed her, "though no doubt you may believe them so should you achieve your dream. Is this truly why you married me—to be closer to your Saxon lover?"

Frey merely looked at him, her face pale and composed, her eyes steady on his, revealing nothing of her thoughts.

"Then don't answer!" Blaize exclaimed with an angry gesture. "You answered clearly enough last

night. So be it. You shall go to the Welsh marches, if
that is your desire. And should you find your lover,
and should you choose to fly away with him, then
never fear that I might raise a hue and cry after
you, for I shall not. I heartily repent me of this
marriage, lady. You may go to Nicol of Linscote.
You may go to the very devil, for aught I care!"

He grabbed his cloak from its peg and went out,
shutting the door with a sharp thud behind him.
Frey closed her eyes, wondering how much more
she was supposed to bear.

Then, and only then, did a tear drip down her
temple into her hair, an oblation to girlish dreams
that were lost forever.

After a while, a servant brought breakfast of
soft white bread, milled from the finest wheat,
with a dish of rich butter, a honeycomb dripping
with golden sweetness, and a jug of watered wine.
Though Frey had little appetite she forced herself to
eat since she knew she might be hungry on the
journey to Triffordd.

As she was finishing her meal, a scratching on
the chamber door prefaced the welcome appearance of Hilda—dear, cheery Hilda, whose company
lifted Frey's depression a little.

"I've been attending to those two boys you
brought with you, my lady," Hilda chatted as she
tidied the bed. "Put both of them in a tub and gave
them a good scrubbing down. Not that they liked it
much—especially the older one. Will, is it? I had to
box his ears for him in the end. That made him
behave. His little brother didn't need any more
telling after that. They're not bad lads, as lads go,
under all that dirt and sulky manners. They'll do
well enough at Triffordd once they settled to the life."

"At Triffordd?" Frey wiped sticky honey from
her fingers with a napkin of embroidered linen,

turning wide eyes on the maid. "Has my lord decided that they are to go with us?"

"Indeed he has, my lady. Young Will's to help out with the pack train, though they reckon he'll make a fine soldier one of these days. And little Tam's to be a page at the castle, running messages for the knights. It's all arranged."

"I see." Feeling disconsolate, Frey turned away and drained the last mouthful from her wine cup. She was allowed nothing of her own, not even a say in the fate of the two Saxon boys she had rescued. Blaize commanded everything, it seemed.

From behind her, Hilda said softly, "Don't fret about them, my lady. They'll do well enough. Better than they would have done on the moors alone, or with some robber band. I told them they must never forget they owe it all to your kindness. At least now they'll have a place to stay, and work to do. As for family, why . . . I'll take them under my own wing, if they'll let me."

Puzzled, Frey swung round on the stool to face Hilda. "I thought you said Will and Tam were coming with us to Triffordd?"

"So they are."

"But you're in the countess's service. How can you care for the boys if you're here in—"

Hilda laughed, her face bright with pleasure. "Oh, my lady, don't you know? Why . . . I'm to go with you, too!"

"You are?!" The news brought such relief and pleasure that Frey's own face lost its troubled look.

"Lord fitzHugh has asked the countess to release me," Hilda explained, "and the countess has agreed. She has enough servants round her and she was never very fond of me, seeing I'm Saxon. So I'm to be your maid and your companion, if—" She hesitated, flushing as she concluded somewhat shyly, "if you're agreeable, my lady."

"I can't think of anything that would please me more!" Frey cried, jumping to her feet and throwing out her hands before clasping them at her breast. "Oh, this is the most heartening news I ever heard! In truth, I've been apprehensive of journeying to Wales and staying in a military garrison without the company of another woman. But Hilda . . . what of you? You'll miss your friends here. Glad as I should be to have you with me, I wouldn't wish you to be unhappy."

"Bless you, my lady, I'll not be unhappy! Far from it!" Hilda's cheeks glowed an even more vivid red than usual and her eyes shone. "My Robin—my husband—is among the garrison at Triffordd—been there all winter, and me leagues away at the court in Winchester with the countess. I haven't seen him for months. Now I'll be able to see him every day. Oh, I can hardly wait!"

Her overflowing joy was infectious and made Frey smile. "Then I'm happy for you, Hilda."

"Thank you, my lady," the maid returned, dipping a deep curtsey. "And may God bless you and your lord for all your kindness to me." She straightened, adding briskly, "I've promised him I'll take good care of you. Don't you fret, I'll make sure no more harm comes to you while I'm near."

This assertion caused Frey to wrinkle her brow, unable to follow the maid's reasoning. "Harm?" she repeated blankly. "Oh . . . you mean when I was ill in York?"

Seeming disconcerted, as if she wished she hadn't mentioned the subject, Hilda stumbled over an incoherent reply, color ebbing and flowing in her face.

"But I didn't blame you for that," Frey said. "I know you meant well. Was my lord very angry with you?"

But Hilda seemed reluctant to discuss the

matter. She twisted her apron between her hands and muttered something indistinctly, unable to meet her mistress's eyes.

"Well, never mind it," Frey said, assuming that the maid was embarrassed to be reminded of a mistake which might well have cost Frey her life. "It's over. If Lord fitzHugh has arranged for you to come to Wales then he must have recovered from his annoyance. I'm very glad you'll be with me, Hilda. Very glad indeed."

A moment longer Hilda fidgeted uncomfortably, chewing on a corner of her apron. Then, "And so am I!" she burst out with what seemed unnecessary fervor. She glanced at the door, leaned closer to Frey and lowered her voice as she added, "For if he'd left you here as he planned, I wouldn't like to say what might have—" She stopped herself, a confused look in her eyes as she straightened and turned away to fuss over the perfectly straight fur coverlet. "I mean, you'll be safer at Triffordd, my lady—with Lord fitzHugh, I mean. A woman should be near her man, shouldn't she?"

"Why . . . yes," Frey said, wondering what the maid was suddenly so agitated about. "Yes. And I'm glad you'll be with your Robin again, too. But if we're to make a start on the journey today we'd best not be tardy. My lord will be annoyed if I cause him delay. Please . . . get out some clothes for me."

She began to wash her face and hands, glancing round with a towel blotting her cheeks as Hilda made a little sound and, bending to the floor, swept out from beneath the bed the shredded shift which Blaize had torn from Frey the previous night. As she glanced at Frey over it, her eyes danced with mischief.

"You'll need new clothes if he keeps treating them like this, my lady," she laughed. "Oh, I knew how he would be. A fiery man—that's what I said to

Berta in York. The good Lord give my lady
strength, I said, for fitzHugh's a fiery, lusty man.
Just like my Robin. No wonder you look so tired
this morning. Still, it's a pleasant tiredness."

Bundling up the shift, she stuffed it into her
apron pocket and bustled about her duties.

A pleasant tiredness, Frey thought with a sigh.
How wrong Hilda was. For Frey it was becoming
more a tiredness of heart and soul, a sad emptiness
that she suspected was to be her fate for the rest of
her life.

The chests—all three of them—were packed and
taken away, with Hilda warning the bearers to take
care as she followed to supervise the loading. She
was taking her new duties as personal maid to Lady
fitzHugh very seriously.

As Frey waited alone in the bedchamber, with
the cry of gulls beyond the window and the sea
breeze bringing the shouts of men about their work
in the harbor, a soft click came almost inaudibly.
The latch lifted and the door opened to reveal a
slender figure with golden braids hanging from
beneath a blue veil threaded with gold.

Melissande!

The lady-in-waiting came into the room, carefully closing the door behind her, blue eyes
regarding Frey with a bright hostility that she did
not trouble to conceal. Her open hatred sent a cold
tremor of disquiet up Frey's spine.

Melissande spoke haughtily, in French, saying
something about the countess and her baby son. Did
Frey understand?

"Yes, I think," Frey replied in her own halting
French, wondering at the reason for this unexpected visit from a lady whom she knew to be
her rival and her enemy. "You say Countess Arlette
is . . . is occupied with her baby."

Coolly, Melissande agreed that this was quite

correct. And since the countess had other, more important, things on her mind, she continued, she had sent her lady-in-waiting to say her farewells to Lady fitzHugh—and to bring a parting gift as a token of friendship and family affection.

As she mentioned a gift, Melissande produced something from the draping folds of her wide embroidered sleeve.

The gift was an object that dangled from a thin leather thong and as Melissande came nearer Frey saw that it was an amulet, shaped like a gnarled and warty toad. It was rather ugly, but Frey had seen such things before and had been given to understand that their intent belied their looks: made of wood, these kind of amulets were meant to be worn as good luck charms, to drive away demons and despair.

Why the countess should consider she needed guarding from evil things Frey could not imagine. She did not much care for the gift; however well-intended, it remained an ugly thing to behold. But it would have been bad manners to refuse any gift from the countess. No doubt Arlette had meant it kindly, Frey thought, telling herself that she ought to be flattered, especially when the earl's wife had shown no real interest in her until now.

Making it clear that she was merely the countess's messenger, and an unwilling one at that, Melissande glided forward with the amulet and reached to tie it around Frey's neck, murmuring under her breath words that Frey could not catch. Her sweet perfume came cloyingly in Frey's nostrils, catching at the back of her throat. She recalled that she had detected a hint of that same perfume on Blaize last night.

The memory reopened wounds that had had no time to heal. Blaize loved Melissande, but Melissande was already married to another man and therefore out of his reach. So it was Frey, his substitute wife, who would travel with him to Wales while Melissande remained behind. Was her jealousy to be wondered at?

Frey caught herself feeling almost sorry for her fair rival, feeling an empathy with Melissande. Fate had been unkind to them both, as it often was to women of their time. Who was the most unhappy—the hopeless lover or the unwanted wife?

Having fastened the thong in a knot, Melissande stepped back as if to admire the way the charm lay against Frey's breast. Long lashes veiled her vivid blue eyes as she dipped a deep curtsey and said, "*A dieu, beldame fitzHugh.*"

The choice of words, and the throaty tone of her voice, struck Frey as odd. *A dieu*—"go with God"—had nuances of finality. It was as though Melissande expected never to see her again.

But Frey had no time to ponder over the puzzle; another incident intervened. As Melissande turned for the door, Hilda returned.

Serving maid and lady-in-waiting both stopped short, seeming disconcerted by the meeting. The ingenuous Hilda, who could never hide her feelings, paled visibly and Melissande hissed something which made the maid edge away from the door. The slender, velvet-clad figure slipped away leaving the tapestries wafting in her wake and Hilda closed the door behind her, looking worried as she turned to Frey.

"Oh, my lady! What did *she* want?"

"She came to say goodbye, on behalf of the countess," Frey said, wondering what could be wrong with everyone that morning. The air seemed alive with undercurrents and Hilda was unwontedly edgy. Or was it only that she, Frey, was suffering from an excess of nervous imagination? "Are you afraid of the lady

Melissande, Hilda?'' she asked in bewilderment.
"What was it she said to you?"

Hilda's eyes slid away from hers as the maid
went to pick up the travelling cloak. "It was
nothing, my lady," she prevaricated. "Just—'Get out
of my way.' She's angry with me over something I
did."

"Why, what did you do?"

Hilda shrugged. "It's not important, my lady.
And, begging your leave, there's no time for
talking. Will you put your cloak on now? Lord
fitzHugh expects us in the courtyard."

Frey swung the heavy cloak round her, slipping
her arms into the sleeves and allowing Hilda to tie
the ties. Catching sight of the frog amulet hanging
at Frey's breast, the maid caught her breath and
lifted troubled eyes that asked questions.

'It's a good luck charm," Frey said, denying the
doubts that moved like snakes in the back of her
own mind. The amulet was harmless; of course it
was. To imagine anything else would be foolishness. "Surely you're acquainted with such things?
The countess sent it to me as a parting gift."

"It came from the countess? Oh, I see." Hilda
seemed relieved. "Then that's all right, my lady."

The great hall was as busy as it had been the
previous day, with people crowding in, most of
them intent on reaching the ear of the earl with
petitions and grievances. Few of them took note of
Frey as she quietly made her way among them. But
as she approached the arched opening to the stairs
she was surprised when Earl Hugh himself broke
away from a group of men and insisted on giving
her several wet kisses on either cheek, smiling at
her and saying in French that his son was a lucky
fellow, or some such flattery. Frey blushed and
curtseyed in reply, hardly knowing how to deal
with the man. She heard him laugh as he moved

back to the knot of men with whom he had been
talking.

"He likes the ladies," Hilda muttered darkly. "I
feel sorry for his wife. Not that she seems to care
much. Now that she's given him his only legitimate
son and heir, she goes her own way."

"Yes, I thought the lady Melissande mentioned a
baby," Frey replied. "How old is he?"

"He was born last harvest. They call him
Richard."

Born last harvest? Frey thought in surprise. But
the countess had spent the winter in Winchester!
"Did she take so small a baby with her to court?"
she enquired.

Hilda looked astounded. "Indeed not, my lady!
She left him here with his wet nurse."

"Oh—of course," Frey said, berating her own
stupidity. "I had forgotten that great ladies do not
suckle their own children. I'm unused to the ways
of nobility, Hilda."

"Well, don't worry, it'll be different at
Triffordd," the maid comforted. "You'll set your
own rules of conduct there. I'm not sorry to be
leaving this place, either. I was never very happy
here. My home's where Robin is, and that's at
Triffordd."

And where, Frey wondered, was her home to
be? A wave of near unbearable homesickness swept
her as she remembered Ketilfiord and her family.
Even the vinegarish Edith had not scorned to nurse
her babes at her own breast—sickly Lucy, who had
died, then young Wulfnoth and next little Eadric.
Edith had once said that the pleasures of suckling
were a compensation for the pain of birthing. That
was something great ladies must miss.

All at once Frey found herself facing the
thought of herself bearing a child—Blaize's child!
Already a baby might be growing in her womb,

seeded by passion but not by love. Dear God . . . she
could not decide which emotion beat most strongly
in her breast at the idea of bearing Blaize's
child—was it excitement, or was it sheer breath-
catching terror?

Forcing the panicky thoughts away, along with
her longing for home, she went on down the stairs
that wound inside the wall's thickness and came at
last to the inner courtyard, where she was obliged
to set her mind fully to the journey ahead. The place
was busy with masons hammering as they worked
on completing the keep; knights and men-at-arms
came and went about their duties, and by the gates
a crowd of jostling people argued vociferously with
the earl's stewards as they pleaded for an audience
with Hugh of Chester. There were horses, too, including the enlarged pack train which Blaize
fitzHugh was taking with him to Triffordd.

Blaize himself was standing by Frey's palfrey,
waiting to help her up to the saddle. The sight of
him brought back memories of all that had
occurred between them the previous night—his
forcing her to undress while he watched, and then
the darkness, redolent with the acrid tang of
extinguished candles, and his cool sensuality
rousing her to intense heights of desire and fulfillment. She felt her face burn as she came near
enough to touch him and experience again the
vibrant life-force that seemed to reach out and
encompass her, claiming her as his property.

But whatever Blaize was thinking he hid it
behind veiled eyes. After one bleak glance at her he
bent and cupped his hands for her foot. All he said
was, "Make haste, my lady. We must be away."

XIII

It was an inauspicious day for journeying, with rain falling across the city and its harbor, sweeping in opaque, soaking waves across the estuary and hiding all sight of the sea. That rain, driven by a swirling wind, drove against Frey's face and made her bend against it, her hood drawn round her face. Tiny trickles of water seeped down her cheeks and found their way down her neck.

A great company rode out from the castle—knights and soldiers with their crimson and white pennants aflutter, servants and laden mules and packhorses. Toward the center of the procession Frey rode on her palfrey with Hilda beside her. Blaize was somewhere ahead among the knights of his personal guard, who included Sir Henry and Sir Simon, and Frey had been glad to see Will and Tam, both scrubbed clean and wearing decent warm clothes, accompanying the pack train.

Along the crowded, twisting streets of Chester, citizens stopped to stare at the cavalcade, some of them hailing various members of the party whom they recognized, wishing them farewell, God's speed, and swift victory over the Welsh. It was a sharp reminder that this was no outing for pleasure. The castle of Triffordd was a military garrison, intended for defensive purposes. These men were bound for war.

Hilda, who was looking forward to seeing her Robin after nearly two years of enforced separation, nevertheless turned nervous as the city walls fell further and further behind and finally merged with the mist while ahead blue mountains clustered on the horizon behind veils of sweeping rain. "I've never been inside Wales before, my lady," the maid chatted, as if to take her mind off her fears.

"Well, neither have I," Frey replied, wiping a raindrop from the end of her nose before it could trickle further. "We shall partake of this new experience together."

"They say the people there are wild, and crafty fighters," Hilda reported. "They don't stand and fight in the open like our soldiers do—fair and honorable. No, these Welshmen attack suddenly from cover, like brigands. My Robin told me so." Frowning worriedly over the fears her imagination roused, she peered at Frey from the shelter of her own rain-dark hood and soothed herself, "But they won't dare attack us while we're on the road, not with so many soldiers in the train. It would take an army to do that. A few brigands would be cut down before they could get near us. Wouldn't they, my lady?"

"If there were any real danger," Frey said, "I doubt that my lord would have brought us along with him, Hilda."

This assurance seemed to comfort the maid, at least for a while.

At first they turned inland, following the broad river Dee away from its estuary until they reached a place shallow enough to ford. The horses splashed through the river, plodding obediently on through the rain, and took the road that led westward, toward the distant mountains that loomed nearer and higher with every hour that passed.

For a while the cavalcade passed ·through
cultivated lands and scattered villages which had
long been settled and civilized, but as they neared
the marches that divided England from Wales the
woods closed in on either hand and when they
crossed the bridge over Offa's dyke—the ancient
fortification that marked the border—they came to
wilder, less inhabited forests. Here the trees had
been cut well back from the road, to hamper any
enemy with ambush in mind.

The silent, mist-shrouded forests brought back
Hilda's fears and she began to chatter again, constantly glancing to either side as if watching for
lurking brigands.

Despite the fierce resistance of the uncivilized
Welshmen, the coastal areas of their country were
slowly being brought under Norman domination.
The Normans were gradually pushing their
influence along the coast from the south and from
Chester to the west, and each time an area was
conquered a mound was thrown up, surrounded by
a palisade, and a wooden castle was built, sturdy
and stern, to house a garrison that would hold the
newly won land. When the central mountains had
been surrounded, then the last pockets of resistance
could be starved out from their rocky fastnesses.

This aim was what preoccupied Blaize and his
men during the fighting season and would do so
until the last petty prince had been winkled out of
his mountain fastness and either slain or persuaded
to swear fealty to the Norman king.

The travellers spent the night at one of the
wooden castles, giving Frey her first notion of what
frontier life might hold for her. This place was
crowded with soldiers and possessed very few
comforts. Rain dripped constantly onto its thatched
roof and its walls seemed to have a million cracks

where drafts crept through. Frey and Hilda slept in
the castellan's chamber off the main hall. Apart
from a few servants—cooks and laundresses—they
were the only women in the castle; the lord of
Rhuddlan had left his lady to enjoy the more
civilized life in Chester.

By morning the weather had cleared and a
bright sun shone down from a sky chased with
white clouds that slowly shredded to leave clear
blue above. Frey saw Blaize only briefly, when once
again he helped her up to her palfrey. He barely
looked at her. He was as cold and impersonal as if he
were made of stone. But that suited her very well,
she told herself bitterly. She preferred him cold
when the alternative was a counterfeit of caring.

They still kept to the lowlands of the coast,
gentle hills covered in fields and woodlands where
in the settlements life went on to the rhythm of the
seasons in a routine that was familiar to Frey. But all
the time to the south of them the mountains drew
closer, rugged summits lifting from deep, impenetrable forests, seeming to be watching and
brooding. The tree-clad wilderness became an
almost living presence, threatening danger.

"That's where those Welshmen hide," Hilda
vouchsafed, looking askance at the tangled wilds
away to their left. "You must take care never to
stray into those forests, my lady. They say that if
some unwary traveller should hack a path through,
it will just grow over behind him and cut him off.
Only the Welsh know the secret ways of those
forests. My Robin told me so."

It was evening, the sun hanging low ahead amid
a nest of golden cloud, when at last the company
emerged from a stretch of open woodland striped
with lenghtening shadows and came within sight
of a shallow valley. Here a spread of fields laid its
stripwork of greens, and a sprawl of thatched

habitations clustered near a place where the road forked. The right fork led away along the coast, as Blaize had once explained to Frey; the left wandered off toward the deep, dark forests, heading for the mountains. But as a focal point that drew all eyes, overlooking valley, village and junction of roads, there towered the double palisades of a sturdy fortress.

A palpable feeling of relief and pleasure rippled along the train and men could be heard exclaiming. "It's Triffordd!" Hilda echoed their cries in a glad voice. "They said we would reach it by nightfall. Oh, my lady, it's Triffordd!"

Frey felt as though she couldn't breathe. Her heart seemed to be beating in her throat, trying to suffocate her. Here then, at last, was the place where she must live her joyless life with Blaize. It looked strange and alien.

She started in nervous alarm as, from the wooden towers and ramparts of the castle's outer palisade, a sudden trumpet blared brazenly, warning the garrison of the return of their castellan. One of Blaize's escort lifted a horn to blow a reply, the sound jubilant as it rang out across the valley. The leading knights of the company dug in their spurs, increasing their speed, smiling at one another, riding eagerly past the spring-green fields and staring peasantry, with lances at the salute and pennants aflutter.

Beyond the plank bridge which gave access across the deep, dry moat, huge gates swung silently open and the thunderous rhythm of hooves on planks echoed out as the company passed through into the broad acres of the outer bailey. Here were grassy areas for practice at arms, sheds for stabling, and buildings that housed smiths, saddlers and armors. Other thatched buildings formed barrack quarters and storehouses, from

which men who had overwintered here now
emerged to greet their returning fellows. This
courtyard was set on a slight slope, leading up to
where another stout palisade with watchtowers
and gatehouse protected the inner bailey and the
main keep whose thatch Frey could see above the
fortifications of the stockade.

As the first gates closed behind them, the train
divided itself, some of the servants and men-at-arms
riding away along with the string of packhorses.
Frey sought the slight forms of Will and Tam, but
the boys seemed contented enough with the
packman. Meanwhile Blaize fitzHugh, with his
main guard—his wife and her maidservant among
them—was riding on to where a drawbridge rattled
down across a natural cleft in the rocky outcrop on
which the castle was built. Hooves clopped
hollowly on the bridge and Frey saw the watch,
armed with spears, standing guard along the
palisade as she passed through the gatehouse and
into the inner courtyard.

Here the space was more confined, built with
kitchens, dormitory huts and more storerooms
around the two-storied central keep. People milled
about, servants about their work, soldiers about
their duties, or taking their ease playing with the
dogs. A knot of men waited by the keep to greet
Blaize as he and his knights rode up.

Apparently he was too interested in hearing
news of the winter's activities to attend to his wife;
it was Sir Henry who came to help Frey dismount,
smiling one of his shy smiles.

"This is your place now," he said in French.
"Your place. You're mistress here. You
understand?"

Frey managed a smile. "Yes, I understand.
Thank you, Henry." But as she looked about the
place, seeing only functional wooden buildings and

men swarming over muddy trodden ground, with no sign of a bush or a tree, let alone a garden, she wondered if the place would ever be home for her.

Her eye fell on a stocky fellow wearing the leather jerkin of a common soldier. He was seated on a log and had been busy oiling his lance; now he was halted in mid-motion as though turned to stone by some enchantment, staring at Hilda as if he didn't believe his eyes. Hilda's face, Frey saw, was aglow with an almost uncontainable joy as she returned the soldier's look. Very slowly, he put down his lance and stood up.

"Is that your Robin?" Frey asked, touched by the ocean of feeling that flowed between the pair.

"Yes, my lady," Hilda managed, never taking her eyes from her husband.

Frey gave her a little push. "Then go to him. Go before you burst! Attend me later."

"Oh yes, my lady! Thank you, my lady!" Bobbing a curtsey, Hilda broke into a run, darting straight for the man whose arms opened wide to hold her and swing her off her feet, hugging her tightly.

"Ah, love!" Sir Henry said with a heartfelt sigh, drawing Frey's attention to his pleasant face, which was suddenly wreathed in sadness. "How sweet it is."

"You have—" Frey sought for the word in French, "—a wife?"

He smiled ruefully, bashfully, as if ashamed to confess it. "And two small sons. In Normandy."

Understanding that he missed his family, Frey laid a hand on his arm, murmuring something to soothe him as she turned to see where Blaize was. Across yards of ground, past the shoulders of several men in between, she met her husband's expressionless eyes and knew he had been watching her—he was waiting for her to join him.

Had he witnessed the little scene between her and Henry? His stony face gave no clue to his feelings.

She picked up her skirts, lifting them clear of the dirt, and with her head high and her eyes calm she trod through the mud to Blaize's side, half expecting some bitter comment about her attachment to Henry. But all Blaize offered in greeting was a flat, "Here are some people you should meet, my lady."

He introduced her, first to his deputy, who had held the castle over the winter, then to others of his officers, the steward of his household, the sergeant of the guard, the bailiff. All of them bowed politely, their faces full of curiosity as they covertly studied their new mistress.

Finally, Blaize laid his hand under her elbow and turned her to face the keep, saying, "You will wish to see your new domain, my lady. Come."

The hall of the keep of Triffordd was on the ground floor, reached by an iron-studded door and a screened passageway that separated the main room from the buttery where the wine was kept and decanted. It was not very different from the hall at Ketilfiord, except that it was more sparsely furnished. No hangings softened the unpainted plaster of walls where some half-literate soldiers had used charred sticks to scratch their names along with other messages and signs. There was no dais for the high table, no carved chairs, not even a covering of rushes to grace the pounded earth floor; only a meager scattering of dry grass caught the scraps and dirt of Triffordd, and the only seats were rude benches ranged around the walls, with trestle tables leaning nearby ready to be erected at mealtimes. Clearly it was a functional room, intended as a meeting place, a dining place and a sleeping place for the knights and sergeants of the

garrison. And for its lord and his lady, too? Frey
wondered.

Some of her feelings must have shown on her
face, for Blaize read her thoughts with unnerving
accuracy.

"I warned you it was a home for rough
soldiers," he said. "We have our duties in the field
to attend to, which leaves no time to think of
fripperies. However, you may be relieved to hear
that the castle does provide private quarters for its
commander. They lie above this hall. This way."

He bowed slightly, gesturing her to go first,
back through the crudely screened passageway and
out by the main door, to where Frey had already
seen stairs climbing up the outside of the keep,
sheltered under a slanting wooden canopy. She had
assumed the steps led to some sort of guardroom
but apparently she had been wrong. Still feeling as
though her heart was dead inside her, as though
she would never experience emotion again, she
climbed the stairs and unlatched the door at the top.

She found herself in a solar furnished with
stools and a small table, with, in the end wall, a
metal-lined fireplace with a basket for logs. The
narrow window looked out across the muddy
courtyard to the turreted palisades and the valley
below, which had been cleared of vegetation for
some distance, so as to provide no cover in which an
enemy might conceal himself. A bleak place, she
thought; or was it only her depression that made it
seem so?

Blaize's bootheels thumped on bare floorboards
as he walked across to a further door, opened it and
stood by it watching her with unreadable eyes.
"Your bedchamber is here."

Curiosity drew her across the room to peer
through the door at what lay beyond. The bedchamber, too, was spartan, except that the bed was

wide enough for two and covered with blankets
and furs. The room could be improved—as could all
of the castle—with a little work on hangings, bed-
curtains, cushions and other homely comforts such
as a woman needed even if soldiers did not.

Oddly reluctant to enter the bedchamber, Frey
glanced at her husband, wondering at his choice of
words. "*My* bedchamber?"

"Yours," he affirmed in a toneless voice that
conveyed his total disinterest in the subject. "You
shall have your privacy. I'll sleep in here, on a
pallet. The only thing I require of you, lady, is an
outward appearance of wifely respect, at least in
front of my men—and the servants."

She ventured another glance at his face but,
seeing his expression opaque and guarded, she
inclined her head in acquiescence, murmuring, "As
you will, my lord." Telling herself she hated him,
she swept past him, into the bedchamber, taking
care that not even her cloak should contaminate
itself by touching him.

Aware of Blaize still watching her from the
doorway, she walked to the window and looked
out, realizing from her elevation above the countryside that this side of the keep was defended by a natural steep hillside—almost a cliff face—that fell away
into deep woods where spring had employed a rich
palette of fresh young greens to paint the leaves.
And beyond those woods, away in the west, a
golden glow of sunset filled the sky, gilding the
distant line that was the sea.

At least the view would be a pleasant thing to
gaze upon, Frey thought. She would enjoy
watching the seasons change in those woods,
though she had a feeling that might be the only
pleasure she was vouchsafed in this military outpost.
Unfastening her damp, heavy cloak, she folded it so
that the fur lining was outermost and turned to

throw it across the bed.

"It will do very well," she conceded with a sigh beginning to massage the muscles in her shoulders "Faith, but I'm so tired!"

"Hilda should be here to help you," Blaize said. still standing in the doorway as though reluctant to enter the area he had deemed her private ground. "Where is she?"

"She's with her husband," Frey said, stretching her stiff neck. "I gave her leave to be with him for a while. It was only charitable after they've been apart for so long. I—" She forced herself to look fully at him for the first time. "I must thank you for allowing her to come with me. She will be a great comfort."

In reply, he made a derisive bow. "A husband's duty must be to consider his wife's comfort. Since you and Hilda became such—" the words trailed off as he caught sight of the amulet dangling at her bosom. His eyes narrowed as he peered at it across the room, demanding, "What hideous thing is that?"

During the journey, Frey had all but forgotten about the amulet. Now she touched its toadlike contours, her hand fastening around it as if to guard it from Blaize's gaze. "It's a good luck charm. The countess sent it to me—it was her parting gift."

"Let me see." His brow had furrowed into a frown as he strode across the room and when Frey involuntarily backed away he growled in his throat and grabbed her shoulders, his eyes piercing her with a furious look. "Let me see!" he repeated in a warning undertone, and she unwrapped her hand from around the charm, turning her head away from him.

Blaize took the amulet in his hand, turning it this way and that to examine it. "It's an ugly thing! A gift from the countess, you say? A good luck charm? Why should she give you such a thing? It's not her usual sort of gift. Usually she scatters jewels among her favorites."

"But I am not among her favorites," she reminded him. "The gift was a token. Nothing more. It's of no importance."

She wished he would move away. His nearness discomposed her, swamping her with heady memories that made breathing difficult; they were after all in a bedchamber with a bed nearby and he was her lawful husband whatever vows of disinterest he might have made in his anger. Some errant part of her hoped he wouldn't feel obliged by honor to keep to those vows. Feeling her skin break out in a delicate sweat that was not entirely caused by unpleasant sensations, she kept her head down, her gaze on the amulet, small and wizened against Blaize's long brown fingers.

"Did the countess give it to you herself?" he asked.

"No," she managed, her voice tight with apprehension. "No, the countess was too busy to bother with someone as insignificant as I am. She sent . . . she sent one of her ladies."

"Which one of her ladies?"

Frey glanced up at him, seeing his dark eyes hard as pebbles in his olive-skinned face. "It was," she said faintly, "the lady Melissande."

She saw his hand close so tightly around the amulet that his knuckles showed white. "What?" he bit out, and when she glanced up again she saw him glowering in a sudden fury. "Take it off!" he ordered. "Take it off!" He jerked the thong, hurting her neck, and she threw up her hands to ease the pain, lifting her face in fright and dismay.

What was wrong with him? "My lord! Please!"

Blaize tossed off her restraining hands and twisted the thong round her neck until he could

reach the tight knot with which Melissande had
tied it. Exclaiming impatiently he picked at the
knot, and when it resisted him he drew his knife
and severed the thong. Then he whipped the
amulet away from Frey and strode with it to the
window, from where he hurled it with all his
strength. Frey saw it lift over the palisade and fall
out of sight, beyond the steep cliff, to vanish among
the trees far below.

Shocked to be so brutally robbed of a gift—even
a gift she didn't particularly cherish—she laid a
hand to her sore neck and cried, "Will you deny me
even a charm to bring me luck? Or could you not
bear to be reminded of Melissande every time I
wore the amulet? You love her, do you not? If she
were not already wed—"

"Enough!" The roar cut her off. He stood quite
still, his back turned to her, his every muscle tautly
bunched as if to do some violent deed. Then after a
long, pulsing moment he drew in a ragged breath,
forcing air to fill his lungs to capacity in an effort to
calm himself, then his shoulders relaxed and he
glanced round over his shoulder with hooded,
inscrutable eyes, to say, "We shall sup shortly. You
had best rest for now. I'll send Hilda to attend you."

With that, he strode past her and departed, his
footsteps loud on the boards in the solar.

Blaize spent that first evening planning tactics
with the leaders of his knights and eventually,
weary from the journey and the strain of facing so
many new things, Frey retired to her bedchamber,
where Hilda helped her to undress and put on a
warm robe; the April evening was chilly so near
the coast and the mountains.

The dressing chests and other belongings had
been brought up by servants and now the apartments looked a little more homelike with a games

board on a table and a lute standing in one corner.
More chests stood around the walls of the solar,
providing storage and seating, and someone had
spread a thin rush mat on the floor in the center of
the room.

As Hilda was brushing out her mistress's long
red hair, the door opened and revealed the tall
figure of Blaize, somber and still-faced as he waited
in the doorway.

Frey felt her heart skip and then begin to pound
at accelerating speed.

"You can go, Hilda," she said in a low voice.

The maid glanced from her suddenly tense mistress to her silent, brooding master, bobbed a deep
curtsey to each and departed with a soft, "Good
night, my lady. My lord—"

Momentarily Frey caught herself envying the
maid her uncomplicated joy; then she was facing
her own less happy situation. She stood up, shaking
the curtain of long hair back from her shoulders.
Blaize had once said he liked her hair loose. Was he
admiring the shining red tresses now, and the way
her nightrobe clung to her curves?

His face remained inscrutable. It might well
have been carved from the Welsh rock on which
his castle was founded. But she sensed that behind
that control he was fully aware of her apprehension
and perhaps coldly, cynically amused by it.

As soon as the outer door had closed behind
Hilda, Blaize bowed mockingly to Frey, saying
merely, "Good night, my lady. Sleep well." He then
closed the door between them, leaving himself in
the solar.

Hardly breathing, Frey strained her senses for a
clue to his movements beyond the door. She heard
him open one of the big chests, heard a pallet slide
to the floor, his belt hit the boards, his boots clump
down first one and then the other. After that there

was silence.

And at dawn the next morning, before Frey was awake, her husband left the castle at the head of a column of his knights, leading the first of the summer forays against the Welsh.

This was the pattern of their life from that day on: Blaize rode forth for days at a time with his men, pushing the Welsh still further back into their mountains and helping to consolidate what had previously been won; Frey remained at the castle, occupying herself in learning the domestic duties of chatelaine of the household. And when Blaize did come home he slept in the solar, as he had promised he would, leaving her to the privacy, and increasing loneliness, of the bedchamber.

Frey was pleased to find that among the supplies they had brought with them on the packhorses more items of household comfort waited for her to order their distribution. There were two carved chairs for herself and Blaize to use at table; there were goblets and silverware, crisp linen tableclothes, sheets, blankets, and bolts of fabric for clothes and hangings. Now that he was wed, it seemed, the castellan of Triffordd had decided to bring a touch of luxury to his formerly spartan stronghold. For that, if for little else, Frey was grateful to him.

The men of the garrison did not disguise their pleasure at having their castellan returned to them. Lord Blaize fitzHugh was a popular commander, it seemed, honored and respected for his fairness in dealings with all ranks of his men. And it soon became apparent that Frey's arrival also meant a great deal to the lonely knights and soldiers of castle Triffordd. She reminded them of their own wives and families, some of them as far away as Normandy. Her courage in coming to Wales gave them new heart for their task of conquest, and her presence in the fort obliged them to curb the worst excesses of rude behavior and language. Lady fitzHugh was to them a symbol of things nobler and finer than usually existed in a military outpost.

Very soon, young Will and little Tam found their niches among the household. Will became attached to the falconer and began to learn to handle the hawks which were kept for the pastime of hunting in what few leisure hours Blaize could find; and Tam stayed most of the time near the keep, running errands for the steward and for Hilda. The maid, and her husband, grew attached to both lads and took them very much into their care.

During the past winter, when bad weather had inevitably brought a hiatus in the fighting, when snow blocked the mountain passes and the roads were either ice or mire, then the castle had been manned by a small force of men who kept the watch and organized a few random patrols when blizzard and storm permitted; now, the return of the spring and fairer weather heralded the resumption of the real business of the fort—subduing the Welsh and encroaching further into their territory, so that they were driven ever deeper into their mountain eyries.

Frey discovered her feelings on the war to be ambivalent. Once, she remembered, she had applauded the bold Welsh and their continued resistance against foreign intruders who had conquered and brutally used her own people the Saxons; but now that she was here on their borders a part of her felt that the Welsh were her enemies too. On their journey to Triffordd she had shared Hilda's unease as they passed through the edge of those tangled forests, the hairs on her neck prickling as she imagined unseen eyes watching her from thickets along the way; even here at the

castle she was constantly reminded, every time she
glanced from a window, of the proximity of the
mountains and the forests. And perhaps she also
feared the Welsh because she was now the wife of a
Norman lord who must wield his sword in the
struggle against the brigands.

Blaize seemed only too eager to risk his life in
the service of the king, and the Welsh would
probably be eager to capture such a prize. She tried
not to listen to these thoughts; they brought only
further confusion and dismay.

When she had been young, back home in
Ketilfiord, everything had been much simpler, all
black and white and easily understood. Normans
had been by definition evil and therefore to be
hated; anyone who opposed them had conversely to
be a trusted friend. But the older she grew the more
blurred the boundaries between good and bad had
become, the more difficult it was to decide what she
ought to think and believe about anything. Life, she
was discovering, was no longer a question of Saxon
and Norman, right and wrong, white and black;
there were murky areas of gray.

It was so in personal relationships, too, Frey
thought sadly. Nothing was nearly as straightforward as she had once naively believed.

Among the officers of the garrison several of
the knights, including Henry and Simon, were
serving Blaize for the required period which they
owed him annually in return for lands they held
from him, the homes where they had left their
families. He was their overlord, as his father the
earl was overlord of Ketilfiord.

In addition there were about a dozen bachelor
knights—unmarried men without inheritance of
their own; they served at arms in return for pay
and keep, and in the hope that some day their lord

might grant them a fief of their own, so that they might marry—as Nicol had once hoped to merit an award of lands from the earl. Perhaps he was still hoping. Even if it were true that Philip of Linscote had been a traitor—which Frey still did not believe—the earl in all fairness could hardly continue to punish his brother for it.

Had Blaize arranged all that, she wondered, simply to put Nicol forever out of her reach? She found it impossible to answer. He hadn't denied the accusation, and yet . . . Perhaps she didn't *want* to believe him capable of such deviousness.

Once, soon after arriving at Triffordd, Frey asked among the knights bachelor if any of them knew or had heard of a man named Nicol of Linscote. None of them recognized the name; they seemed curious as to why their lord's wife should be enquiring about a poor knight. Her explanation that he had once been a neighbor of hers sounded feeble even to her own ears, so she stopped enquiring.

Though she had first agreed to marry Lord fitzHugh with the idea of finding her former friend, the idea had since lost its appeal. Nicol, she was discovering, had been part of another life that was finished long ago.

She kept busy to prevent herself from brooding over her fate. She managed the servants, who were mostly English with a few Welsh from the village; she kept an eye on supplies and checked the purity of the water in the well—when she saw young Tam drop a handful of pebbles into the water she herself soundly boxed his ears for it; she supervised and helped in the embroidering of cushions, and of hangings for the high table end of the hall, and for her bed; and she ordered the plaster in the hall to be painted with scenes of the Knights of the Round Table. Though the resulting daubs had not much artistic merit at least they did cover the obscene scribblings.

Apart from these domestic duties, when necessary she helped in the sad task of tending the wounded who came back from battle.

Seldom did a patrol come in without at least one man hurt in greater or smaller measure. Once a blood-stained company rode in to report three men dead in a sudden ambush by Welshmen. Frey needed all her nursing skills.

If the right herbs were not available in store, she went herself to look for them in the woods below the cliffs, usually in the early mornings while the dew was fresh. Sometimes she took Hilda with her, out by the postern gate and down the steep path in the rocky cliff, and at first one of the guard insisted on coming with her. But after a while the soldiers became accustomed to their mistress's forays; no harm could come to her so close to the castle; she was allowed to be alone with the woods and the dawnsong.

Such outings became a comfort to her. They made her feel less confined and gave her a chance to breathe the country air she had always loved; among the greenwoods she could recall her happy days at Ketilfiord and for a little while put aside her fears for Blaize—but never for long. Every time he was absent she was haunted by the knowledge that he was out there somewhere in mortal danger.

Outwardly, she played her role with calm efficiency, and when Blaize was absent himslf he always left either Sir Henry or Sir Simon behind to help and advise Frey. She found their company cheering. Also, they were rapidly helping her to become fluent in spoken French.

And of course there was Hilda, chatty and apple-cheeked, whom Frey soon came to regard as a friend. It was good to have another woman with whom to discuss household affairs. Hilda was always nearby, except at times when her husband rode in from patrol; then she begged leave to spend a few hours with him, as eager as he was to make love in any quiet spot they could find. She always came in glowing, evidently relishing her husband's attentions; her one sorrow was that she had never conceived a child, but that gap was rapidly being filled by her fondness for little Tam.

Frey's own apprehensions on the subject of pregnancy had long since vanished: there would be no babe to fill her arms and her aching heart—not yet. Perhaps not ever; Blaize seemed set in his decision never to trouble her again in that way. Since she had thrown Nicol's name in his face, that terrible night in Chester, he had done his best to ignore her very existence.

Blaize had become the total soldier, the commander with only duty on his mind. When he did come home he slept on his pallet in the solar, though he was seldom home for more than two or three nights together. Always some urgent duty took him out for more forays into the wilds—into danger of being wounded or even killed. He seemed to relish the thought of violent action, to welcome its hazards.

It was a deadlock Frey had no idea how to break, though increasingly she fretted over his safety and knew an overwhelming relief each time he rode in unharmed.

Three summer months passed. August came hot and still, then abruptly the weather broke and storms shook the rock on which Triffordd stood. Lightning stabbed out to sea, followed by rolling thunder that seemed to drum from coast to mountains, echoing back to the purple-black sky. Frey stood at the window of the solar watching

rain drench the trees in the woods, battering the
leaves while gusts of wind swept by, its damp
breath tugging at Frey's veil. She found herself
thinking, as she did so often, of Blaize out there
somewhere. She hoped he was in shelter, not
caught in a struggle with the fierce Welsh fighters
who cared nothing for bad weather.

A deafening clap of thunder directly overhead
made her throw her hands to her ears and turn
from the twilight world outside, crying, "Oh, why
doesn't it stop?!"

Hilda looked up from her tapestry frame.
"Don't fret, my lady. Lord fitzHugh will be safe
enough." She cast a glance at the rain pouring down
beyond the window. "And my Robin, too, please
God. It's not easy to rest knowing your man's in
danger."

Arms folded tightly around herself, Frey paced
the room agonizing inwardly about Blaize's well-
being. Let him come home, she prayed. Oh, please,
let him not be hurt, or catch a fever.

"Though there's many a lady as doesn't give it
another thought," Hilda added. "I've heard the
countess laughing and singing when the earl's off
in the thick of it. It wouldn't trouble her if he was
killed—but then their marriage was made for
reasons of state, not for love, like yours and mine."

Frey glanced at her maid's kerchiefed head,
rapt in concentration over her nimble needle. How
wrong Hilda was. She and her Robin loved each
other, for sure, but for Frey and Blaize it was
different. She wished she dared confide in Hilda and
ask how a woman was supposed to endure a
marriage that was no marriage.

When Blaize was away she spent her days
trying not to think of him wounded or dead because her imagination drew images too frightening
to face. She always promised herself that when he

came home she would be welcoming, even let him make love to her if he wished. But one look at his shuttered face and dark, disinterested eyes made her retreat behind the screen of distant politeness which had become her usual manner with him. He treated her more coldly than he would a sister. They existed, each of them in a separate world—he with his soldiering, she with her housewifely duties. Beyond that, nothing was left between them.

But wasn't that what she had wanted?

"Why don't you work on your embroidery, my lady?" Hilda suggested. "The storm's making you restless. You can't go to supper looking so pale and distressed. All the men look to you to keep up their spirits for them."

"Do they?" Frey asked.

"Of course they do." Hilda looked up in surprise. "Surely you know it, my lady. You're making their lord happy, that's all they care. If he's happy, so are they. They respect him. You might say they love him, in their own rough way. I know my Robin does. He won't hear a word against his lord. He says lord Blaize treats all of them like human beings, high or lowly."

Yes, Frey had noticed the way the men responded to Blaize and it had made her proud. He was a strong commander, but he was just.

She sat down on a chest by the wall, picking up a piece of silk she was embroidering for another cushion. But she only sat staring at the stitching, too distracted to find any enjoyment in the work.

"But he's not, is he?" she said eventually, the words seeming to be dragged out of her.

"My lady?" Hilda sounded puzzled.

"He's not happy," Frey amplifed. "Hilda . . . I don't know what to do." Her eyes drowned in tears as she looked across and found the maid watching her in dismay, but now that she had begun she knew she must speak of the things that had been troubling her for so long. "Between my lord and me . . . it's not as it is with you and Robin."

"Oh, my lady." Hilda's round face was soft with sympathy. "I was afraid it might be so, but it wasn't my place to mention it. Do you want to talk about it? What can be wrong? You love him, and—"

"But I don't!" Frey croaked. "That's the trouble, don't you see? There's nothing between us. Not even affection."

Hilda stared at her, blinking rapidly. "Forgive me, my lady, but that's not so. Why do you worry so over him? Why do you hurry to groom yourself when he rides in? Why have you taken such pains to turn this castle into a home for him? Why do you watch him with such pain in your eyes? I've seen it. I've wondered."

Wrenching herself to her feet, Frey went to the window, breathing in deeply of the rain-damp air. The wind blew a fine mist of drops to cool her face and though the center of the storm had moved on lightning still glared in the distance and more dark clouds gathered.

Was it love that ailed her? she wondered. Was it love, this ache inside, this longing for one human being whose absence made her feel so empty and yet whose presence was so painful that at night she shed tears in her lonely bed? She was confronted by a truth she had refused to see before: love had crept up on her, whether she willed it or not.

"And he loves *you*," Hilda said through the steady drip of rain. "Perhaps he has other things on his mind, what with the Welsh and everything, but men are like that. It doesn't mean he doesn't care. Why . . . he could have had any lady he wanted. Any lady at all."

"No, not any lady," Frey put in dully,

remembering Melissande. "Not if she was already married."

"But you weren't married, were you?" the maid commented. "No, you were free and waiting for him. It was the talk of the earl's court that Lord Blaize turned down all the heiresses his father offered him after his first wife died, because he wanted to wed with a Saxon lady from some place in Yorkshire that nobody had ever heard of."

Frey swung round to frown at her maid in disbelief. "What?!"

"He was the butt of jokes all over the city," Hilda assured her, "until he brought you back and showed them what a prize he had—a lady born and bred, with grace and beauty as fair as any princess, for all she might be lacking in wealth and dowry. There was many a knight in Chester talking of going over to Yorkshire to see if he couldn't find a wife just like the lady Aelfreya."

"Oh, come!" Frey cried, finding all this impossible to believe.

"But it's true, my lady!" Hilda cried. "Lord Blaize isn't the only one to see you and love you. Just lucky for him he was there first. That's what he said—'For if I can't have her I might as well be dead.'"

Frey caught her breath, scorn on her lips; but Hilda was too ingenuous to have invented such a thing. "When did he say that? *When*, Hilda?"

"Why—" The maid was wide-eyed with surprise to find her mistress so ignorant of her husband's real feelings. "Why, in York, my lady. When you were so sick he was near mad with fear of losing you. Didn't you know that?"

"But he was angry with me!"

Hilda snorted. "Angry with himself, more like. He seemed to think he'd frightened you. Men are queer creatures. When they're hurting most, that's

when they act like bears, to cover up soft feelings
they're half ashamed of."

It could be true, Frey thought dazedly,
remembering moments of tenderness from Blaize.
Had she been wrong to doubt him? Had she mis-
interpreted his relationship with Melissande? Oh, if
only he had spoken openly of his feelings for her,
how different everything might have been. If she
could believe that he cared . . .

But if it had been so, it was true no longer.
Whatever he had felt for her the feeling had finally
died, along with his desire, that night in Chester.
And she herself had killed it.

XIV

With little hope of success, Frey decided to make one final attempt at some kind of reconciliation with Blaize. Her chance came when he rode in at dusk two days later.

Unfortunately for her, Blaize was exhausted after almost two weeks' campaigning in difficult terrain and terrible weather, and the loss of five of his men had left him dispirited. Among the wounded was Hilda's husband Robin, suffering from an arrow-wound in his arm—not a serious injury but enough to make Hilda frantic with worry. Frey gave her maid leave to stay with Robin when, after supping as usual with the entire household, she and Blaize retired to their private apartments above the main hall.

As always, she felt unsure of herself now that she was alone with her husband. This dark, powerful stranger had shadows under his eyes, and a thick growth of black beard. He had not changed his clothes for days. Frey followed him into the bedchamber and poured water for him to wash, watching as he wearily stripped off his tunic and undershirt. His body showed the marks of the heavy armored hauberk he wore in the field; a place on his collarbone was rubbed raw from the edge of the metalled leather. If he would allow it,

she thought, she would soothe that hurt with
ointment.

"I prefer to wash in private," he said, dismissing her with one brief glance from expressionless eyes.

"But, my lord—" she faltered.

"I said leave me!"

Frey, too uncertain to argue, retreated into the
solar.

By the light of expensive beeswax candles, she
picked listlessly at her embroidery. Every time
Blaize came home it was the same: she planned to
change things but his cold manner proved too
daunting for her. He did not love her. If he had ever
felt anything for her he could not have been so hard
and distant, not for so long. This impasse had
endured for almost four months now. For all he
cared, it could go on forever.

Eventually Blaize came in wearing a long loose
robe of linen, carelessly tied by a leather girdle at
his waist. As if she were not there, he opened one of
the chests, took out his thin straw pallet and a
blanket, and laid them on the floor.

"My lord—" she ventured.

He looked at her incuriously, deep circles of
weariness driven under his eyes. "My lady?"

She ground her teeth in helpless anger. How she
hated it when he did that—when he was so very
polite that it came as an insult. "If you wish—" she
tried again. "You need a proper rest. Surely your
bed would be more comfortable?"

"*My* bed?" he queried, and gestured at the
pallet. "This is my bed."

"Then *my* bed, if you would have it called so."

"Thank you. But after sleeping on the ground
for a fortnight I might find a mattress too soft. The
pallet will do. At least it's dry and warm in this
room. I'll not rob you of your bed."

Frey got to her feet, her head feeling tight, her

hands twisted round folds of her skirt. "I meant—"
She couldn't say it.

"You meant what, my lady?" he enquired, all
civility.

Nothing stood between them but air, yet even
so Frey was aware of an impenetrable barrier
through which she could not hope to break. Calculated weeping was not in her armory of weapons,
and temper only made matters worse, as she had
discovered. Oh, it was hopeless. Hopeless! Hilda
must have misunderstood whatever he had said in
York, and the gossip in Chester must have been
ironical, not flattering. Blaize had never loved his
penniless Saxon bride.

What had she hoped for? To have him make
love to her? If he did so it would only be as a means
of assuaging the needs of his body. She didn't think
she could bear to have that happen again. So she
sighed and said listlessly, "Nothing . . . Nothing."

A bitter smile curled his lips. "Did you intend to
invite me to share the bed with you? A pity you
should choose to do so on a night when all I want is
sleep. Were you the Queen of Sheba herself I would
have to decline your generous offer tonight. But you
may sleep easy, my lady, with your conscience at
rest. It was a brave try."

"It was not my conscience that—" she began
dully, knowing her face had reddened under his
scornful gaze.

Obviously Blaize didn't believe her. He gave her
a contemptuous look, saying, "I need my sleep. I'll
bid you good night, lady."

He threw off his robe and, unabashed by his
own nakedness, lay down on the pallet and pulled
the blanket over him, composing himself for sleep.

Frey fled for the bedchamber, slamming the
door behind her. Since she had thought only of him
and not, for once, of the consequences to herself, his
rejection was all the more hurtful.

* * *

She wept bitterly into her pillow as she did so
often when Blaize came home. She kept thinking,
maddeningly, about him unclothed, thinking of
smooth, muscled flesh that would be so exciting to
touch, to stroke, to kiss. She remembered a night in
a tent when she had slept warm and safe in his
arms, when the following morning they had made
such sweet love that all her misgivings had been
swamped. She remembered other occasions, too—in
York, in the cave on the moors, and that night in
Chester when he had excited her beyond all reason.

The thoughts got into her dreams, and in her
dreams she welcomed him joyfully into her arms,
exchanging kiss for kiss, caress for caress,
mounting toward that final moment of unity
when . . . when she woke with such a terrible ache
inside her that she almost cried out aloud for him.
Blaize . . . if only her handsome knight would come
back to her and be tender as he could be at times,
then she would forgive him anything. She would
forget about Melissande, content herself with whatever crumbs of affection he had to give. Anything
was better than this gnawing loneliness of being a
wife in name only.

She slept again and woke at first light, feeling
drained. This torture could not be endured any
longer, she thought. If this was love then it was too
painful; it must be done away with. She knew a
potion that was supposed to accomplish this
miracle. It was based on hawkweed and succory.

She rose and dressed, tying her hair into one
loose braid down her back before she crept into the
solar, where her husband still slept soundly. Often
on his return from patrol he would sleep until noon.

She paused at the sight of him sprawled in total
relaxation, his hair dishevelled, his jaw darkened
by his beard and his body naked but for the blanket
which, in his sleep, had become twisted about his

loins. Pain twisted inside her, compounded of tenderness and despair. He was growing thin; his ribs showed and his body was marked by weals and bruises which she would gladly have soothed if only he had let her come near.

Only now did she begin to realize how deeply she had grown to love him, all unknowing. He meant everything to her. But she couldn't bear the pain of loving him when he no longer wanted her. There must be no more nights like this last one when she lay restless, tormented by dreams of a physical oneness that could never be. In future, she would have the remedy at hand. The decoction would soothe her heated blood and help her find sleep.

Forcing her tears back, she went out to the stairs in the cool dawn light, and thence to the postern gate in the palisade above the cliff. No one took much notice of the lady Aelfreya, who was often about early in her search for herbs. Only young Will came ambling across the courtyard rubbing sleep from his eyes, offering to accompany her.

"You shouldn't go out alone, lady. It's not safe."

Frey rumpled his hair and cuffed his shoulder. "The Welsh wouldn't dare come so near. But you can come and guard me if it pleases you."

One of the soldiers of the watch came down from the ramparts to unbar the postern gate for her, asking if she wished for an escort.

"I have my sturdy Sir Will," Frey replied, watching the lad blush at her teasing. "Don't concern yourself. We shall not be long."

"Then take care, my lady," the man said. "Stay within call," and let her through the gate, with Will a pace behind.

She found herself on the familiar path that angled down the rocky face and into the woods below. Having made this journey many times, she no longer feared for her own safety. No Welshman had ventured within miles of castle Triffordd, not for many months—they were too afraid of the strong garrison commanded by Blaize fitzHugh.

Having at one time or another had reason to seek most of the herbs with which she was familiar, Frey knew where she should look for her hawkweed and succory. But now that she was free of the castle all haste deserted her. She breathed deeply of the dewy air, enjoying the morning as the sun came up over the borderlands. Birdsong clamored in her ears as she walked amid the undergrowth beneath the trees.

"Do you like the woods, Will?" she asked.

His somber young face brightened. "Oh, yes, my lady. We had woods like this at home. When my mam was alive—" He stopped himself. He never talked about the past. It was as if he had closed a door on it and wanted never to reopen those old wounds.

"I know," Frey said sadly. "The woods bring back memories for me, too. That's one reason I like to come down here."

She had been thinking of other woods and another dawn, when she had been alone with Blaize of Bayonne and had fought both him and the desire he roused in her. She had responded to him irresistibly, then when it was so wrong; now, when it might have been so right, everything had gone awry for them.

But still she loved the woods, tangled and green, pearled with moisture. Early sunlight slanted among the trees in long, hazy swaths, pricking rainbows among spiders' webs jewelled with dew. Leaves quivered in a slight breeze. Birds sang their joy at the beginning of another day . . .

And then, directly in front of Frey, a man stood up from behind a bush.

She stopped, hands flying to her throat. She

uttered a little startled cry. The man was roughly dressed, dark and unkempt, with an evil look on his face. He had a bow slung round his shoulder, a quiverful of arrows strapped behind him.

A brigand!

At once, young Will stepped past her, bracing himself to guard her as he dragged the short knife from his belt and took up an aggressive stance. The man laughed, showing a mouthful of blackened, broken teeth, and spat into a bush, saying something unintelligible.

A sound to one side made Frey catch her breath and spin round. More figures had materialized behind her—and to both sides. They encircled her and Will. She felt like a trapped fawn.

"Put the knife down, Will," she advised. "Please! There are too many of them. There's nothing you can do."

The lad shot her a questioning look then slowly, reluctantly, dropped his knife in the grass, causing the first man to grunt approval. The circle of men began to close in.

"*Stay within call*," the castle guard had advised, Frey remembered. And if she called, would the watchman hear her?

She opened her mouth, but as she screamed hard hands grabbed her. She heard Will shout. She struggled, but she was held fast. Will, too, was caught and held. That was all she saw. Something rough and dank-smelling closed over her head and shoulders. She screamed again. A blow to her head silenced her as more hands fastened on her, winding bonds around her.

Denied sight, her other senses came to her aid. She heard the brigands' voices. They were speaking in Welsh. She caught the name "fitzHugh" and that alarmed her. She must bring help! But when she screamed again another mighty blow to her head shut out light, sound and sense. She didn't even remember falling.

When consciousness returned, Frey found herself still bundled in that vile-smelling sack, lying across a horse as if she were a saddle-pack. The horse was moving under her at a steady walk. Her head hurt abominably, but as her senses awakened one by one she heard her captors chatting among themselves in their own language.

She was a prisoner of Welsh brigands. What did they mean to do with her? And what had they done with young Will?

After an interminable time of uncomfortable jolting, until she felt sick, she was relieved to feel the horse stop. Strong hands lifted her down and laid her on long grass. Her bonds were untied and the stinking sack removed from her head. Gasping long breaths of welcome fresh air, she blinked at the figures around her, and at the deep forest glade that surrounded them. Wherever they were, they had come a long way from Triffordd.

To her relief she saw Will not far away, his face pale and blood drying in a long streak trailing from his scalp. His hands were lashed behind him and he was tethered round the waist to the saddle of one of the shaggy horses, but at least he was alive, and still with spirit enough to wink broadly at her, his look bright and encouraging.

The men were all chattering among themselves, grinning and full of self-satisfaction. They were short, dark, shaggy people. Their little, equally shaggy ponies were even now being led away along a forest track that seemed to close up behind them as branches swung back into place, making Frey recall what Hilda had said about forest pathways that grew over behind unwary strangers and trapped them. One thing was for certain—even if she did manage to escape, she could never find her way back to Triffordd.

The brigands, she saw, were all armed with short bows and quivers full of arrows. Several had cudgels thrust into their belts, and one of them had a fine broadsword—stolen, no doubt—thrust into a rough leather scabbard. This one seemed to be the leader of the band. He was heavily bearded. His tunic, though dirty, was of a soft blue linen, his cloak of virgin wool, and around his wrists he wore thick bronze bracelets; the rest of his band wore simple brown homespun with few adornments.

The leader came up to Frey and spoke to her in appalling French, evidently ordering her to get up. Frey understood his gestures and tone of voice rather than his words. With aching head, still feeling nauseous, she got stiffly to her feet, her bright hair coming loose from its hurried braid.

"You're fitzHugh's woman?" the man rasped, still in what passed for Norman French.

"I am Lord fitzHugh's wife," Frey answered loftily in the same language, fixing him with a defiant glare.

"Ha!" The syllable contained both satisfaction and contempt before he turned away and spoke to his men, apparently confirming that they had captured the right prisoner.

Belatedly, it occurred to Frey that these men had been lying in wait for her. She had walked into a well-laid trap. But how had they known that she often walked the woods in the early morning, seeking herbs? Had they kept a close watch on the castle, or was there a traitorous informer at Triffordd?

The leader looked again at Frey, his blue eyes vivid against tousled, greasy dark hair and thick unclipped beard. "You come," he said, signaling to his men.

Two of the band pushed into the forest to lead the way while the leader took Frey's arm and forced her to go ahead of him, between bushes and onto a narrow, overgrown track that was barely discernible amid the lush growth of the forest. The other four men came behind, one of them dragging Will on his tether, as Frey saw when she glanced back to check on the lad. The leader jabbed his fist into her back to make her keep going.

Soon she began to understand why they had left the horses behind; the way became tortuous, climbing steeply through thick undergrowth, past trailing, snagging brambles and small trees, skirting rocks and leaping trickling streams. By the angle of the sun, Frey judged that two or three hours must have passed since she was captured. Her stomach felt empty and she was aware of a growing thirst. She had not had breakfast that day.

Eventually, when her throat became unbearably parched, she paused by a tiny waterfall and cupped her hands for a drink of the icy water before she was ungently made to move on. They were passing now among mountains whose craggy tops lifted way above forest-filled gorges. Frey wondered if this was the sort of terrain that Blaize patrolled. If so, there was little wonder he and his men came home so tired.

What was Blaize doing now? What must he be thinking? Did he care at all what she might be enduring?

After a particularly arduous climb, she collapsed breathless on a boulder, brushing sweat from her brow, gasping, "What is it you want with me?"

"*Quoi?*" came the ill-mannered bark.

Frey repeated the question in French, almost shouting it at the man in her extremity of fear and exhaustion.

"Never you mind what we want," the leader growled, or words to that effect. "Move on. We've still got a long way to go."

Through thickly tangled trees on slopes littered

with red pine needles, they came at last to a gorge so deep that despite the sun's height the bottom of the vale remained in shadow. Frey was obliged to scramble down that steep hillside, moving from tree-trunk to tree-trunk to prevent herself from going too fast.

Halfway down the gorge, a rough, unstable bridge of wood and rope had been built over a deep, fast-flowing river that murmured darkly in the bottom of its chasm, an occasional flash of white foam showing through shadows and overhanging branches. The bridge swayed so much that Frey feared she might find her end in that rushing spate, but at last she was across and found herself facing a climb so steep that she was forced to use her hands to pull herself up with the aid of rocks and tree-roots, always with the man behind pushing at her, urging her on in impatient Welsh.

Finally, when she thought she couldn't climb another yard, she saw the sky opening up ahead, where the trees were thinner. One of the men behind her played a trill on a reed pipe and was answered shortly by a similar trill from a lookout among the rocks above. A few minutes later, Frey emerged into sunlight in a clearing, on a broad rocky apron of the hillside from where several caves opened off.

Here there were people, most of them unkempt and dressed in rough homespun—men, women and children turning from their tasks and games to stare as she stumbled forward with a hand shading her eyes. The people appeared to be delighted by the sight of their captive as they crowded round to congratulate the kidnappers on their success.

The bearded leader of the bandits took Frey's arm, pushing her through the crowd toward the largest of the caves, from which another man appeared—evidently a man of some importance among these hill people. He was as roughly dressed

as the rest; the difference was in the way he carried
himself, and in his coloring—where the others were
dark in varying degrees, this man had fair, mouse-
colored hair and a long, reddish beard.

He began to say something, but stopped
abruptly, eyes of a pale washed blue widening in
disbelief as they lit on Frey's face.

He exclaimed, "Frey!"

And only then did she recognize him in his
ragged homespun garb and his untidy beard.

The man was Nicol of Linscote.

At first Frey thought her exhaustion must be
producing hallucinations, but however hard she
blinked the vision would not go away. Here indeed
was Nicol of Linscote, in the unwashed flesh, with
his hair untrimmed and his beard unshaven for
many months. What was he doing here with the
Welsh? Was he a prisoner, too?

She dismissed the idea as soon as it came. Nicol
was no prisoner, nor even a stranger among these
people; he was exchanging conversation with the
leader of the band that had kidnapped her and he
was speaking what sounded like fluent Welsh.

Had he turned traitor and joined the enemy?
Frey hated to believe it, but it seemed the only
answer.

Even as he spoke with the leader of the
brigands, his narrowed gaze was turned to her,
scanning her up and down as if, like her, he could
not believe what he saw. He had changed in the
three years since last she had seen him. This was an
older, harder Nicol, all muscle and sinew, a mature
man she found impossible to relate to the callow
youth she had once known.

"But is this the truth?" he asked her incredulously as the Welshman stood aside. "You're
fitzHugh's wife?"

Frey lifted her head, looking him in the eye. "I

am." She was surprised by the pride in her own voice. Wulfnoth's daughter, proud to own herself the wife of a Norman baron. How much had changed!

Nicol turned and made an angry gesture at the people who stood staring. He snapped orders in Welsh, making the cluster of onlookers begin to disperse; then he turned back to Frey, thoughtfully pulling at his bottom lip as he took her arm and drew her toward the cave.

She resisted him, twisting away from his hand and looking around for Will, who seemed to have vanished. "The boy! What have they done with the boy?"

"Oh, he's all right," Nicol assured her, grabbing her in a firmer grip and propelling her into the cave. "Don't worry, no harm'll come to that brat. We've a little job for him to do. Maybe it was lucky that he was with you."

Inside the cave, rough cushions of sacking filled with straw were scattered on the ground around a fire whose smoke drifted up in a column, drawn through a narrow cleft in the roof of the cave. Frey guessed that the smoke would disperse among the trees above and be lost in the winds, thus providing no guide for an enemy who might be seeking the location of the camp—not that an enemy would have much hope of finding this place so deep in the forested mountains. An enemy . . . or a rescue party.

Suddenly the hopelessness of her situation struck her, added to hunger, thirst, bodily discomfort and plain weariness. Her shoulders slumped and her chin drooped to her chest as she closed her eyes against a rush of tears.

"You're exhausted," Nicol said with concern, as if all at once he regretted her predicament—and his own part in bringing it about. "Sit down, Frey." He guided her to one of the cushions and watched her sink down on weary legs before seating himself beside her. His voice came incredulous: "*How* did you come to be fitzHugh's wife? Did something happen to Reynold? Are you an heiress? Did you inherit Ketilfiord?"

"Reynold is well and has two sons to follow him," Frey said, slowly lifting her head to look at him. "Emma will soon take her vows as a nun, and I . . . Oh, does it matter how I came to be here? What I cannot understand is *your* being here—among these Welsh brigands."

"They're not brigands—they're fighters in the cause of freedom," he argued, and his mouth tightened in a petulant way she remembered all too well. "As to why I'm here . . . I live here. I fight with them against the invaders."

"But *why*, Nicol?" she persisted. "Tell me what drove you to join them. What happened to you?"

His eyes flashed with a bitter, defensive anger. "Did you expect me to continue obediently in the service of Hugh the Wolf after he disinherited me? I had nothing left then. Nothing to hope for."

"But you might have won lands of your own as a reward for your service!" Frey cried.

"Lands of my own? Lands rewarded to a Saxon? Under Norman rule? It was a childish dream, Frey! It could never have happened."

"But it could! It is already happening for some people."

"It could never have happened for me!" he shouted at her. "Oh, my brother Philip was right to try to raise a rebellion. We Saxons have gone soft, turned into fear-filled slaves by these bastard Norman barbarians!"

Frey's heart seemed to quiver as yet another illusion cracked and fell apart. "Then it's true that Philip planned treachery?"

"Of course it's true!" he told her with flashing eyes. "We talked of it often, he and I. *Both* of us

planned to lead an uprising. Father had lost his
stomach for fighting—like your brother Reynold.
But if Philip had lived, and come into his inheritance, Linscote would have drawn to it all
Saxons who abhor living like curs on scraps. Aye,
and I'd have been proud to join them. We'd have
marched, as our fathers did in the early days. But
when Philip died and that hope was taken from me
I joined the Welsh, who have not gone soft. Some
day we'll drive the Normans into the sea, or back
beyond Offa's dyke. Aye, and maybe then the
Saxons will rise again to join us!"

"I think not, Nicol," Frey said quietly, alarmed
for the passion of hatred which she sensed in him.
"Oh, I understand how you feel, but this is another
hopeless dream. The time for fighting is long past.
Our people did fight. Our people failed. The
Normans are here to stay. We'd best work with
them, not against them. Together we'll make our
England stronger than it ever was. What good can
come of shedding blood, and yet more blood, until
the land runs red? When defeat comes we have to
accept, and try to build from it."

He peered at her incredulously, his mouth half
open. "What have they done to you, Frey? I never
thought to hear you speak like this."

"Nor I," she admitted ruefully. "But I've learned
to face reality. Not all Normans are cruel barbarians, Nicol. They're people, as we are. That
much I do know."

As he began to argue, a girl appeared in the cave
mouth, her buxom figure cutting off some of the
light so that both Frey and Nicol looked up as she
came in carrying two plates of food. Long dark hair
hung untidily round her face and over her
shoulders. She wore a simple brown gown tightly
gridled at the waist to show off full hips and
breasts. She might have been pretty if she had
washed, and if her blue eyes had not spat hatred,

but the pout of her full mouth gave her a sulky look as she pushed one plate at Frey and gave the other to Nicol.

The girl remained near Nicol, one hip thrust out as she stood with a hand possessively on his shoulder. She glared jealous defiance at Frey, but Nicol spoke curtly to her, removing the hand from his shoulder and obviously telling her to go away. She flounced off with a final flash of blue spite.

The food—some sort of stewed meat and a hunk of dark rye bread—looked less than appetizing though its aroma made Frey's stomach growl and reminded her she had not eaten all day. She stared at the brown mess on the plate, saying evenly, "Is she your woman?"

After a brief hesitation, Nicol said stiffly, "And why not? You didn't wait for me, did you? In spite of all your promises."

"Circumstances prevented me."

"Huh!" he snorted. "Circumstances like fitzHugh, I suppose! I do seem to remember you qualified your promise—you would wait, unless some wealthy lord came asking for your hand. And he did, it seems, though I can scarce believe it. God's eyes, he's the earl's son! Oh, a bastard, I grant you, and he'll not inherit the earldom now that the Wolf has a legitimate son, but even so . . . What dowry did you bring?"

"Only what I had," Frey said, hating him for the way he spoke about Blaize.

Blaize . . . his image filled her mind and all at once she was seized with a longing for him that was a piercing pain inside her.

Now that she had seen Nicol again it was all too clear to her that she had never felt anything for him but the most tenuous friendship. Old Ula had been right about that: Nicol had been a means to an end—an excuse and a companion for mischievous escapades when she had been young and wild and

given to folly. He had never meant the tenth part of
what Blaize now meant to her.

"Do you expect me to believe that he married
you for love?" Nicol was saying, laughing scorn-
fully.

"And why not?" Frey demanded, stung. "You
loved me once yourself—or claimed to."

But Nicol did not respond to the bait. His
laughter had died and his eyes narrowed again—on
crafty thoughts of his own. "By God, if he cares for
you then we can have him! He may be fool enough
to come after you himself. The earl's own son! *That*
would be a victory for us. We could deal a body
blow direct at Hugh the Wolf—his own son's head
as a gift from the Welsh."

"No!" As he began to rise, Frey caught at his
sleeve in terror, her face lifted in appeal. "Nicol, no!
Please! Do what you will with me, but—"

"By God!" He wrenched free of her grasp with a
harsh laugh. "You care for him, too—for that dog of
a Norman. He's turned your stupid empty head.
How very touching." Putting down his plate, he got
up and strode away, shouting for someone named
Caradoc.

She had never known Nicol at all, Frey thought,
never guessed the depths of treachery and evil in
his soul. If by her foolish talk she had put Blaize's
life in danger she would never forgive herself.

But she could not believe that Blaize would be so
foolhardy as to come after her, and certainly not
alone. Perhaps he wouldn't trouble himself even to
attempt to find her in these impenetrable forests.
Lately he had displayed the utmost indifference to
her well-being and she recalled how he had once
coldly told her that she could, "*go to the very devil,
for aught I care.*"

As she was about to give in again to exhaustion
and despair, the dark-haired girl reappeared,
gesturing at Frey's untouched food and saying

something. When Frey made no reply, the girl snatched the plate and thrust out a horn cup of water, managing to spill some over Frey's yellow linen gown.

Frey took the cup, saying, "Thank you," but the girl was looking at her clothes covetously and suddenly spun round to run from the cave. She returned with Nicol, gesturing and speaking agitatedly, obviously demanding something, pointing to Frey and then pulling at her own ill-fitting garment.

Nicol shook his head. "No. I said, no!" The girl screamed something at him and stormed away, while he came to resume his seat and continue his meal. "She wants your clothes. But we're not common robbers. We're soldiers, even though we're reduced to living in caves and dressing in rags. Prince Caradoc's been tossed out of his kingdom, but we'll be back there before long."

"*Prince* Caradoc?" Frey repeated in disbelief.

Nicol gave her an uncomfortable sidelong look. "That's what he is. The Welsh have many princes. But one of his knights has seized his castle—temporarily. We'll get it back in time."

"Just who are they fighting—the Normans or themselves?" Frey asked. "Some fine friends you've found for yourself, Nicol. They squabble with their own kind . . . They kidnap women . . . What is it they want with me?"

"You're our hostage," he said with a sullen flash of pale blue eyes. "We'll send you to your husband for fresh supplies in return for your safety. You've seen how badly we're in need of more food and equipment. You'll stay here until we hear from him."

"How long will that be?"

"Depends how quickly he responds. He'll have the message before sunset—we've dispatched that brat they caught with you to take it to him."

"You've sent Will?" Thank heaven, then the boy would be safe!

"I told you he'd be useful. FitzHugh'll have the night to think about it, then if he knows what's good for him he'll be sending out a packtrain as your ransom. We'll go down the mountain to meet it tomorrow. And if your husband comes in person—"

"He won't!" she broke in sharply. "You were wrong. He doesn't care about me. He won't come. You may not even get the supplies you need. Blaize—" Even saying his name was hurtful, making her heart twist with fear for him. "Blaize may be glad to have seen the last of me."

Nicol's frown said he was beginning to believe her. "You'd better pray that's not so. If there's one thing we don't need up here, it's another useless mouth to feed. If fitzHugh doesn't cooperate, Caradoc will give you to his men, or toss you into the gorge. Or both."

The thought sent a chill through her. "Would you let him do that?"

"How could I stop him? And why should I try? You're nothing to me now, Frey. You've turned traitor. Married to a stinking Norman! Once you would have died sooner than accept such a fate."

"He's not Norman!" Frey said sharply. "Not entirely. His mother was a Saxon."

This surprised him, though after a moment he laughed harshly. "Then he chose the wrong blood to cleave to." As another thought struck him he paused and looked her over with renewed curiosity. "I know Caradoc and his men are scared of him, but for you to feel the way you do . . . he must be something special, this fitzHugh. What's he like?"

"You've seen him," she said dully, twisting at her loosened hair.

"No, that I have not—not close enough to know

him again."

"I don't mean here. I mean you saw him three years ago—back in the woods near Ketilfiord. The last day you and I were together. When I was unhorsed and the dark Norman knight came along—" She couldn't go on; the memories were too painful.

But she had said enough. Now Nicol was frowning again, no longer like a sulky boy but like a cruel, vengeful man with plans and schemes moving behind cold eyes. "That was fitzHugh? By God's eyes! I should have killed him then!"

"And risked a charge of murder?" she demanded, taunting him. "You sheathed your dagger soon enough when you noted his rank, as I recall."

His scowl darkened and he leapt to his feet, a hand on the knife at his belt. "Are you calling me a coward? I'll show you the truth. Let him come. Just let him come and I'll tear out his heart with my bare hands." He leaned over her, his teeth bared in hatred. "He and his kind have robbed me of everything—my lands, my rank, my pride. Even you have been taken away from me. So let him come and by God I'll show you how a true Saxon behaves with Norman scum!" He whirled away, yelling, "Myfanwy!!"

The girl appeared at the cave mouth, looking sullen until she heard what Nicol had to say. Then her face brightened and she advanced into the cave beaming triumphantly at Frey.

From behind the girl, where he was a thin dark figure against the brightness of the day outside, Nicol said, "I've told her she can have your clothes. Best let her take them or she'll rip your eyes out."

Myfanwy stripped Frey of everything, including her stockings and garters, exchanging the garments for her own misshapen gown. It hung on Frey like a sack, the neckline low and loose, the rough wool irritating her skin. Her shoes did not fit Myfanwy, who threw them back in disgust; but the Welsh girl managed to wriggle into the muslin shift, tearing it a little in her eagerness, then the undertunic, which she left unlaced, and finally the yellow linen gown which was tight at her hips and had to be left unlaced in order to accommodate her cushiony bosom.

Still, Myfanwy seemed pleased with her stolen finery. With a smirk at Frey she swayed out to show herself to her companions.

Frey spent an uncomfortable night in the cave surrounded by several of the Welshmen and their women and children. She hardly slept; she was too restless, thinking about the coming day.

A messenger had come back from Triffordd with news that Will had delivered his message, causing a rush of activity at the castle; Lord fitzHugh was preparing a train of supplies to exchange for his wife.

"We told him exactly how to go about it," Nicol informed Frey. "There'll just be one packman, all on his own, making for a place we've decided on. There'll be eyes in the woods, everywhere. If he plays us false, you'll be the one to pay for it. But I don't think he will. A few supplies are little enough to pay for the safe return of his dear wife. We'll be there to meet the packtrain at noon. So be ready. We'll be leaving straight after breakfast."

After all, Frey thought miserably, Blaize could not ignore her plight without arousing the displeasure of his men, who had grown fond of her these past four months. And deep in a hidden, secret place of her heart, she treasured the memory of what Hilda had said about Blaize's professed feelings for his bride. If he had cared once, perhaps he would be concerned about her, if only a little.

Perhaps he might wish to have her safely back. Perhaps.

After a meager breakfast of thin gruel and cold water, most of the men dispersed into the woods to keep watch for possible treachery, leaving the women with ten "soldiers" who included Nicol and Prince Caradoc—the blue-eyed, bearded man who had led the kidnapping party and who spoke such execrable French.

Of them all, Caradoc seemed to be the only one with a shred of civility left in him. That morning he appeared to be sorry for Frey's plight and did his clumsy best to help her feel better. To begin with he dispatched one of the women to accompany her to the nearest stream, where she was allowed to wash in comparative privacy.

When she returned, she sat braiding her hair on a rock by the cave mouth. Caradoc approached her, struggling for words, seeming to be apologizing for any indignities she might have suffered.

"What's he's trying to say," Nicol informed her as he strolled up, "is that he took this course out of desperation, because his people were starving. It's not his way to wage war on helpless women. And he's sorry about your clothes, but he's sure you've got plenty more at home, whereas Myfanwy has nothing." He looked her over, his expression almost sneering. "But you look fetching enough to me. After all, fitzHugh's seen you in peasant's garb before. At least this time you're dressed like a woman, not like a lad in breeches."

With that jibe he went away, taking Caradoc with him.

Frey stared at the thickly wooded slopes around her, her eyes stretched wide to prevent the tears from coming. Memories of Blaize brought her only pain. Would she ever see him again?

What would the end of this day bring?

XV

Before the sun had climbed halfway up the sky, Prince Caradoc's ragged band of Welshmen, with their captive Lady fitzHugh, were making their way back to the forest glade where Frey had been untied the previous day. The return journey proved just as tortuous as the original trek. The difference was that this time Nicol of Linscote was with them; it was he who walked with Frey, occasionally helping her over an awkward spot, but mostly hustling her along with half an eye on the position of the sun. The message to Blaize had, it seemed, specified the time of the meeting as noon.

To keep her mind from panic, Frey tried to memorize the path they were taking, so that she could tell Blaize and his men how to find their way back to the caves: she was no longer confused as to where her loyalties lay. But the route they were following was different from the way she had been brought. There were few marked paths, few landmarks in the forest. After a while her memory became so crowded with impressions that she knew she would never find the way again.

After what seemed hours they came to a spot all closed in by trees and bushes. One of the men was sent ahead, presumably to check that all was clear. Now Frey's hands were bound in front of her and

Nicol took charge of her, leading her on into a glade
where the sun gilded swaying leaves and lush
grasses. The others took cover. Frey saw them
notching arrows to their bows, ready for any
trouble, as they vanished into the undergrowth.

She was placed by a huge spreading oak tree
whose lower branches swept to the ground. Nicol
stayed close beside her, holding her arm in his left
hand, with a dagger drawn in his right as they
waited. Under the sound of a breeze among lush
summer leaves, and birds calling and twittering,
the silence seemed profound, but Frey guessed that
the quiet was deceptive. The woods were thick
with Welshmen. Those who had left the camp early
that morning had been coming here, to lie in wait
and guard the meeting place against Norman
treachery.

Before long, sounds of branches swishing and
swaying, brushing together, warned them that
someone was coming. A sharp whistle that was
uttered by no bird came from the trees where
Prince Caradoc had ridden. It was answered by a
similar call from elsewhere, and then a real bird
flew up, calling in alarm. The clatter of its wings
startled Frey and she found her heart thumping in
apprehension. Let Blaize not come, she prayed
silently. Let him not walk into this trap. Please!

She saw movement among the trees, a rider
followed by a string of horses. The man who rode
first into the glade was evidently one of Caradoc's
band, astride one of the shaggy Welsh ponies; he
must have acted as a guide for the last stages of the
journey of the packman who followed him, astride
a palfrey and leading the first of a string of packhorses laden with heavy sacks.

Frey's heart had almost stopped as the men
came in sight. Now she released her breath in relief:
Blaize had not been so foolhardy as to come himself;
the only man he had risked was the packman, who

bent round-shouldered over the lead horse's neck, wearing a rough mantle with its voluminous hood raised to cover his head.

But even as she applauded her husband's prudence, Frey could not help but be saddened that he had obeyed the kidnappers' instructions so well. She hadn't wanted him to come himself, of course she hadn't. That would have been too dangerous. But his absence only seemed to prove to her once and for all how very little he cared.

The packman dismounted, slowly and awkwardly, evidently afflicted by rheumatism that stiffened all his joints. As he slid to the grass, the glade began to swarm with Welshmen who surrounded the packtrain and began to unload the horses. They were laughing, calling to each other in triumph. So much for the almighty fitzHugh. They had really outfoxed him this time.

Ignoring them, the packman shambled away from his horses, making across the glade to where Nicol was holding Frey.

Nicol spoke to the man in Welsh and, eliciting only a shrug of incomprehension, said, "You're Saxon?"

"Aye," a gruff voice answered from the shadows of the hood. "I'm to take the lady back with me."

Frey felt herself start. Her heart leapt and suddenly began to pound at such breathtaking speed that she feared Nicol might feel it. No amount of gruffness could disguise that voice, not from her! This was no packman, bent and aged—this was Blaize fitzHugh, come riding alone into the heart of enemy territory to fetch his wife.

He did care! A part of her exulted, even while the rest went crazed with terror for him. She was hotly conscious of the hidden bowmen waiting with arrows poised. If Nicol realized who the packman really was, Blaize would have no chance of escaping alive.

He reached out a hand to take her arm, the rough sleeve pulling up a little to reveal Blaize's hand, strong and shapely. But Nicol drew her out of reach, using her as a shield as he brought his dagger close to her throat. His left arm circled Frey's waist.

"Not yet, old man. Not yet," he said over her shoulder. "We'll wait until they've unloaded."

While Nicol watched his companions melt into the forest with their sacks of booty, Frey's glance met that of her husband. From beneath the edge of his disguising hood his dark eyes returned her look alertly, bolstering her courage with silent approbation. Her heart swelled with love for him and fear for him, even as she tried to warn him with her eyes: *Be careful, Blaize! Oh, my love, be careful!* How foolhardy, yet how incredibly brave he was to have come himself.

To her alarm, she noticed that he had straightened his stooping posture slightly, giving a hint of his real stature. She guessed that beneath the voluminous, patched cloak every powerful muscle was tensed for action. But if he gave away his identity he would be killed instantly. Nicol had talked of presenting Earl Hugh with the gift of his son's severed head!

Close to her ear, Nicol taunted her, "Well, it seems you were right. Your brave Norman didn't risk himself—or any of his men—to save you. That's how much he cares. Why don't you stay with us, Frey? With me? You were always a free spirit. You'd enjoy the life. And we could be together, the way we always planned ever since we were children in Yorkshire."

She heard Blaize's indrawn breath, saw him straighten further as he stared at Nicol, evidently recognizing him for the first time. He would betray himself if he didn't take more care!

To divert Nicol's attention, she began to struggle, saying fiercely, "I would not stay with you if you were the only man in the kingdom! Traitor! Thief!"

The dagger's blade came perilously near her face and she caught her breath, staring at the wicked edge on the knife. In the same moment, Nicol's left arm clamped hard about her waist, nearly stopping her breath.

"Then we must *oblige* you to stay," he said through bared teeth, and began to pull her back toward the undergrowth with him, adding to the hooded "packman," "Now move away, fellow, unless you want me to cut your lady's throat. Go back to Triffordd. Go back and tell your lord that his wife is too valuable a hostage to exchange for only a few supplies. Prince Caradoc wants swords—and lances—and a supply of gold. And tell this also to your lord—Next time he must come in person. In order to save his wife he must come and claim her himself."

Frey saw the rage burning in Blaize's eyes at this treachery, but she understood why he was held impotent—it was because of the dagger at her throat. The blade could have her life before Blaize could ever stop it. She had never felt so close to him as she did then, as if she could read his thoughts in every small movement of the tall frame he had incautiously drawn up to reveal his full height.

But if she could read those unconscious signals, so could Nicol. She heard his sharp intake of breath as he dragged her further away, his eyes fixed on the cloaked and hooded figure, and when he spoke his voice was ragged with an emotion that Frey could not identify at once. "Take off that hood!" he ordered. "Take it off."

Very slowly, Blaize lifted a hand to brush the hood away from his dark hair, revealing his face which was almost ugly with hatred. His eyes fixed murderously on Nicol.

"It *is* you!" Nicol exclaimed, and Frey smelled
the fear on him—that was what it was, an almost
superstitious fear of Blaize fitzHugh, the earl's own
son, lord of the fortress of Triffordd. That fear
made Nicol's voice crack as he yelled, "Caradoc! It's
FitzHugh! Take him. *Take him*!"

Suddenly the woods around her erupted with
furious howls. Men emerged from hiding and
closed in from all sides—men wearing iron helmets
and metalled jerkins, men brandishing swords and
spears. Norman soldiers! Frey realized. Blaize's
men!

But even above that noise Frey heard the rush of
an arrow. She saw it fly, straight at Blaize. Saw it
strike him full in the chest. Saw him reel. Saw him
fall . . .

A scream tore from her. She began to struggle
with Nicol, no longer caring for her own safety. She
must force Nicol to let her go. She must go to Blaize.
Blaize . . .

Then, miraculously, she saw her husband leap
up from the grass where he had fallen. From
beneath the folds of his ragged cloak he drew out a
heafty broadsword. Surprise and relief held her still
in Nicol's grasp. Nicol, too, had paused to stare in
horror at his new-risen foe.

Sunlight glinted off the keen edge of Blaize's
sword as he regarded Nicol with a glowering,
vengeful look. But he was still hampered by the fact
that Frey was held as a shield for his enemy, with a
dagger near her throat and with her hands tied.

But his men were dealing with the Welshmen.
Frey heard Sir Simon yelling in glee as the glade
emptied and the sounds of flight and pursuit came
crashing back through the forest.

As though sensing that victory was at hand,
Blaize threw off his rough cloak, disclosing the

loose sleeves of a linen undershirt, with over it a
leather hauberk sewn with iron rings, the
armoring lapped over in rows to form a close and
well-nigh impregnable mesh. That was what had
saved him. The arrow must have glanced off the
armoring. Thank God! Frey thought, sagging in
relief—a movement which made Nicol hold her
tighter as her weight threatened to unbalance him.
She sensed his indecision and his growing fear. He,
too, knew that the day was lost to him.

"Treacherous dog!" he spat at Blaize.

"There would have been no treachery had you
kept the pact—the supplies in exchange for my
wife," Blaize grated. "Your greed was your
undoing. Now let my lady go, Saxon coward! Will
you hide behind a woman's skirts?"

"See how brave he is, Frey," Nicol said hoarsely.
"With a broadsword in his hand while I have only a
dagger."

The taunt made Blaize glance at Frey. She shook
her head and, guessing his intent, croaked, "No!
No!" But to her horror he tossed his sword aside
and drew his own knife, poised on the balls of his
feet like a dancer, ready to strike.

"Now we're equal, Nicol of Linscote," he
growled, his eyes afire with anger and bloodlust.
"Knife against knife. Man against man. Let go my
wife!"

Frey could feel Nicol's pulses thudding in fear.
He was sweating, terrified of releasing her and
facing Blaize man to man. Vile coward, she thought
in contempt. If her hands had not been tied she
would have scratched out his eyes.

Gathering her strength for one swift action, she
drove her elbow into Nicol's midriff. At the same
time she lifted her foot and brought it down hard
on his instep. The sudden attack caught him off
guard. An "Oof!" of surprise escaped him. He

doubled over, winded, trying to soothe his foot, all of which obliged him to loosen his hold on her. Frey thrust at him, broke away, and threw herself to one side, rolling on the grass. She sensed Blaize launching himself to stand guard over her, the knife flashing in his hand.

Nicol had sprawled against the tree and was half crouched there, trying to get his breath. His left hand was pressed to his sore middle, but his right still held the dagger ready. He stared in fright at the dark figure menacing him, while Frey lay watching, hardly daring to breathe. The two men seemed to hold their deadly tableau for an age.

Suddenly, in desperation, Nicol drew back his arm and hurled his dagger. Blaize dodged aside. The knife narrowly missed him and curved across the glade. But in that moment Nicol broke and ran. He ducked into the forest, which seemed to swallow him whole.

Blaize started after him.

"Blaize!" Frey cried in fear.

He stopped on the edge of the tangled woods and spun to face her with burning eyes in a face turned livid by hatred. His voice cracked across her nerves. "Do you beg for his life even now?"

Frey stared at him dumbly, not sure why she had stopped him. Perhaps Nicol deserved to die, but she didn't want to live the rest of her life in the knowledge that Blaize had killed him because of her.

But at that moment they both heard Nicol scream, "No!" The cry ended in a choking gurgle. Bushes cracked as if a body had fallen among them. Stricken, Frey stared at her husband's grim face. Both of them knew that Nicol of Linscote had met the end his treachery deserved.

Out from the forest strode a smiling Sir Simon, wiping fresh blood from his sword with a handful

of grass. "I got the Saxon traitor, too," he said,
pleased with himself. "We've slain nearly all of
them, my lord, and recovered most of the supplies.
Shall we continue to search for the ones who fled?"

Blaize shook his head. "No. It's enough. One
nest of rebels decimated. You've done well, Simon."

He came to kneel beside Frey and with his
dagger cut the rope that bound her wrists, though
he avoided her eyes and kept a quivering silence
between them. When she was free he moved away,
leaving her to rub some life back into her numb
wrists and hands while he recovered his sword. His
men were now returning to the glade, some
slightly wounded, others unharmed, all of them
elated by the victory.

It was Simon who helped Frey to her feet,
Simon who steadied her when she swayed with
momentary weakness. She kept thinking about the
girl Myfanwy, wearing her stolen finery, waiting
for Nicol to return. But most of her mind was on
Blaize. He was very much in command as he
organized the reloading of the packtrain and the
withdrawal of his men from the scene of their
triumph. But from her he might as well have been
as distant as the moon.

"I was relieved to see you," she told Simon. "But
how did you come here? How did you manage to
surround them without being seen?"

His blue eyes gleamed with laughter. "We
know more about them—and about their forests
and their secret ways—than they guess, my lady.
When they gathered this morning to watch this
place, my men and I were already here, waiting to
close the noose. They all walked into a trap they'd
set themselves. Caradoc's not very clever, nor was
that Saxon henchman of his. All we needed was half
a chance."

"I see," Frey said. "Well, I'm grateful, Simon.

And what of Will? He wasn't harmed, was he?"

"No, the lad's well enough. Angry with himself for not guarding you better, but it'll be a good lesson to him. He wanted to come with us. Had to be forcibly held back. He'll be glad to see you safe. But then—" as he paused he afforded her a languishing look, "we are all glad for that, my lady."

Frey brushed off his ardent declarations, in no mood for his foolery even though she knew it was sincerely meant. She didn't doubt that he, and the rest of the men, were relieved to have her safe. Only Blaize's feelings were in doubt. And only Blaize's feelings really mattered to her.

Horses were brought up, including Blaize's stallion. An air of satisfaction pervaded the company as they began to ride away—soldiers, packtrain, and finally Sir Simon, who sent a cheery wave at Frey before he disappeared into the greenwood.

Only then did Blaize take further notice of his wife. He picked up the long rough cloak he had discarded and tossed it at Frey. "Put that on."

"I'm warm enough," she replied with a dispirited sigh, convinced that nothing had changed between them. He had come to find her, but only because it had been his duty to do so; he appeared to care nothing for the ordeal she had been through. "I'm too warm. It's hot."

"And I too am hot in this hauberk," he reminded her. "You need the cloak for modesty, not for warmth. That rag you have on is barely decent." At the thought, he moved to take her by the shoulders and all at once his eyes were alight with anger. "Did he touch you?"

Frey stared at him, so startled she was unable to think. "Who? Simon?"

"No, not Simon," he raged, shaking her. "Your Saxon lover. Nicol of Linscote. Up there in the mountains. Did he touch you? Did he make love to you?"

"No!" Frey cried, affronted.

"Then what became of your own clothes?"

"A woman at the camp took them! Nicol's woman!"

"Ah." The monosyllable contained many nuances—including, she fancied, relief: was he jealous? The hard hands on her shoulders relaxed. He released her and moved away. "Come, my lady. We must go home."

With the cloak wrapped around her, so long that it trailed round her feet, she trudged behind him to where the stallion waited. Blaize mounted in one effortless swing and then shifted as far back in the saddle as he could. His face was a dark, unreadable mask as he held out a hand to her.

"You intend me to ride in front of you?" she asked in perplexity. "I'd be more comfortable behind."

"I think not. Sideways you'd be in constant danger of slipping. And no wife of mine shall be seen riding astride. But if the thought of being in my arms is so distasteful to you, you may walk at my stirrup."

He meant it, she could see, but she was much too weary to walk any distance. Knowing she had no choice, she accepted his helping hand, using his boot for a foothold as she climbed up to sit across his lap. His arms looped round her as he gathered the reins and made the stallion walk—slowly, so as to conserve his strength in the heat.

For some time they travelled without speaking, but when the silence became too much to bear Frey said, "I know why you're angry, my lord. It was foolish of me to venture from the castle alone. But I've been out in the woods on many a morning. No

danger threatened me before. How could I know
they would be waiting?"

"You could not have known," Blaize answered.
"But the guard should have been more alert. You
must never stray out alone again. Though . . . as it
has turned out, you helped us to win a significant
victory. Caradoc's band has been an irritation at my
borders for many months."

She made no reply, feeling both chastened and
annoyed. She had not expected him to be so reasonable. Obviously he didn't much care for the danger
she had been in, only that her capture had, in the
end, proved useful to him. Yet on his behalf she had
endured agonies of fear back there in the glade.

They rode on.

The forest was still, even the trees seeming to
rest in the heat of an August afternoon. Eventually,
knowing that Blaize was too stubborn to be the first
to speak, Frey ventured, "My lord—"

"My lady?" he answered.

Goaded beyond endurance, she cried, "Oh, I
hate it when you speak to me so politely!" She
struck at him with her fist, and yelped as her
knuckles encountered the armored rings of his
hauberk. Thrusting her injured hand to her lips,
she glanced up at Blaize's face and fancied she saw
the corner of his mouth twitch.

"And don't laugh at me!"

Briefly, he afforded her a mock-surprised look,
all wide eyes and injured innocence. "I?"

"Oh, I hate you! I hate you!" she stormed, and to
her own irritation burst into tears.

She might have leaned on him had it not been
for the armor that was like a barrier between them.
She swayed helplessly, trying to stem the tears with
her hands. But for all the effect her distress had on
him, he might have been armored all through.

Again the silence of the forest surrounded
them, flickers of bright sunlight glittering amid

deep shade. Then after a while they came to a stream in a tiny clearing dappled with light, with leafy branches arching above, forming an airy bower.

Blaize halted the stallion, said, "We'll rest a while," and slid from the saddle to stand with his arms held out invitingly.

Through sore, reddened eyes she looked at his unreadable face, hating him, loving him, worn out by the conflict inside her. Then she reached out and let him help her down, feeling his strong hands at her waist as he placed her on her feet on the grass and let her go. She trailed across to sit by the stream, trying to catch water in her cupped hands.

Silently, Blaize offered her a cup he had taken from his saddlepack. Frey took it without words and scooped up some of the clear cool water, drinking her fill while her husband tied the stallion to a bush from where it too could reach to drink from the stream.

When she glanced round, she saw Blaize unbuckling his sword belt and then shrugging out of the heavy, ironclad hauberk. He dropped the armored jerkin to the ground beside the horse with a clinking of metal, leaving himself in a linen shirt loosely laced across the breast, worn outside breeches and thonged stockings.

He sat down three feet from her, accepting the cup of water she mutely offered, and she watched as he drank thirstily.

"Since you hate me so much," he said, his head bent over the empty cup in his hands, "why did you not stay with your swain when he offered you the chance?"

"He was not my swain," Frey said dully.

"But you came to Wales to be near him."

Sighing heavily, she unfastened the cloak and let it fall around her on the grass, feeling the breeze move through the loose weave of the peasant gown, cooling her. "So I told myself."

"And wasn't it so?" he asked with a sidelong glance.

"I no longer know. I'm no longer sure of anything. I'm tired, sore and aching. And, my lord, I'm sick at heart."

"Well, you may console yourself that you did all you could to save his life."

She turned on him with an indrawn breath of agitation. "You take pleasure from misunderstanding me, my lord! That is *not* what . . . Oh—" she laid her head in her hands, despairing, "What does it matter?"

"I thought we were speaking of Nicol of Linscote," Blaize said. "If that's not so, what is it that's troubling you? Tell me, lady."

"Do you not know?" Lifting her heavy head she regarded him sadly. "My lord, I'm heartsick from battling with you all these months. I can endure no more. You should have left me in Chester, as you once said you would. Neither of us is finding joy in this marriage."

"Joy?" His lips thinned and suddenly his face was bleak. "Was it joy you expected to find when you married a stranger? No, lady—you wished to find your lover. Well, now you've found him, and it seems that you had little pleasure in the meeting. All your dreams are dust—like mine."

"Yours?" she queried with a weary laugh. "You said a soldier does not indulge in such foolishness."

"Aye," Blaize said, as if to himself, his gaze on the stream. "So I did."

Frey watched him for a while, puzzling over him. What a strange man he was—an enigmatic man. It occurred to her that she had never understood him. Unconsciously she allowed herself the bittersweet pleasure of drinking in the sight of him—the strong lean lines of the body beneath the loose shirt; the dark hair curling errantly round his ear and onto his brow; the profile sturdy, carved as in oak, yet with a vulnerable curve to his mouth. A part of her longed to touch him, to remind him of the desire he had once felt for her. But she was too unsure of herself to reach out to him and risk another rebuff.

But his comment about dreams nagged at her. Eventually, driven by unbearable curiosity, she asked, "What dreams did you ever hold in your heart, my lord?"

"Oh—" he shrugged, as if deriding youthful fancies. "I had thoughts about a girl I once met."

"A girl?" Despite her efforts to prevent it, jealousy surged through her. "What girl? Melissande?"

He glanced at her briefly, saying, "No, not Melissande," before he returned to his contemplation of the rippling stream and tossed a few stalks of grass to float on the surface. He watched them sail into the distance, then said as if to himself, "There was another girl. A beautiful, spirited girl. A girl as hot-tempered as wildfire, cool as mountain streams, proud as a princess, elusive as mist. In my vaunting arrogance I thought to capture her and tame her. But all I did was break her spirit. And now she hates me." Moving very slowly, he turned to look at her with clear, fathomless eyes, making Frey hold her breath. "And you, lady? What dreams were yours? To be wed with Nicol of Linscote?"

Frey shook her head, mesmerized by the look in those depthless brown eyes. The moment was now, or never, if only she could find the right words. "I dreamed," she managed despite the catch in her throat, "of a knight with dark eyes. A man I could never have, and ought not to think of as I did. He was too far above me. He was a Norman—and I had been taught to hate and fear all Normans. And he frightened me, because he made me feel things I had never felt before—things I had no wish to feel, not for him."

She saw the changes in his expression as she spoke—surprise, disbelief, and then dawning hope—and she saw him turn and get to his knees as if to stand up, only to stop himself and remain poised there.

He said hoarsely, "When I heard, in York, that you were to be betrothed to the merchant Geronimus, I rode to prevent it. I rode with jealousy boiling in my blood."

Frey blinked at him, astounded, remembering that sunny day he had ridden into the Ketilfiord valley as if demons pursued him. "Is that why you came?" she asked in a faint voice.

"Didn't you guess? I couldn't have borne to know you were married to that fat, fawning merchant. But you were so cold with me, so haughty. Even when I saved you from the Viking, still you denied feeling anything for me."

"But I believed you to be married! You were a Norman. A knight. How could it ever be? And you didn't speak of love—you spoke of wanting. You vowed to make me submit."

"To marriage with me!"

"Oh, no, sir," Frey argued fiercely. "It was not marriage that you had on your mind."

He scrambled a little closer, searching her face anxiously. "Perhaps not, not then. I was angry. My blood was hot for you. I thought you had already known love with other men, and I had felt your response to me, even though you denied it. And then . . . then you told me you were faithful to Nicol of Linscote."

"I said that to make you leave me be! You confused me. You frightened me."

"But would you have married him? If I'd been able to persuade my father to give him the manor of Linscote, in spite of his brother's treachery, would you have accepted Nicol as husband?"

Frey stared at him, wondering if she could believe the implication in the way he had phrased that question. "Did you try to do that—to stop the earl from disinheriting him?"

"Aye." He made an irritated gesture, as if he had not meant to raise the subject. "I tried. I thought it was what you wanted. But then I learned that Nicol had turned traitor, left his post and joined the Welsh, so—"

"Before he was disinherited?" she gasped. "He joined the Welsh *before* he knew he could not have Linscote?"

"Aye," Blaize informed her with disgust.

"But why didn't you tell me so?" she cried.

He looked away, only to flick his glance back again with renewed heat. "Would you have believed me? Wouldn't you rather have believed that I was lying, to turn you against the man?"

She thought about that—about the way things had been between them then—and sighed heavily. "Yes, perhaps I would."

"So . . . he was lost to you. An outlaw. So I decided to marry you myself, and make you forget about him. I decided to make you love me instead of him."

"Oh, Blaize!" she cried, tears blurring her sight. "Love cannot be forced. Love must be won. When I realized who you really were—a marcher baron, lord of Bayonne, castellan of Triffordd . . . the power you had over me terrified me. I wanted my dream back. I wanted my handsome knight. But he was gone forever and in his place was a stranger— the earl's son."

"Is that why you wept on our wedding day?" he demanded.

"Of course it is! So much had happened to bewilder me. But—" Her hands clenched in her lap as she informed him forcefully, "But I was not distraught enough to poison myself. I swear I took nothing to make me ill. It was the philtre, and too much wine."

Blaize sat back, leaning on one knee, his face suddenly grim with remembrance. "Aye, I know."

"You know?!" she gasped, astounded.

"After you so tardily informed me about the 'love-philtre,' I questioned the servants. But by that time Hilda was gone with the countess and the others knew nothing about any potion. So after I took you to the Abbey to see your sister on that last evening, I visited the apothecary."

"So that's where you went," she sighed. "But afterward you seemed so . . . distracted."

"I had much on my mind," he told her, frowning into the distance as he recalled the events. "What I discovered was disquieting. A potion had been procured, it's true. It was bought by a woman who wore a dark cloak with a hood drawn round her face to conceal her identity. She paid gold for one of the man's more noxious mixtures—an irritant for the stomach, which I guess was intended to make both of us ill and ruin our wedding night. Of course, the apothecary had been well bribed to hold his tongue."

"But he told you the truth?"

With a wry smile, he gave her a gleaming sidelong glance. "He soon spoke up when he had my knife at his throat. But he could not tell me who the woman was, though he described her as best he could. Before I could discover the full truth, I was forced to wait until we reached Chester, where I spoke with Hilda. She suspected nothing wrong. She too had been sworn to secrecy, but when I told her that the mixture had not been a love potion—as she had been told—then she quickly enough informed me of the identity of our enemy."

Frey was trembling; the story could have only one explanation. "Melissande?"

"Aye, Melissande," Blaize agreed grimly. "It was done to repay me for spurning her. Since she came to the earl's court she has set her traps for me—to no avail, I assure you. It is not in my nature to play the lapdog, especially with the wives of men I hold in high honor. So she conceived her plan of vengeance. She gave the potion to Hilda saying it was a gift to help us find more pleasure in each other. Hilda trusted her. She suspected nothing, not even when you were so ill."

His eyes filled with remembered anguish as he reached to take hold of her shoulders. "You might have died of it, Frey. You were the victim of Melissande's malevolence and I—God forgive me—I accused you of trying to poison yourself. I could not bear to have you so afraid of me, yet I seemed unable to reach you. I . . . I do not find it easy to speak of my feelings. When I needed soft words, I found only angry ones, which made you more afraid, and me more angry. And all the time I believed you to be experienced in love and wilfully denying me comfort."

Unable to speak for the emotion that choked her, Frey let her hands rest on his shirt, adoring the firm warmth of the body beneath.

"I discovered I was wrong," he went on, his hands working on her shoulders, his eyes devouring her face, "but then you reminded me of Nicol of Linscote—the man you had told me was your one true love. Can you understand how it was for me, to believe that you still cared for him? I despaired, I was angry again. I thought to leave you behind in Chester and forget you. I let you ride with Henry and with Simon, and was forced to hear you laughing with them, as you had laughed with father William—but never with me! I tried to harden myself against the pain. It was impossible. And when we reached Chester, and I learned who was responsible for making you ill—"

"Is that what you were talking to Melissande about, at the celebration? The two of you, alone in a shadowed corner . . . And I thought you were speaking of love to her!"

"Not so!" he denied passionately. "Not so! I told her I knew what she had done. I vowed that if she harmed you again she would pay dearly for it. She only spat venom at me. I dared not leave you in Chester so close to her. I was afraid she might yet work some evil against you."

"That's why you were so angry about the amulet!" she realized. "You thought it might have an evil spell on it?"

"Aye, I did. And so it may have done!"

Frey felt the blood drain from her head at the thought. If she had gone on wearing that amulet, who knew what ill luck it might have brought. "But why didn't you say so?!"

"I should have done," he replied raggedly. "Yes, perhaps I should have done. But my thoughts were not clear, Frey. They had not been clear for a long time. At the castle of Chester that night, I wanted . . . Oh, how I wanted to be tender with you. But you kept goading me about Melissande until . . . I planned to humiliate you, to make you want me and then to reject you—as you had rejected me."

"But you couldn't do it," she recalled, her fingers moving on his dear face, round his ears, in his hair, loving the way he felt.

Blaize trembled, letting his arms slip round her. "Indeed I could not," he breathed in a harsh whisper. "But it was not the way I wanted it to be, with anger between us. You did respond to me, but I know it was against your will."

"Blaize—" she whispered and, unable to hold back any longer, reached to touch her lips to his in an agony of tenderness.

But having borne her kiss for a moment he

eased her away, his eyes wide and very dark as he gazed at her. "No. No, not yet. Let me say it all. I was bitterly wounded, it's true, to be told you had come with me only in hope of finding your lover. I told myself I no longer cared. I steeled myself to behave as though I felt nothing. But it has been a sore trial, Frey. Staying out in the field when I might have come home. Enduring hardship and loneliness sooner than endure the pain of being with you. And then, yesterday morning . . . to have you vanish . . . to be told of a scream from the woods, and then to search in a fever of fear, only to learn that you were being held captive—" He swept her into a tight embrace, saying passionately, "Oh, my love, I was so afraid of losing you forever."

Her senses seemed to explode into life as his mouth took posession of hers. She clung to him, expressing her own remembered fears in the way she responded, twining her arms about him, touching him, pressing her body close to his as they knelt together on the grass. She felt him untie the rope girdle at her waist, felt him stroke a hand beneath the rough gown, sending shivers along her thigh and round her hip. He slipped the loose gown over her head, paused to throw off his shirt and took her in his arms again, kissing her, easing her down onto the sward.

"I want you," he groaned against her throat. "Oh, I need you, Frey."

"I need you, too," she whispered, twining her arms about his naked shoulders and burying her face in the warm dark silk of his hair. "Oh, my dearest lord—"

And then there were no more words, nor any need for words. They spoke in terms more intimate, in touch and sigh and movement, until for Frey nothing existed in all the world but this one man she loved. Blaize . . . and the mutual joy they had of each other.

* * *

Some long time later, they moved on. Now the armored hauberk was strapped behind the stallion's saddle and Frey nestled close in her husband's arms, enjoying the intimacy of his body moving against her through light clothing. She reached up to kiss his throat and saw him smile down at her, his dark eyes tender with a love she had once thought she would never find in him. Her handsome knight. Hers now forever.

Sighing contentedly, she clasped her arms about him. "Don't ever leave me, Blaize."

"I didn't leave you when you hated me," he replied. "How could I leave you now?"

"I never hated you. Never. I loved you always." She held him tighter as the thought came that he might be taken from her without his willing it, by a sword thrust, or by a Welsh arrow. That noon she had thought him pierced. She would never forget the agony of that moment.

"I thought you dead," she said. "When that arrow struck . . . Dear heaven, how could I have lived without you?"

He held her close, his cheek on her hair. "I wondered the same, when I knew you were captive. You must not wander alone again in the woods. Always take an escort. No herbs are worth the risk of losing you."

"Yesterday morning I gave no thoughts of risks. It seems a stupidity now, but all I thought of was finding where hawkweed and succory grew."

"Hawkweed and succory?" He gave her a wry indulgent smile, tilting a mocking eyebrow at her. "For what? Another potion?"

She played with the loose lacings of his shirt, letting her fingers smooth his flesh. "Those are the main ingredients for a remedy that will cool the fevers of unrequited love."

His smile widened. She could see that he under-stood her well enough, but he said, "Indeed, my lady? And which of my men has been lusting after you now, that you must practice your witchcraft on him?"

"Oh, all of them, my lord," Frey teased. "All of them!"

Blaize laughed, and she laughed with him, re-joicing in the blending of their voices ringing through the trees. Then his laughter died, his arms tightened about her and the look in his eyes became fiercely possessive.

"If I believed that to be true, I'd hang the entire garrison. Has any man dared to speak of love to you?"

"None of them would dare," she assured him. "They have too much regard for you. Besides, I've been too absorbed in my misery over you to notice any other man."

"Even Henry?"

The question astounded Frey. Had Blaize been riven with envy over her innocent friendship with the gentlest of his knights? "Especially not Henry!" she exclaimed. "He's faithful to his wife. He adores her. He was lonely, as I was. If I'm not to be allowed even to smile on another man without your sus-pecting—"

He stopped the horse and drew her full into his arms, bending his head to kiss her long and deeply. "So long as you smile on me, too, I shall try not to object. But on others you must bestow no more than smiles. The rest is for me alone."

"The rest," she said, twining her arms round his neck, "is all for you, only for you, my beloved lord."

Holding her with deep dark eyes, he stepped down from the stallion, pulling her with him, and carried her to a shaded bower where he made sweet love to her once more.

It was a very long time before at last Frey was brought home to castle Triffordd, safe in the arms of her dark conqueror.